DEATH

AT THE

ABBEY

D0176354

THE LADY OF ASHES MYSTERIES

Lady of Ashes

Stolen Remains

A Virtuous Death

The Mourning Bells

Death at the Abbey

ALSO BY CHRISTINE TRENT

By the King's Design

A Royal Likeness

The Queen's Dollmaker

Published by Kensington Publishing Corporation

DEATH
AT THE
ABBEY

A Lady of Ashes Mystery

CHRISTINE TRENT

WITHDRAWN

KENSINGTON BOOKS
www.kensingtonbooks.com

This book is a work of fiction. Names, characters, places, and incidents either are products of the author's imagination or are used fictitiously. Any resemblance to actual persons, living or dead, events, or locales is entirely coincidental.

KENSINGTON BOOKS are published by

Kensington Publishing Corp.
119 West 40th Street
New York, NY 10018

Copyright © 2015 by Christine Trent

All rights reserved. No part of this book may be reproduced in any form or by any means without the prior written consent of the Publisher, excepting brief quotes used in reviews.

All Kensington titles, imprints, and distributed lines are available at special quantity discounts for bulk purchases for sales promotion, premiums, fund-raising, educational, or institutional use.

Special book excerpts or customized printings can also be created to fit specific needs. For details, write or phone the office of the Kensington Sales Manager: Kensington Publishing Corp., 119 West 40th Street, New York, NY 10018. Attn. Sales Department. Phone: 1-800-221-2647.

Kensington and the K logo Reg. U.S. Pat. & TM Off.

eISBN-13: 978-1-61773-646-9
eISBN-10: 1-61773-646-5
First Kensington Electronic Edition: November 2015

ISBN-13: 978-1-61773-645-2
ISBN-10: 1-61773-645-7
First Kensington Trade Paperback Printing: November 2015

10 9 8 7 6 5 4 3 2 1

Printed in the United States of America

For Carolyn McHugh

Thank you for many years of friendship, encouragement, and fun day trips, as well as for discovering the intriguing 5th Duke of Portland, and thus providing the idea for this story.

Acknowledgments

As the Lady of Ashes series enters its fifth volume, it is only proper that I thank five people at Kensington Books who have been very instrumental in the caring and feeding of the series.

First and foremost, my editor, Martin Biro, has been an advocate of my books. His keen judgment never ceases to surprise me, and my books are made all the better for his insights.

Kristine Mills is responsible for the marvelously atmospheric design of the covers. I literally tremble with joy each time I hold a new cover in my hands.

Paula Reedy, my production editor at Kensington, shepherds many manuscripts each year, yet always gives mine meticulous care and attention.

Copy editor Mary Beth Constant is an unsung hero in the production process, saving me from numerous historical goofs during the course of this series.

Finally, I extend thanks to Steve Zacharius, Kensington's CEO, who has spent the better part of the past few years on the front lines defending and nurturing the publishing industry. Despite how busy he is, he answers every e-mail. Even mine.

Turn the Page Bookstore in Boonsboro, Maryland, continues to champion my books, and I cannot think of signing occasions I enjoy more than those with Janeen Solberg, Beth Rockwell, and the rest of the crew there.

This story came to life over several meals at the Olive Garden in California, Maryland, with my husband and my brothers-in-law, Christopher Trent and Paul Trent. The superb staff there not only kept me well supplied in Italiano Burgers (sadly no longer on the menu), but were always kind and considerate in making the restaurant a conducive place for us to brainstorm.

As always, my draft manuscript was edited with sharp eyes by my sister-in-law, Marian Wheeler; my brother, Anthony Papadakis;

my mother, Georgia Carpenter; and my much-cherished husband, Jon. I am so fortunate to have them taking on the burden of painstakingly reviewing my manuscripts, usually with me in the background frantically repeating, "Are you done yet?" Why none of them has disowned me yet is beyond me.

Finally, I am thankful to *you*, dear reader, for without your enthusiasm for this series, Violet Harper's adventures would still be a flight of fancy in my imagination.

Sola gratia.

Cast of Characters

VIOLET HARPER AND HER FAMILY AND FRIENDS

Violet Harper—undertaker
Samuel Harper—Violet's husband
Mary Cooke—mourning dressmaker and Violet's friend

WELBECK ABBEY STAFF

Edward Bayes—estate purser
Margaret Bayes—Edward's wife
Martin Chandler—falconer
Mrs. Garside—cook
Miles Hudock—footman
Judith—kitchen maid
Mr. Kirby—butler
Gilbert Lewis—a young estate worker
Mrs. Neale—housekeeper
Olive—parlor maid
Parris—head gardener
William Pearson—the duke's valet
Ellery Reed—estate manager
Burton Spencer—another young estate worker
Molly Spriggs—the girl with the lantern

FRIENDS, ENEMIES, AND BUSYBODIES

James Appleton—Worksop Priory's vicar
Jack LeCato—a government agent
Colonel George Mortimer—the duke's old army friend
Peter Saunders—Worksop Inn's innkeeper
Polly Saunders—Peter's daughter

HISTORICAL PERSONAGES

Lord William John Cavendish-Scott-Bentinck—5th Duke of Portland
Lord Henry William Scott-Bentinck—the duke's younger brother
Lady Howard de Walden, née *Lady Lucy Joan Cavendish-Scott-Bentinck*—the duke's sister
Frederick George Ellis, 7th Baron Howard de Walden—Lady Lucy's eldest son
William Gladstone—prime minister
Evelyn Denison—Speaker of the House of Commons

All is vast, splendid, and utterly comfortless.

—AUGUSTUS JOHN CUTHBERT HARE (1834–1903),
ENGLISH WRITER AND RACONTEUR WRITING ABOUT
WELBECK ABBEY

1

October 16, 1869

All Violet Harper wanted to do was have a peaceful luncheon at
Worksop Inn with her husband. Instead, she was summoned
away from her half-eaten fish pie to the most magnificent estate
she'd ever seen, owned by the most eccentric man she'd ever met,
to care for the most bizarre corpse she'd ever been called upon to
undertake.

Violet and Sam had been in North Nottinghamshire for almost
four weeks, with Violet touring the countryside while Sam worked
tirelessly to get his coal mine into operation.

He had leased an abandoned mine that was situated on the Nottingham coalfield, a productive stretch of coal that ran beneath
Nottingham. Sam had encountered more difficulties than he'd expected—given that the mine already existed and merely had to be
updated and reopened—mostly because of the difficulty in hiring
workers. Many locals were already employed at one of the various
other active collieries, and a large number of healthy, strapping
men worked at Welbeck Abbey, the enormous local ducal estate
owned by the 5th Duke of Portland.

Rumor had it that His Grace employed hundreds of workers—
not including household staff—for a variety of projects around the
estate. But for what, Sam had no idea.

Violet, though, was about to find out, as Portland's valet stood before her table, as rigid and correct and well groomed as such a servant should be in his work attending to a peer of the realm. The worry lines in his forehead, though, belied his calm exterior.

"Mrs. Harper?" he asked.

Violet put down her fork, which was speared with morsels from the steaming mix of fish chunks, butter, cream, and breadcrumbs, by far her favorite dish at Worksop Inn. In fact, Mr. Saunders, the widowed innkeeper, was kind enough to cook it up especially for her even when it wasn't part of the day's offerings.

"I am," she replied in cautious acknowledgment.

The man bowed and introduced himself as William Pearson, the Duke of Portland's valet. "Your presence has been much commented upon in town, Mrs. Harper, as your, er, profession is most unusual."

Very delicately put, she thought, which was surely to be expected from a servant in a high and trusted place, as a duke's man would be.

"I had no idea my presence was so noteworthy," she said, hoping the man would finish his greeting and be on his way. Already her fish pie was losing heat, the savory trail of steam from the center opening dissipating quickly.

Pearson, in his correct and formal manner, turned to greet Sam, wishing him well in the formation of his coal mine. Sam's look of surprise told Violet that he'd had no idea that his activities were already well known in the area.

Unlike in the busy, chaotic world they had recently left behind in London, everyone here seemed to know what everyone else was doing, and they were especially attuned to the arrival and activities of strangers.

Finally, Pearson got to his point, his voice dropping to a nearly inaudible level. "If you will, madam, your services are urgently needed at Welbeck. There is a carriage waiting for you outside. . . ."

Violet was instantly alert, her fish pie no longer of prime importance. "Someone has died at the duke's home? Was it from an illness or perchance an accident?"

"I'm afraid I cannot say, madam."

He couldn't? Or wouldn't? "What is the person's age? Is it a man, woman, or child?"

"Again, I am unable to say." Pearson's expression was pained. Had something disturbing occurred at Welbeck Abbey? She tried once more as she glanced at Sam, who was shaking his head in a "you're about to be embroiled in someone else's problem again" sort of way.

"Has the local coroner been summoned?" Violet asked, which would determine whether the duke thought the death was suspicious.

"Mr. Thorpe is away in Derby, visiting his ailing mother. We don't know when he'll be back. In any case, Mr. Thorpe is a civil engineer by way of trade, and what is needed is an undertaker."

Most coroners were appointed to their positions, often selected for their stature in society—and the major canal, railway, and waterworks projects of the past few decades had greatly increased the reputations of civil engineers. Only rarely was anyone who understood death or human anatomy made a coroner. Violet had often thought that undertakers should be regularly appointed to such posts, but unfortunately, there were enough charlatans in her profession that it did not enjoy a sterling reputation.

"I see. I'll need my bag," she said, rising briskly. Reluctantly abandoning her fish pie, but having the good sense to ask the innkeeper to wrap it as an evening snack, she left Sam with the valet and went up to their room to retrieve her undertaking bag— a large black leather satchel containing the cosmetics and tools needed to bring a corpse to the bloom of life. Violet had learned to never travel anywhere without it, precisely for unexpected moments like this.

She swiftly changed out of her burgundy-and-green-striped dress into her regular black crape undertaking dress—clothing she also never traveled without—and grabbed her black top hat with ebony tails from inside the room's armoire. Once she had tied the hat's ribbons under her chin and made sure the tails flowed sedately down her back, Violet Harper was thus transformed from carefree tourist to somber undertaker.

"I knew it couldn't last for long," Sam lamented as she reentered the dining room twenty minutes later. She typically wore black every day, for she never knew when her services would be called upon, as they suddenly were now.

Violet had largely laid aside the dreary clothing since they had arrived in Worksop. She hadn't wanted to mislead her fellow tourists at the Long Eaton lace factory or the Sherwood Forest nature walk into thinking she was a woman in deep mourning engaging in entertainments highly inappropriate to such a time.

Sam had daily and delightedly expressed his appreciation for seeing his wife in bright colors for a change. Now here she was, back to her business black.

"It's just for today," she assured him.

Sam's wry glance as he stood to say good-bye suggested he thought otherwise. However, Violet was now too consumed with the thought of the person and unfortunate family who needed her care at Welbeck to be overly concerned about him. The past month had been the longest period she'd gone without preparing for a funeral since becoming an undertaker more than fifteen years ago, except for her interlude of traveling from London to Colorado with Sam four years ago. She had to admit to herself now that she was feeling a nervous tingle at donning her business clothes again and heading off to tend to someone who needed her.

Violet waved absently to her husband and followed Pearson out to the ducal carriage, hoping that whoever had departed had not come to an unnatural end.

As she and Pearson traveled south in the duke's carriage, Violet surreptitiously took in her surroundings. The conveyance was not only plush and luxuriously outfitted but also remarkably comfortable. Even the royal coronation carriage, as expensive and detailed as it was to carry the monarch, couldn't rival this one for pleasing accommodation.

"His Grace is very kind to send such a splendid carriage for me," Violet said to the valet, whose brows were still knit in worry, hoping to coax him into some sort of conversation.

"Yes, the duke is very kind," Pearson replied absently as he stared out at the fields, now barren of crops for the season.

She tried again. "Our innkeeper tells us that His Grace has many . . . unusual . . . building projects in progress."

Pearson nodded without looking at her. "He employs around fifteen hundred workers for their construction. That doesn't include those of us in the household staff, of course."

Fifteen hundred workers at one time on a country estate! What in heaven's name is the duke building? A cathedral? Violet wondered.

Their six-mile carriage ride neared its conclusion at a simply marked post indicating the way to Welbeck Abbey, which sent them east down yet another road to the house, which she could already see about a half mile in the distance. Violet was stunned by the level of activity occurring on the grounds before the Abbey, though. It was as if she had slipped through a magician's fingers from Nottingham's bucolic fields and forests into a buzzing hive of men and equipment.

Most remarkable were the enormous piles of dirt set amid the backdrop of wooded copses, which were now largely devoid of leaves. Men were busy shoveling the dirt onto wagons attached to what looked like miniature locomotive engines, to be drawn to points unknown. "What is that?" she asked over the din of construction, pointing as delicately as she could at the strange contraption.

"What? Oh," Pearson said, startled out of his reverie. "That's a traction engine. It runs on steam and can haul heavy loads more efficiently than horses."

"Remarkable. And what are the dirt piles?"

"That's earth removed for the duke's tunnels, and it will be used to build up the embankments of the lake behind the house."

"Tunnels? What tunnels?" Violet was thoroughly confused. What need was there of a tunnel on this gently rolling property?

Pearson didn't reply, and her attention was immediately diverted away as they rolled past the most mammoth oak tree she had ever seen in her life. Not only did it have branches that extended out nearly fifty feet to either side of the trunk—and Violet could only imagine how impressive they were in the summer, filled with bright green leaves—but the main trunk was so extraordinarily large that a passageway had been cut into it.

The duke's valet, apparently now paying attention, noticed Violet's awe and said, "That's the Greendale Oak. It is known as the Methuselah of trees. The opening was cut through in 1724 on a wager made by the Earl of Oxford that a hole could be made large enough for him to drive a carriage-and-pair through it."

"Remarkable" was again all Violet could manage to breathe.

Pearson nodded. "It is slowly dying, though, from the damage done to it, which isn't easy to see in the autumn. Welbeck is famous for its ancient oaks. Sir Christopher Wren obtained timber for the building of St. Paul's Cathedral from this park."

They were now in full view of the house, which would rival any of the queen's palaces in size and grandeur, with its three stories of stone jutting proudly up from the ground. Violet imagined it was built in a square around a courtyard, although it was impossible to know from her vantage point. Off to their left was a pair of long buildings that reminded her of a college dormitory. Staff quarters, perhaps?

They passed through a stone entrance gate, which prefaced a wide lawn with identical plantings on either side of the drive. Little was in bloom now, except for some fiery-red dahlias with golden centers and several patches of black adders sporting tall bottlebrush spikes of deep purple.

Before they reached the front entrance of the house, though, the carriage veered off to the right and Violet instantly bristled in annoyance. Did Pearson plan to take her to the rear entrance of Welbeck? It was Violet's position that she was not a servant but a temporary member of a grieving family, and therefore she always confidently approached the front door of any home of mourning that she was visiting.

The carriage pulled to a stop about halfway down this side of the house, between a lesser entrance and a vast garden, divided up into various squares, each containing different plantings. One square was full of rosemary, sage, and thyme that faintly scented the air. Others were bursting with fall vegetables—broad beans, peas, fennel, sorrel, and tomatoes.

Apples and pears dangled heavily from trees lining the back of these plantings, which Violet realized comprised a kitchen garden.

Pearson had brought her to the *kitchens?* Heavens, she hoped beyond hope that they were not storing the body down here.

Pearson had already stepped out of the carriage with her undertaking bag and was waiting to help her out. She took his offered hand, and exited onto the gravel path. Once again, she had entered another world, as the sawing, banging, and hammering were only distant turbulence from where she now stood. She was pleased that, as horrified as she was at the thought that a body might be lying in state in a duke's kitchen, at least it didn't have to endure construction noises.

Pearson escorted her down a set of steps to the basement door, where they were greeted by a heavyset, goggle-eyed, middle-aged woman who was sweaty and breathless beneath her stained apron.

"Mrs. Garside," Pearson greeted the woman, "this is Mrs. Harper, the undertaker. Mrs. Harper, may I present Welbeck Abbey's cook to you?"

The cook's expression was confused, unsure what status an undertaker had, so Violet immediately stuck her hand out to shake the other woman's. "How do you do?" she said, immediately regretting it because it was the greeting of someone in a higher class, and Mrs. Garside now looked utterly stricken over how to address the undertaker. Violet followed up with, "I'm pleased to make your acquaintance," and the cook wiped her palm against her apron before taking Violet's proffered hand.

"Inside, if you please, Mrs. 'Arper," the cook said in the Nottingham dialect Violet had come to know well. Mrs. Garside stepped back through the doorway and Violet followed with Pearson behind her, still lugging her bag. They were in an anteroom twice the size of her lodgings in Worksop, probably where all deliveries were made so that no visitors could see into the rooms beyond. Violet was instantly struck by the delicious aroma of roasting chicken. Her stomach responded, reminding her that she had regrettably abandoned her fish pie before she'd made serious acquaintance with it. Several doorways led off the anteroom and the hallway beyond, and as they proceeded along the hallway she could see the various rooms necessary for serving a sprawling ducal estate with hundreds of workers: a pantry, a scullery, a dairy room, a pastry room, the main kitchen area, the housekeeper's room, the butler's room, and, largest of all, the servants' hall, where the staff could eat in shifts.

Women in starched aprons and caps, as well as young men in uniforms, bustled back and forth past them, most giving Violet curious glances but too busy to wonder much about the downstairs visitor. Or perhaps they were avoiding Mrs. Garside, who was muttering incessantly that "No good can come upon this 'ouse after this" and "It's an 'arbinger of more death, I can tell you that much."

As the cook waddled past the rooms, she was working herself up to the point that Violet thought she might have to intervene to calm the woman.

The farther Mrs. Garside went down the hall, the more relieved Violet felt, thinking that they were going to proceed up a rear staircase to either a bedchamber or dining room, more appropriate locations for a body. Unfortunately, Mrs. Garside stopped before they reached the stairs and turned left into a small room lined with locked glass cabinets painted white. Inside the cabinets were all manner of serving dishes in a variety of patterns.

Violet had no time for scrutinizing the serving ware, though, for it was who was on the table in the center of the room that captured her full attention.

Or, should she say, *what* was on the table.

2

Violet was speechless. She turned to Pearson, who had followed her and Mrs. Garside into the room and placed the undertaking bag on the floor. "Surely you don't mean that I am to undertake . . ." She couldn't even complete the sentence.

Lying before her on a kitchen towel was . . . a raven. A bird. An ebony member of the avian species. Someone had taken great care to arrange it so that it looked as though it was huddled down to roost. But still, it was an animal, for heaven's sake! Not even a beloved pet but a wild bird.

Pearson cleared his throat, and looked more uncomfortable than ever. "If you don't mind, Mrs. Harper, Aristotle was His Grace's favorite raven—"

"You've got to tend to 'im, Mrs. 'Arper, and give 'im 'is proper respects," Mrs. Garside pleaded, wringing her hands together. "We're already under the threat of doom because of 'is death."

Violet took a deep breath and began to compose herself. Surely there had to be a sane explanation for why she had been summoned to a ducal estate to prepare a *bird* for a funeral. "You led me to believe there was an actual body waiting for me at Welbeck," she said, turning to Pearson in accusation. She had sacrificed Mr. Saunders's fish pie and time with Sam for *this?*

A young kitchen maid about fifteen years old suddenly appeared in the doorway. "Mrs. Garside, I've filleted the monkfish for the staff's dinner like you told me and oh—" The girl's eyes widened as she realized there were three people crowded around the dead raven's body.

"Go on now, Judith," Mrs. Garside instructed. "Dig up some leeks and slice them like I showed you for the fillets."

The girl needed no further encouragement and scampered right out.

Pearson tried again. "You see, Mrs. Harper, His Grace was concerned by the staff reaction to Aristotle's untimely demise."

"Couldn't someone have merely disposed of the carcass in the woods?" Violet hated to put things so bluntly. She barely restrained herself from adding that undertaking was for humans only.

Mrs. Garside *tsked* as she shook her head woefully. "Oh, surely you know 'ow a dead raven means death and destruction."

Whatever was this woman prattling about? "No, I'm afraid I don't."

Mrs. Garside eyed Violet suspiciously. "Come now, Mrs. 'Arper, you're an undertaker. You should know that ravens are the best luck the queen's got. They're protected at the Tower down in London, because as long as there's ravens there, the country won't fall to a foreign invader. It's the truth," Mrs. Garside added, apparently seeing the disbelief registered on Violet's face. "The ravens 'ave been protecting the Tower since the time of the Conqueror, and there's been no invasion since then." She nodded her head firmly one time in emphasis. "Since 'Is Grace keeps a rookery 'ere, it stands to rights that we've been protected all these years, but Aristotle's death is the start of something 'orrible, I just know it."

"Mrs. Garside," Pearson said, "perhaps if you could leave us so I might explain to Mrs. Harper the circumstances of Aristotle's death, she can better care for him and perhaps advise us on how to avoid any further deaths."

Mrs. Garside nodded with a loud huff. "Yes, Mr. Pearson, I'll take my leave, but mark my words, the bird is trouble. I've a mind to cover the mirrors and stop the clocks." The cook left the room as she had come in, muttering about other methods beyond mirrors and clocks she could employ to ensure the bird's spirit didn't get confused and remain trapped in the kitchens.

Violet whirled on the valet in exasperation. "Why didn't you tell me in the first place that it was a bird you wanted me to see? This is a task for a taxidermist, not an undertaker. You can hardly expect me to believe that a duke actually expected a dead bird to be prepared for a funeral. I have never—"

"Mrs. Harper," Pearson interrupted in a low tone, "please allow me to explain. If I had informed you that the deceased was but a common raven, would you have come here with me?"

"Of course not!" Violet was still contemplating a hasty exit back to Worksop Inn.

"No, I suspected as such. However, His Grace wants to calm down the staff, who are nervous and excitable over the idea that a dead raven means a calamity for the household. You witnessed for yourself Mrs. Garside's agitation. He believes having an undertaker come and conduct a formal funeral will help the staff put it behind them."

"A funeral! For a raven?" Violet shook her head in disbelief. "Why not just capture another one and add it to the flock? Why the pomp?"

"Because, madam, Mrs. Garside found Aristotle herself, dead on a window ledge facing the kitchen gardens, and it took no more than ten minutes for the rest of the staff to know about it. This is far beyond replacing the bird with another," Pearson said. Violet wasn't sure from his tone if he was treating her with the patience he would show to an argumentative child, or if he was shaken by the notion of a curse and trying to convince himself of the validity of what he was saying.

"Please, if you will just tend to Aristotle, His Grace would be exceedingly grateful. He will, of course, pay whatever your charges are for an appropriate funeral."

What in heaven's name was an appropriate service for a duke's dead bird? Was he expecting burial in an actual churchyard? Violet could only imagine *that* conversation with the local vicar.

Pearson must have seen her wavering, for he pressed his point. "There is something else. I don't think it is that significant, but you should know that Aristotle was an intelligent bird, and only five years old. His Grace says the bird should have lived to at least twenty years. The Tower ravens are rumored to live up to forty years because of their pampered living conditions."

There was a problem with Pearson's claim, though. "Don't birds frequently die without warning or cause?" Violet asked. "It doesn't seem all that unusual."

Pearson acknowledged her question with a nod. "True, but Aristotle has no apparent injuries, and His Grace wants to be certain that nothing untoward happened to him."

"What of Mrs. Garside's claim that ravens protect the Tower—and Welbeck Abbey—from foreign invasion?"

Pearson shook his head. "It's a legend, is all. Started a few years ago by some wag, but now nearly given gospel status. I'm surprised Mrs. Garside didn't tell you ravens protected Eden, as far back as she takes the tale."

Violet nodded, understanding how simple rumors, if well told again and again, can become legends. "Well," she allowed reluctantly, "I suppose that since I'm here, I may as well see what I can do to make Aristotle . . . comfortable."

Pearson's relief was palpable as his shoulders relaxed ever so slightly. He thanked Violet, then left her alone with Aristotle.

Violet stared down at her charge, pondering everything the valet had said. What bothered her most was Pearson's comment that the duke wanted to ensure nothing unfortunate had happened to the raven. Did he actually suspect his prize raven had been intentionally killed?

Violet tapped a finger to her lips, involuntarily shaking her head in disbelief. She wasn't seriously about to investigate the death of a raven as a murder.

Was she?

Violet was flummoxed as to what to actually do to undertake a bird. She put her reticule down on the table and gingerly ran her hands over the bird's body and under his wings, feeling for any protuberances or oddities. His feathers were still very sleek and shone almost iridescently. He was quite gorgeous. She gently rolled Aristotle onto his back and ignored his sightless, beady eyes. His talons were curled up and stiff. She'd never thought about it before, but she guessed animals experienced rigor mortis, just like humans.

Out of habit, Violet began talking to Aristotle as she examined him. "Now, sir, you look fine and healthy to me, and I admit I've no idea what to do to improve your appearance. I certainly cannot use any cosmetic massage on your feathery face, and embalming is completely out of the question, as I'm afraid it would be too ridiculous. No offense intended, sir. Ah, I see a bit of your ebony beak has broken off. Were you in a fight? Did you crash into the kitchen window and break it? Did you attempt to eat something you shouldn't have? I think a little bit of clay to fill in the area, with a daub of Heavy Black Number Two, should fix you right up."

Perhaps the bird died from accidentally ingesting something poisonous to him. Violet worked to pry open his beak and looked inside his—was it a mouth? "Hmm, I can only imagine how much rotting flesh has passed through here, sir."

She saw nothing there. She rubbed his gullet beneath his beak and was startled to feel something hard and solid lodged inside it.

"Now what is this, Aristotle?" Violet asked curiously as she attempted to work whatever it was up out of his throat and into his mouth. "Perhaps you really were out dining on improper foods. Isn't it true that you ravens love shiny objects? I'll bet this was all just a simple case of you discovering—Ah, here we are." Violet reached her little finger in and scooped the offending object out of his mouth.

"What have we here?" she said, holding up what appeared to be a small scrap of colored porcelain with smooth edges. She dug into her undertaking bag for a cloth to wipe it off. The shard was white with part of a blue-and-green pattern on one side of it. Part of a teacup or saucer, perhaps? It was probably part of something that had broken and then been thrown into a refuse pile or badly buried in the kitchen garden. Maybe the bird had seen the sun reflecting off its surface and swooped down for it. Ravens were like crows, attracted to glittering objects. If the shard got lodged in his gullet and was too large for him to digest, it would have effectively choked the poor thing. That would explain how he ended up on the kitchen window ledge, as well.

"Aristotle, you have given everyone a scare, but I think we now understand what happened to you." Violet dropped the shard into her reticule, where it shared space with a kitchen knife. Violet had added the weapon during her previous investigation, and decided that it should remain there permanently for protection. The shard, however, she intended to discard later, once she informed the master of the estate of her conclusions. Perhaps now that a very simple explanation was to be had, all of this nonsense about preparing the raven for a funeral could be put to rest. She quickly pulled out a bit of clay and the proper paint and a brush from her bag, and set to work on repairing the bird's beak. She had no idea what else to do for him.

The odor of roasting chicken wafted over her once more. Violet could picture the browning, crispy skin, the chicken's juices dripping succulently into the iron pan in a golden pool of exquisite flavor. Perhaps she could convince Mrs. Garside to offer her a nibble.

Speaking of Mrs. Garside, Violet decided it was time to find the cook. First, though, she quickly rearranged Aristotle's body back into the roosting position in which she'd found him, then stepped back into the hallway, where she nearly collided into a maid carrying a stack of dishes. With an apology for her clumsiness, Violet asked where Mrs. Garside was, and the maid nodded down the hall. "In the roasting room, madam."

The roasting room? Violet had no idea that a ducal estate had such specialized kitchen rooms. She went where the maid had indicated, and found herself in an overly warm room, about fifteen feet square, containing two kitchen ranges and an enormous, old-fashioned fireplace along one wall with three revolving spits set at two-foot intervals above the ground. Each spit contained a half dozen chickens, which explained the intensity of the aroma down here. Fat and juices dripped lazily into large pans below.

What Violet couldn't explain was the sight of Mrs. Garside, her broad back to Violet, bent over and using a bellows in front of the fireplace. Was Violet mistaken, or was the cook pumping air into a grate in the wall nearby? How peculiar.

"Mrs. Garside, excuse me," Violet said.

The cook rose unsteadily from her crouched position and turned. Her face was scarlet from the heat of the flames, a routine hazard of her occupation, Violet supposed. Mrs. Garside brushed away a lock of frizzy hair that had fallen out from under her cap as she laid aside the bellows. "Yes, Mrs. 'Arper? Is Aristotle all fixed up now?"

Violet supposed Aristotle was as "fixed" as he could be. "Yes. You'll be pleased to know there was no evidence at all that he was purposefully injured. I believe he just had an accident."

Mrs. Garside looked doubtful.

"I would like to see His Grace now if he's here," Violet said.

"Oh, 'e's 'ere all right. I'll get the 'ousekeeper, Mrs. Neale." Mrs. Garside swept past Violet back into the hall. "Judith!" she shouted above the din of everything else happening. The girl appeared from nowhere.

"Yes, Mrs. Garside?"

"Go fetch Olive, and 'ave 'er ask Mrs. Neale to come down when she 'as a moment. Tell 'er it's about Aristotle. Then come back 'ere and get to minding the spits again."

Judith ran off to do the cook's bidding.

While they waited, Violet asked about the quantity of roasting chickens, which were almost overpowering in their delectable fragrance as she stood near them. "Does the staff eat whatever the duke and his family eat?"

"No, we're 'aving monkfish tonight. And 'Is Grace doesn't have any family living 'ere."

"Ah, His Grace is having a dinner party, then?"

Mrs. Garside snickered, but quickly caught herself and became serious once more. "No, madam, 'Is Grace isn't 'aving guests."

"But . . . surely the duke cannot eat nearly twenty chickens tonight by himself."

"No, but he likes the smell of them. All of the time."

Violet cast her glance at the bellows, which was propped up against the wall beneath the grate. Surely the woman didn't mean that—

At that moment, an elderly woman entered the room, wearing the most ostentatious chatelaine Violet had ever seen. It hung from a pale-blue sash, and multiple keys, from large gate keys down to the tiniest jewel casket key, dangled and clinked together as she walked.

"Olive said you wished to see me for an important matter?" the woman demanded imperiously, as though exceedingly put out to have been summoned to this hot and stuffy room.

Mrs. Garside was appropriately deferential in her tone, but Violet didn't think the cook was particularly frightened of the other woman. "Yes, Mrs. Neale. This 'ere's Mrs. 'Arper. She's the undertaker seeing to Aristotle, and she wants to speak with 'Is Grace."

Mrs. Neale wrinkled her nose distastefully at the mention of the dead bird. "I see. I'll talk to Mr. Kirby."

After Mrs. Neale swept out, jingling her way into the hall toward the staircase, Violet asked, "Who is Mr. Kirby?"

"'E's the butler of Welbeck Abbey. 'E's in charge of the male staff in the 'ouse."

"I see." In the manner of large houses, protocol had to be followed, and it appeared as though the butler would be the one to escort her to the duke.

Mr. Kirby appeared promptly, and once again Violet was introduced. He was much more gracious than Mrs. Neale. "Thank you for coming, Mrs. Harper. The duke will be glad of it, I'm sure. I'll send Hudock down to you." The butler left, almost instantly replaced with Judith, who ducked into the room and took turns at each spit, checking on how each of the chickens was faring.

Apparently it was not the butler who would escort her after all. "Who is Hudock?" Violet asked, exasperated by how many people were required for her to see the duke.

"Miles 'Udock, 'e's one of the footmen," the cook said. "A little lame-brained, but thinks 'e will replace Mr. Kirby one day. Silly boy. Mr. Kirby serves this family, as 'is father did before 'im, and 'is grandfather before that. I imagine it will be another Kirby in the butler's uniform just as sure as it will be another Bentinck behind the ducal crest one day. Now if you'll pardon me, I must return to my birds."

Mrs. Garside turned and retrieved her bellows and began operating it next to the grate again. In a quick minute, a young man in a uniform arrived, looking down and brushing invisible specks from his jacket. He acknowledged Violet's presence with a nod and took her to see Lord William John Cavendish-Scott-Bentinck, the 5th Duke of Portland.

3

Violet was thoroughly confused when the footman led her back outside again. Were they not to access the house through the servants' staircase? Was she actually to be taken to the front door this time?

However, instead of walking back in the direction of the main entrance, Hudock went to the left, as though to head to the rear of the home. Perhaps the duke was taking tea in a rear garden?

But the rear gardens, dominated by a large fountain overlooking acres of finely manicured shrubbery, were empty except for a gardener on his knees, tugging at a stubborn root. "Parris," the footman said in greeting as they passed. The gardener squinted up at them and nodded in return.

The footman continued leading her away from the house. *Where are we going?* Violet wondered, trying to block out the noise of construction going on around the estate. Although she could hear the hammering of nails, dragging of carts, and shouts of laughter emanating from the front of the house, the rear gardens were peaceful. Between the gardens and the welcoming arches of the rear stone entrance was a multilevel terrace, with artfully arranged potted shrubbery struggling to mask the disarray of construction elsewhere.

Behind the gardens was an expanse of lawn, and behind the lawn was a copse of barren trees. Hudock led her around the copse, to one of the most remarkable sights Violet had ever seen. It was nearly bewildering in its complexity. Men stood near horse-drawn wagons mounded with fresh dirt, shoveling out a long and narrow lake while men below moved the dirt around all along the embankment. In an area where the lakeside was not being filled stood a tall, stooped man wearing a brown coat at least ten years out of fashion and a black silk hat at least two feet too high. He held a black umbrella over his head with one hand and a wood oar in the other as he shouted encouragement and instruction to several rowboats out in the lake. Those boats were populated with uniformed male servants, who were doing their best to row according to the man's commands, despite the constriction of their tight jackets and trousers.

This man couldn't possibly be . . . No, it just wasn't conceivable.

Yet Hudock walked straight for the man, only stopping when he was about six feet away, clearing his throat several times until he was noticed.

"Yes?" the man said, as Hudock instantly dropped his gaze, avoiding direct eye contact.

"Your Grace," Hudock said deferentially, his eyes still downcast. "May I present to you Mrs. Violet Harper, Aristotle's undertaker?" he offered before backing away, presumably to return to his duties.

The duke was distracted by something on the lake and turned his attention away without acknowledging Violet's presence.

"Bernard, no! Pay attention to your oar. Don't let it slap against the water, let it gently glide in. Like this." The duke demonstrated the proper movement with the oar while still keeping the umbrella over his head. He moved awkwardly, like a mechanical toy soldier.

Violet had no idea which rower was Bernard, for they all responded in kind, checking their oars and trying to imitate their employer. Some of the low-slung boats were slicing through the water; others were moving in near circles. It would have been comical if it weren't so . . . bizarre.

"You wish to speak to me about Aristotle?" Portland asked without preamble, startling Violet out of her concentration on the hapless servants.

"Yes, Your Grace," she replied, as she finally had the opportunity to see his face. She guessed he was near seventy, but his height made him an imposing figure, despite his slightly stooped shoulders.

"We won't speak of it here, where the servants may be listening. We will go inside."

Violet had no idea who could possibly hear them. "Yes, Your Grace."

Portland had a nose so long and broad that it probably prevented the sun from ever reaching the man's lips. What was most peculiar about him, though, was that, in addition to his large features and outmoded clothing, the man would not make direct eye contact with Violet. He continuously gazed off to one side, or tilted his head up in the air as they spoke to each other. His efforts were probably made easier by his pouch-like eyelids, which hooded his eyes from view.

Portland returned his attention to the rowers, who seemed exhausted from their ordeal. After a few more minutes of instruction, during which Violet wondered if she should wait or if perhaps she had been dismissed, Portland finally dropped his oar. He pulled a whistle from a wide-flapped pocket on the exterior of his coat and blew it. The shrill, piercing noise made Violet cringe, but inspired near body heaves of relief out on the water as the rowers started their boats toward shore.

"Come," Portland commanded, walking off toward a rear entrance of the house.

With her reticule and undertaking bag in tow, Violet struggled to keep up with the man's stride as he moved purposefully, the umbrella still perched high over his top hat, despite there being no rain and it not being a particularly sunny day.

Portland paused at the door long enough to allow Violet to precede him through. The footman who opened the door kept his eyes cast down in the same manner that Hudock had. Was this a sign of fear? Was Portland a cruel taskmaster? And what was all of the rowing instruction for?

Well, it was of no matter to Violet. She simply needed to report on the dead raven, see him buried, and return to her sightseeing around Nottinghamshire.

Unfortunately, her plans were not to be realized.

* * *

Violet had to refrain from gasping as she entered Welbeck's house. The interior was under as much construction as the exterior. Walls were being replastered, repapered, and sometimes moved entirely. Huge carpets lay rolled in stacks, waiting for oak flooring to be fully installed in intricate variations of herringbone patterns. Furniture sat shrouded, awaiting their final resting places.

Remarkably, the din of hammering, sawing, and talking ceased instantly in each room into which Violet and Portland entered, with the workers casting their eyes down, if not turning their backs completely and waiting for the undertaker and the duke to be gone.

Although many rooms of Welbeck were under renovation, some were not, and Portland paused inside a grand, spacious dining room, as if debating with himself whether to meet with Violet here. It was quieter in this room, removed from much of the other construction underway.

The center of the room held a banquet table that was so long, Violet counted eighteen chairs precisely placed on each side of it. The ceiling soared, as majestic as any cathedral's, and the walls were covered with splendid paintings. In fact, there were more than enough portraits to represent a guest for each dining chair. As Violet began to take notice of particular portraits, she had no doubt that some of them were by the likes of Rembrandt and Reynolds.

Her attention was drawn to three portraits, identically framed and hanging over the mantel, where ordinarily there would just be one life-sized portrait as the focal piece of the room. They were of three young women, each wearing the same pearl ear bobs and fashionable seventeenth-century clothing.

"You are admiring the Cavendish sisters, I see," Portland said, his face away from Violet and concentrating on the portraits. "Those are Jane, Frances, and Elizabeth Cavendish. They were great-granddaughters of Bess of Hardwick."

Every schoolchild knew who the formidable Bess of Hardwick, a notable figure of Elizabethan society, was. Through a series of four well-made marriages, she had become fabulously wealthy, dying at age eighty as the Countess of Shrewsbury. She was most renowned for having served, along with her last husband, the 6th Earl of Shrewsbury, as a jailer for Mary, Queen of Scots.

Hadn't Violet heard that Portland had the Cavendish name included in his own? "They are relatives of yours, sir?" she asked.

"Indeed." Portland smiled, but it came across as more of a grimace. "They were daughters of my ancestor William Cavendish, a nobleman at the court of James I and a friend to Charles I. The sisters married very well. No doubt the thought of possessing some piece of Welbeck Abbey's fortunes—as well as their own personal charms—made them very desirable in the eyes of suitors."

Violet had to admit that all three girls were very beautiful.

"You're an undertaker," Portland continued, "so I'm sure you can appreciate the fact that Elizabeth's funeral was attended by nine mourning coaches. They were reputedly filled not only with her nine children, but with a complement of gentry and nobility. Quite a young woman she must have been."

And quite a rich young woman to have had such an ostentatious procession, Violet thought.

"Ironically, Elizabeth died in childbirth for her tenth child, while Frances was completely childless. Hmm." Portland cocked his head as he gazed at Jane's portrait. "I think Jane died of seizures."

Portland's informative history lesson was very interesting, but Violet needed to get back to town. She was also famished. Was that the aroma of roasting chicken she smelled once more? To the left of the fireplace was a grate identical to the one in the basement, except this one was painted to match the yellow walls, whereas the one in the kitchen was in its natural black iron state.

Mrs. Garside had done her work well. Violet pushed the thought of her hunger to the recesses of her mind so she could wrap up her current duty.

"Your Grace, if I might . . ."

"What? Oh, of course." Portland held out a chair for Violet, as if they were to dine together. She sat, dropping her undertaking bag behind the chair next to her, and he moved to a chair across the table from her. Still he had difficulty meeting her gaze. This was becoming very disconcerting.

"I examined Aristotle—" she began.

"He was my best raven. Did Pearson tell you that? A sorry loss, the bird was. Made more so by all of the gossip about him down-stairs."

"Yes, Pearson did mention it. You will be glad to know that I be-lieve I have uncovered the cause of his death, which should dispel any rumors." Violet reached into her reticule and pulled out the shard of porcelain. "I believe he choked on this, which I found in his gullet."

Portland examined it in her hand as best he could across the table, but refused to reach out and touch it. "Ravens do love shiny things. Aristotle was very well trained. My falconer could get him to do tricks, hopping through rings and even flying obstacle courses. I don't suppose another will rise to take his place. Do you know of the legend surrounding ravens, Mrs. Harper?"

"That England won't be conquered as long as they live at the Tower? Yes, Your Grace."

Portland was pensive. "I had a rookery installed for my own en-tertainment, but the staff think that the idea extends to Welbeck Abbey, too. However, I shall have Kirby announce to them that he accidentally swallowed a . . . what is it, exactly?"

Violet studied the shard once more. "A piece of porcelain, I'd say. Perhaps from a broken teacup or saucer? I imagine Aristotle found his way into some discarded goods."

"Mmm. The servants may still have some ridiculous idea that there is a curse upon the estate because we've lost a raven for rea-sons other than old age. They will need the comfort that a formal service can offer. Pearson says you have agreed to conduct Aristo-tle's funeral, which I would like to hold tomorrow morning."

Violet detested the thought of a bird burial being referred to as a "funeral" and felt the whole ordeal was nonsense, but bit her tongue and respected his station. "Yes, Your Grace."

"May I request, then, that you stay as my guest overnight here at the Abbey? I'm sure you will have preparations to make for Aris-totle's funeral."

Preparations? She simply needed to find a small crate and line it with a newspaper. "My husband and I have lodgings back in Worksop, so I don't think—"

"That's fine. I'll send someone to town to give your husband a message and pick up your things. There is a finished guest room somewhere upstairs, I'm sure. Kirby will help you."

Portland stood, nodded vaguely in Violet's direction, and left her at the table, alone except for that delicious aroma that would not go away. She wasn't sure what had just happened to her. Had she somehow committed to staying overnight in this unfinished colossus, just to inter a dead raven? Was there some strange animal graveyard on the grounds? Perhaps it was part of the construction plans.

Well, if she was to be trapped at Welbeck Abbey for a day, she might as well go see Mrs. Garside for a sampling of the chicken that had been taunting her hunger for the last hour. As marvelous as it smelled, it just might make the overnight stay worth it.

Once Violet had secured Aristotle inside a box that had previously held a shipment of nails, she set the box directly in the center of the table where she'd found him. She draped a tablecloth over the box in some effort to make it look as though he were lying in state. Satisfied with her efforts to undertake Aristotle properly, she then partook of a side of chicken in the servants' hall that more than lived up to the tantalizing promise of its aroma.

Her hunger now satiated, Violet actually wanted something to do to exercise away all she had eaten while waiting for her belongings to arrive. Perhaps it might be of benefit to show a few of the staff members the porcelain shard, just to confirm that it came from the duke's collection. It would also help impress upon the kitchen staff what Kirby had announced when he came downstairs earlier while Violet was eating.

She left her undertaking bag in the room with Aristotle and wandered into the main hallway, where servants were bustling to and fro with cleaning supplies and linens. She stopped several of them and showed them the porcelain shard. They all shook their heads at it, saying that they didn't know where it might be from.

Violet was just about to locate Mrs. Garside to ask her opinion when a parlor maid in her twenties approached her. "Madam, I'm Olive, and I'm told you want to identify some porcelain. I assist with His Grace's collections and can help you."

Violet showed Olive the shard. Unlike her master, Olive didn't hesitate to take the piece and hold it up in the air, trying to catch it in the light and get a better look at it. Finally, the girl frowned. "This doesn't look like anything of His Grace's, but it's such a small piece. . . ."

"Have any sets been thrown away recently?"

"No, madam, His Grace wouldn't do that." Olive seemed shocked at the very thought of it.

"Can you show me his porcelain patterns? Together we might be able to tell what set this shard belongs to." Violet had no idea why she was pursuing this. Boredom, perhaps?

Olive, however, looked intrigued by Violet's suggestion. After hurrying off to get the housekeeper's permission for the task, the parlor maid returned and escorted Violet up the servants' staircase into the main floor of the Abbey.

Violet followed Olive through another set of rooms, different from those she had seen earlier. These rooms might have been parlors, or bedrooms, or smoking rooms, or libraries, or any of the other types of luxurious chambers contained in a stately house. It was impossible to tell because, although they were all finished— their walls and ceilings painted and embellished with moldings, their floors laid and varnished, and their windows adorned with graceful draperies—they were all utterly empty.

Except for paintings. A countless number of them, just as Violet had seen in the dining room, covered the walls in a priceless hodge-podge.

As they passed through several of these rooms, Violet noticed one other item. In one corner of every room, standing lonely and erect like a sentinel, was a commode. Each was adorned with a luxuriously padded seat and cloaked in a walnut edifice.

"What is this?" Violet asked, walking to the commode in one room and pointing to it.

"You don't know?" Olive asked in surprise.

"Of course I do. I mean, why is this the only piece of furniture in the room?"

Olive shrugged. "His Grace's orders. He likes things the way he likes them. In here, madam."

They entered a storage room as large as Violet's lodgings back in London. It had a window on the opposite end from the door, and both long walls were lined with cabinets, where glass-plated fronts displayed their wares. From top to bottom, the cabinet shelves were stuffed full of numerous sets of china in a wide variety of patterns with dozens of place settings each. It would put the sumptuous offerings of the renowned Bainbridge's to shame.

After Olive quickly opened each of the cabinets with a large brass key, Violet began comparing the shard against each pattern in turn. There were a few patterns of blue and green that seemed similar, but it was hard to tell because the shard she had was so small. *Perhaps it belongs to this one with ribbons along the edge in a Scottish tartan pattern,* she thought. *Hmm, no, that isn't right.*

Another hopeful pattern was that of exquisite majolica, with various scenes of Italian Renaissance life painted across them. Although the dishes incorporated rich cobalt blue and bright emerald green, none of it was quite right. She moved on to the next pattern.

While Olive waited respectfully to one side, twisting the key in one hand, Violet thought to engage her in conversation. "Without us counting the various place settings to see what might be missing, which would take days, I suppose this is the only way to match this little piece I have."

"Yes, madam," the girl said dutifully.

"You're certain that there haven't been any pieces chipped or broken recently that would have ended up in the kitchen garden?" Violet held the shard up to a plate whose centerpiece contained a burst of flowers and fruit spilling out of a Grecian urn. It was a riot of vibrant colors, but it still wasn't a match.

Olive shook her head. "The duke doesn't throw away much."

"But surely he would have broken dishes tossed." After that declaration was met with a blank stare, Violet had another idea. "Can you tell me which pattern was used for his most recent dinner party?"

The girl tried to keep her face steady, but Violet saw the expression of incredulity there. "There are no dinner parties here, madam."

"What do you mean? He has dozens of china patterns here." Violet put the shard back into her reticule, indicating that she was finished with her inspection here, which had resulted in nothing.

"Yes, but there are no parties at Welbeck Abbey." Olive began locking up the cabinets.

This made no sense. "None at all? Not even, say, a wedding celebration for a close family member?"

"Especially not that, madam." Olive raised her eyebrows quizzically and held up the key, as if to ask if they were finished in the storage room. Violet was not.

"Well, what about the china that the duke eats on daily? Where is that kept? Downstairs?"

Olive gave her an odd look. "His Grace? Why, he don't eat on any of it, madam. He uses the crockery the rest of us use."

Violet had never heard of such a thing. What she knew of Portland thus far made him an utter paradox. First she'd witnessed him drilling his servants in rowing, then seen that both he and his staff couldn't seem to look at one another, implying that there was something odd about the man at best, cruel at worst. Now Violet was discovering that the duke reduced himself to eating as humbly as those same servants—not to mention that he was willing to spend money to give a bird a fancy burial to soothe his servants' fears, and to spend vast amounts of money renovating rooms, only to use them as picture galleries.

What in heaven's name was going on here at Welbeck Abbey?

Violet followed Olive back through the empty rooms whose walls were replete with masterpieces, then back down the servants' staircase. Down in the kitchens, they ran into Mrs. Neale, who silently held out a palm, into which Olive placed the key, curtsied, and went off to her duties without a glance at Violet.

"So, Mrs. Harper," Mrs. Neale said with a disdainful sniff as she reattached the key to its proper place along her chain, "did you find what you were looking for? You should know that I absolutely never let keys out of my sight. This was a great exception I made. I was busy making out an order for the coal man when Olive came to me, and His Grace has given orders that you are to be properly accommodated while you are here. That's only until tomorrow, correct?" Mrs. Neale wrinkled her nose in distaste.

No one ever seemed to enjoy having an undertaker under his roof, with the exception of the perpetually mourning Queen Victoria. However, Violet intuitively sensed there might be something else behind Mrs. Neale's open resentment. "Just until tomorrow morning, in fact. I need to find out where His Grace would like Aristotle to rest. Is there some sort of animal burial ground on the estate?"

"I'm sure I don't know—my time is spent inside, not outside. I've never heard of a bird being buried. I think he buries his hunting dogs in a special place across the lake."

Perhaps Violet needed to speak directly to the duke again. As directly as could be managed. She had one final question.

"Is there a chapel at the Abbey?" It seemed a reasonable assumption as many wealthy estates had chapels purpose-built for their families and staff.

The housekeeper frowned. "You mean the underground one?"

"Underground?" Violet frowned in puzzlement. "There is a chapel beneath Welbeck Abbey?" That was curious. Why would the duke—or one of his ancestors—have built one in secret?

"That's none of my concern and I shouldn't have mentioned it," Mrs. Neale replied. "I pay no mind to any of His Grace's doings down there."

His "doings"? It sounded as though the duke had some sort of strange laboratory down there. Was he conjuring spirits, like the queen's favorite servant, John Brown, liked to do? Or was there something else macabre happening at Welbeck Abbey?

Try as she might, though, Violet could see she would get nothing further from Mrs. Neale, who now stood there with her lips clamped shut, refusing to say more. Finally, with a sigh, Violet asked if she could see the duke once more, and once more they enacted the intricate dance of summoning Mr. Kirby, who escorted her himself to the duke's quarters.

What she saw there had Violet questioning her own sanity.

Portland's "quarters" consisted of four rooms in a remote part of Welbeck that was still under construction. In fact, Kirby had to gently hand Violet up across boards precariously positioned over a large gaping hole in the duke's antechamber, beneath which was more construction. Before he knocked on the door at the other end of the room to announce her presence, Kirby said, almost apologetically, "You must understand, madam, that His Grace is rather shy." That was not enough to prepare Violet.

They entered a room that, while spacious, was sparsely furnished in worn leather chairs and sofas and some scarred tables that looked as though they belonged in a St. Giles tavern. Unlike in the dining room, the walls—painted a pale shade of salmon— were devoid of any artwork whatsoever, although the requisite commode stood proudly in a corner. Halfway across the room stood a wood screen, with acanthus leaves and swirls carved through the wall-to-wall structure, providing a shadowy look at what lay on the other side. It reminded Violet of a bank teller's screen, only more elaborate and more concealing. It was also the only piece of genuine décor in the room.

"Kirby?" came Portland's voice from the far end of the room. Violet saw a flash of something dark behind the screen.

"Yes, Your Grace. I have Mrs. Harper here. She wishes to speak with you once more about Aristotle."

"Yes, yes." Shadows moved again, and it seemed as though Portland had taken a seat next to the screen. Why the subterfuge? Hadn't Violet just met the man face-to-face a short while ago? Of course, now that she thought about it, the duke hadn't ever looked her in the eye.

Kirby showed Violet to a chair next to the screen. It had a ripped back, was missing buttons in its tufts, and was totally unbefitting a man of Portland's stature. She sat down at the edge of the seat, to avoid having the torn leather snag the back of her dress. Kirby offered an apologetic smile and left. The gentle clicking of the doorknob sounded like a ricocheting bullet in such a barren room.

Portland did not invite any conversation, so Violet assumed it was her responsibility to initiate it. She cleared her throat. "Ahem, Your Grace, I wanted to let you know that Aristotle is . . . ready. Also, I did attempt to investigate where the porcelain shard may have come from, but to no avail."

The duke made no response of acknowledgment. With dogged determination, she kept going.

"I need to know where you wish to have him buried on the grounds of the estate. Do you have an animal burial ground? Also, do you wish to have a service in Welbeck's chapel?" It made Violet's stomach turn to speak so seriously of such a bizarre situation.

The duke did not respond. Had he even heard her? It was impossible to think that he hadn't. Maybe it was best to sit quietly until he said something. The quiet, though, was painful. There wasn't even the sound of a clock ticking to fill her ears. How correct it was when people said that silence could be deafening.

She then noticed the aroma of roasting chicken yet again. Was it really wafting up this far into the house? Violet glanced around surreptitiously and saw a familiar grate in the wall.

Good Lord, she thought. *If I lived here I'd gorge myself every day on chicken meat.* How did the duke remain so lanky? He must be active around his estate, beyond teaching his servants how to row boats. Perhaps he even—

"No service in the chapel," Portland said, interrupting her thoughts. "We shall bury him in the ravens' graveyard near the rookery so he can be near his brethren."

There was a special, separate cemetery just for his birds? She shouldn't be surprised. Violet was only disappointed that he hadn't said anything else about the underground chapel as she was interested in seeing it. Before she could even figure out how to delicately ask a peer of the realm about his buried house of worship, a knock at the door interrupted, quickly followed by Kirby's reentry.

"Your Grace, Colonel Mortimer is here to see you. He says it is important, and I believe he is quite serious."

As if the day hadn't been peculiar enough already, Violet now had the discomfort of encountering one Colonel George William David Mortimer, a man who made Violet believe she had truly entered a distant, grotesque world filled with all of the eccentrics of Great Britain. Outside of the royal family, of course.

4

Colonel George Mortimer had never been a man to panic, and he was certainly not about to start now. Lying on his side in the dark, with no noise around him save his own thoughts clamoring wildly in his mind, he couldn't quite convince himself that he wasn't dead at the moment.

Egads, did he feel dreadful, confined in this space as he was, his face against something hard and unyielding. His tongue was thick and dry, and he could barely open his mouth, so tightly was the roof of it stuck to his tongue. His head throbbed as though he had been clubbed with a tree trunk. Wait, was that what had happened? He recalled being outside very late. There were shadows, angry whispers, and then . . .

Right. Now he remembered. In fact, he recalled everything from the previous night. He almost wished he were still unconscious. The question was, what should he do about it?

He opened his eyelids. At least, he thought he opened them, but it was still pitch-black around him. Good Lord, had he completely lost his eyesight, too? Wait, no, there was a small shaft of light winking at him. Mortimer closed his left eye and squinted his right. Realization dawning on him, he reached out an arm.

Just as he thought. He brushed aside the floor-length bedding that draped to the floor, and light from the cottage filtered down to him. Mortimer was lying under his own bed. How the deuce had he ended up there?

He crawled out from beneath the bed and struggled up to a standing position as he adjusted to the sunlight flooding the room. The floor mirror informed him that he was covered in dust and had cobwebs in his thick, drooping white mustache and in what remained of his hair. Perhaps he should take up the offer of having one of the parlor maids visit his place on occasion.

What was he thinking? What if a maid had come upon him just now? She would have run screaming in terror, bringing all of Welbeck Abbey in to see the very dead—or very drunken, depending upon how she saw it—Colonel Mortimer stuffed under his own bed. She might have noticed other things, too, that might bring him embarrassment. No, a few cobwebs were worth his total privacy.

Mortimer turned to one side and examined his girth. When had the mirror become such a liar? Well, there was no time to think of it now; he had far more important issues to worry about. He made himself a pot of tea inside his two-room cottage, which was small but had been refurbished with running taps and a hot-water boiler. He also had his own privy outside, whereas most of the other cottagers living on the estate had to share with at least one other.

With his clothes and hair dusted out and a warm cup in his hands, Mortimer thought about last night. What could he tell Portland that wouldn't implicate him? The body was sure to be found soon, if it hadn't already been discovered and the local police brought in. He tapped the side of his teacup as he stared out at one of the ravens from Portland's rookery swooping down after something nearby.

Wretched birds, he thought, with their endless croaking and knocking sounds. Why didn't Portland limit himself to normal birds, like hawks, falcons, and owls? Why these black thieves?

The raven flew off, having apparently secured whatever had attracted it. Mortimer remained at the window, though, contemplating, until finally he realized what he must do. Setting aside his cup and saucer, he strode out of his cottage. Heading across the side lawn of Welbeck Abbey, passing by the kitchen gardens, he reached the main house. He'd been fortunate that Portland had offered him this place to live for as long as he wanted it.

A footman, Milo or Milton or something, saw him approach and opened the door before he had to hammer the enormous lion's-head door knocker. What with the incessant pounding already in his brain, the harsh sound of the knocker would have probably made him unconscious at this point.

The footman's expression—quickly hooded, of course—told Mortimer exactly what his appearance was. Well, that would make him that much more convincing to Portland, who would not be inclined to believe his story.

The butler, Kirby, appeared from nowhere. The man had a sixth sense about him and showed up in the unlikeliest of places when you least expected him. Mortimer explained that he urgently needed to see Portland.

"His Grace has another guest at the moment," Kirby said, unruffled.

"I don't care if the Archangel Michael has come to visit, I *must* see him right away." Mortimer crossed his arms in an aggressive stance. Kirby relented, although Mortimer had the distinct sense that the butler was merely placating him like a child, not responding in fear.

He followed Kirby through the usual trek of never-ending construction to Portland's dismal rooms. As he entered through the door the butler held open, Mortimer couldn't believe what he saw. Sitting on the near side of Portland's screen was a beauteous dark-haired woman dressed in mourning. Had the body been discovered and his family and the police summoned that quickly? Was this his widow? It seemed impossible that so much could have happened already.

Unless he had been unconscious longer than he thought. What time was it? For that matter, what *day* was it?

Well, it didn't matter, this was his moment. Mortimer launched into his story.

Violet was aghast at the man who had just entered the duke's quarters. This Colonel Mortimer was wild-looking and unkempt, his eyes wide with fear or distress and the left side of his face scratched as though he had been on the losing end of a fight with a wild animal. Yet he carried himself with strange self-assurance. He also stank of liquor, and his bloodshot eyes furthered the impression that the man was still in his cups, or had been recently. It was a thoroughly disrespectful way to intrude upon a peer.

Violet clasped her hands in her lap as Portland dealt with the man.

"What has happened, dear friend?" the duke asked from behind the screen.

The colonel stood next to Violet, nearly enveloping her in his odor. She maintained as dignified an expression as she could as the colonel addressed Portland without acknowledging her presence.

"John, I have witnessed something terrible, something unspeakable." The colonel's voice quavered, but it seemed forced to Violet. Who was he that he addressed the duke so casually and was called "friend"? And he did not seem to think it odd that the duke was hidden behind a screen.

"'Unspeakable'?" Portland said. "You have seen a great deal in your life. What could be worse than the horrors we witnessed in Burma together?"

Portland's voice was soothing, and his manner entirely different from what Violet had experienced with his staff. Violet tried to summon up history. Hadn't there been a series of conflicts in Burma back in the '20s? She couldn't remember her childhood lessons well enough, though, to recall what the strife had been over. Territory, maybe. British pride, more than likely.

"Nothing, I suppose, except that this impacts you. I believe I saw a murder being committed last night."

The room fell silent, as though the very furniture—what little of it there was—were in shock over the colonel's words.

Violet immediately had a thousand questions, but first it was imperative that she see whoever it was. The misfortune the late individual might have suffered was being compounded every second that it was left alone with no one to care for it. She also hoped to heavens that the colonel, who appeared half crazed, wasn't referring to Aristotle's death.

She kept all of her thoughts to herself, though, waiting for the duke to respond. Finally he did, but not in the way she expected.

"Are you sure?" Portland asked slowly. "It was not . . . a vision, perhaps?"

"Definitely not. I saw a man being strangled. I think he was being strangled. It was dark and it happened so quickly."

"This is indeed dreadful, George. It occurred on the grounds of Welbeck?" Portland was remarkably calm at this calamitous news.

"Yes. I was taking a late-night stroll and came upon two figures arguing. Then I saw the larger of the two attack the other, and the second one dropped to the ground. The first man fled and I—I—" Colonel Mortimer took a heaving breath.

"You had an episode?" Portland asked gently.

"Forgive me, John, I don't know what came over me."

"Remember back in '25, when we fought against Bandula's foot soldiers? Remember his fighting elephants?"

The colonel nodded, and Violet presumed Portland saw him do so.

"That nincompoop strode back and forth in front of his men in full insignia under a gold umbrella, an easy target for our guns. He got exactly what he deserved, didn't he? It didn't take long for all of the provinces to fall after that, I tell you. Lucky for us, since their thick forests and jungles would have eventually snared us, eh? I remember you once shot a python who was making his way for me. Wouldn't be here today if you hadn't done so," Portland reminded him gruffly.

"I remember," Colonel Mortimer said, wiping a tear from one eye and seemingly calming down.

This had to be the most bizarre conversation Violet had ever witnessed—two old friends discussing a murder through a screen. Both of them should have been anxious to find the body, but instead the colonel was busy apologizing for encountering the crime, and Portland was mostly concerned with consoling him by reliving their past exploits together.

Violet could take no more of this.

"Your Grace," she said, standing abruptly. The colonel's shocked expression suggested that he was just noticing her for the first time. His bloodshot eyes moved incongruently, as if each was independent of the other. A single tear rolled from his right eye, unchecked, and dripped off his chin.

Yes, there was something seriously odd here, but Violet had more pressing matters to concern her.

"I believe it is imperative that we find whoever was murdered, don't you?"

Portland coughed. "Of course. I just wanted to ensure the colonel was not—"

Violet no longer cared about the colonel's delicate sensibilities. "Yes, Your Grace. Perhaps if the good colonel could show us exactly where the murder occurred . . . ?" She knew she was inserting herself where she didn't belong, but her greater concern was for the body.

"In due time, Mrs. Harper," Portland assured her. "George, are you quite all right to get back to your cottage on your own?"

"I think so. Yes, I can make it."

"I'll tell Kirby. He will know what to do."

Kirby will know what to do? Violet thought. *Are people regularly done in at Welbeck?*

The colonel nodded to Violet and left, having not actually spoken to her once. The door clicked behind him, and she was once again in the silence with Portland. He made no move to summon Kirby or anyone else. Was he waiting for her to leave before he informed the staff that there was a dead body on the grounds? The man was incomprehensible.

As she was wont to do when agitated, Violet started pacing back and forth in front of the screen, abandoning all pretense of deference to the duke.

"Sir," she said without pausing, "I hope you will permit me to accompany Mr. Kirby to wherever this body is. I should like to help prepare it, speak with the family, go to—"

"Please calm yourself, Mrs. Harper. We must see first if there actually *is* a body."

That stopped Violet. "What do you mean?"

Portland sighed. "You must understand that Colonel Mortimer has been my friend since our time together in the Grenadier Guards. I would have stayed in the army much longer if my brother hadn't died, forcing me to return home to assume the Marquess of Titchfield title in anticipation of eventually becoming duke. Regardless, George and I share many memories. Other than Pearson, he is nearly the only person I can tolerate. He knows me, understands my past, and expects nothing of me."

"Of course, Your Grace," Violet murmured. What did she know about the friendships formed in the ranks of the peerage?

"But George suffered terribly in the Burmese War. We were establishing proper control over northeastern India, you know, but the Burmese were violently opposed to us doing so. The colonel led a group of men on a secret mission to assassinate General Bandula, commander of their forces, prior to Bandula making it so easy for us. George's men were discovered before they could complete their task, and brutally slain before his eyes. Only George and a trusted lieutenant escaped the slaughter. Worse, George was blamed for the mission's failure and asked to quietly resign his commission, even though we soon killed Bandula."

Violet began to see what made the colonel so agitated yet secretive about witnessing a murder. What if he were to be blamed again? She began to feel some sympathy for the colonel, as well as respect for the duke's circumspect handling of the situation.

"After he left the army, George turned to drink and also suffered black periods of great insomnia. He married, but Esther died not two years later. I've often wondered if George's episodes wore her out. He came to me over a year ago, penniless, and I offered him a cottage here at Welbeck for as long as he wants it. I know that he sometimes wanders out at night, unable to sleep.

"And now, Mrs. Harper, you know why I am hesitant to sound the alarm. George may have been mistaken in what he saw. We have never had anything so sordid as a murder on the grounds. My workers are respectable townspeople. Whatever he saw, it is causing him great mental anguish, and I want to prevent further distress until we know what has really happened."

Not to mention that the servants were already on edge over Aristotle's death, and rumor of a murder would make some, like Mrs. Garside, ready for an asylum stay.

Violet could hardly believe it, but she found herself actually agreeing with Portland's approach. Still, if there was a body lying somewhere, requiring attention . . .

"Your Grace, I'm sure we can be discreet and not arouse the servants' suspicions, but I must insist that if there is a dead body on the grounds, I need to see it."

"Yes, I believe George will have returned safely to his cottage by now for a good nap, so if you wish to find Kirby and accompany him quietly, you may."

But nothing seemed to occur quietly at Welbeck Abbey. As Violet walked through the house, a footman appeared from nowhere and discreetly followed her. As she reached the front door, a man in the homespun clothing of an outdoor worker burst through it, past the footman's "You cannot enter this way!" and skittered to a stop in front of Violet, panting.

Remembering himself, the stranger pulled off his cap. "Begging your pardon, ma'am. Mr. LeCato said there was an undertaker lady here and I was to find you. There's a body, ma'am, a dead one. Come quick."

The two footmen gasped, and Violet knew that within moments the entire household would be in an uproar.

"Show me," she urged, hoping she could get there before all of Worksop had turned out to see whatever indignity the corpse had suffered.

As she followed the worker outside, it occurred to Violet that perhaps Mrs. Garside had a point about Aristotle's death portending doom for Welbeck Abbey. Only Violet didn't realize yet how extensive that doom would be.

Violet walked behind the worker as quickly as she could without appearing to be panicked. Her efforts didn't matter. By the time she reached the location where the body lay, a small gaggle of onlookers had already formed, including Mr. Kirby, who was, mercifully, in the process of covering the deceased's face with a handkerchief.

The body was loosely covered in the dead leaves from a nearby oak, and was barely visible in the quickly descending October sun.

Violet estimated that it was nearly three o'clock already. Thank goodness the body had been found before nightfall.

They were not far from the house, alongside a section of tunnel that had obviously been completed, hence the body's lying undisturbed for nearly a day, since workers were busy elsewhere. The tunnel, easily traced by a small mound running along the ground, looked as though a behemoth of a mole had burrowed it and then someone had placed a three-foot glass dome every thirty feet, presumably for light. As the darkness set in, gas lamps came on belowground, inside the tunnel, casting an eerie trail of dotted light that ran for nearly a hundred yards.

Violet shivered to think of the various oddities she had encountered in the past few hours. Every moment brought something new and generally unnerving. But at least the light would help illuminate her present work.

As the butler rose from what he was doing, she opened her mouth to ask a question, but Kirby spoke first, absentmindedly, as if remembering that his duty was far more important than any tragedy that had befallen the estate.

"Mrs. Harper, your belongings have arrived, and you have been placed upstairs in the Old English Black Room. Mrs. Neale took the liberty of having your large bag moved from the kitchens up to your room," Kirby said, as though he were greeting a simple weekend guest, and not as though they were both standing over a bloodied body with several of the staff waiting to see what the lady in black might pronounce.

Violet, confused, simply nodded and said, "Whose body has been found?"

Kirby, though, not to be loosened of his butler's persona, replied, "May I introduce Mr. Jack LeCato to you, madam? He is an agent of Her Majesty's government, helping to oversee construction here at Welbeck."

The queen had installed someone at a remote estate in Nottinghamshire to supervise some odd underground construction projects? That didn't sound likely. A man in his midforties with a handsome, if deeply lined, face greeted her. "Mrs. Harper, we are fortunate you are on the estate at this exact moment. One of the footmen found the body and reported it to me, and, having heard you were here, I sent him to find you."

"Who is this?" Violet asked again.

"Burton Spencer," LeCato said. "He works for Ellery Reed, Welbeck Abbey's estate manager. Someone has gone to fetch Mr. Reed in town."

Violet knelt down and gently pulled away the handkerchief from Spencer's face. He looked to be no more than seventeen or eighteen years old, despite his brawny build.

The crowd gathered on the spot was growing, with sweaty men pressing in for a closer look. Between the receding sun and the looming spectators, Violet could hardly see anything, even with the glow emitting from underground.

Sensing her distress, LeCato turned to address those who had gathered. "Return to your quarters, all of you. Mr. Reed won't like to know that you've been standing around gawping." He was perfectly pleasant about it, but Violet could hear the strength of an iron locomotive in it. She wondered again why the queen had sent him, then returned to her work before the sun was completely gone.

Except for Kirby and LeCato, the men moved off, grumbling. Violet put all of her attention to Spencer as the butler and the queen's man looked on.

She put her hands on either side of Spencer's face and spoke softly to him. "I see you've been bleeding, but"—Violet pulled a hand away and examined her fingers against the light of the tunnel; there were just a few crusty bits of blood on them—"your blood is not fresh. You have been here some time, haven't you, Mr. Spencer? Give me a hint as to what happened to you."

She turned his head from side to side and gently probed his scalp. As she did so, she heard a loud clacking noise; then a swarm of ravens raced overhead, cawing as they flew toward the sound. That, combined with the dimming light and the dead body cradled in her arms, left Violet very unsettled. Was Mrs. Garside correct about the mantle of doom settling over Welbeck Abbey? She shivered to dispel the silly notion and returned to her task.

There was a definite wound on the back of Spencer's head, but was it his cause of death or incidental to a fall? Hadn't the colonel said he witnessed a strangulation?

"I need more light," Violet said.

In his remarkably efficient manner, Kirby slipped away and returned almost immediately with a large lantern attached to an iron ring. He set it on the ground next to Violet, and it bathed Spencer in a warm glow. If it weren't for the matted hair on the back of his head and his gaping mouth, she would have sworn he had an angelic presence.

Violet slowly lifted Spencer's chin for a better look at his neck. She found none of the bruising or welts that would have indicated a strangulation. As near as she could tell, Spencer had fallen, disturbing the scattering of leaves that subsequently landed on his body as they fell back to earth with him.

He must have hit his head on a sharp stone or brick. Violet lifted the lantern with one hand and asked the men to brush away the leaves surrounding Spencer without disturbing his body.

"Without disturbing him, Mrs. Harper?" LeCato said. "I'm sure he won't notice what we're doing."

"Nevertheless, you will be respectful of Mr. Spencer. He deserves dignified treatment from this point until the moment he is buried."

Violet didn't need daylight to know that LeCato was rolling his eyes at her. It was the usual response she received from her commands to treat the dead in a reverent manner.

The men did as she requested, though, and she held the lantern up, moving it around the area near Spencer's head.

"There!" LeCato said, pointing. Violet trained the lantern in the direction indicated. Two feet away from the body was a bloodied rock with a sharp edge. She hefted the stone in her hand. This would certainly do serious injury to—or cause the death of—someone who fell against it. And yet . . .

"I guess that explains it," LeCato offered. "Poor boy. He was just clumsy and paid dearly for it."

Violet said nothing. The duke should be the first to know her thoughts on the matter.

Kirby was already taking action, brushing the leaf debris from his hands and straightening his jacket. "I shall inform His Grace straightaway that there has been an accident on the estate."

"Wait," Violet said, her single word causing Kirby to freeze mid-motion. "Does Mr. Spencer have family in town? I will need assistance having him delivered to his home."

Neither Kirby nor LeCato seemed to know anything about Spencer, other than having vague recollections of seeing him about on the estate. "I shall ask His Grace," Kirby said, as if somehow the duke would have a better idea of who a random worker was than anyone else.

Kirby left Violet and LeCato with the body and the lantern while he picked his way through the dark back to the house.

"I hear you practice in London, Mrs. Harper," said LeCato. "I find a woman undertaker to be quite unusual." His tone suggested he wasn't quite sure whether he approved.

Violet was quite used to this reaction, too. "Yes, I learned the trade from my late husband, and now I own—"

The light of a swinging lantern distracted her, and in moments they were joined by another man, tall and lanky, who looked grizzled beyond his years from outdoor work.

"Reed," LeCato said curtly. "Good of you to take notice of your worker."

"I was in town," the other man said with no further explanation, then addressed Violet. "Are you the undertaker? I heard it was a woman."

Violet rose to her feet and offered her free hand to the man. He took it reluctantly and quickly dropped it, his attention now on the prone body. "Who is this?"

"One of your workers, Burton Spencer. He has a head wound caused by this." Violet showed him the rock.

Reed set his own lantern down, bent over to take a look at Spencer's face, and, hands on his knees, muttered a foul oath. He then cursed Spencer. "How could you be so stupid, boy, to let this happen? What did I tell you? What did I tell you?"

Violet was appalled by the man's behavior. "Sirrah! I will ask you to show the deceased some respect. We do not chastise the dead for any wrongdoing they may have committed. We only wish them well into the afterlife."

Now she was the target of incredulity by both LeCato and Reed, but she didn't care. "I will not have any body under my care spoken to in such a manner," she repeated emphatically.

"You have no body in *your* care," Reed spoke grimly through gritted teeth. "This is *my* worker. Don't dare to tell me how to treat Welbeck's people. I'll have you know I oversee more than a thousand men on the duke's construction projects, and I'll not be upbraided by a chit in a black dress."

Of all the unmitigated nerve, to speak in such a way in front of the deceased! Violet lowered her voice, out of respect for the body. "You deserve an upbraiding for your unkindness. However, for now perhaps you can be helpful and tell me whether Mr. Spencer has family in Worksop or somewhere nearby. He needs to be taken home and prepared for his funeral. I will do so, unless you believe you are qualified for it."

Reed frowned and was silent several moments. "He didn't have any family that we knew of. He lived here on the estate. You'll have to take care of him here, and I suppose His Grace will decide where to bury him."

The butler came scuffling back up to them once more. "I spoke to His Grace," panted a breathless Kirby. "He does not know anything about Mr. Spencer and suggested that we speak with—ah, Mr. Reed. His Grace said you—"

"I told her," Reed growled curtly.

"Thank you, Mr. Kirby," Violet said. "Would you be so kind as to ask His Grace if I might call on him when I'm done here? Also, Mr. Spencer needs to be taken out of the elements. Hmm." She thought for a moment. "Gentlemen, I need your assistance in carrying Mr. Spencer."

"To where?" LeCato asked. "The servants' quarters?"

"No. We are going to place him in His Grace's dining room," Violet said firmly, ignoring the chorus of protest by all three men, who assured her that the duke would have her run off the estate in a dog cart for such a thing.

"He will not," she replied, with more assurance than she felt.

She intended to share her thoughts about Spencer's death with Portland, and contend with his reaction from there. But for now, the young man would be placed in elegant surroundings, probably the finest he had ever encountered.

She followed the men, who had lifted Spencer's lifeless body and were carrying it toward the house. She paused, though, held up both lanterns, and turned slowly in a complete circle, looking around at the scene before her. Where had Colonel Mortimer's vantage point been to have witnessed Burton Spencer's death? The other side of the tunnel roof? From the wooded copse a hundred yards away? It seemed impossible that he could have seen anything without a lantern, and if he had a lantern, wouldn't Spencer and his attacker have noticed the colonel?

There was something wrong with the colonel's claim. The dreadful thought that he might have had a hand in Spencer's death rose in her mind, but if that were true, why would he have come confessing that he had witnessed the crime? Why wouldn't he simply have stayed locked away in his cottage and professed shock when the body was discovered?

And for what reason would an old military pensioner need to kill an estate worker? None of this made any sense. The only thing Violet knew for sure was that the colonel was lying. She just didn't know what he was lying about. Yet.

She struggled to catch up with the bleak little funeral entourage, which had moved to one side to use the light coming from the tunnel to guide their way. Violet moved in front of them and held up the lanterns while they finished the journey to the house.

In the distance, she heard the penetrating screech of a barn owl, which reminded her of Aristotle. It was impossible to think now that there would be a funeral for a bird. At first light tomorrow, Violet planned to march into the kitchens, pick up the box containing the raven's remains, and quickly inter him in the burial ground next to the rookery. Undoubtedly the duke's mind would be elsewhere once he realized one of his workers was dead.

Not just dead. Murdered.

5

As Violet had expected, Portland was disquieted by Spencer's death. He was even more distressed by Violet's pronouncement that she had had Spencer placed on the table of his newly remodeled dining room, and that she would prepare him there in the morning.

By the time Violet voiced her suspicion that Colonel Mortimer had not engaged in complete truth telling, she could sense Portland's agitation behind the screen.

"Why would you say such a thing?" he asked.

"Because, although I do believe Spencer was murdered, it most certainly was not by strangulation. His head was bloodied by a rock, which I believe he was struck with before he fell to the ground."

"How do you ascertain this?" She could hear that the duke was now breathing heavily behind the screen.

"Because it was lying two feet away instead of directly under his head or close by. I think someone struck him—in anger or in a planned way—then panicked, dropped the rock, and ran."

"I see." He wheezed several more times, then said, "So you are suggesting that George was not just having an episode, and that he didn't merely witness an accidental death?"

"I don't suggest it, sir. I am convinced of it." Violet hoped he wouldn't go apoplectic at her assertion.

"Good Lord, what do I do?"

"Well, sir, you should probably send someone for the police."

At that, Portland was aghast. "I couldn't possibly do so. Have men traipsing about the property, poking their noses wherever they want, questioning my servants? Questioning *me?* Unthinkable. No, this must be handled another way." He paused and said slowly, "You, Mrs. Harper. You have already discovered that Spencer did not die of a fall. I'm sure I can rely on you to discover the perpetrator. Discreetly, of course. After all, you will at least be staying long enough to manage Spencer's funeral, will you not?"

Violet saw that all of her plans to visit the nearby Creswell Crags to view their Ice Age cave art, and to travel down to Edwinstowe to walk through the ancient Church of St. Mary, were not going to materialize anytime soon. Her holiday was quickly turning into work, but Sam was so busy with his colliery that he probably wouldn't mind. She hoped.

After all, there was a corpse that needed her, and that tug on Violet's heart was nearly a maternal instinct. Taking care of Spencer and seeing justice for him was far more rewarding than a church's pamphlet for her scrapbook.

"Yes, of course, Your Grace, I will see to Mr. Spencer's funeral and will discover who committed this crime against him."

"Very good. I am certain that the colonel had nothing to do with it."

The duke's defense of his friend was admirable, though probably misplaced. Her first concern, though, was Spencer's funeral. "Shall we hold Mr. Spencer's service inside Welbeck Abbey's chapel?"

Violet heard the sharp intake of breath from behind the screen. "Indeed not! I am shocked that you would advocate such a thing, and now you have suggested it twice in one day. No one is permitted to use the chapel. Go see the vicar at Worksop Priory and have him buried in the churchyard there. Tell Reverend Appleton I'll give him whatever donation he wants."

After that outburst from the duke, her next suggestion—that, under the circumstances, it was best to just bury Aristotle quietly—was surprisingly met with a simple "Yes. Quite right."

Violet left the duke's presence, already wondering if she'd made the right decision to become further involved at Welbeck Abbey. Why was no one allowed to use the chapel? And why did everyone behave as though it were perfectly normal that the Duke of Portland could not interact with other people in a normal fashion but rather must do so behind a screen?

After a check on Spencer to be sure his body was not splayed out at odd angles on the dining room table, which had a tablecloth hastily thrown between it and the corpse, Violet allowed herself to be escorted to her rooms by Mrs. Neale. The door plaque read, "Old English Black Room," and although it was located on an upper story with Portland, his suite overlooked the rear gardens and lake, whereas she was at the front of the home, overlooking the long drive and the ongoing tunnel construction.

"Am I in this room because it is complete, or because the name is a play on my profession and dark clothing?" Violet asked.

"Neither, madam," Mrs. Neale said as she shook out one of her dozens of keys and inserted it into the lock. "His Grace is a well-known horseman and has named the guest rooms after extinct breeds. We all get lessons in them. Let me see, William the Conqueror was responsible for the Old English Black breed by crossing some of the brutes he brought over the Channel with some English mares, if I recall correctly. The other rooms on this floor are the Norfolk Trotter, the Irish Hobby, and the Cheval Navarrin."

"Are those rooms also finished?" Violet said as she followed the housekeeper into the darkened room.

"Yes, this wing of the house is complete." Mrs. Neale bent over a table and turned up a lamp. It illuminated a chilly room with tall windows framed in thick, fringed floral draperies in deep reds and blues, a canopied bed, an oversized walnut armoire, and a Turkish carpet that covered much of the herringboned floor. Spectacular landscapes covered the walls. A doorway at one end led to another room, which Violet supposed was a sitting room, as she could see a writing desk and several chairs in it. As with the other art-filled but otherwise empty rooms that she had traveled through earlier, there was an elaborate commode in one corner.

"His Grace provides magnificent quarters for his guests," Violet said. "Does he entertain often?"

"Never," Mrs. Neale replied tersely, pulling aside the fire screen from the fireplace and using a poker to turn over the dying embers of a fire that must have been laid hours ago. "Where is that Olive? I told her to start this fire and keep it going."

"I suppose that's my fault, Mrs. Neale, since she was helping me look through the dishes." It seemed like a lifetime ago that Violet had thought the shard Aristotle had choked on was of any importance.

"That's no excuse for the girl. She should have been able to manage both. I'll have her bring up a carafe of water, unless you prefer sherry?" When Violet shook her head no, the housekeeper went to the doorway. "Will that be all, Mrs. Harper?"

"Yes, thank you." With Mrs. Neale gone, Violet arranged her clothing in the room's armoire. Sam had done an admirable job of selecting things for her. She set her undertaking bag near the door to the hallway since she would need it first thing in the morning.

Olive knocked at the door, carrying a tray with not only water but also a pot of tea and some buttery scones. The girl looked as though she had been well chastised as she added more coal to the fireplace from a bucket on the hearth. Soon it was blazing again.

"Have a pleasant evening, madam," Olive said aloofly, having lost any vestige of her earlier friendliness.

Finally alone, Violet went into the sitting room and looked through the writing desk's drawers. As she'd hoped, it was well stocked with paper, pens, and ink jars. She set to work, outlining what had to be done for Spencer's burial.

Presuming that his fellow estate workers would wish to pay their respects to him, Violet knew she had to plan on a fairly large entourage. Let's see, the duke wanted it to be held at Worksop Priory, which must be at least five miles away if it was in the center of town. Should it be a walking procession, or should she ask the duke for carriages to transport mourners back and forth?

Normally, this would be a third-class funeral, but the duke was paying for it, so it should be something more. Perhaps when she went into Worksop tomorrow to visit Reverend Appleton, she could find some black plumes to attach to the horses pulling the hearse wagon, which would have to be fashioned from equipage already in the duke's mews.

Ah yes, she needed a coffin. She would also telegram Boyce and Sons tomorrow from town and ask them to put a stained pine box, with interior and exterior velvet trimmings, on the next train to Nottinghamshire.

There was so much to be done, and Violet was at a great disadvantage to be working so far away from her shop. Speaking of her shop . . . she then made a list of various items she needed from Morgan Undertaking. That would go into another telegram to Harry Blundell, her business partner.

Once she was satisfied that she had Mr. Spencer's funeral in hand, she undressed—always blissfully happy to be rid of her corset—put on her nightgown, and climbed into the bed. The bed was extraordinarily plush and comfortable. The duke hadn't spared a dime in renovating this room, just as he had surely spent a king's ransom on the dining room.

As she snuggled down, she wondered briefly how it was that men like the duke managed to hold so much wealth. Portland was spending fantastic sums to maintain and renovate his estate, with workers buzzing about like bees in a hive, and there seemed no end in sight to what he was doing. It was almost as if he had access to the Crown's treasury and its seemingly endless supply of the nation's wealth.

6

The following morning, having dispensed with Aristotle in a quickly dug little square of ground under a tree near the rookery—a fitting location, she thought—Violet returned to the dining room to attend to her more important work, tending to Burton Spencer.

Despite his size, he looked like a tiny doll on the enormous table. The portraits on the wall looked like mourners gathered around to grieve his loss, an image Violet rather liked.

She pulled away several chairs so that she could stand directly against the table as she worked. One of the parlor maids had left a full washbasin and several cloths on the floor in anticipation of Violet's work, which the undertaker appreciated.

"Now, Mr. Spencer," she began, placing her hand over one of his as she smoothed out the tablecloth with her other hand, "I know that you have suffered great indignities over the past day or so, and I am quite sorry for it. I want you to know that today I plan to make you look most presentable. You should also know that His Grace is paying for your funeral and that everyone at Welbeck Abbey will be in attendance, I'm sure, to pay their respects to you. You are not forgotten in your death."

Violet patted his knuckles and said, "I hope you will not be offended, but I must undress you in order to clean you. I will be discreet, I promise."

His shirt was a loosely constructed piece of yellow nankeen, and she was able to remove it over his head relatively easily, despite his stiff weight. Although Spencer had the height of an older man, his chest and stomach gave the impression of a more immature one, with no sprouted hairs nor any of the roughened skin or scars that most working-class men had developed by their twenties. What Violet did see on Spencer horrified her.

In the middle of his chest was fierce bruising, as though he had been slammed in the torso several times. She gently laid her hand on his chest, which didn't even cover the spread of purple.

This had happened before he fell, but she would estimate not long before. The bright coloring told her it had not had time to fade into the greenish-brown hues that accompanied a bruise's healing. It couldn't have happened after death, or the bruise would have never formed.

More importantly, it wasn't possible that this was the result of his backward fall against the rock. The only conclusion Violet could make was that Spencer had been struck—perhaps repeatedly?— shortly before he died.

Her thoughts were interrupted by Hudock announcing Ellery Reed into the room. Violet was immediately on edge, but in a sign of humility, Reed swept his dusty, brimmed cap from his head as Hudock departed, a sign of humility. All of his hubris and disdain from the previous evening were gone.

"Mrs. Harper," Mr. Reed began awkwardly, "I've come to apologize. I—" His glance darted to where Spencer lay, shirtless. "I was unspeakably rude last night. I don't know what came over me. I was—May I see him?"

Violet nodded and stepped aside as Reed approached the table. Reed stood gazing down at Spencer for several minutes, lost in either thought or prayer. Finally, he stepped away from Spencer and looked up, his eyes moist.

"As I was saying, ma'am, I wasn't myself last night. When they came to fetch me, I thought they were either playing a prank on me or that Spencer here had just gotten himself into trouble. When they're older you just have to contend with them drinking, but the younger ones get into all sorts of mischief. It's a constant chore to keep your workers in line. When I saw that it really was

one of my men, dead like that, I'm afraid I didn't react very well."
Reed gazed at Violet. His eyes were a pale brown, almost as if their
color were fading away from so much strenuous outdoor work. A
tear gathered in the corner of one eye, and Violet turned away so
that the estate manager was not unmanned in her presence.

"Think nothing of it, Mr. Reed," she assured him, picking up
one of the cloths the maid had left and covering Spencer's bruising
with it.

Reed continued, "I've not lost a worker in two years, you know.
In fact, I've only lost three since coming to Welbeck Abbey five
years ago, and those just to illness or an overabundance of liquor,
never an accident. What happened to Spencer is . . . impossible."
He sniffed, and Violet knew he was still restraining tears behind her.

"Accidents are an unfortunate part of life," she said to console
him, not ready to share her suspicions with anyone yet, particularly
a man who was already distraught over the loss of a worker in his
charge. "I don't believe he suffered much." A small lie, if Spencer
had been attacked the way she believed he had, but it was an offer
of comfort.

Reed nodded. "Will there be a funeral here?"

Violet turned back to face him. "Tomorrow the procession will
go from here to Worksop Priory."

"I'll make sure the men are ready."

"You said that he has no family nearby," she added.

"No, none."

"I could use something, Mr. Reed," she said. "Another suit of
clothes for Mr. Spencer. Is that something you can find for me?"

Reed seemed happy to have a role to play, and his grizzled face
broke into a smile. "Yes, I can send along something." With that,
Reed left and Violet returned her attentions to caring for Spencer.
By the time she was done washing him, Hudock was once again
tapping on the door, with a freshly laundered shirt and homespun
trousers. "From Mr. Reed," he said, avoiding any glance over at the
dining room table.

Violet redressed Spencer and tied a string around his left ear,
brought it under his chin, and tied the other end around his right
ear to keep his jaw shut. After a couple of drops of adhesive along

his eyelids to keep his eyes shut, she pulled out her case of cosmetic massages.

"You are well weathered from the sun for someone so young, Mr. Spencer," she said, examining her various color pots. "I think that Earth Number Two—no, Number Three—is the right one for you."

She applied the cream to his face and forehead, then combed his freshly washed and dried hair. "Sir, I believe you are ready for your ceremony, and you may rely upon me to get you to Worksop safely."

As Violet cleared up her supplies, set the used washbasin and cloths outside the dining room door for pickup by whichever maid wandered past, and headed back to her room, she considered what had transpired over the last day. It was baffling, from the duke's oddities to Colonel Mortimer's confusing claim of a murder, to her realization that someone had indeed been killed.

Had it been an accident, or had someone maliciously attacked Spencer? If it was just an accident resulting from an argument, why hadn't the other party immediately run for help?

Violet shook her head. She'd spent too much time investigating suspicious deaths, and now she assumed that everyone had dark histories and motives.

And yet it was obvious that Spencer had been abandoned after he fell, although no one had taken pains to try and hide his body. Did the killer want Spencer to be found? If so, why? Was there something of importance about Spencer that was not obvious at a cursory glance? He certainly carried nothing of value upon him. In fact, he carried nothing at all. After all, he was merely an estate worker.

Moreover, what about the ostensible witness to Spencer's death, Colonel Mortimer? Was he merely mistaken about exactly what he had witnessed in the dark shadows, or had he intentionally misled the duke?

Violet tucked her undertaking bag back inside her bedchamber's armoire before heading out to visit the vicar. At least inside a church there would be calm and peace for a few minutes. Maybe Reverend Appleton could offer her a blessing, or a few words of comfort.

* * *

Violet stopped to send her telegrams to Harry and to Boyce and Sons, then shopped for black ostrich feather plumes at a milliner's shop before walking to Worksop Priory. The church was located in the center of town as so many were since towns frequently centered around the fairs, festivals, and other activities sponsored by a local chapel or cathedral. It had a magnificent nave and appeared to have been recently restored, although it was obvious that many parts of the church and its outbuildings still required repair, even three hundred years after Henry VIII's rampage. Violet supposed that sacred spaces were not candidates for hasty rebuilding projects. That, or most of the local men were busy at Welbeck Abbey.

The Reverend James Appleton was probably as old as the duke, but had a head full of snowy white hair and a step full of vigor. Had it not been for his lined face, Violet would have thought he was half his age.

"Yes, I've had word about the tragic accident at Welbeck," he said, inviting Violet to sit down in his cramped study, which was heaped with Bibles, yellowed parchment manuscripts, translations of classical ancient works, and sacramental supplies: chalices, candles, and linens. It was as if the Almighty had blown a mighty breath through the door, leaving His marks behind in a jumble.

Violet sat in an old leather chair and immediately jumped up at the feeling of something sharp poking her. She lifted the cushion to find a gold-plated crucifix beneath it. The shape of the Christ was very realistically portrayed on it.

"Ah, a thousand apologies, Mrs. Harper. I wondered where that went." Appleton took it from her and inserted the base of it inside a staff and then placed the staff on the wall behind him, with the horizontal bar of the cross resting upon two nails. "So you wish to have Mr. Spencer's funeral tomorrow?"

Appleton pulled a ledger from the bottom of a tottering pile of books. He was obviously experienced at doing so because the stack wobbled precariously for several moments but did not collapse. "My curate is away, so I've been handling details large and small. Let me see . . ." The vicar patted himself until he found his gold, wire-rimmed glasses on top of his head. Putting them on, he flipped through his ledger until he found the page he wanted.

"Hmm, yes, the ladies' benevolence group was planning to have a meeting here tomorrow, but we shall put them off for a few days, shan't we?" He drew a line through an entry in the ledger and scribbled something else. "His Grace should not be kept waiting. He is a great benefactor to our parish, you know."

Most peers were. In fact, in previous centuries, parishes owed their entire existence to whichever lord held sway in their locality.

Violet nodded at the vicar. "This would normally be a mere third-class funeral, but since the duke is bearing the expense for it, and it will be well attended by all of Welbeck's workers, it is my plan to make it a bit more . . . elaborate."

Appleton raised an attentive eyebrow. "His Grace is covering the service? Yes, that is very interesting. Do you know whether Mr. Spencer is Anglican or one of these nonconformist types?"

Nonconformists were those of any sect—typically Baptists, Presbyterians, and Methodists—who dissented from the Church of England's governance.

"Actually, I do not know," she replied. "No one seems to know much about him."

Appleton pursed his lips. "Hmm. Well then. Yes." He scribbled down something else in his ledger. "I believe it wise to assume Mr. Spencer was a faithful adherent to the Church of England. His Grace despises nonconformists."

"Really?" Violet asked. Here was a new fact about Portland to add to a growing list of his curious qualities.

Appleton smiled appreciatively at her interest. "His Grace has a great affection for the Anglican church and its special place in the history of the Lord's blessing upon His people. The duke doesn't care much for how the sheep are being led astray by those who practice outside orthodoxy. Entirely too radical, His Grace says, and one cannot help but be in complete agreement with so pious a man. In fact, last August he gave two thousand pounds to the National Protestant Union, which is trying to prevent the horrid disestablishment of the Irish branch of our church." As he spoke, Appleton began waving his hands to emphasize his points. Violet watched helplessly as his left hand bumped into a pile of books, from which the top one fell to the floor.

Violet jumped up and retrieved the volume for him, reading the title aloud as she handed it back to the vicar. *"High Church, Low Church, and Broad Church: An Examination of the Merits and Shifting Attitudes Toward Ceremonial Worship.* I had no idea there was such great debate," she said politely, not realizing what she was about to unleash.

"Oh yes." Appleton was warming to his own theological discourse. "As you probably know, the church appeals to three sources for authority: scripture, reason, and tradition." He ticked them off on his fingers. "Low churchmen tend to put more emphasis on scripture in their services, the Broad churchmen on reason, and the High churchmen on tradition."

He nodded to emphasize that tradition was the proper choice. "Why, the Low Church doesn't even portray our Lord on the rood." He looked back at the crucifix hanging on the wall and uttered a sound of disgust. "The infiltration of Broad ideas, where the laity believe they can decide for themselves what is proper, has caused no end of damage, and I blame a lot of these nonconformist churches for it."

"I imagine that not every parish commits to one form or another," Violet murmured, lifting the watch pinned to her dress and making an obvious show of examining the time. How was she to get the conversation back on course?

The vicar took no notice of her discomfort, so impassioned was he. "Of course, some say that as long as both clergy and laity are ready to jump into prayer, work, and sacrifice, the mode of service makes no difference. Of this, I am not convinced."

He stopped to draw a breath, and Violet jumped in. "Perhaps we might return to a discussion of Mr. Spencer's funeral, sir," she said.

"Ah, quite right you are, Mrs. Harper. I'm afraid I am a bit enthusiastic—and concerned—about doctrinal changes in the church. Now, where were we? Yes, Mr. Spencer's service. I believe that in order to please His Grace, it should be a High Church service. . . ."

Violet and the reverend discussed the estate worker's funeral for another half hour; then Violet was finally able to make her escape, pleading a myriad of duties that awaited her at Welbeck prior to tomorrow's services.

"Thank you for such a delightful discussion," the vicar said. "I don't know when I've enjoyed such stimulating conversation."

Violet wasn't sure she had made a statement of any note, as his esoteric topic was, in her mind, immaterial to the question of whether the flock was faithful, and especially irrelevant to the co-ordination of poor Mr. Spencer's funeral.

As he escorted her out of the church, the reverend continued his instruction on the proper forms of worship, even calling out to her as she passed through the gate, "Mrs. Harper, I have another interesting volume that presents a case for making church attendance compulsory again in society, if you would like to borrow it."

Violet accepted the church's teachings, but her life's work was caretaking dead bodies, not dusty books full of arguments. She simply smiled and waved as she kept walking.

She was almost back to Welbeck Abbey when she realized that—quite unbelievably—she had forgotten to mention to Appleton that Spencer had possibly been murdered. Would it impact where he wanted to bury Portland's worker? She was not about to return to town to ask him about it, lest she be asked to commit to more theological engagement. Perhaps he might ask her to write a treatise on the correct form of baptism or some other fine point of theology.

Baptism was a sacrament best left to priests. Violet Harper could only be of help to the church after the sacrament of extreme unction.

A sacrament, she soon realized, she would encounter more than once during her stay at Welbeck Abbey.

7

The next morning, Violet awoke before light to prepare for Burton Spencer's procession. After putting on the best of her undertaker gowns, this one trimmed with broad, deep ebony velvet stripes around its crape skirt, she threw open the window of her room and stuck her head out. All was blissfully quiet, as construction was halted for the day in honor of Spencer's funeral.

The day was cool and the air was acrid from the coal smoke drifting from the multitude of chimneys around the house. It didn't matter to Violet, though. She cherished days such as this, where she could achieve her greatest aspiration, to place someone in his final resting place with dignity and honor.

She sometimes wondered if it was wrong to become so excited about a funeral. Reverend Appleton would have much to say on the matter, for sure.

She secured a quick breakfast of porridge and sausage from Mrs. Garside, then began the work of finding men to put Spencer into his new coffin—which had arrived on a late train last night—and carry him out solemnly to the makeshift hearse. It was pulled by four horses adorned in magnificent plumage, and attended on either side by Mr. Reed and Mr. Kirby.

The estate's male house servants and outdoor workers, all wearing black armbands distributed by Mr. Kirby, fell into a natural procession line behind the hearse as it began its long, slow walk into town. Portland had stated quite clearly that he would be in attendance, but Violet didn't see the ducal carriage anywhere. Was he walking in the processional? It didn't seem likely, as the ridiculously tall top hat was nowhere to be seen floating above the crowd of mourners.

Violet scurried up the line to catch sight of him, but he was nowhere to be found. How curious.

Colonel Mortimer was in attendance, leaning heavily on a cane as if in great grief as he walked with Portland's valet, Pearson. Violet's husband always walked with a cane, because of an old war wound to his leg, so she was familiar enough with their use to know that the colonel didn't require it.

Why, then, the great demonstration of infirmity over Spencer's death? What was the man trying to prove?

The procession wound its way to Worksop, with Violet now trailing respectfully behind everyone else. In typical fashion, people emerged from their homes and shops to watch the spectacle. This was probably considerable entertainment for the townspeople, given how many of their neighbors and friends worked at Welbeck and were in the procession.

As they neared the church, Violet once again hurried past the line of mourners to be the first one at the gate. To her great surprise, the ducal carriage was already there, waiting patiently across the street. It was an enclosed carriage, and the windows were covered in thick drapes. There was no movement or sound from within. In fact, if there were not a horse and driver attached to it, she would have assumed the carriage had been abandoned.

Violet approached the conveyance, but the driver shook his head sternly in warning not to come closer.

Very well, it was none of her concern what the duke did. She merely had to bury Mr. Spencer.

Naturally, not everyone fit inside the priory. Despite its size, many stood outside, listening through the open windows to the reverend's words as he spoke blessings over Spencer's coffin.

The coffin was then carried out to the churchyard, and Violet lingered at the rear of the great circle formed around the freshly dug grave, leaving Reverend Appleton to have his moment of eminence over the lowering of the coffin into its permanent home.

Standing near her were several men who had also chosen not to be closely involved in the interment: the hobbling Colonel Mortimer; the queen's man, Jack LeCato; a grim-looking Ellery Reed; and another man she'd never seen before.

"Good morning, gentlemen. Mr. Spencer is fortunate to have such a pleasant day for his ceremony."

They gave her odd looks, and Reed snapped at her, "I've always thought gloomy, rainy days were supposed to be the most appropriate ones for funerals, not cool and crisp autumn days that seem to beg one to take a stroll through a park." His face turned scarlet. "Pardon my rudeness, Mrs. Harper. This has all been so sudden . . . and difficult."

Violet nodded in sympathy. She had encountered all manner of reactions by the grieving, although Reed seemed to be swinging between calm and storm more wildly than most people did.

She looked pointedly at the man she didn't know, and LeCato quickly spoke up. "Ah, Mrs. Harper, do you know Martin Chandler, the duke's falconer?"

Violet exchanged greetings with the man, who must have been in his early twenties. He was handsome in a careless way, as though he was vaguely aware that he had melted pools of azure for eyes, an inviting smile, and a sturdy physique, but didn't much care because there was so much else on his mind.

As it turned out, it was mostly birds on his brain.

"Mrs. Harper, aren't you the undertaker who has been on the premises? You took care of Aristotle."

"Yes, I did. The duke's raven is buried with the others near the rookery."

Chandler cocked his head to one side as if in serious assessment. "Madam, you yourself resemble a raven in that black dress and hat. The long tails suggest a raven's wings."

Chandler might have been handsome, but he wasn't particularly tactful. Comparisons of Violet to a crow or other bird were usually made by those who were angry in their mourning and were lashing out at her, not by casual observers.

"Indeed," she replied, and changed the subject. "Colonel Mortimer, do you not feel well today, sir?"

"What? I'm fine. Oh, you mean this?" He lifted the cane. "Just an old injury, reminding me of its residence in my hip."

The colonel was lying. He might have some lingering injury—perhaps from the Burmese War—but it had nothing to do with his carrying of a cane today. What kinds of dark secrets did the man keep?

"I'm glad to know you are well. Which reminds me, is His Grace ailing? I do not see him here in the crowds."

"He will no doubt be along soon," the colonel said cryptically. "In any case, I believe I have paid my respects. I must be getting back so I can rest. That walk was a bit much." He tipped his hat toward Violet and ambled off into town.

Once more, she was struck with a deeply uneasy feeling about the colonel.

Violet turned her attention to LeCato. "Sir, have you enjoyed your stay at Welbeck Abbey? I have discovered it to be a very impressive estate, despite all of the construction in progress."

She hoped he would offer a clue as to why he was installed on the ducal property, but she was not to be rewarded with any pertinent information.

"Yes, it is most magnificent, with a grand history worthy of kings. Are you aware of its connection with our monarchs stretching all the way back to William the Conqueror?"

"I know that Henry VIII dissolved it as a religious house."

"It was made a manor during the reign of William, then the abbey was built during the time of Henry II. After the dissolution, the abbey came into the hands of the Cavendish family, and they turned it into a glorious country estate. Both James I and Charles I were lavishly entertained there. During the Civil War, William Cavendish was a fanatical Royalist, but also a coward. He was in charge of a garrison located at Welbeck, but when the Roundheads came to Nottinghamshire, he fled in terror to the Continent with his purse and a couple of his favorite servants, abandoning his three daughters—whose mother had just recently died—and leaving them at the mercy of Cromwell's soldiers."

"Surely not!" Violet said, although she had experienced enough of the upper class to know that they didn't necessarily lay claim to integrity and honor. "You must be referring to the Cavendish sisters whose portraits hang in the dining room. I was aware that they were wealthy young women who made good marriages, but not that they were at the mercy of the enemy."

"Well, old Cromwell was a pious man, even if he was austere and responsible for years of English misery. After his man, the Earl of Manchester, took over Welbeck as his headquarters, Cromwell sent strict instructions that the girls were not to be molested in any manner. Thus left alone, they were able to hide the family silver, manage the family finances, and send letters to their father, right under the Puritans' noses. Neither Cromwell nor Manchester ever knew that they were harboring Royalist vipers in those three angelic faces."

"Were the daughters reunited with the father once Charles II reclaimed the throne?" Violet asked, fascinated by this slice of English history despite herself.

"Unfortunately, no. The sisters continued writing loving letters to Sir William for years, even though he had remarried and showed no intention of ever returning to Welbeck."

"You know a considerable amount about the Abbey," Violet observed. Had he been thoroughly instructed in it for some reason? Was this Violet's opportunity to learn more about the duke? "His Grace must be very busy, with so much to run and no wife as his helpmeet," she ventured discreetly. Fortunately, neither Reed nor Chandler seemed interested in her question.

"He is an . . . interesting . . . man. Whereas his ancestors were obsessed with expanding the home itself, His Grace is concerned with more unusual projects."

"You mean these tunnels I have heard so much about? I have seen the skylights of one of them." Violet remembered that Mrs. Neale had been reluctant to discuss Portland's underground activities.

"Yes, he has had miles of tunnels built, and intends to build many more."

"Where do these tunnels lead?"

"Various places on and off the estate. In fact, there is a tunnel that runs from the house toward the Worksop train station."

"Truly?" Violet was agog. Even given that a tunnel could skip the twists and turns of overland travel, it still must be a single tunnel of at least two miles.

LeCato nodded. "There are also many more projects beneath the earth."

"Such as a chapel?"

He raised his eyebrows in surprise. "You've seen it?"

"No, but I've heard of it. His Grace did not want Mr. Spencer's services held there. Perhaps that is because it is too small?"

LeCato shrugged but offered no opinion. "Well, the chapel isn't the most elaborate underground edifice he's built."

Violet prodded him for more information about what other subterranean structures existed, but LeCato was vague. She tried another tactic. "Why do you think it is that His Grace builds so much beneath the earth, where no one can see it all?"

"That is a question the prime min—many people—would like to have answered, Mrs. Harper." He then added wryly, "Perhaps you will inform me if you discover the answer to it?"

Violet had no idea how to respond to this. Was she being asked to spy upon the duke? She would not do so. The man was her customer, and his worker's care was entrusted to her. Besides, her time at Welbeck was almost done. She offered a distracted "hmm," then changed the subject. "It seems a tragic postscript in the history of the Abbey for Mr. Spencer to have died in such an unfortunate manner."

LeCato either didn't care about Spencer's death or wanted to avoid the matter completely for he replied, "It would appear that the coffin has been lowered. Time for the return journey, eh?" and strode off to join the crowds, followed closely by the estate manager and the duke's falconer.

While some of the mourners crowded around the reverend to compliment him on the service, and others milled around, waiting for guidance on what to do next, Violet headed out of the churchyard gate. She needed to alert the Welbeck Abbey driver that he could begin the journey home with his empty hearse while she assembled the mourners back into some likeness of an organized procession to follow it home.

Welbeck's servants and construction workers flooded out into the street in a hardly containable mass, made worse by what happened next. The ducal carriage sprang to life, pulling in closer to where the hearse was. One of the windows lowered, and a gnarled old hand—obviously Portland's—began throwing coins into the street.

The people reacted immediately to this, rushing forward to grab the shillings, sixpences, and farthings as they jangled against the unevenly cobbled pavement. As the money was quickly scooped up, the hand appeared again and again, scattering more silver and bronze coins.

Violet felt as though she were in some strange medieval pantomime, where the lord of the land was offering alms to the poor as part of his responsibilities to his estate. Except this was a modern, nineteenth-century town, for heaven's sake, not some centuries-old feudal estate. Why did Portland feel compelled to do such a thing?

Violet shook her head. Members of nobility had depths that were impossible to plumb. For now, she had to worry about getting this completely disorganized throng back to Welbeck. Contemplating Portland's motives could wait for another day.

Violet returned to Worksop once everyone else had returned to the Abbey. She was glad to be back at Worksop Inn with her husband, finally having the opportunity to start and finish a dish of fish pie as she and Sam discussed what had happened during their past couple of days apart.

She explained to Sam what had happened with Aristotle the raven, and the subsequent suspicious death of Burton Spencer, as well as the Duke of Portland's eccentricities and Colonel Mortimer's odd behavior.

"So you don't believe that the colonel actually witnessed Mr. Spencer's murder, and that in fact he may have had something to do with it," Sam said as he lifted his glass of ale to wash down his beef stew.

"I'm not entirely certain what I think. I just don't see how the colonel can claim that he saw Mr. Spencer being strangled, when it is obvious that Spencer was struck repeatedly in the chest and then fell upon a sharp rock. Even in the dark, how would the two actions look alike?" As she scooped the last creamy morsel onto her fork, Violet wondered how it would look to ask for an additional portion of fish.

"And you plan to do something about it," Sam said. It wasn't a question.

Violet bit her lip. How well he knew her. "I was thinking I might return to the Abbey tomorrow to do some more investigating in the area where Spencer was found. Maybe there will be some evidence that was impossible to see in the darkness, despite the light from the tunnel."

"What tunnel?" Sam asked.

Violet told him about the skylights over the tunnel she had seen, as well as LeCato's claim that there were miles of tunnels crisscrossing the property.

Sam's interest was palpable. "Are they still digging tunnels?" he asked.

"I believe so. Mr. LeCato said that—"

"What method are they using for creating the tunnels? Cut and cover? Drill and blast?"

Violet had no idea what he was talking about. "I'm sure I don't know. He never told me—"

"Perhaps they were using a bench tunneling approach?"

"It's not anything anyone saw fit to tell the undertaker, Sam. I don't think—"

"Don't you see?" Sam said excitedly. "The duke—or the estate manager—might well be interested in employing dynamite. I could help them be more efficient at it, with less risk and loss of life than in whatever method they are using now. I'd like to go with you tomorrow, sweetheart, and have you introduce me to the estate manager so I can propose it."

"I—I'm not sure exactly where Mr. Reed's office is. I suppose I could ask Mr. Kirby. . . ." Violet wasn't sure how she felt about the idea. She was hesitant about Sam's enthusiasm for dynamite, although, if he was going to be blasting anyway, wouldn't blasting fairly shallow walking tunnels be safer than the deep shafts needed for a colliery?

Sam, however, was thoroughly warming to his own idea. "If I could convince Welbeck Abbey's estate manager—Mr. Reed, you say?—that dynamite is a good idea, and then the duke was on hand to witness its benefits, why, I might have a whole new way for promoting dynamite in Great Britain. Imagine the influence such a great peer could have if he supported it. I tell you, it's been damnably slow getting this colliery started. Far more difficult than I had anticipated."

"I thought you were enthusiastic about it. Remember all the trouble you went to in securing financing for it in London?" Violet knew she was stalling for time as she thought this out, not sure how she felt about bringing Sam along. Would Mr. Reed feel obligated to entertain her husband as penance for his churlish behavior? Would Portland believe Violet to be taking advantage of the privilege she had in taking care of one of his workers?

Who knew what they would think about using dynamite? Queen Victoria herself had been horrified at the prospect when Violet had once told her that Sam was pursuing it.

Violet's thoughts were muddled, and she knew it. But ultimately, she needed to do this for her husband, no matter what her concerns were.

"Of course. I'd be happy to do it." Violet wasn't at all happy about it, but wanted to please her husband. If she knew the troubles that lay ahead for Sam, though, she would have stamped her foot in protest.

8

It was with great trepidation that Violet now stood in Mr. Reed's cottage, which served as both his office and his home, and stood a distance behind the kitchen gardens. The small building stood amid several other wood cottages with thatched roofs, and all looked as though they had been built in recent years but purposely made to look old and pastoral.

With things back to normal after yesterday's funeral, the roar and clanging of construction continued unabated around them. Reed seemed not to notice it, Sam looked thrilled, and Violet felt queasy.

Within moments of introduction, Sam was deeply animated in his description of dynamite and its potential for Welbeck's underground projects, and Reed was nodding in interest, seemingly unperturbed by Sam's drawling American accent. With Violet all but forgotten, she decided to leave the men to their discussion, which would probably end up lingering over cigars and whisky, despite the early hour.

Besides, there were intermittent clouds already brewing, so she might as well take advantage of whatever sun was left to examine the area where Mr. Spencer had fallen.

No one questioned Violet's unexpected presence as she made her way back past the tunnel, which she now saw led from somewhere beneath the house to a set of stables in the distance. No one, actually, even seemed to remember that Spencer had died mere days ago. He was already forgotten like the fallen autumn leaves—once young and green and soaking in life, then quickly swept up by the wind, never to be seen again.

The grass was still damp from the morning's dew, and soon her hem was wet from pacing methodically back and forth across the area of the lawn where Burton Spencer had been found.

There was still the stain of blood where his head had lain. The rock was no longer here. Had Violet dropped it somewhere after showing it to Kirby, Reed, and LeCato?

She retraced the general steps they had taken to get Spencer's body to the house, but couldn't find it. Well, perhaps it wasn't important.

She could find nothing else of any interest near the death site. Discouraged, she went back to Reed's cottage to collect Sam, but the two men were still in deep conversation, standing over a large map, which they were marking up with charcoal pencils.

Violet decided to seek a cup of tea from Mrs. Garside. Unsurprisingly, the cook and her kitchen maid, Judith, were in the roasting room, billowing the aroma of golden chicken up into the house.

"Mrs. 'Arper, you 'ave returned," the cook said, but there was no malice in her voice. Instead, she seemed to welcome the undertaker's company. Violet soon understood why as she waited in the kitchen garden beneath a walnut tree whose bounty had been recently harvested, if the scattered shell pieces were any indication. Upon bringing a tray out to Violet, Mrs. Garside's voice turned conspiratorial.

"I was right, then, wasn't I, madam?" the cook said, setting the tray on a folding table next to Violet's lawn chair and pouring out steamy, fragrant souchong tea.

"Pardon me, you were right regarding what, Mrs. Garside?"

"Oh, Mrs. 'Arper, it's no use being coy with me. You know I'm meaning 'Is Grace's bird, Aristotle. 'Is death 'as already brought a bit of doom to Welbeck, 'asn't it? What with that Burton Spencer falling and 'itting 'is 'ead."

Violet wasn't sure how to respond. She wasn't about to tell Welbeck's cook that she suspected foul play.

"I don't think Mr. Spencer's death, although tragic, constitutes doom for the estate," Violet said, sipping her tea, its smoky aroma enveloping her. Souchong leaves were high-quality, and this pot was good and strong, made from new leaves, not reused ones that a servant would have for preparing tea downstairs, which indicated to Violet that Mrs. Garside was showing her a large degree of respect by brewing upstairs tea for her.

"It's just the beginning, you mark my words, madam. There's more to follow." The cook nodded her head sagely. "It's lucky you're 'ere to bury all the bodies. I 'ear yesterday's service was lovely. You'll need to stay on longer for the others."

Violet couldn't bring herself to tell Mrs. Garside there was no reason for there to be other deaths on the estate, for the cook spoke with unshakable assurance. Instead, she simply replied, "I shall keep my eyes open for any further bodies."

Satisfied, Mrs. Garside topped off Violet's cup and returned to the kitchens.

With the ever-present construction noises soon receding to a dull throb in her mind, Violet closed her eyes and simply enjoyed the warmth of the cup in her hands. It was impossible to keep her mind blank, however, and her thoughts drifted to the events of the past three days. Had it really been just three days since she had arrived to bury a bird? She shook her head. That was the strangest undertaking request ever made of her. But it had ensured she was on the premises when Spencer died, hadn't it? That had certainly been a divine stroke of fate.

Although if someone had murdered the estate worker, the killer might not leave fate's handiwork alone, and instead take matters further into his own hands.

"What did you do to earn a fatal beating, Mr. Spencer?" Violet whispered softly. "Was it done in the heat of the moment, or had you earned someone's hatred over time?"

She brought the warm cup to her lips again, tapping the side of it as she drank.

A sudden thought came to her and her eyes flew open. Putting the cup on the tea tray, she reached for her reticule and dug through it, finally retrieving the porcelain shard she had found in Aristotle's gullet.

It occurred to Violet that when she had compared the shard to all of the duke's dish sets in the storage room, she had merely held it up against the various porcelain designs, trying to match them. She hadn't actually held any of the dishes in her hand to, say, compare heft or thickness. Perhaps Aristotle had choked on a piece of the servants' dishware.

Although, hadn't Olive told her that His Grace ate on that, as well? The maid should have recognized it in either case.

Furthermore, did it really matter what specific shard from a soup bowl or dessert plate the raven might have choked upon?

Nevertheless, Violet liked for all of her undertaking jobs—no matter how strange—to wrap up tidily.

She lifted her teacup again and drained it, then lifted the cup in her left hand and the shard in her right, twisting and turning them in comparison.

Now that is strange.

The shard was . . . different. It was of fine quality, better than that of the teacup and probably more like that of the stored, unused sets, yet it had an odd, translucent quality she hadn't noticed before. What factory produced porcelain like this?

Or was it even porcelain?

If it wasn't, what material *was* it? Something used in constructing the duke's tunnels, perhaps? A substance that might be readily found in the rookery if one knew where to look?

Violet had met the falconer, Martin Chandler, at the funeral. Perhaps it was time to pay him a visit.

The falconer was not alone at the rookery, which was located a couple of hundred yards north of the house and consisted of three different structures, all painted deep brown and attached to wire-mesh enclosures. To Violet's surprise, the parlor maid, Olive, was with him inside one of the enclosures, and if Violet was any judge of facial expressions, Olive was deeply enamored of Martin Chandler.

Chandler looked up quizzically from where he stood inside at a large, waist-high table, on which sat perches at varying heights, with ravens resting atop three of them, their long black talons curved tightly around the branches.

"Mrs. Harper? Have you come for falconry lessons? I can retrieve one of our red-tailed kites for you." Chandler offered a lazy smile.

Violet smiled thinly, even as Olive, who had been seated watching Chandler, now stood up and went to be next to him, as though offering herself as a physical barrier between Violet and the falconer.

"No, I'm afraid I've come on a specific mission. I was wondering if you could tell me a little about the habits of ravens. What they eat, how far away they travel, what their nesting habits are, and so forth."

Chandler continued to look puzzled, while Olive's glare was full of daggers. Did the poor girl actually think Violet was here to flirt with the young man? Well, it was flattering to think that Olive considered her a threat, as misplaced as the parlor maid's notions were.

"Do you plan to acquire a bird for yourself?" the falconer asked as he buried his right hand deep into the feathers above the shoulders of a raven that had hopped down from its perch onto the table, still tethered to the branch by a chain. As Chandler scratched the raven's skin beneath the layers of plumage, the bird acted ecstatic, raising its wings to give Chandler easier access to its skin, and cackling in delight as it bobbed its head up and down.

"No, I'm just curious about ravens," Violet hedged, "now that I've actually undertaken one of them."

"I know all there is to know about them." Chandler said this without pride or arrogance, but in the easy manner of someone who knows his business.

"For how long have you been His Grace's falconer?" Violet asked, a question she knew had nothing to do with the birds, but one more pertinent to her investigation.

He shrugged. "Near to three years, I suppose. My father was the falconer before me, but he got gout pretty bad, and couldn't work with the birds anymore. It nearly killed him not to handle them anymore, but the master gave him quarters here on the property for the rest of his life, so he was fair happy enough."

"Do you enjoy training them as much as your father did?"

Another shrug. "It's respectable work. I expect to come into some money soon, and then I'll be in a position to marry. That will make me even more respectable."

Next to him, Olive blushed bright pink, and Violet had to admit that the color on her high cheekbones made the girl quite attractive.

"I congratulate you on your upcoming happy event, sir. Are the birds confined to the rookery most of the day, or do they spend much of their day flying?"

"It depends upon which of His Grace's birds you mean. The kites, peregrines, and eagles spend much of their time on the ground except for when I send them out to feed or am training them for hawking. The ravens fly about more freely, and many of them like to perch in that grove of trees." He pointed through the enclosure at some high treetops near the rear gardens. "I use this to call them home."

Continuing to rub the raven, Chandler dug out a wooden device from his trouser pocket. Was this what was responsible for the loud clacking noise Violet had heard when the large flock of them passed overhead as she investigated Spencer's body? "His Grace keeps the ravens largely for entertainment—they can perform tricks, you know—and to take care of carrion. They are nasty eaters, will consume most any decaying flesh." Chandler stopped scratching the bird and offered his fore and middle fingers to it. The raven squawked its displeasure at no longer being stroked, but hopped on and allowed itself to be settled back on its perch. Chandler removed a second bird, which cawed in pure delight at having its turn.

"What prey do they hunt?" Violet asked. Perhaps they looked for mice and other small creatures in kitchen gardens and ended up with porcelain shards in their gullets. . . .

"They look for smaller birds, rodents, and eggs, but they are lazy. Most of the time, they prefer to just scavenge. In fact, they will guide other animals to prey that is too big for them to take down, and encourage the larger animals to attack the prey. When the attackers are done, they will feed on the leftovers. That's why they aren't trained with the other birds, which are taught to capture and kill small game."

Had Aristotle picked up the shard from the carcass of an animal that had ingested it first? If so, it would be an impossible task to figure out where the shard had come from and Violet might as well give up now.

Nevertheless, it was worth asking one more question. She removed the shard from her reticule and held it up. "I found this in Aristotle's gullet. Do you have any idea what it is?"

Olive sidled even closer to Chandler. "Remember I told you I helped her look through the storage closet for a match?"

Chandler nodded as he took the piece from Violet and examined it, flipping it several times through his fingers while continuing to stroke between the second bird's shoulders. Violet wasn't sure she could manage to perform two completely independent tasks at once like that.

Finally, the falconer shook his head and handed the shard back to her. "Ravens are known to pick up shiny objects, so I'm not surprised that Aristotle did so, but I don't know what this is. None of the others have brought anything similar back to the rookery. Aristotle was a clever boy, though. He could play games and do tricks, such as making his way through a series of obstacles to reach a morsel of food. He also liked to look at himself in mirrors and would go through obstructions to reach a looking glass. Perhaps he had to make his way through some impediments to get to your little piece of glass, which he thought was a treat or reward."

Violet doubted that was it, but thanked the falconer for his time so she could return to Sam, who was surely finished with Mr. Reed. Olive's relief at her departure was palpable.

Sam could barely contain his excitement when Violet returned to the estate manager's cottage. His eyes flashed with joy as he ushered her inside to where the air was thick with celebratory cigar smoke. "Sweetheart, did you know that the duke plans to open up an underground roller skating rink west of the house? Apparently, he likes for his servants to take regular exercise."

First the rowing lessons, now this? "Why does he intend to build it underground?" Violet asked.

"Most of the duke's projects are underground," Reed said. "He is quite . . . modest, and prefers that his construction not be visible to others. He considers them to be for his own enjoyment and for that of his household staff."

So much money invested in buildings and tunnels that would only be used by essentially just a handful of people. Portland was a strange man, and becoming more eccentric in Violet's eyes with each passing glimpse into his world.

"Anyway," Sam continued, "Ellery immediately saw the value of dynamite in tearing open the pit required for it. In fact, he recommends that work be started on it right away."

So her husband and the estate manager were already on a first-name basis.

"I'm to return tomorrow with James and Philip to mark it out, set the holes, and blow them." James and Philip Ward were twin brothers Sam had employed to help manage the opening of the colliery.

Reed smiled. "We've been celebrating our agreement, but it seems to me that food is in order. Will you join us for luncheon, Mrs. Harper?"

Over broiled hare and stewed celery in cream sauce brought out to them by Judith, Sam and Reed continued their conversation about how many rounds of blasting to do, where to drill holes for placing the dynamite, and what estate staff should be on hand to help. They were as excited about it as Violet was when she found a new brand of cosmetic massage cream. She let them prattle on as she wandered into her own thoughts about the porcelain shard, Spencer, Martin Chandler, and Colonel Mortimer.

Eventually, though, the two men realized that they had an uninterested party at the table, and changed the subject.

"I know you must think His Grace is peculiar," Reed said, addressing Violet as he laid his fork on his plate and took a sip of ginger beer, "but he is actually a generous and thoughtful master to his workers. Every man receives a donkey and an umbrella to ensure he has no trouble getting to work, and he has established a widows' and orphans' fund to care for the families of workers who die. If Burton had had a wife, I have no doubt His Grace would have already installed her in her own cottage on the property."

"He *is* generous," Violet murmured, wondering if Reed intended to offer any of the bread pudding Judith had left under a glass dome on a side table.

"I believe many of his projects are devised by him just to keep men in the area employed. In fact, it's said that any man can come to Welbeck and expect that he won't be turned away," Reed boasted. "I probably manage the work and pay of more men at Welbeck than on any other estate in England."

Now Violet's attention was diverted from the pudding. Reed was certainly eager to defend the duke from—what? Criticism? Blame? Something else? He was gainfully employed by the duke, so he did have reason to extol the man's virtues.

Sam was also diverted, but in a different manner. "That explains much about my difficulties with my colliery. I knew there was competition from other mines along the Nottingham coalfield, but I found that the largest challenge for labor came from this estate. I couldn't for the life of me understand how one house could require so many townspeople. I've been blamed near having to hang up my fiddle on the whole thing and abandon the mine."

Reed tried to suppress a smile, and it was evident that his sympathy for Samuel Harper was overridden by his pride in working for such a grand—and magnanimous—peer of the realm.

Sam, though, was too wrapped up in his own rumination to notice Reed's amusement. "This estate must produce a vast amount of wealth to enable the duke to continue hiring and building without end."

Violet winced. It might be de rigueur in America to discuss how success was achieved, but it was highly improper to inquire about a peer's prosperity. Reed, though, didn't seem to mind. "Yes, His Grace has made a variety of wise investments. His latest was in government consols to support the 1867 expedition to Abyssinia to see several imprisoned missionaries freed."

"Consols?" Sam frowned.

"High-quality government bonds, typically used to fund wars and building projects when tax revenue at the moment of need isn't enough."

"Ah, similar to our treasury notes," Sam said, nodding in understanding.

"Yes. His Grace purchased a vast amount in consols, but has lately been turning them back in to regain the principal in order to maintain the pace of his construction schedule. I hear that the Crown is short two million pounds in revenues for the past year in having to repay him."

This was yet another interesting tidbit Violet hadn't known about Portland. Was he really risking his investments and standing with the government to ensure he had funds available to keep men employed on his estate? Perhaps it was no wonder that they were generally willing to overlook his eccentricities.

"His Grace is truly generous," she repeated, and she wasn't even thinking about bread pudding anymore. She was actually thinking once more about Colonel Mortimer. How far had Portland's generosity extended to his old war friend? The duke seemed to have three passions: construction, church, and charity. Was it remotely possible that he somehow knew the colonel was mistaken in what he had witnessed the night Spencer died, and was giving the man protection out of loyalty to their past camaraderie? Was one of the men covering something up for an unknown reason, or was Violet's vivid imagination just running away with her again?

The men returned to their discussion about the next day's dynamite, and by the time luncheon was over—with servings of bread pudding finally consumed—it was agreed that Violet would stay over at Welbeck once more since Sam would be busy until the morning in securing everything in town for the next day's tunneling.

This time, Violet was happy to stay at the Abbey, for she had decided that a particular visit was in order, to set her mind at rest. Or perhaps she would be poking a stick in a hornets' nest, and risking getting badly stung.

* * *

Once Sam had departed for Worksop, Violet set about on her plan, first asking as to where Colonel Mortimer's cottage was. To her surprise, she learned that it was in the same cluster of cottages where Reed's was.

This meant that she was doing a great deal of walking back and forth across the estate today, although her waistline could certainly benefit from the effort.

Violet took a walking path that led from the rookery to the rear gardens of the house and beyond. As she walked, she remembered the grove of trees near the rear gardens to which Chandler had pointed, saying that the ravens enjoyed perching there. If Aristotle spent much time there, perhaps that was where he had picked up the shard, and maybe she could find the rest of the item, thus finally putting to rest that nagging question about what the raven had swallowed.

As with most of the other flora on the estate, the silver birches in this grove, with their paper-tissue bark, were stripped of leaves. Some of those leaves still remained on the ground beneath the canopies, curled and withered. They crunched and swished beneath her booted feet as she futilely kicked them around, looking for a cup, shattered plate, or anything that might match the fragment in her hand.

Was she merely chasing phantoms?

The telltale screeching of ravens grew louder until several of them lit on the uppermost branches of the birch trees, like gargoyles of death watching over her movements. She involuntarily shivered despite the sunshine of the day, and immediately admonished herself.

Violet Harper, you are an undertaker and have no fear of death, and you especially have no fear of mindless birds.

As if reading her thoughts, one of the ravens hopped down through the branches until it reached a low one right over Violet's head. It cocked its own head and stared at her as if to inquire what she was doing under *its* tree.

"I need to find the rest of this," Violet said, pulling the shard from her reticule and holding it up for the raven's inspection. "Can you help—" She stopped herself. "What am I saying? I must be mad to seek a bird's assistance."

She sighed. Perhaps everyone who came to work at Welbeck Abbey developed a touch of madness.

She returned to her fruitless search in the dirt and leaves, and soon realized that she had discovered yet another bizarre thing. There were dozens of small holes dug into the earth under the trees. They were deep, but only a few inches across. Had some burrowing animal done this? Violet couldn't imagine what creature it could have been. Moles dug tunnels much like Portland did. Mice and chipmunks burrowed into holes, but these weren't the random sort of holes she would expect from the rodents. These holes were in much more of a deliberate pattern.

Violet gasped aloud, causing the raven to squawk and ruffle its feathers in alarm. It hopped completely around the branch in one fluid motion to stare at her with its other eye.

Violet had lost most of her interest in the bird, though, as she knelt down and picked up a tiny piece of porcelain, practically glowing white against the dark ground around it. Yes, it was the same material. With great anticipation, she held the other shard up to it, turning it until it fit almost perfectly against the piece she'd just found.

She couldn't believe it. No wonder neither she nor anyone else had been able to determine what fine dining ware the original fragment had come from. She glanced up at the raven, which leaned over to examine what was in Violet's hands. "Korrrrr," it said softly, as if it, too, realized the significance of what Violet held.

The fragment wasn't from dining ware after all. She held the two pieces together and realized that they combined to make a glass eye.

It was well made, the blue and green of the iris distinct yet blending together around the dark pupil almost artistically. It didn't look as though it was meant to be in the shape of a round eyeball, but instead was more of a prosthetic covering that would merely be inserted into the eye socket and attached to, what, a muscle?

Violet tried to remember if she had ever undertaken a body with a glass eye before. She had seen many prosthetic limbs and teeth before, but not an eye. Whoever wore this must be proud of it, for its artificiality wouldn't be apparent to anyone giving the wearer a cursory glance.

But who could the glass piece possibly belong to? Would he not be walking obviously about with an eye patch now?

She frowned as she thought of something. When Colonel Mortimer had visited Portland to tell the duke of having witnessed a murder, Violet had noticed that the colonel's eyes seemed to move independently of each other. Did he wear a glass eye? But when that occurred, she already had the shard in her reticule. Unless he had an additional prosthetic.

But . . . both of his eyes had been bloodshot, evidence of heavy drinking. A glass eye couldn't change its own appearance in that way.

The colonel's face had also been scuffed up. Now she truly wondered how that had happened. The man had claimed he witnessed a murder, and indeed Spencer's body was found near a tunnel located to the south front of the estate. Violet now stood far to the west. If the glass eye belonged to him—and she wasn't sure it did—it simply wasn't possible that he lost it while witnessing Spencer's murder.

Violet's thoughts turned very dark as she began to suspect the colonel of an exceedingly evil deed.

Had Mortimer killed Spencer here, dragged him over to the tunnel where he was sure to be easily found, and lost his prosthetic eye in the process? Had there been an altercation between the two men that resulted in the terrible bruising on Spencer's chest?

What of the rock Spencer had fallen against? Was that an intentional display by the colonel so that everyone would think Spencer had died in a mere fall?

The problem with all of this theorizing was that Violet could not reason out what the colonel's reason could be for killing the young man.

She rose and went to the birch tree, leaning her back against the trunk as she continued to examine the two shards and puzzle out what exactly it was she had discovered. The raven grew bored of watching her, and flapped off its branch to join its mates in the treetops with one final, guttural squawk.

Is there more to find in this area? Violet decided to expand her search a bit farther into the grove of trees, hoping she wouldn't stumble upon any adders sleeping curled up in the denser underbrush, or twist an ankle in one of the many holes in the area.

She had no idea what she was even searching for with her feet as she continued shuffling through the growth that was clearly not part of the head gardener's responsibility to keep trimmed. More glass eyes? The weapon used to bruise Spencer? A written confession to the murder?

Her boot connected with something solid. She would have thought it was a tree stump except it wasn't as hard as that. In fact, there was something familiar to it. She knelt down once more to inspect what was half buried under the leaves, brushing them aside until she found—

Violet staggered backward, and let out a loud gasp that sent the ravens scattering out of the trees in a burst of screeching and cawing. They couldn't possibly be any more startled than she was.

9

Lying before Violet was the body of another man. She blinked in disbelief. Who was this? Who had left him so carelessly in the woods like this, in a shallow grave where he might be preyed upon by animals and made to suffer the chill and rain? For certainly he had not covered himself up.

Although still trembling, once she had sufficiently recovered from her shock and choked down her outrage, Violet fully uncovered the body and began an inspection of the man. He was of larger than average height and build, and probably in his late thirties, considerably older than Burton Spencer. His clothes were worn but fit well. There were what appeared to be paint smudges on the right thigh of his trousers.

She held up one of his hands. It was rough and calloused. "Sir, I am guessing you are one of His Grace's hardest-working outdoor men." She rubbed the gray hand between her palms. Rigor mortis had passed. She leaned over and slowly sniffed the air around him, trying to separate out the telltale odor of decomposition from that of rotting leaves. It was impossible to be certain, but she thought that this man, like Spencer, had been dead no more than three or four days.

She had an idea. "Will you allow me to open your shirt, sir, to see if you are bruised like Mr. Spencer?" Violet unbuttoned the black-and-white-striped shirt and pulled it back, exposing his chest and shoulders.

There was no bruising on the man's chest, but what was this on his right shoulder? She bent to take a closer look. Why, it was a tattoo, and an odd one. It seemed to be a hill with a tree growing out of the top of it. What in heaven's name did it represent?

Violet had more immediate concerns. First, how had the man died? With a knot of dread in her stomach, she reached her hand behind his neck, gently probing the back of his head. There was definitely a mass of crusted blood.

It seemed likely that he had died by the same hand that had killed Spencer. How were these two murders related? Did the two men know each other, beyond both presumably serving as estate workers? Had the colonel actually murdered them? Or was the colonel perhaps involved in one but not the other?

Another thought occurred to her. What if this was the murder the colonel had actually witnessed? Spencer's body had been discovered first and so she had simply assumed he was the one to whom Colonel Mortimer had referred. And the colonel had never been summoned to identify the body, so that assumption had remained in place.

Had Violet's mental accusation of the colonel been completely off the mark? She checked his neck for marks of strangulation. Nothing. Nevertheless, she needed to report this.

"Sir, forgive me, but I'm afraid I will have to leave you alone once more while I go to fetch help. I promise that you won't remain here long."

She rose, and her first thought was to go to the duke right away, for surely he would want to summon the police this time. Her second thought, though, was to continue on her original mission to the colonel's cottage. She would report the body to him and see what his reaction was. After all, the corpse could not be helped now, and it might be illuminating to witness the colonel's reception to the news.

Colonel Mortimer's reaction to her visit, however, was unlike anything Violet could have ever expected.

The colonel's cottage was larger than any of the others around it, although it shared their thatched-roof styling. Like the others', its exterior was immaculately groomed. The duke must be spending inordinate sums to maintain the complicated landscapes surrounding the main house and all of these outbuildings.

As Violet raised her hand to knock at the door, she wondered who lived in the surrounding homes, other than Mr. Reed, the estate manager. Widows, orphans, other displaced relatives? Perhaps more of the estate's crucial employees?

The door opened, and Colonel Mortimer appeared from behind it. His condition was even more dreadful than when she had met him in Portland's quarters. Violet self-consciously pressed a hand against her reticule, to make sure she still felt the outline of her knife inside, should something go awry.

"Colonel? I'm Violet Harper, the under—"

"Yes, I remember." He stood back and pulled the door farther open, so Violet stepped in. A lone gas lamp burned in the room, which was full of the overstuffed furniture, patterned rugs, and bold floral wallpaper that were currently popular. The cottage lacked any framed photographs, but more than made up for it with shelves full of liquor bottles and glasses.

She supposed she should credit him for not hiding his tippling.

"I've discovered a body," she said without preamble as he shut the door behind her, enveloping them in murky shadows. Violet felt that the cottage wanted to cry out in its loneliness.

The colonel raised an eyebrow, which framed one of a pair of bloodshot eyes. "I know this, Mrs. Harper. We just had a funeral for Mr. Spencer."

Liquor fumes from his breath settled over Violet like a noxious miasma, confirming her suspicion that he was drunk.

"I don't mean Mr. Spencer, Colonel. I mean to tell you that I've found a second body."

The colonel weaved back and forth. "I didn't find it this time."

"No, Colonel, *I* found it. It's a man whom I think is probably a work—"

"I didn't have anything to do with it, either."

Was Colonel Mortimer telling her something specific, or was he merely rambling in his intoxication? One thing for certain, his pair of bloodshot eyes conclusively proved to Violet that the glass eye was not his. But was it true that he'd had nothing to do with this second murder? Perhaps she should try to set him at ease with her visit.

"I must confess to you, sir, that I found a broken glass eye, and I was certain it belonged to you, except that both the day I met you and at this moment, your eyes have been particularly red, so I know it cannot be yours." She reached into her reticule and pulled out the two broken pieces.

To her surprise, the colonel roared with laughter after a mere glance at them. "Of course it's mine, madam."

"But—"

"Care for a nip? I'm dry as the Sahara myself." He went to one of the laden shelves and searched through the bottles. Violet wasn't sure if he was looking for a specific type, or merely a bottle that was at least half full. He finally selected a bottle of dark liquid. He held it up for Violet's approval.

"No, thank you," she demurred politely.

"Are you certain, madam? It's rum made from the finest molasses Barbados produces. No? Very well, then." The colonel poured himself a generous glass of it and sniffed appreciatively before taking a gulp.

Was Violet going to have to wait until he drained the glass before he explained about the glass eye? "Sir, you said that this belongs—"

"Ah yes, just a moment." The colonel left the room with his glass.

Violet planned to count to ten, and if he didn't return by then, she would simply have to leave and report the death to Portland. The body was, after all, still lying inelegantly in the copse.

Colonel Mortimer returned, though, before she reached the number six, with his drink in one hand and a glass-covered tray in the other. The tray reminded her of her own portable glass cases, which she used to exhibit mourning pins, bracelets, hairpins, and handkerchiefs to her customers. However, Violet had never seen a display such as what the colonel now held.

The tray was divided into twelve compartments lined in satin. Each compartment but two held a different glass eye. Despite herself, Violet put a hand to her chest. "Oh my," she breathed, as ten eyes of varying pupil width and iris shade stared up at her.

The colonel laughed again, enjoying her discomfort. "Quite a collection, eh? There is an ocularist in Munich who makes them for me. Look at this one," he said, putting down his rum to open the case and take one out. "See the yellowing in the white portion here? Makes it look jaundiced, doesn't it? I wear it when I'm not well."

The colonel put that one away and set the case down next to his glass. "When I have a little nip or two, my eye can get a bit bloodshot, so I always insert this one"—in one fluid motion, the colonel popped out the prosthetic in his left eye, presenting the piece with its red lining around the iris to Violet like a gift—"so that others are not disconcerted when they don't match. Clever, isn't it?"

As Colonel Mortimer spoke, Violet was fascinated by the fact that his eye socket wasn't completely empty, but that there was still muscle moving about in it. So that was why his glass eye wasn't a ball to fit inside the cavity, but was more like a plate to fit over what remained behind his lid. However, she was being distracted from her real mission here.

"Yes, but I remind you that there is a body in the woods between the rookery and the house, someone who needs to be recovered from where he lies. Perhaps I should have gone to His Grace—"

"No, no, I will accompany you and alert whoever is appropriate." The colonel was suddenly—and remarkably—recovered from his sotted state.

"There's one more thing, Colonel. I should tell you that I found the glass eye near the body." Violet hoped her revelation would startle him if he was the guilty party, but he was nonchalant.

"I must have lost it when I witnessed the attack. I remember waking up the following morning and having to put in a new one, but I didn't attach any significance to it."

Violet's mind worked furiously as she led the colonel back to the grove of birch trees. If what the colonel said was true, then perhaps this second body really was the victim of the murder he had witnessed, which meant that Burton Spencer was—what? An independent attack? Had Spencer witnessed the first murder and put himself in mortal danger as a result? She thought about the condition of the second body. She would have to estimate that it had been there no more than three or four days. Rigor mortis was gone, but with the cool October air it had not gone into any serious decomposition. If only—

"Mrs. Harper, is this the place?" the colonel said, interrupting her flow of rambling thoughts. She looked up and realized she was about to march straight past the trees and on to the rookery.

"Yes, of course. Let me show you where the corpse is. I presume a man such as yourself is not squeamish about these things."

"I should say not," he huffed, blowing more liquor fumes over her as he indignantly straightened his jacket.

Violet moved into the underbrush, with the colonel at her heels. *Let's see, another ten feet in this direction, then straight across from the bramble of thorny blackberry bushes, and then—*

Wait, was Violet confused? She stepped off again, concentrating harder on her position relative to the birches. Yes, this was the right spot.

"Mrs. Harper?" the colonel asked.

This was simply impossible. Was she on the verge of losing her mind? Had she not just inspected the body of a man with a tattoo on his shoulder?

And yet . . . the body was gone.

10

"**I**—I don't understand," Violet protested in disbelief. "I just inspected this body not an hour ago. What could have possibly happened to it? Bodies don't just get up on their own, despite what mystery novelists would have us believe."

"Have no fear, dear lady, I have been the victim many a time to visions that were not real." Colonel Mortimer offered an expression of sympathy, which only served to irritate Violet.

"I am never in a polluted state," she snapped. "And I did not have a vision. There was a dead man here. I saw him, I touched him, I spoke to him."

Mortimer looked at her sideways. "You spoke to the body? Did it answer? Perhaps you are more in need of rum than you think."

Violet resisted the urge to disparage the man, who she knew meant no harm. However, she was as tense as a mouse in a room full of tabbies. Where was the tattooed man? Who or what had moved his body? Was it possible that someone else had come across the body and hurriedly reported it to the duke? Perhaps it was lying on the dining room table at this very moment, waiting for her to formally attend to it.

Yes, perhaps that was what had happened.

The colonel pointed up. "Evening is settling in. Perhaps you were confused by what you saw, Mrs. Harper. In the shadows, a deer might have looked like a human being."

Violet was aghast. She had cared for hundreds—perhaps thousands—of bodies in her lifetime as an undertaker, and he thought she could mistake a wild animal for a human being?

"Sir, the body had the tattoo of a hill with a tree in the center of it located on his shoulder. I hardly think England's deer population is visiting the docks to have tattoos drawn on their shanks."

The colonel frowned. "A tattoo, you say? Of a treed hill? Perhaps it was actually a volcano? Hmm, this is interesting."

"It is? How so?"

The colonel seemed unwilling to share his thoughts, though, and reverted to his previous theme. "People make mistakes all the time when there isn't strong sunlight to provide clarity on the situation. No doubt you simply had what His Grace refers to as 'an episode.'"

Her pounding heart and uneasy stomach didn't think so. And the colonel had certainly been insistent that *he* had not made a mistake in the dark, with only one good eye to back up his assertions. However, the first thing to do was to check on whether the body was at the house. She took a deep breath to regain her calmness. "Colonel, I apologize for disturbing you during your . . . private time . . . for no apparent reason."

"No apologies necessary. I think you may have been confused. I *did* witness a murder here, but it was just the one, not two of them. I may be an old one-eyed warhorse, but I am not a lunatic. I know what I saw."

Yet he thought Violet had mistaken a deer for a human, which would make her a complete Bedlamite. Regardless, she didn't know what to make of his assertion at this point. She needed to find Portland right away.

"May I walk with you back to your cottage?" she asked.

"Perhaps it might be wise if I went on my own. Otherwise, I might find it gone when I arrive." The colonel chuckled at his joke, offending Violet in that he not only didn't seem to care that there might be another dead estate worker but also was mostly concerned with having been vindicated in witnessing a murder.

As he walked away, Violet realized that he didn't have his cane with him, and was moving quite well—despite an occasional drunken stumble—across the expansive lawns of the estate. With the colonel ambling back to his bottle, Violet walked back toward the house, and it occurred to her that the colonel almost seemed happy by what had just happened.

She waited until he was long out of view before heading to the house, but she didn't have far to walk before she came upon yet another unusual sight, which was becoming only too common at Welbeck Abbey. The duke was out walking along a gravel path in the rear garden, wearing his typical brown overcoat and ridiculously high hat. Despite the mild day, he once again carried an umbrella over his head.

None of that, of course, surprised Violet anymore. What did was the young woman in a hooded cloak walking about ten feet in front of him, carrying a lantern that was far too big for her to handle. Light from the lamp well illuminated Portland's path, as it swung unsteadily from the chain in the girl's hand. Violet was instantly reminded of the Brothers Grimm tale of Red Riding Hood, except that here the girl carried a lantern instead of a basket.

Presumably the duke was not the wolf.

There was no time to worry about that for the moment. Violet rushed up to Portland, causing him to exclaim aloud at her sudden appearance. "Matthew, Mark, Luke, and John, what do you mean by sneaking up on me like that, Mrs. Harper?"

"My apologies, sir, but there is an urgent matter I must discuss with you."

Portland waved at the lantern carrier. "Molly, wait a moment. I see that my walk is to be disturbed this evening."

Without waiting for him to grant her leave to continue, Violet plunged in. "I saw a body earlier—another body—in the copse near the rookery. I went to Colonel Mortimer's cottage and had him accompany me back to the body, but when we returned, the corpse was gone. I am wondering if perhaps someone else found it and brought it to the house."

"You say you found yet another body on *my* property? That is impossible. No, I refuse to countenance it."

Why was it that most members of the upper classes believed that the world could only operate in a manner that pleased them, and that it wouldn't dare do otherwise?

"It may seem unimaginable, Your Grace, but it is so. May I presume you have no such body inside the house?"

"Of course not. Mrs. Harper, why did you summon the colonel instead of me?" Portland asked.

Violet bit her lip indecisively. This was an excellent question. On reflection, it was precisely what she should have done instead of trying to vindicate her suspicions of the colonel. "I—I—know that you are close friends, and believed he might know if such a thing had occurred. I didn't wish to disturb you any more than I already have."

"I see." Portland's tone was penetrating, even in the shadows.

Violet was a terrible liar and she knew it. It was best to move the subject along. "Your Grace, it is imperative that we find this body. What if it is one of your workers?"

He nodded. "That would be a grave circumstance, indeed. Why don't you show me the location where you found him? Perhaps in the setting sun it was easy to mistake his location. With Molly illuminating the area, we'll find him for sure. Molly?"

The girl came forward with her lantern, and once again Violet led the way back to the grove of birch trees. Once again, there was no body, despite the good Molly's best efforts to shed light everywhere.

In fact, the more Violet thought about all of the mysterious doings at Welbeck Abbey, the darker it all seemed.

After a half hour of searching the relatively small area, even Portland had to admit there was no one there. "Perhaps the man you found had fallen down in a drunken stupor, but woke up and left before you returned."

Yet someone else questioning her abilities. "Sir, I have been an undertaker for many years. I am confident in knowing when someone is deceased."

"No, I think there is merit to my suggestion. Sometimes men can be so insensible from too much liquor that they do not wake for days. You had the misfortune of him waking in that narrow space of time in which you sought out the colonel. Besides, in your profession, do you not use bell coffins to accommodate such situations where mistakes are made?"

Violet cringed at the reference to the possibility of an undertaker not recognizing the signs of death, having recently experienced just such a situation, but avoided responding to his sardonic comment. She realized that the only way to convince Portland that there was actually another dead body on his estate was to somehow produce it. Which she intended to do, only she had to figure out how to find the poor man. For now, perhaps she should bring up another of her suspicions.

"Sir, speaking of the colonel, I feel obligated to tell you that shard I found in Aristotle's craw was a piece of one of Colonel Mortimer's glass eyes. I presume you knew he wore one."

"Of course. He told me that he lost his eye in a hunting accident several years ago. Poor man, he's had the most unfortunate luck." He motioned to Molly, who began walking back toward the house, with Portland ten feet behind her. Violet fell into step with him.

"Be it that his luck is lamentable, I have my concerns about his . . . trustworthiness."

"Whatever do you mean?"

How should Violet characterize it? "I find something suspicious in his statements and behavior regarding Burton Spencer's death."

"Mrs. Harper, come now. George is a trusted friend. I have known him for decades and can state positively that he would never, ever do anything that would cast dishonor upon his person. Why, we fought together in the Burmese War against General Bandula, who had fighting elephants and who—"

"Yes, Your Grace, I remember. The colonel was instrumental in ensuring you weren't strangled by a python." It was dark now, and getting quite chilly. It was time for her to return to her quarters, to sit by the fire that was surely waiting for her, to sip a glass of sherry, and to think.

Portland might trust Colonel Mortimer implicitly, but Violet didn't. Even if he weren't guilty of murder, there was still something off about the man.

11

❧

"Would you like a tour of the underground?" Ellery Reed asked the next morning, uttering words that made Violet nearly delirious at the prospect, despite her anxiety over the missing body.

"Most certainly," she replied for her and Sam.

As promised, Sam had returned with James and Philip Ward, as well as several other workers and a wagonload of dynamite and other materials. While the Ward brothers directed the unloading of the wagons, Violet and Sam followed Reed to a tunnel entrance—or, rather, an exit, located near the two rows of dormitory-style buildings, which Reed confirmed were servants' quarters. The tunnel was worked into the landscape in such a way that it almost looked like a natural stone formation rising up and welcoming them to the mystical grotto below. Belowground, though, were no ancient Greek mosaics and spouting dolphin heads, but a remarkably wide space that led into infinity. Violet couldn't see the end of the stonework tunnel, despite the paned-glass ceiling domes above them approximately every six feet, which provided the tunnel with enough daylight that Violet could pick out the stone's marbled pattern.

The gravel crunching beneath their feet as they walked three abreast was unsullied by animal droppings, plant debris, or any other dirt, almost as if it were being swept clean each day.

"This will take us beneath the house, to the grand ballroom, chapel, and guest rooms," Reed said. "We are in the servants' tunnel, which runs alongside His Grace's private tunnel. The other one has a pavement surface, naturally."

"Naturally," Sam said, drily. "Why are there two?" Welbeck held few surprises for Violet anymore, but for Sam it was still new.

"His Grace prefers his own tunnel, which is sizable enough to enable his largest carriage-and-four to pass through, with no danger of a groom on the raised rumble seat being injured. He doesn't like to encounter anyone when he makes his trips to town."

"Who could he possibly encounter from here to Worksop other than a neighbor or two?" Sam persisted.

"One never knows what may happen," Reed said. "His Grace used his passageway for Spencer's funeral, which enabled him to avoid the procession."

"He wanted to avoid his own servants and staff?" Sam was running off with the topic like a fox with a mole in its jaws.

Reed took no offense, though, and instead shrugged. "As I said, His Grace is private in the extreme. Workers are fortunate to have a place here, so no one thinks about it anymore."

They crunched on to a point where the tunnel actually split into three directions, a marvel of workmanship in Violet's mind. "We'll go this way," Reed said, heading to the right.

"Where do the other passageways go?" Violet asked.

"The one to the left ends at the stables, and meets up here to deliver equipage when His Grace desires it. The other tunnel leads to the worker dormitories."

They proceeded on through the tunnel until they came to a set of arched, Gothic double doors set in the wall on their right. "This is the ballroom," Reed said, opening one of the doors and allowing the Harpers to precede him in.

Violet had no idea what to expect, yet it was positively breathtaking. Unlike in the tunnel, the ceiling here was tall—but flat—and coffered, with rows of squares filled with glass alternating with squares from which dangled sixteen opulent crystal chandeliers.

Had they been walking on a downward incline this entire time, to enter a room with such a high ceiling?

Reed turned a key set into a wall plate, and the chandeliers all hissed with gas, showering the room in a glow befitting Buckingham Palace. What they illuminated shouldn't have surprised Violet but did.

Like in the dining room, this room's walls—which was probably sixty feet by eighty feet, if she had to guess—were covered over in paintings, many of which Violet guessed were priceless. How much money this family must have spent in artwork!

Positioned in a rectangle around the room, approximately ten feet away from each wall, were overstuffed viewing chairs and couches, all in the same floral fabric, atop the glossy wood flooring, which seemed to call out longingly for slippered feet to glide across it.

This time, Violet jumped in with questions before her husband could. "Didn't you say this is the ballroom?"

Reed nodded. "It is accessible from the house only through means of a lift."

"But . . . it looks like a picture gallery. I feel as though a museum guide might approach me at any moment with a penny guide to the collection."

Reed smiled thinly, as though he had heard her comment many times before. "His Grace does not have many visitors, so he uses the ballroom in this manner to be more useful to him personally."

Violet and Sam exchanged glances, and she knew her husband was thinking the same thing she was. *Why build a ballroom if you don't intend to host balls?*

Reed led them to a corner of the room that contained a discreetly placed glass case resting on top of an elegant mahogany table. "Here are the prizes of His Grace's entire collection," he said.

Violet peered into the slanted glass top as Reed described the contents. "These pearl drop earrings and silver gilt chalice belonged to Charles I. He used the chalice prior to execution at Whitehall. You can see the inscription on it."

Violet knelt to read.

KING CHARLES THE FIRST RECEIVED THE COMMUNION
IN THIS BOULE ON TUSEDAY THE 30TH OF JANUARY, 1649,
BEING THE DAY IN WHICH HE WAS MURTHERED.

Oh my. What a treasure. She would have been surprised if the British Museum had not attempted to purchase it.

Next to the earrings and chalice was a letter. The writing was faded and difficult to read, but what was obvious was the closing, which read, *Your very good friend, Mary R.*

Violet was agog at what lay in the duke's possession.

"He holds many letters from the Stuarts, although this one from the Scottish queen is his most prized one. Ironic, since he is descended from the queen's jailer."

"He keeps them here in his basement?" Sam asked in amazement.

Reed nodded. "They are quite as safe here as anywhere else, and don't receive much light or dust or fluctuation in temperature."

Violet couldn't argue with the logic of that.

"When he builds his planned library, His Grace will of course move these items there," Reed added. "He has many old volumes boxed away."

Undoubtedly, Reed meant an underground library.

They then followed Reed across the length of the room to another set of double doors, these with a glass transom over them. They passed into another tunnel, which had a series of doors leading off of it. Reed opened each one briefly for them to stick their heads in for a glance. Each room was approximately twenty feet square with a large dome light in the center of the ceiling. But that was where the similarity ended, for each of these bedchambers was decorated in vastly different fabrics and furniture, each one themed to its own color palette or design pattern. One room had delicate Sheraton-style furniture and was done in pale blue; the next had a heavy walnut poster bed and was swathed in burgundy and gold. By the time Violet had seen ten of these rooms, she was overwhelmed and exhausted.

The other similarity she realized was that all the rooms appeared as though they had never been slept in. Or even had their carpets trod upon.

Already anticipating her next question, Reed said, "His Grace is a private man. He doesn't entertain."

Sam shook his head in disbelief. "Never in all my dad-blamed days . . ." He kept the rest of his thought to himself.

They proceeded farther down this tunnel, the floor of which was done in alternating black and white marble tiles so that it felt like they were inside a grand country home, until they reached its end, which stopped at yet another pair of rounded, Gothic double doors. Wooden crosses hanging upon the doors announced where they were.

Unlike the ballroom or guest rooms, the chapel was almost stark in its simplicity, with a dozen rows of oak pews and a preacher's box. Overhead—the only nod to ostentation—the dome skylights were done in stained glass and a magnificent, if oddly placed, crystal chandelier. The ornate fixture had at least a dozen branches radiating out and reflecting light in an ornate mirror at the head of the nave where a crucifix might hang.

"Does His Grace have private services for himself here on Sundays and holy days?" Sam asked.

"Dear me, no," Reed said. "He attends chapel at Worksop Priory."

Sam muttered something unintelligible.

Violet, though, was distracted again. Why, was that the odor of roasting chicken, discernible even down here? She sniffed the air as unobtrusively as she could. Yes, it was. In fact, she realized that the wonderful odor had followed them here from the ballroom. No wonder Mrs. Garside had so many chickens cooking at once all the time, if she was wafting the smell to all parts of the house. The estate must have a very productive hen house to keep this going twenty-four hours a day.

"I imagine the dynamite has been unloaded by now," Reed said, escorting them out of the chapel and back the way they had come. "I'm eager to see it in action. Combined with the advanced steam machinery we have on the estate, it has the potential to help us get twice as much land moved in half the time as is being done at places like Thoresby Hall or Clumber Park."

"Where are they?"

"Both estates neighbor Welbeck Abbey and, along with Worksop Manor and Welbeck Abbey, make up what are called the Dukeries, straddling Nottinghamshire and Derbyshire. None of them have the extensive building projects of His Grace." Violet heard the pride in Reed's voice.

Little did she realize that, a short while later, all of Reed's pride would evaporate, leaving him with only anger and bitterness.

Once they were aboveground, Sam went to direct his workers on where the shot-firing would take place to blast the holes for the skating rink. Shot-firing was his recently learned method for clearing rock and earth. As Sam showed James and Philip where to dig the holes to place the dynamite sticks—which had long wires that attached to a detonator a long distance away—Violet allowed Reed to escort her to a safe viewing place atop a grassy hill.

She sat down and spread her skirts around her, noticing that many estate workers were finding their way to the hill for observation. Word must have spread quickly about what was to take place.

Knowing that Reed would wish to join Sam and observe how he chose where to dig holes and insert the dynamite, Violet decided she had just a few moments in which to conduct her business with him. "Mr. Reed," she said, "I was wondering if any of your other workers have gone missing in the past few days?"

Reed had been about to leave to join the dynamiters, but spun back around on his heel at Violet's inquiry. "Another worker? What do you mean?"

She countered with another question. "Do you have a worker with a tattoo of a hill or volcano on his shoulder?"

"Yes, that sounds like Edward Bayes. He spent time in the navy before—Wait a moment." Reed's expression was confused. "Mrs. Harper, what are you suggesting? Is Bayes . . . ?" He made a choking sound as if he could hardly get out his next words. "Has Bayes died, too?"

"I believe so, sir, but I'm not sure." Violet rose to stand next to him. "I found his body late yesterday."

"Where is he? If he's one of my men, I can identify him."

"Yes, well, I went to go get help, and when I returned with Colonel Mortimer, the body was gone."

Reed's expression was even more baffled. "You sought the colonel's help instead of mine or His Grace's?"

How Violet wished she could erase the way she had handled the situation. "Unfortunately, yes. But His Grace is aware of the situation, and now I plan to resume searching for the body—Mr. Bayes's, I now presume—just as soon as the estate is cleared from the dynamiting."

The estate manager nodded, too stunned to even respond to the news that he might have a second death on his hands. Instead, he said, "I believe I will join your husband at the blasting machine." Sam and his workers were congregated near the small piece of equipment that would create the grand explosion people were gathering to see as if they were here to witness a circus performance.

On impulse, Violet rose and said, "I will join you, as well."

"Mrs. Harper, it is safer here on the hill." Reed put out a hand as if to stop her.

"Nevertheless, I will go with you."

He shrugged, and she followed him to where Sam and the Ward brothers stood, now interestingly joined by Jack LeCato, talking behind a temporary metal wall with an observation glass in it. Sam nodded to acknowledge her presence, but was too tense for conversation as he constantly stepped out to issue instructions to his workers, who were digging last-minute holes and shoving in dynamite sticks.

The long trails of wires leading back to the blasting machine looked like an invasion of adders, which reminded Violet of the holes she had seen under the birch trees. But there weren't dynamite sticks in those holes . . . were there? Who even had access to the explosive materials besides Sam and his workers? Besides, why would someone want to annihilate a grove of trees? Unless . . . unless there was evidence of some sort to be destroyed? If only she could fathom what.

She made a mental note to go back and check the holes she had found.

"Retreat to safety!" Sam shouted at his workers as someone else blew a horn. They all scattered away from the area that would soon constitute the beginning of an underground skating rink for all of Welbeck Abbey's workers. Sam himself rejoined them behind the metal wall, surreptitiously kneading his bad leg. Violet made a second, more important mental note that she needed to retrieve her bottle of Mr. Johnston's Essence of Mustard from her luggage and rub some of the pungent oil into Sam's old battle wound.

Now there was an eerie silence in the air, save the distant cawing of ravens, as all of the spectators realized that something monumental was about to occur, and a collective breath was held in a mix of gleeful anticipation and utter terror of what the dynamite would do.

Even Violet found herself not breathing, wondering what the combination of noise, smell, and theatrics would produce.

Sam crouched over the blasting machine, placed a hand on either side of the wooden plunger handle, and pulled it up from the top of the detonator. Violet heard a strange whirling sound emitting from the machine. Counting loudly to three, he pushed down hard. The whirling continued, and Violet knew from Sam's description of the machine that it was sending a discharge down the wires to the dynamite securely lodged in its strategically placed locations.

It took only moments for Violet to witness the greatest spectacle of her life. The deep, reverberating boom was accompanied by dirt shooting up in the air in great, jagged streaks, like lightning in reverse. The streaks held motionless in the air for the briefest of seconds before plunging back down to the ground in the cloud of earth that was also billowing below it.

The amazing vision turned instantly into horror as Violet realized there was more than just dirt falling back down to the ground.

There was also a body.

12

With no regard for the shouts of Sam, Reed, and LeCato, Violet sprinted as quickly as her skirts would allow her to the explosion site. She tripped over a fallen branch, but managed to regain her balance before falling and embarrassing herself in front of an audience of hundreds, who would soon be following her as soon as they realized what she'd seen.

As she neared the central point of the excavation, dust quickly settled into her eyes and her nose, stinging them and making her cough violently. She wiped her sleeved arm indelicately across her face, wiping away as much as she could, as she continued to bumble her way to the site.

She'd only had a moment to see the body, but was certain it was a man. Where was he? She thought he had gone down—was it here? No. Over to this side? No. She looked around wildly. *Please, God, do not reveal that on his descent the man . . . came apart.* Wait, wasn't that a scrap of billowing shirt? Yes, there he was. She scrambled a few feet farther, to one edge of the dynamited area, falling down on her knees next to him.

As she frantically brushed dirt away from the body's face and hair, she didn't know whether to laugh in relief or cry in frustration and heartbreak.

The black-and-white-striped shirt . . . the volcano tattoo . . . Violet had just found the missing man from yesterday.

She didn't even have an instant to consider how he had gone

from the woods to the explosion site, for the men who had been behind the metal wall were upon her, and she could hear the gossiping and exclamations of concern from the estate workers behind them.

"Violet, what in tarnation do you think you're doing—ah!" Sam pulled up short next to her. Before he could say anything further, Ellery Reed barged between them to see what they were hovered over.

"Good Lord!" he exclaimed, putting a fist to his face. "Edward Bayes. It really *is* him. What in heaven's name is happening here, Mrs. Harper? Honestly, there has been nothing but carnage and ruin since you arrived—what?—a mere four days ago." His voice was rising on the edge of agitation.

Sam, meanwhile, was as pale as Edward Bayes. Which explained why he didn't ferociously rise to Violet's defense as he ordinarily would do.

"Mr. Reed, I may be an undertaker, but I hardly think my presence has been the cause of these deaths. You've simply been fortunate that I was present to assist. In fact—"

Violet was interrupted by Jack LeCato, who inserted himself into the situation. "Ellery, I realize you are upset, but you must realize that your judgment is clouded. The problem is not Mrs. Harper's presence at Welbeck; it is Mr. Harper's dynamite, which has killed someone, after we were assured that it is a perfectly safe method for excavation."

Now it was Violet's turn to blanch. No wonder Sam was in shock. He didn't realize . . .

She rose once again, sure that she was quite a sight with bits of clay and rock dusting her hair, face, and dress, but spoke as forcefully as her appearance would allow. "You are mistaken, sir. This man, Mr. Bayes, died prior to this. You are falsely accusing my husband of an unsafe procedure and you owe him an apol—"

LeCato clucked his tongue, which irritated Violet in its arrogance. "It is appalling that this experimental explosive is responsible for the death—no, murder—of one of the duke's employees. Weren't we to understand that dynamite was supposed to be *safe?* It is obviously as perilous a substance as any black powder ever used. I shall recommend to His Grace that all work on the skating rink cease immediately."

"Experimental!" Violet was on the verge of exploding herself. "I'll have you know that my husband—"

"Violet, enough." Sam had found his voice once more, and it was deathly low. "Mr. LeCato is right. I have staked my entire reputation with Mr. Reed—and, ultimately, the duke—on the notion that dynamite is not just quick and effective, but perfectly safe. This is disastrous."

She tried again. "Sam, you must listen to me. This has nothing to do with your blasting. Edward Bayes died yesterday. Or perhaps several days ago, I'm not sure. I found him yesterday buried under a pile of leaves, but he disappeared from the wooded area after I went to fetch help—then he turned up here. I don't know how his body got here."

Violet's mind raced. Who had moved Bayes here? And *why* was he moved?

Her questions were compounding with each passing minute.

Sam, though, was studying her in curiosity, but whether it was because she had offered him a life preserver, or because she had gotten tangled up with another corpse, she didn't know.

The estate workers who had gathered to view the blasting stayed back at a respectful distance, but Violet heard them muttering about trouble coming in threes and the third thing coming was sure to be the worst of them all. Some grumbled that the minute they'd heard the plan to dynamite out a tunnel, they knew no good would come from it.

Yet they had all come in a crowd to watch.

One complaint she overheard disturbed her above all the others.

"It comes back to the raven, don't it? Its death spells doom for all of us 'ere at Welbeck."

Violet wished she could shout from the rooftops that Aristotle's death had been an accident, that the bird had simply ingested a shard from a glass eye, and that it wasn't possible for a mere raven to determine the fate of thousands of people.

Instead, she sighed. Who knew? Perhaps at this point Welbeck's superstitious workers had a better grasp of things than she did.

* * *

William John Cavendish-Scott-Bentinck, 5th Duke of Portland, captain in the Grenadier Guards, and renowned horseman, waited patiently as Pearson helped him into his overcoat. He owned six of them, all the same shade of trampled mud, all made by Mr. Henry Poole in London, whose family had founded Savile Row at the turn of the century.

Portland had Mr. Poole make one each year when the duke went to stay at his London residence, Harcourt House. Mr. Poole had received the royal warrant from Her Majesty this year and, in his newfound vanity, had attempted futilely to convince Portland to adopt the smoking jacket fashion the Poole house had created for the Prince of Wales.

Portland was loyal to his queen, but Poole's suggestion that he begin wearing gaudy Japanese silk to prove he was worthy of lounging about in a London club like Victoria's son was taking things a bit too far. Poole complained that Portland's penchant for his unfashionably long and drab coats proved he was at least twenty years out of date in fashion.

Better that than to be a dandy, he silently retorted, suppressing the thought that there had been a time long ago when he would have enjoyed the admiring glances of ladies. Before Adelaide Kemble happened, of course. Portland swept the thought of her away, too, just as Pearson was now quickly running a brush down the sleeves of his jacket.

"There you are, sir, ready to watch that new Arabian gelding being broken. He must be nearly seventeen hands high," Pearson said, stepping away and offering Portland a tentatively encouraging look. His valet was one of the few people—including George— whom Portland could tolerate having around him for more than a few moments at a time. Other people simply made him uncomfortable.

Oh, and that Mrs. Harper, she was strangely comforting, although what Mr. Poole would have to say about her own fashion, one could only wonder. She was almost as careless in her dress as he was. Well, perhaps not careless, she just didn't seem to value any socictal opinion on her appearance. Perhaps that was why he didn't mind having her around. She was a kindred spirit.

"Thank you, Pearson," Portland replied. "Yes, I do believe that horse will prove to be a good—" His words were interrupted by a deafening boom and the rattling of the window panes. Even the covers of the room's gas lamps vibrated and threatened to break.

"What the—?" He hardly had those words out when, as if in delayed reaction, a few small chunks of plaster fell from the ceiling to the carpet beneath their feet. One piece struck him in the shoulder, sending white chips and dust down the arm of his jacket, which had just been brushed so carefully.

"Your Grace, I believe the skating rink area has just been dynamited," Pearson said, retrieving his brush and going back to work on the jacket as though nothing startling had just happened. It was the mark of an excellent servant, and Portland appreciated him all the more. What he did *not* appreciate, however, was hearing the term "dynamite."

"What did you just say? What do you mean that the skating rink is being dynamited?"

Portland regretted his sharpness, for now Pearson looked nervous, although he didn't cease grooming his master for even an eyeblink. "Well, sir, Mr. Reed hired Mr. Harper to come in and demonstrate the use of dynamite for excavating the skating rink, instead of how they've been doing it, with pick and shovel."

That was quite a liberty Reed had taken. "You knew of this plan?"

"Yes, sir." Pearson's eyes were downcast. "Word moved around quickly that there was to be an explosive used on the estate."

"And yet no one thought to consult me and obtain my permission?" Again, Portland regretted the sting of his words to his valet, who was not responsible for what had just happened. Reed, though, would be smarting soon from his unconscionable actions. If only Portland were of a mind to fire workers who angered him, but he liked the reputation he enjoyed among the Worksop townspeople, that a position at Welbeck meant security for life.

However, that didn't mean Portland wouldn't tongue-lash Reed severely. The estate manager enjoyed great autonomy in running many aspects of Welbeck and Harcourt House, but inviting a man in to—

"Wait. Did you say it was a Mr. Harper who brought in the dynamite?"

"Yes, Your Grace. He's the undertaker's husband." Pearson stepped away to assess his master's clothing once more. Satisfied that all was neat and tidy, he put the brush away in a grooming kit.

Portland, though, was incredulous. "The undertaker is married to a dynamiter?"

"No, sir. I mean, yes, she is married to him, but I believe he is the newest colliery owner in Nottingham. That is what I've heard downstairs, anyway."

This is outrageous, the duke fumed. The undertaker had brought in her explosives-handling husband, and together they had convinced Reed to employ it *at Welbeck Abbey?* Was Reed mad to have entertained the idea? Everyone knew that dynamite was very dangerous. The queen herself was repulsed by it and had announced it publicly.

The household staff must be upset. Kirby must be informed of the dynamite—although he probably already knew of it—and sent to calm them all, especially the women. Portland himself had more important things to do.

"Pearson, my hat. I must see for myself what has happened. Someone will be out on his—or her—ear today."

Violet saw the look of grim determination on Portland's face, and wondered how word of another body being found had traveled so quickly up to the man's quarters. She was prepared to tell him that this was the same body she had mentioned last evening, but Reed not only bested her by speaking first, he changed the subject entirely away from Bayes's body.

"Your Grace, I must apologize if you have been disturbed. I had no idea the sound could be heard so far away."

Apparently, Portland had not yet seen the corpse that lay behind Reed and Violet, and also must not have heard about it, for he launched into a castigation of Sam over the employ of dynamite at Welbeck Abbey. It was a long and rambling speech, full of accusations and recriminations for the utter destruction of this part of the estate and the near demolition of the house itself, as well as his overcoat.

Violet's husband stood stoically, taking the verbal punishment over his audacity in bringing his faith in dynamite to Welbeck like St. Stephen enduring a stoning for his religious faith.

A brief flash of Sam's eyes, though, told Violet that he wouldn't endure Portland's rhetorical beating to the death. She hoped the duke would be done soon, lest her husband put on an equally vigorous defense of his faith in dynamite, and then the true explosions would begin. Sam shared Violet's unfortunate habit of speaking his mind, even when it was inconvenient and improper.

However, this was the most animated Violet had ever seen the duke, and she realized from his words that his greatest concern was for the safety of his workers, an admirable trait in a person of power, considering how many people were mangled and mauled in coal mines alone each year. And once the duke realized a body was involved in this incident, she couldn't imagine his response.

Which made Violet shudder once more as she considered Sam's new venture.

The duke wasn't finished, though, and once he was done with her and her husband, he turned the tirade to Ellery Reed, who wasn't nearly as impassive as Sam, and immediately leapt to his own defense.

"Your Grace, I again offer a thousand apologies. I didn't speak to you ahead of time because I did not wish to trouble you with an affair I assumed would not be as . . . astonishing . . . as it proved to be. You must believe that my only goal was to bring efficiency to the digging out of the skating rink."

Violet felt sympathy for Reed, whose position was in grave jeopardy, and hung on which breeze Portland might follow in the next few moments. However, how daft was Reed to have authorized this without having ever talked to the master of the estate?

Fortune followed Reed, however, as Portland visibly calmed down. "Right. Well. Mind your post and your responsibilities from this point forward."

Reed accepted his acquittal with a deferentially bowed head.

By this point, Violet was becoming agitated. Portland had given over his spleen regarding the explosives, but no one seemed willing to address what lay behind her. Why hadn't the dead body received attention first? Now it was Violet's turn to enter the fray. "Your Grace, as unsettling as the dynamiting was, it pales in comparison to the discovery of Edward Bayes's body."

Portland furrowed his brow. "Bayes, you say? Is this one of my workers, Reed? Found where?"

Violet, Sam, Reed, and LeCato all moved aside so that Bayes's body was visible. In his shock, all of the color drained from Portland's face and he instinctively took a step back from the now-battered Mr. Bayes. "M-Mrs. Harper, is this—is this—the body you referred to yesterday evening?"

"Yes, Your Grace. He had certain identifying marks on his body that proved to me he is one and the same. Mr. Reed identified him as one of the workers here."

Portland's gruff manner had completely disappeared, and he was once more the shy and eccentric peer she had first encountered on the estate. "How—how did this happen?" He took a handkerchief from his pocket and mopped his forehead, tilting his hat precariously backward.

Reed opened his mouth to speak, but Violet jumped in once more. "We aren't sure, Your Grace. I believe when I discovered him yesterday that he was already dead, but if Mr. Bayes was in his cups, as you suggested, perhaps he woke up, walked away, and once more passed out, this time in the vicinity of the blasting site. But the condition of his body was such that—no, I am quite certain he was dead."

There was another point to be made, too. "Besides, Sam and his men would have easily come upon him while clearing the blasting site, wouldn't they?"

"Obviously not," Reed commented drily, but Violet was not deterred.

"Furthermore," she continued, "if the man were alive a few minutes ago, how could he possibly have been so deeply asleep that he wouldn't have heard the clearing horn?"

Reed laughed without mirth. "You clearly have little experience with estate workers, Mrs. Harper, who are capable of consuming gallons of spirits in their free time. It doesn't strike me as odd whatsoever that Mr. Bayes could have drunk himself into an insensible stupor. Wouldn't you agree, my lord?"

Portland nodded slowly. "Yes, I can see how this would be so. Nevertheless, it is a terrible thing, terrible. How his family will long for him, no matter how reprehensible his behavior might have been. Heavy drink kills a man quickly or kills a man slowly, but it always kills the man."

They were all silent, waiting for what the duke would say next. Violet wasn't about to offer her opinion that drink had had nothing to do with Bayes's death.

Finally, Portland sighed in resignation. "Mrs. Harper, you will of course take care of things . . . ?"

"Yes, Your Grace. I will visit whatever family he has right away." Violet was certain that behind his words was an unspoken request for her to look into Bayes's death.

"I will spare no expense on a third-class funeral for him," Portland added, which was a contradiction, given that a third-class funeral was always a very simple affair for those who could not afford better and were not entitled to the trappings of a first- or second-class service.

"He has a wife, Margaret," Reed said to her. "She lives in town in a cottage just down from the telegram office and not two blocks from the priory. You cannot miss it, for the front door is painted orange. Sir," he said, turning his attention back to Portland, "I presume you will . . ."

"Yes, yes." Portland nodded much more vigorously, and Violet was certain his top-heavy hat would come crashing to the ground. "Mrs. Bayes and her children can be settled into whatever empty cottage is available on the estate. And now, I must return to my rooms. This has all been . . . exhausting . . . to say the least."

Portland turned away and took just a few halting steps before stopping, tilting his head, and returning. "In all of this distress, I believe I failed to ask: What was the outcome of the dynamite experiment? I see dirt and rock everywhere, but was it effective?"

LeCato spoke for the first time since insulting Violet prior to the duke's arrival. "Your Grace, if I may say so, the experiment was an utter failure. Your entire staff was disrupted for the morning"— he waved a hand to indicate the workers who had started dispersing the minute Portland had shown up—"and the grounds have been irreparably harmed. It seems to me the entire project has been halted as a result of its use, and should perhaps remain halted until we can be sure there have been no other workers harmed. Or killed." LeCato's voice suggested a man who was practical in the extreme, although Violet would not forget his earlier insult.

An expression passed over Portland's face that Violet couldn't read. "How interesting of you to say so," he replied coolly. "Mr. Harper, perhaps you can show me what you did. You, as well, Mr. Reed."

Violet knew that the rest of them were dismissed, which was perfectly fine with her, for she needed to complete the sorrowful task of talking to Mrs. Bayes. First, though, she wanted to inspect the holes under the birches again.

She sought out Mr. Kirby and asked if she might have the use of a wagon and driver for her solemn task of carrying Bayes's body to town. Learning that the equipage would be brought around in about fifteen minutes, Violet returned to the scene where she first had found Mr. Bayes.

She needed no more than a few moments to realize that there was no dynamite planted anywhere. Why, then, were the holes there? Another thought struck her. Were they markers? If so, what did they mark? Violet stood back in an attempt to see some sort of pattern in the holes, a nearly impossible task with all of the leaves on the ground. Weren't holes dug to mark foundation areas for homes? Perhaps the duke planned to build some cottages here.

Yes, perhaps it was that innocent, and Violet was worked up because she had found them near the colonel's glass eye and poor Mr. Bayes's body. It was time to put that concern to rest, and concentrate on the rest of her day, which would no doubt include a grief-stricken widow and dazed, confused children.

Mrs. Bayes, however, was anything but grief-stricken.

13

Mrs. Bayes was shocking, both in her appearance and in her speech. Dressed in glaring bright colors—making her a near perfect match for her orange front door—the new widow's first response upon seeing her husband lying in the wagon was to shake her fist at him and screech a string of obscenities at him.

"You bleeding oaf, you 'ad the wits of a stupid goat and you smelled like one, too" was the most polite phrase Margaret Bayes used. The tirade went on for several minutes in the now-familiar Nottinghamshire dialect, with the scarlet-faced woman not even stopping to take a breath.

Violet directed the driver to help her move Mr. Bayes into the house before the neighbors spilled into the street to see what all of the commotion was. The undertaker was already seriously questioning whether the corpse would be safe in the Bayeses' dining room, a small, crowded affair with nine chairs set around a table meant for six.

The danger being Mrs. Bayes, not the venue.

After Mr. Bayes was situated in the dining room and the driver had gone back to the carriage to wait, the woman continued railing inside her tiny, dark parlor, which contained little more than a threadbare settee and two mismatched chairs under its low, dank ceiling. Several children, all about a year or two apart in age, stood in a doorway leading from the parlor to a corridor beyond, but scattered at the sight of their mother calling down Satan and his minions upon their father.

"Mrs. Bayes, please, let us talk," Violet said, in the soothing tone she adopted when faced with the wildly grieving. This woman was a bit more turbulent than most, raging and howling like a storm that rushes in from the coast and batters everything around it.

"I am terribly sorry for the loss of your husband and what it means for your family." Violet kept her voice low and remained still. Soon, Mrs. Bayes also quieted down, having expended her rage and fury, at least for the moment. However, the woman still shed no tears of sorrow. Violet knew that some people would not grieve in public, even if "public" meant before one other person inside the privacy of home.

"I want to assure you," Violet continued, "that His Grace is devastated by your husband's death, and will pay the entire cost of the funeral."

Mrs. Bayes nodded stonily. The tempest seemed to have blown itself out and was headed back out to sea.

"Do you want to know . . . what happened?" Violet asked.

The woman shrugged carelessly. "I can guess. 'E was sotted up and fell in front of a 'orse van, or got 'imself into a fight with a brute ten times bigger than 'e was. I always told 'im 'e'd come to no good end."

Violet was in a quandary. Was it better for the woman to believe that her husband had died in a manner that upheld her obvious belief in his waywardness? Would there be an odd comfort in that for Mrs. Bayes? It wouldn't be a lie to tell her that her husband had been found at the dynamiting site, where it was already believed he had stumbled in drunk. Or should Violet speak truthfully and tell the woman that she had discovered Mr. Bayes with a bloodied head last night and that his body had promptly disappeared, only to resurface at the dynamiting site? What would such a revelation do to this woman's precarious state?

Before she could decide what to do, Mrs. Bayes spoke again. "'E was gone for a few days, so I didn't think anything of it. Edward was forever wandering off to 'is own purposes and coming back when it suited 'im. I'm not a bad wife, just so you know. I cook for the children, I clean, I go to market. But 'im, no, Edward wasn't reliable at all. It would be just like 'im to get 'imself killed and leave me with everything to do."

The condition of her home suggested that Margaret Bayes probably put more thought into these activities than actual effort, but Violet wasn't exactly the best mistress of the house the world had ever known. Besides, she didn't herself have a passel of children to care for on top of it all, so what did she know?

As if on cue, a wailing erupted from another room. With a resigned sigh, Mrs. Bayes rose from her chair and disappeared for several minutes, and eventually the crying stopped.

When she returned, Mrs. Bayes seemed to have forgotten the manner of her husband's death and was focused on practical things. "I've 'eard 'Is Grace 'as a widows' and orphans' fund, to pay the family of dead workers a stipend each month. Even if Edward died of 'is own foolishness, will 'Is Grace still make good on the money? I could sure use a few quid each month."

Violet was surprised by the hint of craftiness in Mrs. Bayes's voice, although given the woman's circumstances, maybe it shouldn't be that much of a shock.

"His Grace assured me personally that you and your children are welcome to a cottage on the estate, to occupy for the rest of your life."

Mrs. Bayes smiled, while gently shaking her head in disbelief. "Well, ol' Edward, 'e's finally doing in death what 'e's supposed to 'ave been doing in life."

Perhaps with that bit of good news for the widow, it was time to discuss Edward Bayes's funeral. Violet pulled her funeral service book from her large leather undertaking bag. She had had the driver stop by the inn so she could retrieve the bag on their way to visit the widow, and was now very glad she had brought it with her to Nottinghamshire, along with her professional black clothing.

Violet hovered in the book between the Working Class and Tradesman sections, and finally decided that Portland's instructions meant that the funeral should be working class, as befitting the man's station, but well done. She laid the book open in her lap to that section. Each section of the book, which started at Poor and ran up as far as Society and Titled, contained drawings of coffins, mourning fashions, flowers, and memorial stones appropriate for that class of funeral. Violet always felt a twinge of guilt at having to indirectly remind the grieving of their station in life, even in the face of the great equalizer of death.

"You will have a simple black hearse, containing a small viewing window, with one horse wearing a single black ostrich feather." Violet pointed to an engraving of the hearse.

"That's better 'n just a cart, isn't it?" Mrs. Bayes asked.

"Yes, madam, much better. You can also be provided with your own mourning coach for transporting you to the church." Violet expected Mrs. Bayes to demur, given that she was so close to the church and because she presumably had quite a number of children to manage who would not all fit inside the coach.

Instead, the widow seemed struck. "Lawd, me in a coach. I never 'ad such good fortune when Edward was alive."

Well, if Mrs. Bayes wanted to enjoy the coach, they might as well do the traditional funeral ride through the small town instead of taking the coffin directly from the house to the church. Such a display was typically reserved for only the wealthy or well known, but surely Violet could justify to Portland that Edward Bayes had become instantly famous in a town like Worksop. "Your husband and the entire funeral party will travel from your house through as many streets of Worksop as possible, to give your neighbors an opportunity to offer their blessings."

"Yes, that would be fine, most fine." Violet suspected the widow would struggle to refrain from grinning the entire time.

"The coffin will be elm, painted black, with a black velvet pall over it. I will place a spray of flowers over the coffin. You will have a coachman and an attendant wearing black gloves, hat bands, and arm bands. You will need six pallbearers, whom I will also outfit similarly, to carry the coffin from the house to the hearse and from the hearse to the grave. They should be chosen from immediate friends of Mr. Bayes's, and should be near to him in age. Do you know six men who can serve?"

Mrs. Bayes nodded. "I just need to send one of my boys down

to the Lamb and Chalice to ask, and no doubt six of the lushing-
tons will put down their tankards long enough to do it."

Violet dreaded the carnival performance the funeral would
surely be. "Would you like the service held here at home or at the
church?"

Mrs. Bayes looked around her tiny parlor and then back at Violet incredulously. "I can't 'ardly fit my young ones in here, much
less the gaggle that will come to stare at Edward."

Violet agreed completely and made a note to see Reverend Appleton again, hoping she could do so without engaging in more
theological conundrums.

"Speaking of the clothing to be worn by funeral attendants, I
must ask, do you have clothing that will suffice as widow's weeds,
or will you need a dressmaker's visit?" Violet doubted this woman
owned somber garments and was certain the duke would happily
pay for a few dresses to carry her through two years of mourning.

But Violet was once more taken aback when Mrs. Bayes said,
"There's no worries there. I 'ave just the right thing to wear," and
refused to discuss additional accoutrements, such as jet earrings or
necklaces, mourning brooches, bonnets, tortoiseshell-handled fans,
or any other items that would identify her as a new widow.

Violet gently suggested that she accept a gift of a black-edged
handkerchief from the duke, for which, once more, Violet was certain he would happily pay. Sensing that the woman needed more
social guidance than most, she also dispensed advice that she
would not normally presume to do with any grieving widow.

"It is, of course, essential that you do not receive or pay visits for
at least six months," Violet said, hating her words, for she remembered how much she had detested that much mourning over her
unlamented first husband. "Also, you must not attend the theater
or other public places of amusement, unless it is a sedate musical
performance."

Fortunately, Mrs. Bayes took no offense and shrugged her way
through that and the rest of Violet's suggestions, only finally becoming animated at the idea of an outdoor repast with her friends
and neighbors following Mr. Bayes's interment at Worksop Priory.

Violet's next question, though, sent the widow back to indifferent shrugging.

"Is there anything the vicar should know about your husband as he prepares the service?" Violet asked.

"Besides 'is love of Star Brewery porter? What else is there to know?"

Violet had to tread carefully here, for she didn't want to send Mrs. Bayes back to howling. "Is there anything about Mr. Bayes's life—where he was born if not in Worksop, how he came to be employed at Welbeck Abbey—that the vicar could mention to those in attendance at the funeral? I noticed that your husband has a very peculiar tattoo on his right shoulder, and thought you might know—"

"Oh, that? It's One Tree 'Ill."

It sounded like an address. "What do you mean?"

"It's one of them dead volcanoes—the kind that once blew fire—all the way over in New Zealand. It 'ad a single tree in the center of it until some dobbie cut it down in the '50s."

Violet was still confused. "And your husband saw a drawing of it in a picture book?"

"Of course not. 'E was there. Edward joined 'Er Majesty's navy to have an adventure, but grew sore tired of it while fighting in the Maori Wars, since all 'e did was sit inside a ship for gobs of time during a blockade at the mouth of the Waikato River."

This was interesting, although Violet wasn't sure it was relevant to anything. "Was your husband born in Worksop, then?"

Mrs. Bayes shook her head. "No. 'E was from Liverpool. After 'is stint in the navy, 'e wandered about from county to county and job to job, finding me along the way. I traveled with 'im, and we brought our young ones into the world. 'E always thought the next town would be the place where 'e would find 'is fortune. By the time we reached our fourth one, I told 'im it was time for 'im to quit 'is roaming and settle somewhere. 'E learned about Welbeck Abbey and 'ow the duke never turned away work seekers, so we ended up 'ere. Edward thought this might be the place to finally make 'is riches, though I don't know 'ow the fool expected to do that as a purser."

So Edward Bayes distributed the pay for the estate's workers. Did that mean anything? He must have hidden his love for drink to maintain such a responsible position. How could it possibly be relevant to his death? It probably wasn't. And yet . . . someone had moved the man's body, Violet was sure of it. Despite Mrs. Bayes's insistence that he was an incurable drunkard, it didn't seem possible that Violet had mistaken him for a corpse, and that he had stumbled off to the dynamiting site.

"Did your husband have any experience with dynamite?" she asked.

"With what?" Mrs. Bayes looked genuinely confused.

"Your husband was found near one of the duke's tunneling sites, which was being dug for a skating rink for the staff."

"Yes, I 'eard about the skating rink. 'Is Grace is always planning up exercises for 'is workers. Edward didn't think much of it, though. Thought it was an insult to make 'im go rowing and batting cricket balls around."

"So your husband had no part in the building of the skating rink?"

Mrs. Bayes's expression was wary "Not so I would know of it, but I didn't follow the man about every second, Mrs. 'Arper. Wasn't any of my business what 'e did for 'Is Grace and Mr. Reed."

"I see. Do you know of any particular friends or enemies he may have had at Welbeck?"

"Edward?" Mrs. Bayes laughed. "'E could easily be best mates with anyone who could fill his tankard."

Violet persisted. "But was there anyone in particular with whom he was especially close? Or with whom he had had a recent argument?"

The woman shrugged. "'E had his occasional row with the falconer. Said the birds was always stealing coins from 'is money box. Falconer called Edward a nitwitted fool. Can't say as I disagreed with the bird 'andler. Once they even got to fisticuffs over some missing paper scrap of Edward's. The falconer promised to poison Edward in 'is sleep."

Interesting. "Would you be willing to come to Welbeck to report your story to His Grace?"

The widow's eyes widened. "What? Me? No, I could never. It doesn't mean anything, anyway."

"It might be important, Mrs. Bayes. I believe His Grace might wish to know if one of his staff might have had reason to harm your husband."

"What difference would it make? Edward lived a fool and died a fool, and the falconer 'ad nothing to do with it. No, I'll not do it. You just told me I 'ave an income, to be mine from now on. I'll not be running tales or do anything to make me look unappreciative before 'Is Grace."

No matter what Violet said, Mrs. Bayes refused to come with her to Welbeck Abbey.

Resigned that her work with Mrs. Bayes was complete, Violet rose, intending to return to the dining room where Edward Bayes lay. "I might suggest that you have one of your sons visit the Lamb and Chalice right away to find some men to hold vigil over your husband in shifts until the funeral." The practice had largely gone out of style, but Violet was still nervous that Mrs. Bayes might exact revenge on Edward once she was alone with him.

Mrs. Bayes called out for Charlie, and a thin boy of about ten poked his head into the room. Mrs. Bayes curtly told him that his father had died, and that he was to run quickly to the tavern to find men to hold vigil and to serve as pallbearers. Violet's heart broke over the boy's confused expression at his mother's bland pronouncement, but he rushed off to do as he was bid.

"I'll prepare your husband now," Violet said, picking up her undertaking bag, which was full of the supplies she would need.

On this, Mrs. Bayes became intractable once more. "No, no one touches 'im." The woman's lips made a thin, sour line. "'E's my husband and I'll wash 'im."

This was exactly what Violet didn't want, but she had little choice in the matter. The woman was, after all, the widow, and no matter what Portland was expending, the widow had a right to dictate this.

"Very well, then, I'll be on my way."

After leaving the gloomy cottage, Violet sent a telegram to Harry Blundell to have him ship yet another coffin and other supplies right away. Afterward, she once more visited Worksop establishments to gather the remaining materials and perform necessary tasks, including a visit to the local newspaper to insert a death announcement in the following day's edition. Her final stop was at a draper's for yards of black crape and ribbon, which she took immediately back to the Bayeses' house, ignoring the driver's chagrin over so many starts and stops. The ribbon she used on the door knocker, a symbolic indication that the dread visitor—that mercurial beast called death—had entered the house.

More importantly, she used the crape to cover up the hideous orange door.

Back at Welbeck, Violet had one final task to perform to put her mind at rest regarding the holes beneath the birch trees, which was to have someone more experienced in earth matters look at them. She quickly learned that the head gardener was Parris, whom she'd passed in the rear gardens when Miles Hudock had escorted her to meet Portland for the first time. That had only been a few days ago, but it felt as though a lifetime of events had happened since then.

She found Parris inside a garden shed, its exterior built to resemble the estate's other cottages. The interior, however, was a single large room, full of dirt-encrusted tools and baskets full of seeds and bulbs being carried over for the winter. He stood before a tall, rough-hewn table, counting out some kind of tree pods.

"Yes?" he asked, taking in Violet's black gown and tall black hat with tails trailing behind her. Recognition slowly dawned in his eyes. "You're the undertaker who buried Burton Spencer."

Violet introduced herself and explained her mission, asking if he would accompany her to the birch grove to see if he could identify the holes she'd found.

Parris nodded slowly, as if deeply contemplating her request. "Yes, I believe I can do that."

Violet could hardly imagine the man's age, so deeply lined were his neck and the skin around his eyes from time spent in the sun. Yet he moved with the spryness of a younger man, despite his leisurely, deliberate speech. He could have been anywhere from thirty to eighty years old.

They walked out to the copse, with Violet hardly able to keep up with Parris's stride. She supposed that the work of managing so many plantings required a man to be nimble on his feet.

She showed him where the holes were, and he squatted down easily before each of them. He spent a few minutes measuring them with his hand and cocking his head to one side to examine them, like the raven that had kept watch over her when she discovered the holes in the first place.

Parris said nothing as he worked, but finally rose and brushed his hands off on his trousers. Violet expected a pronouncement from him, but still he continued in his silence, staring just past Violet as if in deep thought.

Should she wait? Should she prompt him? Did everyone at Welbeck have to be so odd in mannerism?

Finally, she could take it no more. "Mr. Parris, what do you think of the holes?"

He shifted his gaze to her. "Not very deep."

Which was not exactly a thorough explanation and certainly not anything she hadn't figured out for herself. "Do you think an animal could have made them?"

"No. They were made by human hands."

"Can you determine what sort of implement was used?"

He pursed his lips. "Not a shovel."

That much Violet had figured out for herself. This was going to be a torturously long conversation if she couldn't figure out the correct question to ask.

"Have they been recently made?"

He squatted down again, and brushed at some of the dirt built up around the edges of the hole. It was much darker beneath the surface. "No, they've been here awhile. I also found a couple of holes that you missed, that had been loosely covered up."

It was the most verbose the man had been, and Violet was encouraged. "I thought someone might have attempted to place dynamite here, but that is obviously not the case. Can you see what purpose the holes might serve?"

Parris, though, had already run out of steam from his speaking ordeal. "No."

She tried one more approach. "Do you think they might serve as markers?"

"For what?"

Violet tried not to let her exasperation show. "I don't know. Buried treasure? A secret grave? An underground lake? The foundation of a building?"

Parris rubbed a grizzled chin as he considered what Violet had said. She could almost see the gears of his mind working behind his eyes as he evaluated each of her suggestions. Finally, he shook his head. "No."

Was Violet flogging a dead horse by continuing to worry about some random holes in the ground? For all she knew, they had been made by some of the estate workers' children during some sort of invented game. Not that she had seen children playing out and about, but it was the first time she had considered the idea and it made sense to her.

Given that she now had a second funeral—and possible murder—to worry about, she decided that it was time to put the holes out of her mind.

Besides, Mrs. Bayes was to occupy a great deal of her thoughts soon.

14

To Violet's surprise, Mr. Bayes's fellow tavern sitters were very well behaved, and the funeral service was executed in a much more dignified fashion than she had anticipated.

Except for one aspect: that of Margaret Bayes.

Mrs. Bayes was dressed as a . . . Well, she was wearing a . . . Violet was nearly speechless by the woman's showy and ostentatious bodice and skirt. The top was green and yellow striped, whereas the mismatched skirt was solid purple hemmed in mauve. Violet had purchased a handkerchief from a tiny dress shop tucked unobtrusively behind a bookseller in town. That black, lace-edged handkerchief was Mrs. Bayes's only nod to mourning, and now it dangled showily from the bottom of one sleeve.

Violet could only imagine where—or from whom—Mrs. Bayes had obtained the clothing.

Mrs. Bayes's neighbors seemed just as appalled as Violet, evidenced by the number of cupped hands around whispering mouths that Violet witnessed.

As Mrs. Bayes moved about, looking like a twirling circus tent, it was obvious how much she enjoyed the attention she was receiving, even if most of it was disapproval and horror. On the one hand, Violet had a good sense that Mrs. Bayes probably felt great relief at being rid of her soused husband, especially since she now had a comfortable home on a grand estate for life.

On the other hand, the flouting of mourning custom was highly offensive to Violet, and Mrs. Bayes's clothing suggested that the undertaker hadn't done her job properly with her customer. Thank heavens the duke was not in attendance to see how his money had not purchased any decorum for the widow.

"Mrs. Bayes," Violet said as patiently as possible, pulling the woman aside before she entered her mourning carriage, "you told me that you had appropriate mourning clothing for—"

"Oh," she replied airily, "I decided to skip all of that nonsense. I'll be 'ostess to a feast later, you know." Mrs. Bayes stepped into her carriage and settled contentedly into her seat. "And anyway, what I wear concerns none but myself."

Violet imagined slapping the woman across the face with all of her might, but satisfied herself with merely gritting her teeth. "Madam, brightness and merriment make a mockery of grief. Mourning garments are our outward sign of an inward sorrow, and it is our last token of respect and affection that we can pay to the dead."

Margaret Bayes raised a pointed yet mocking eyebrow. "Exactly," she said, shutting the door on Violet as the carriage rolled away behind the clergyman's carriage and the hearse. The widow said no more to Violet throughout the rest of the service and the subsequent picnic.

Fortunately—in Violet's mind—most of Welbeck's staff had been spooked by two deaths so close together, and many of them chose not to attend the funeral, pleading either that they didn't know Bayes very well or that they couldn't afford two days off so close together. Most of those in attendance were probably frequenters of the Lamb and Chalice and other pint-pouring establishments, plus their appalled wives.

Even Edward's tavern friends wore dark colors as a matter of respect, though. And if their respect extended to gorging themselves at the picnic, then by all counts they thought very highly of the deceased. Great quantities of ham, cider, ale, pies, and cakes were consumed in rapid order.

Sam found Violet at the feast following the funeral, where she stood aghast at the proceedings. Mrs. Bayes's neighbors and friends had imbibed enough liquor to forget the widow's flamboyant weeds.

"How was it?" Sam asked from behind her, cupping Violet's elbow in his hand as she watched the festivities from a distance.

"Well," she said, leaning gratefully backward into him, already exhausted from the day's effort, "Mrs. Bayes managed to not throw herself on top of the coffin in her grief, and thus far no one has fallen and split his head open on his tankard, so I suppose all is well." Sam laughed at the sarcasm dripping lethally from her voice.

"A brutal day, it sounds like," he said, kissing the top of her head. "I have something that might cheer you up. Portland is no longer angry at me over the explosion. He says he realizes that everyone involved had good intentions, even though a good worker was lost in the process. In fact, His Grace became quite fascinated by what dynamite does and asked several probing questions about it."

Mr. Bayes was not "lost in the process," Violet thought stubbornly, but remained quiet about that. Instead, she said, "I'm glad for you, sweetheart."

"He mentioned that dynamite might be of use on other tunneling projects of his, even going so far as to say that he might wish to invest in it, should it prove fruitful for him. He suggested that I go shooting with him next week to discuss it further, but I don't believe he was serious."

Violet wasn't so sure. "The duke isn't a casual man, and is not one for spending time in the company of someone he dislikes. Actually, he can hardly tolerate those that he *does* like. I suspect that if he says he wants to talk more on the matter, that he means it. It could be a remarkable opportunity for you, despite the inauspicious start."

Sam appeared unconvinced, only saying, "As long as I no longer dread the weight of a displeased peer on my shoulders, all is well. I have enough trouble with the bank's displeasure that the coal mine isn't even remotely close to operational . . . or even fully staffed. The idea that he would actually finance me is as likely as a cat having puppies."

Sam had struggled with many banks to secure financing for his coal-mining venture, so it was understandable that he was pessimistic about any future endeavors.

At least Violet's current endeavor, that of seeing Mr. Bayes into the ground, had come to a conclusion. It had been memorable only for how disrespectful the widow had been, but Violet supposed she had seen worse behavior before. In any case, Mrs. Bayes was no longer her problem.

As Violet went to bed that night, she couldn't seem to erase the most vivid memory of the funeral from her mind, that of Mrs. Garside—one of few of the household staff who attended—shaking her head and moaning to whoever would listen, "That raven, 'e cursed us. 'E cursed the Abbey, and 'Is Grace, and all of us. There's more to come, I promise you that."

15

Since Portland hadn't actually asked her to leave Welbeck Abbey yet, Violet decided that she had implicit permission to continue her investigation into the deaths of Burton Spencer and Edward Bayes.

Today she was headed back to Colonel Mortimer's cottage, only this time it was not with accusation in her mind but curiosity. Although the colonel thought he had seen the murder of Spencer, Violet was becoming more convinced that he had seen the murder of Bayes, even though everyone believed that Bayes had been killed in the dynamite explosion. Could he possibly provide Violet with any further description of the murder he had seen that night?

The colonel wore a different glass eye. This one was a close match to his natural eye color, with no prominent red streaks or jaundicing, so Violet presumed that meant that the colonel hadn't overindulged the previous night.

What other human being in the world used an ocular prosthetic to display his mood and well-being?

However, true to his glass eye's indication, Colonel Mortimer was in a jolly mood, inviting Violet in and offering to share his plate of sheep's sausage with her, which she politely declined.

"Very well," he said, sitting back down to his breakfast, the odor of which suggested that it had been smoked overly long. "What has you traipsing about the estate so early this morning, Mrs.

Harper? Have you discovered who killed that poor man, Spencer? So many dashedly awful events the past few days, eh? Portland told me about Edward Bayes being found in your husband's dynamiting trick."

Violet didn't care for Colonel Mortimer's referring to Sam's effort as a "trick," but the colonel paid no mind to her poorly veiled annoyance as he continued. "I imagine the word has spread to all of Worksop and the Dukeries about our misfortune here. I just hope it doesn't cause His Grace to cease work on any of his projects."

Violet expressed her hope for the same thing, meanwhile thinking about what it would mean for Sam if Portland really was serious about exploring more dynamite use.

"In the interest of seeing His Grace's plans continue," Violet said, "I am endeavoring to solve the mystery of who it was you saw attack Burton Spencer."

"Yes, the poor man. However, as I have stated, it was late at night and I didn't recognize the man."

"No, but you may have caught a glimpse of the murderer's clothing, or the outline of his face. Perhaps he had a large nose or a protruding lower lip? Anything that would lead to an identification?"

The colonel pushed his empty plate away and leaned back in his chair, closing his eyes and crossing his fingers over his belly. Seconds ticked by.

But a few moments later, he opened his eyes. "No, I remember nothing about Spencer's attacker, except that he was taller—perhaps just overall larger—than Spencer was."

Violet supposed there was no more help to be had from the colonel. She thanked him for his time, but as she turned to leave, she had another idea.

"Colonel, I know His Grace provides cottages to widows of his workers, such as the unfortunate Mrs. Bayes, and that he also has some . . . permanent guests . . . such as yourself. Can you tell me who else stays on the property in such a capacity?"

Violet's thinking was that another "guest" might have witnessed a strange event on the estate without ever realizing it was odd or criminal. Guests would not be focused on daily work, and might be more aware of their surroundings.

She was probably grasping at straws at this point, but it was worth a question.

The colonel, who had risen to escort Violet out, crossed his fingers over his bulbous midsection and closed his eyes once more. Violet hoped he didn't plan on going to sleep in this position, like a horse in a field. However, the colonel quickly opened his eyes again.

"There are two. Old Mrs. Caldwell was a friend of the duke's mother, who is long dead now. Mrs. Caldwell is infirm, though, and rarely leaves her lodgings for any reason. The other resident may be of interest to you, Mrs. Harper. Jack LeCato has only been here a few months, and seems to make a habit of prowling the estate much like you."

Ah! She'd nearly forgotten him, but now Violet was reminded of LeCato's outrage over the dynamite and his involvement with Spencer's body.

"Do you know why he is here, Colonel, and how long he plans to stay?"

"I can't say as I know. Whatever he is doing, it seems to be very secret. I'm not sure Portland even understands why he is housing and feeding the man. Talk to His Grace about him. Better yet, go to the seat of government in London to ferret out what you can, since I understand you are surprisingly well connected in high circles, given your trade."

How was it possible that Portland was permitting a man to reside on his estate without knowing why? In particular, how had this stranger thought it his right to complain about Sam's dynamite to the duke?

Violet regretted not looking into him earlier. She suspected the man would turn out to be far more interesting than she could imagine.

As it turned out, she was right.

*   *   *

Escorted by Mr. Kirby, Violet stepped across the precarious planks once more to reach the duke's quarters. As usual, he was hidden behind his screen, and Violet wondered if he stayed back there even when he was alone.

As near as she could tell, he welcomed her presence, and she was heartened when he asked after Sam, adding that Sam would be returning for a shooting party. Violet looked forward to telling her husband that Portland had indeed been serious about talking to him more about dynamite.

"Your Grace," she began, seated once more with carved wood separating them. It reminded her of a confessional. "I've been doing my best to look into Mr. Spencer's death, and I believe now that Mr. Bayes died under suspicious circumstances. I have discovered that the porcelain shard lodged in Aristotle's throat was actually a fragment from one of Colonel Mortimer's glass eyes. He recalled that he lost it when he witnessed the murder. It broke, and Aristotle picked up a shiny piece of it."

"Poor little beast," Portland said. "He was such an intelligent creature that it sounds unlike him to have been taken in by a shiny scrap of glass. As for Mr. Bayes, are you determined to find mayhem everywhere?"

"No, Your Grace. I'm simply trying to discover the truth. And I believe the truth is that neither Mr. Spencer nor Mr. Bayes died accidentally."

"I begin to think you persecute me."

"On the contrary, sir, I wish to bring justice to the victims and, consequently, honor to your name."

Portland emitted something between a growl and a harrumph, but didn't reply.

Violet cleared her throat noisily. Together, she and the duke sounded like wounded pigs. "I visited the colonel earlier, and he mentioned that Mr. LeCato has been a guest of yours for some time, and that he seems to spend a great deal of time walking about the estate. If I am not being too forward, may I ask what his position here is?" Violet knew she was being entirely too forward, but she asked the question anyway.

"Gladstone sent him" was Portland's curt reply.

What did that mean? William Gladstone was prime minister. Violet had even had the opportunity to meet him during an investigative matter for the queen but didn't know much about the man except that he was wildly popular with the people, and vastly unpopular with Queen Victoria. He was known affectionately as the "G.O.M.," or "Grand Old Man," by his supporters; Benjamin Disraeli, a favorite of the queen's who had vacated the prime minister's seat a year ago to make way for Gladstone, called him "God's Only Mistake." Perhaps it was time to change the subject.

"I see that you have many tunnels crossing your estate. Why, I hear that one can take a tunnel nearly half the distance to the train station in Worksop."

At that observation from Violet, Portland opened up. "Yes, my tunnels have proved useful for many reasons. I can get to many locations on my property without encountering a soul, although I had to walk overland to reach the skating rink site, as you are well aware."

"It is more comfortable to walk underground." Violet hoped she had said it as a statement, and not as an inquiring question.

"It keeps me out of the sun. And the dark. And the rain and wind. I walk outside only occasionally. Besides, I can use my tunnel system to emerge unnoticed anywhere on the estate, and thus track what my men are doing. They never know when I might turn a corner."

"Doesn't Mr. Reed manage your men well enough?" Violet asked, immediately regretting what could be perceived as insulting to either Reed's capabilities or Portland's trust in the man.

Fortunately, Portland didn't seem to notice. "Yes, he is most competent, but I like to have my own eye on things."

Which made Violet pause. Who else at Welbeck Abbey could be using the tunnels to keep his eye on things . . . or for his own nefarious purposes? LeCato? Reed? One of Portland's other workers? Perhaps even a household staff member? Even the colonel hadn't quite cleared himself in her mind, although his guilt didn't seem quite as likely now.

"Well, Mr. LeCato seems to have some very definite opinions about what goes on here, sir."

"No surprise, is it? Meddling busybody." Another harrumph from behind the screen indicated Portland's displeasure at even discussing the man. "He's damnably expensive, and expects things to be . . . just so." Portland was still being cryptic. Was he protecting LeCato, whom he obviously despised? If so, why? Unfortunately, Violet's gentle probing was not enough to make Portland give her any detail, and it would be thoroughly improper of her to ask outright. She tried again.

"In fact, it was he who suggested that Mr. Bayes had been murdered by my husband, using what he called an 'experimental explosive.'"

"I see."

"Additionally, he also said he would recommend to you that all work on the skating rink be halted right away. I assumed Mr. LeCato holds a special position here to make such suggestions to Your Grace."

Portland's only response was to make some sort of nervous tapping noise from behind the screen. It sounded like thick nails drumming on a table. Violet plowed on.

"However, I also know Your Grace to be exceedingly particular about his confidants, which made me wonder if Mr. LeCato was not overstepping his bounds."

The tapping stopped. "'Overstepping' puts it well, Mrs. Harper. I've no choice in the matter, though. Gladstone sent him here."

Again Portland was deferential to the prime minister. Yes, Gladstone might be powerful, but he certainly did not have authority to lodge his own agents at Welbeck for his own secret purposes. Yet Portland seemed powerless to stop Gladstone. It seemed ludicrous that Mr. LeCato could have anything to do with Spencer's or Bayes's death, but wouldn't it be even more ludicrous not to track down every lead, no matter how foolish it might seem?

"As such, sir, I thought I might be of some use to you, in that I flatter myself as having a few connections in London, and may be able to secure an audience with Mr. Gladstone, to discover Mr.

LeCato's purposes." Now it was Violet stepping way beyond her bounds, but searching for the truth sometimes meant ignoring social proprieties.

Portland chuckled behind the screen, his voice low and deep. Violet had never actually witnessed the man being amused. "I was once the member for King's Lynn, Mrs. Harper, until I gave the seat over to my brother George. I have been well acquainted with every prime minister since my grandfather, the 3rd Duke, served as prime minister at the beginning of the century. However . . ."

He went silent for several moments, as if deep in thought. "However, yes, I think having you visit Gladstone would be of great use, great use indeed, despite the fact that I find him to be a scoundrel of the first order. He never responded to any of my letters vigorously recommending against the disestablishment of the Anglican church in Ireland. Imagine allowing the Catholics to run amok over there."

Reverend Appleton had been right when he told Violet that Portland was a staunch defender of the church. But this was of no concern to her now.

Portland stood behind the screen, and Violet automatically rose in response. He seemed suddenly resolved to a course of action. "In fact, you shall leave straightaway. You may have use of a carriage, and I'll instruct Kirby to have you sent through my personal tunnel to Worksop station."

Violet was stunned, and completely unprepared to make a journey to London this very moment. She needed to pack and she needed to see Sam; for that matter, she had to figure out where to go and whom to interview in the event that she would be unable to see Gladstone. "Your Grace, I—I—I'm not quite ready. I'll have to telegram ahead to my day help—"

"Nonsense. You will stay at Harcourt House in Marylebone. My sister lives there, but Kirby will have a telegram sent to her, announcing your visit. She will be most welcoming, I assure you. She is much more amenable to hosting others than I am, you see. Stay as long as necessary, Mrs. Harper, to divine the true actions of LeCato. Your husband will stay entertained here at Russian Lodge, my shooting hut across the lake."

The duke's shooting hut must have been located well behind the lake, for Violet had never noticed it. She imagined that "hut" was a misnomer, and that it was probably larger than the mews at Buckingham Palace.

"I should invite my brother Henry for the shooting. He's quite a hound man, and he looks for any opportunity to bring along his pack of vizslas to hunt grouse and pheasant. We'll have quite a diversion here while you look into the doings of LeCato. I am certain he is a scoundrel of an extreme degree."

Violet was surprised at Portland's stated enthusiasm for the company of others, given his normal reclusiveness, but perhaps the idea of a day shooting caused him to overcome his shyness. Presumably he wouldn't shoot from behind a wooden screen shielding him from both his brother and from Sam.

However, if Violet wasn't mistaken, Portland seemed downright gleeful about sending her to London.

Violet met up with Sam that evening at Worksop Inn for supper. She didn't know what she enjoyed more—telling her husband that he was truly to go shooting with Portland or savoring the fish pie, which tonight Mr. Saunders had stuffed with fresh mussels. It was an expensive delicacy that Violet appreciated with every swallow.

"He actually means to do this?" Sam asked, his forkful of stewed venison poised halfway to his mouth, as though he couldn't decide whether to have it finish its journey or put it down to more aptly express his surprise.

"Yes. He has a shooting hut on the northern part of the estate somewhere above the lake and will meet you there. He plans to invite his brother Henry along."

Sam put his fork down. "I'm to go shooting with the duke *and* his brother? I'm not sure what to think. I wonder if this is a heaven-sent answer to what has been concerning me of late."

"What is that?" she mumbled over an eager bite of her dinner, wondering if Mr. Saunders might come by and offer her another sliver of pie.

"You know that I have been struggling to find good men to work at the coal mine. My only good fortune thus far has been the Ward brothers. I've been despairing of ever getting it running, and then when everything went wrong at Welbeck . . . well, I began to think that perhaps I was downright cursed. Or that others would view me that way. And if that happened, I would never get the mine open. In fact . . ." Sam paused and stared in the distance at a couple of patrons telling ribald jokes over tankards of ale.

"I think I made a mistake in trying to open a coal mine," he said, grimacing as though the words were like sour milk in his mouth. "Perhaps I should have just stayed with trying to convince others to buy dynamite rather than showing it off within my own colliery. This has been brutally difficult, from securing the financing to actually getting to the point of striking an ax against the coal face."

Violet hardly knew what to say. She desperately wanted to say something encouraging to her husband, yet his statement that he might not want to continue with the colliery was like church bells pealing joyfully in her head. How happy she would be if he no longer pursued this business interest.

However, she maintained a steady tone. "So you think that if His Grace is serious about going shooting with you, then he is also serious about investing in dynamite?"

"Possibly. I'm certainly not counting on it at this point. But his endorsement would certainly help me gain credibility."

Mr. Saunders came around with his trolley, presenting Violet with the last remaining piece of fish pie. She accepted it and sliced into the steaming portion with her fork as he refilled her glass of claret.

"Did you like the blue mussels, Mrs. Harper?" the innkeeper asked. "I added them in just for you. Got them from a Lancashire fishmonger."

"They're perfect, Mr. Saunders. It's the best fish pie I've ever had."

Saunders beamed and offered Sam more venison, but her husband was too preoccupied now for more food. Violet, too, became distracted when the front door of the small inn opened and Martin Chandler entered, nodded to Mr. Saunders, and retreated quickly to the rear of the inn where the staff worked.

"Isn't that the duke's falconer?" she inquired. "Is he a guest here tonight?" She found it curious that he would so brazenly come in and make his way to the private part of the inn.

"No, no. He sometimes helps me when he has time," Saunders said cryptically. Violet wondered what skills the falconer possessed that would be of use to an innkeeper. However, it was none of her business.

As Mr. Saunders moved on with his trolley to another patron, Violet forgot about Chandler and continued with her earlier conversation, telling Sam of Portland's plan for her trip to investigate LeCato. "He wishes for me to stay over once more at Welbeck Abbey and take one of his tunnels back to Worksop in the morning, then board a train for London."

Sam concentrated on his wife once more. "That makes no sense. The train station is a few minutes' walk from here. Why not stay over here?"

"You forget, my belongings are still in a guest room at Welbeck," Violet replied.

"Yes, I keep hoping you are imminently returning, but now you are off to the city. How long will you be gone?"

"Just a couple of days, long enough to try to see the prime minister." She spoke with more confidence than she felt. Would Gladstone actually be willing to see her?

"I think it high time you returned here with me," he grumbled in the manner Violet knew was one of irritated acceptance. "But I'll escort you back to Welbeck. Don't be long in London, though. Who knows what news I may have when you return?"

16

Courtesy of the Duke of Portland, Violet took a harrowing ride through his personal tunnel to Worksop station, the clattering of the carriage wheels inside the confined space nearly deafening her during the ride. The groom riding on the rear stand seemed not to notice the bumping and jangling. In fact, Violet was certain she heard the young man laughing behind her.

As they pulled up in front of the station, Violet waited for the groom to open the carriage door, but she waited in vain. After several minutes at a standstill, the driver proceeded forward again, this time very slowly. The next thing Violet knew, the horses were being unhooked and several men were lifting the carriage, rocking her unsteadily until she landed with a thud inside a train carriage.

She rode to London like this, wobbling back and forth inside the carriage as it rocked inside what must have been a train compartment specially made for the duke.

Violet felt positively ridiculous.

With relief, she arrived at Paddington station. There the carriage was lifted out once more by unseen hands and reattached to the horses, which must have traveled with the driver and grooms elsewhere on the train. Within minutes, she was driven the remaining mile or so to Harcourt House in Cavendish Square.

Once more, Violet was assailed by another aspect of how peculiar the Duke of Portland really was. His London home was as tall and stately as the rest of the properties in this exclusive area of London, except that one side and presumably the rear garden were surrounded by a wall that reached nearly eighty feet in the air.

The wall shimmered in the sunlight, and upon closer inspection, Violet saw that it was constructed of ground glass in varying colors. How positively odd.

It was as if the duke had constructed his own personal prison inside London. Given how reclusive he was, Violet could almost understand how the noise and busyness of the city would cause him to retreat inside this grand edifice when he was here.

But it was through the duke's sister, who resided year-round in this unusual sanctuary, that Violet would receive even more disconcerting tidings about Lord William John Cavendish-Scott-Bentinck, and begin to wonder if Sam having business dealings with His Grace was actually not such a grand idea.

Lady Howard de Walden, née Lady Lucy Cavendish-Scott-Bentinck and the widow of Charles Ellis, the 6th Baron Howard de Walden, greeted Violet from inside an overdecorated parlor, rising graciously to acknowledge the undertaker's presence. Was Violet supposed to curtsy to a baroness? Shake her hand? The aristocratic rules of etiquette were so intricate and illogical as to be simply irritating, and so Violet chose to dip her head and shift her body so that it might be taken as a bumbling effort at a curtsy, or perhaps not one at all, hoping that it would suffice.

The baroness was tall and elegant, with hair swept up in a complicated, blooming coiffure that surely took her maid hours to complete each morning. Despite the fact that she must be in her sixties, Lady Howard de Walden was dressed in the latest style, a lavender-and-cream confection with layers of scalloped edging around a full skirt. Violet felt like a dowdy old matron next to the woman, even though she was surely more than twenty years younger than the baroness.

"My brother sent me a note that an undertaker was performing some work for him in London, but he didn't say what it was. . . ." Her regal, plucked eyebrows rose in question.

If the duke hadn't shared it with the baroness, Violet wasn't about to, either. "Yes, His Grace has asked me to visit some people on his behalf, to discover their opinions on certain topics."

The eyebrow rose higher. The baroness didn't believe her. "Isn't it rather odd that my brother has asked you to perform important work for him? I hear that you recently cared for two of his workers—and most admirably at that—but you are, after all, just an undertaker."

Violet considered herself a respectable tradesman, but it was typical for people from all ranges of the social spectrum to view her as *just* an undertaker. "Yes, my lady, but as you are aware, your brother is quite . . . reserved . . . in his relationships. He is not someone who would be inclined to run off to London himself, nor would he consider sending any of his staff. I was more than happy to do it for him, as I have regular dealings in London for my business."

"Is that so?" The baroness was nearly overcome in her curiosity over Violet, but good breeding would not permit her to ask a penetrating question about Violet's relationship with Portland. Instead, she tried the kindness approach. "Perhaps I can help you. I have many important contacts in the city and can make introductions for you."

"You are gracious, my lady, but I am here to visit only the prime minister, if he has time for me."

"Oh. I see. I'm afraid I won't be able to assist you with an introduction to a station as lofty as that."

"That's quite all right, my lady. I've met Mr. Gladstone before."

The baroness frowned, and her expression was one of confusion that someone like Violet claimed to be acquainted with the prime minister. "I see," she repeated, but clearly she didn't. "How is it that you have been introduced to Gladstone?"

Violet knew she shouldn't tease the baroness further but couldn't help herself. "The queen acquainted me with him when I did a personal service for her."

Mere confusion swiftly turned into astonishment. "Pardon me? Did you say you did a personal service . . . *for the queen?*"

"Yes. I recently assisted her in a couple of sensitive investigative matters involving both a diplomat and several of her family members." Violet couldn't help adding, "Of course, I also helped to prepare the Prince Consort's body in 1861."

She could almost see Lady Howard de Walden mentally writing notes to all of her friends to inform them of the most unusual houseguest she had. To the baroness's credit, she didn't sputter or express further astonishment but instead regained her calm. "Ah, I'm sure I was out of the country then. My husband was the Minister Plenipotentiary to Belgium at the time, so we spent a great deal of time abroad with his diplomatic missions. I followed my husband to many important cities—Stockholm, Lisbon, Brussels—although none so important as London itself, of course." The baroness lifted her chin, looking every inch a cultured diplomat's wife.

Violet hoped her stay here would be brief and wouldn't involve too many encounters with the widow. She changed the subject. "Harcourt House is quite beautiful, my lady."

"Isn't it? My brother gave me use of it for the rest of my life. I'll never remarry, of course. Not when there is so much to do in caring for my sons, especially Frederick."

"You have young boys, my lady?" Violet asked, incredulous that a widow of her age would have sons in their minorities living with her.

"No, four of them are married, but I still have my Freddy with me." She reached over to a table and pulled off a framed photograph of a uniformed man in his late thirties sitting astride a horse, with a saber in his white-gloved right hand. He was handsome and well formed, but his lower lip pouted in a manner that suggested an aristocrat who had never been acquainted with the word "no."

Violet murmured appreciation of the man's good looks and handed the picture back to the baroness, who gazed at it fondly once more before setting it back in its place. "He is such a smart and dapper boy, although he chastises me for calling him a boy, since he is thirty-nine now and a major in the 4th Light Dragoons, not to mention that he holds the title of 7th Baron Howard de Walden."

Violet had met this type of widow before, who was fully cognizant of her stature in society. In Lady Howard de Walden's case, it was as the sister of a duke, the widow of a baron, and the mother of the new baron—and resting all of her fortunes in what that son might do.

"His Grace is fortunate to have you here to manage his property."

The baroness's laugh tinkled against the fringed draperies and painted ceiling medallion. "I don't concern myself with managing property, Mrs. Harper. That's the job of my brother's estate manager. I am simply furthering the family's fortunes with my connections."

How much further do they need to go? Violet thought.

"Of course, my brother gave me free rein to redecorate Harcourt House. John is fortunate to even have this house, considering how it came into his possession."

"My lady?" Violet wondered if the duke had run a tunnel from Welbeck to London and taken over the house like a hermit crab moving into a new shell.

"My brother didn't tell you? I thought you were a close confidant." The baroness appeared to relish not only the gossip she had to share but also the dig she was able to make at Violet. "No matter. The house was built in 1722 for the 1st Earl Harcourt, but did not stay in the family long, for the 3rd Earl held a card party here, attended by my grandfather, who won the house during a particularly heated game. My brother doesn't own it outright today, of course. The house was entailed as part of Harcourt's larger estate, but the Dukes of Portland have a leasehold tenancy that will last into the next century."

Violet couldn't imagine putting up, say, her undertaking business as a mere wager in a card game, but then, she wasn't bound by the unfathomable edicts and commandments that the upper classes were.

"The property is most unusual, my lady," Violet said to veer off the topic of lost wagers. "Particularly the wall around the garden."

At this, the baroness was no longer laughing. "That. Yes. My brother erected it so that he could walk through the garden without anyone seeing him from Henrietta Place or Wigmore Street, nor even from the upper story of a neighboring building. I've talked to him many times about removing it—so unfitting of a ducal property, and he only visits on rare occasions—but he won't hear of it. Frederick says he welcomes the privacy, too, so I suppose I mustn't be too fussy about it."

Here was yet another oddity of the duke's: impossibly tall walls to screen himself from his neighbors on his isolated visits to the city. Portland seemed obsessed with shielding himself from others. The duke was very confusing. He seemed to be very generous with his workers and concerned for their well-being, yet he could hardly tolerate the presence of others. It was almost impossible to understand how he chose those whom he could tolerate. Violet mentally ticked off people Portland would endure: his valet, Pearson; the butler, Mr. Kirby; the lantern-carrying girl, Molly; his army compatriot Colonel Mortimer; and now Violet herself, as well as Sam. Presumably Portland was tolerant of the baroness and his other relatives, but Violet wouldn't wager on it unless she saw them together.

It had been less than an hour since she had entered Harcourt House, and already Violet was thinking of wagers, as if she were a carefree aristocrat.

She dusted away the thought as Lady Howard de Walden continued with stories about the duke's London home and her role in elevating its magnificence, interspersed with crafty questions about the purpose of Violet's visit. Violet kept her responses to minimal "Yes, my lady" and "I'm sure I don't know, my lady" statements. The baroness never invited Violet to sit down, and the undertaker was certain she might faint from hunger and weariness, until the baroness finally ran out of ways to interrogate her and summoned a maid to escort Violet to a guest room.

When the dining hour arrived, without sending a maid to ask Violet what her dining preferences were, the baroness had a tray sent to her rather than inviting her to the dining room, thus informing Violet of her displeasure with how the earlier interview went. Violet didn't mind, for it gave her time to read over the list of questions she had been working on during the afternoon.

*   *   *

Who had a reason to kill Burton Spencer? No one, unless perhaps Spencer witnessed something or was blackmailing someone. All speculation.

Who had an opportunity? Everyone on the estate.

Who had a reason to kill Edward Bayes? No one.

Who had an opportunity? Everyone on the estate. Except poor Mr. Spencer.

Violet tapped the rounded end of her fountain pen against her lips. She was becoming more confused by the minute. She hoped Mr. Gladstone would provide answers about Mr. LeCato that would enable her to conclude her investigation. The next morning, though, Violet had far greater concerns than what Jack LeCato might or might not be doing.

17

In the morning, Violet was once again sent a tray. She finished every morsel of the veal kidney omelet and seeded biscuits slathered with quince marmalade set before her, before changing into her day dress, alleviating her standard black with a cobalt-and-black-checked jacket. However, she did tie her undertaking hat with its tails to her head to give her an air of authority. She hoped.

Thus attired, with a black wool cape for added warmth, she marched past the footman standing at the front door, down the steps, and onto the pavement. Violet Harper might not be a welcome guest, but she was a guest nonetheless and entitled to use the front entrance.

The day was chilly, bright, and clear, marred just a bit by coal smoke drifting from chimneys and the occasional smuts drifting through the air. Across the street, the view inside Cavendish Square was unhindered by the bare trees, whose branches made little movement on such a still day. They seemed to be framing the variety of statues, plaques, and pathways inside the park. She decided it was worth a short walk to tour the small square before heading off to Westminster.

To her surprise, the first statue she came upon was a life-sized bronze of none other than Lord George Bentinck, Portland's brother, who had died in 1848, according to the plaque set inside the tall stone block upon which the figure stood. Violet's head reached the bottom of his feet, making Bentinck grand and imposing in his collared cape that draped casually around his ankles. A half ring of boxwood shrubbery was set back about five feet from the rear of the statue, as if to represent a laurel-leaf crown upon it.

Violet was about to move on down a path to another statue when a dog came bounding up to her, panting and wagging its tail. "Hello there, Mr. Spaniel," Violet said, forgetting about Mr. Bentinck for the moment. "What brings you out on such a fine day?"

She bent down to pet the dog, which had rich chestnut markings running down its back against a pearly white coat, along with floppy brown ears and a chestnut spot on its forehead. "Why, if I'm not mistaken, you are a Blenheim spaniel." The dog licked at her hand as if to affirm that that was indeed what it was. "Have you escaped from your master or mistress? Which of these fine homes is yours?" Maybe the dog even belonged to Lady Howard de Walden.

Before Violet could even decide what to do about the loose dog, which was obviously well groomed and fed and therefore not a stray, she found herself grabbed roughly by her right arm, the arm that had been scalded and scarred in a train accident several years ago. She heard the grunts and mutterings of two men behind her, as one of them yanked her arm behind her back, nearly pulling it out of its socket. At her feet, the spaniel whined in distress.

Violet cried out in pain, but was too startled to do much else. How was it possible that she was being attacked by cutpurses in the middle of Cavendish Square in broad daylight?

Unfortunately, her reticule, containing a sharp and handy knife, dangled from the arm that was now pinned painfully behind her. She was shoved around to the rear of the statue so that she and one of her attackers were concealed from view by the statue's base on one side and the half ring of boxwoods on the other. The second man remained at the front of the statue, clearly watching out for others.

Despite the pain in her arm, Violet had regained her senses. "What is it you want? All I have to do is scream and there will be a dozen officers here to help me."

"And all I have to do is cut your throat and stop your pretty little scream before it reaches its first note," the man said, his voice low and dangerous, as he whipped her around to look at him.

He wasn't what Violet expected. He wasn't filthy, he didn't smell foul, and he wasn't missing teeth. In fact, he looked almost, well, *normal*, with freshly laundered clothing and combed hair.

Normal except for the rather large knife he brandished in his free hand, the tip of it held to her neck. In fact, he gently nudged the point against her skin, and the searing pain of that made her forget completely about her arm.

"What is it you want?" Violet repeated, this time her voice a whisper as she stilled herself, lest the blade make a very unwelcome entry beneath her skin and to vital points therein.

"Watch your belligerence," he growled, using a rather long word for a street criminal. "You hear me well. You and your kind"—he took the knife blade and flipped up the collar of her cape, as if to emphasize its quality cut—"should keep your noses out of other people's business."

He brought the knife back to her neck and lowered his face so that it was mere inches from hers, his murky brown eyes boring into her own dark ones. The malevolence in them frightened her more than his weapon did.

Which reminded Violet of her own knife, still dangling uselessly inside the reticule behind her back.

"What business do you mean?" she asked, wondering if she could distract him enough to dislodge herself from his grip. However, the man was intensely mindful of his task, a task Violet couldn't fathom.

He ignored her question. "It's the fancy ones I most enjoy doing in—"

"Ian!" the other man hissed from around the side of the statue. "There's a police wagon coming around the corner."

The man named Ian uttered several oaths and froze, as if unsure whether to finish his task and risk being caught, or to simply flee and avoid his own trouble. With a final curse, he pushed Violet against Lord Bentinck's statue. Her head struck the back of the bronze cape, and she sank to the ground, blurry-eyed, with no idea where the two men had gone.

It took her several minutes to stop trembling and regain her bearings. Her head and right arm throbbed. She massaged her arm with her left hand but found no relief. By the time she rose on shaky legs, the police wagon and the spaniel were nowhere to be found.

The men, she assumed, were across the Thames by now, to parts unknown.

18

Mildly recovered from the shock and pain of the attack, Violet changed her plans and made her way to Scotland Yard. It was a mile-and-a-half walk, but she used the time crossing through Mayfair and St. James's Park to clear her mind and think through what had happened so that she would have a cogent tale to tell Detective Chief Inspector Magnus Pompey Hurst, her contact at the Yard, with whom she had worked on several investigative matters. In his usual stubborn way, Hurst would undoubtedly try to find a way to accuse Violet of being mistaken, or hysterical, or a victim of misunderstanding, but eventually he would take her seriously.

As she stumbled along, regaining her footing while trying not to draw attention to herself, her primary thought was that her attackers were not a pair of cutpurses on the loose. What was it the man named Ian had said? "You and your kind should keep your noses out of other people's business." What in heaven's name did that mean? The man was a complete stranger to her; she didn't have a nose—or any other body part, either—in his business.

Unless he had been hired by someone else. In an instant, Jack LeCato's face rose in her mind. But why was someone trying to scare her?

Violet entered St. James's Park, passing quickly by the barren trees that now loomed like specters over her, in complete opposition to how they had seemed to invite her into Cavendish Square.

The name "Cavendish" sparked another thought. Ian had growled at her that it was the "fancy ones" he was after. Combined with his comment about Violet and "her kind," well, did he think Violet—who, after all, had emerged from a home facing the park—was an aristocrat?

Another thought struck her cold. Could it be that Ian and the other man had been hired to attack Lady Howard de Walden and assumed Violet was she? But why? The baroness was gossipy and haughty, but such qualities didn't deserve more than a shrug.

Maybe it was time to learn more about the baroness.

Violet entered the large oak doors of Scotland Yard, which added gravitas and dignity to the building they fronted. Within minutes, she was seated at a round table with Inspector Magnus Pompey Hurst and his protégé, Second Class Inspector Langley Pratt, whose fingers were always covered in graphite from note taking, and whose expression was always beleaguered, more than likely due to Hurst's "mentoring." Not only his name but also Hurst's manner and build always reminded Violet of a Roman centurion issuing commands to his legionaries as he led them into war—or, in Hurst's case, investigations.

As Violet began to speak, Pratt's expression immediately turned into concern as he jumped out of his chair. "Mrs. Harper! You need to see a doctor straightaway."

"I do?" she asked, confused. "I'm not ill."

Now Hurst was staring at her strangely. "For the love of God, Mrs. Harper, you're bleeding. Your neck. What happened to you? I thought you had gone away to Nottinghamshire."

Violet brought her hand to her collared neck, and could feel not only the crustiness of dried fabric there but the wet flow of a still-open wound, as well.

Had she received strange glances while walking here? She had been so preoccupied she couldn't remember a single face she had passed on the streets.

Perhaps Ian's knife had laid claim to more territory than she'd thought. The idea that she might have died not an hour ago set her trembling again. Pratt ran from the room and came back with a handkerchief and a cup of water. She accepted both gratefully, and with the cloth pressed up to her neck and several swallows of the cool liquid inside of her, Violet was ready to tell her story.

Except that she wasn't sure where to begin. She took a deep breath. First things first. "The reason I came to London . . ."

Violet proceeded to tell them that she was here at the wish of the Duke of Portland to speak to Mr. Gladstone regarding a man named Jack LeCato, who might or might not have a malevolent purpose at Welbeck Abbey. She then relayed what had happened to her at Cavendish Square. When she reached the point where Ian had said that she and her kind should keep their noses out of other people's business, Hurst interrupted her.

" 'You and your kind'? What? Does he mean lady undertakers? That makes no sense. You must be the only one in London. You don't have a 'kind.' "

Violet could see that they were quickly entering the phase where Hurst would dismiss what she was saying.

"He later said he preferred doing in 'fancy ones.' I think he may have been watching me leave Harcourt House and that he was referring to 'my kind' as aristocrats, not realizing that I am merely a commoner."

Hurst nodded and scratched one side of his muttonchops. "Go on."

"I have a theory. . . ."

At this, Hurst bristled. He never liked to imagine that Violet might be ahead of him on an investigation. "What is that, Mrs. Harper?" His words were patient but laced with derision.

"I believe he may have thought I was the Lady Howard de Walden, the duke's widowed sister who lives there. While my clothing is not as fine as that of the lady in residence, it may have been quality enough to convince him that I was she."

Hurst frowned as he waited for Pratt to catch up on the scrawling he was doing inside a battered little notebook. "Are you saying, then, that the man was actually after the Lady How—What was her name?"

"Howard de Walden. I don't know, I think it is a possibility. Or perhaps he was just a street criminal, but I doubt that. He was entirely too well groomed."

"The most depraved wolves in the world sometimes come dressed in the finest sheep's wool, Mrs. Harper. We will see if there is any word on the street about this Ian fellow, but you shouldn't count on anything."

Violet stood. "Thank you, Inspector. Also, would you be willing to learn what you can about Mr. LeCato?"

"What do you suspect him of?"

Violet bit her lip. "I'm not sure."

Hurst rolled his eyes. "More will-o'-the-wisps to chase, eh? Very well, we will discreetly look into the man, but not in such a way that his reputation is harmed. If he's at Welbeck at Her Majesty's request, it would do the commissioner no good if he was being investigated for a paltry reason."

Violet couldn't argue with that. Hurst agreed to call on her at Harcourt House as soon as he knew something.

From there, Violet walked another half mile south along the Thames to Westminster, hoping the dried blood on her neck had faded into the dark color of her jacket and cape. It wouldn't do to frighten Mr. Gladstone the moment he saw her.

The condition of her clothing didn't matter, though, for she was informed that the prime minister wouldn't have time to see her for three days. Frustrated that her visit to London would be extended, Violet agreed to the appointment offered and consoled herself with the thought that she could use the extra time in the city to visit with her friend Mary Cooke.

That evening, after writing letters to Sam, her daughter, Susanna, and Mary Cooke, Violet was surprised to receive an invitation to attend dinner with Lady Howard de Walden and her son Frederick.

This of course posed the question of whether Violet should inform the baroness of the day's events, but she decided not to reveal anything, lest she make the woman anxious over a potentially isolated situation.

Violet, regowned in her traditional black after handing the blood-encrusted pieces to the maid with a futile prayer that there would be no gossip below stairs about it, was escorted through the main dining room into a smaller breakfast room. The table stood elegantly under a pair of gas chandeliers and was set for three: one at the end and two on either side. It could have easily seated twelve.

Lady Howard de Walden was the only one in the room at the moment and was as exquisitely gowned as ever, this time in shimmering royal blue folds that conformed to her figure so well that it must have been cut and sewn directly upon her. "My lady," Violet said, unsure once more what she was supposed to do. She stood behind her chair, and luckily, the baroness indicated that she should be seated across from her. The head seat was obviously reserved for her son.

A footman stepped forward from the shadows and poured red liquid into a goblet for Violet. The baroness nodded at her, which she assumed was a signal that she could drink. The wine was rich and powerful, so she cautioned herself to sip slowly. "Exquisite, my lady," Violet said in appreciation.

"Were you able to meet with the prime minister?" the baroness asked, not bothering with the platitudes normally employed by her status. "Was he helpful?"

"Not yet, I'm afraid. He won't be able to see me until Tuesday."

"So you were able to secure a meeting, then." Lady Howard de Walden smiled tightly, and Violet wasn't sure if the woman was pleased with Violet's failure to achieve an immediate audience, or if she was disguising disappointment at her guest staying longer. Given that the baroness might have been the target of this morning's attack, Violet decided it might be wise to engage her with kindness and courtesy. Who knew what might happen in the days ahead where the baroness might need her? Or vice versa?

"Will the baron be joining us?" Violet asked politely. "I would be honored to meet him."

The older woman's eyes lit up. "Yes. He is being dressed. He's had a busy day, I'm sure, so he's a bit late. I hope Cook was able to keep the veal warm and moist." A shadow passed over her face, so quickly Violet almost missed it, to be immediately replaced with that forced smile.

"What shall you do with your additional time here in London?"

The baroness asked the question while lifting her own wineglass to her lips.

Presuming this was an attempt to divine how much time Violet would spend inside Harcourt House, she assured her hostess, "I have many visits to make, to a dear friend of mine, as well as to my shop. I expect I will be quite occupied until I meet with Mr. Gladstone."

"Yes, we will all be eager to know what he has to say."

What did that mean?

"I am surprised that Lord Howard de Walden is not married," Violet said, changing the subject and hoping she wasn't being too forward, "given his stature and pleasing looks."

The baroness sighed. "He is quite handsome, isn't he? It's why he's the only bachelor of my children, despite being the oldest. I've picked out a lovely girl for him, but thus far he has been too high-spirited and distracted to consider marriage."

Violet understood this to mean that he probably spent his time gambling, racing, and being obsessed with a myriad of other lofty pleasures. "Perhaps the lady has not captured his heart."

"I don't see why not. Blanche Holden's family may not be quite peerage, but Frederick would do well to have their Palace House in Lancashire among his holdings."

Violet had no time to contemplate the virtues of Miss Holden and her residence, for Frederick Ellis, the current Baron Howard de Walden, made his dramatic entry, a valet on his heels attempting to put a jacket on his master, which the baron shrugged impatiently away. The valet slipped away, jacket in hand, as the discreet footman hurried to pour wine into the baron's glass, which Frederick first sniffed and then drank a long gulp of before sitting down.

"You must be the undertaker I've heard so much about," he said without preamble, looking at Violet curiously as though she were a newly discovered insect waving its feelers from under a bell jar.

The baroness cut in. "Mrs. Harper was unable to meet with Mr. Gladstone today, so she will be with us several more days, until Tuesday at least, Frederick. We've been chatting about your bright prospects in the marriage market."

Frederick turned to Violet and rolled his eyes so his mother couldn't see. "Has Mother been telling you about Miss Holden? I told you, Mother, she has that one ridiculous tooth that juts out sideways. Imagine what little goblins our children would look like. And she isn't even the daughter of a peer."

The baroness's expression was one of mortification. "Frederick, please. We have a guest. . . ." She nodded at Violet, a sign that he shouldn't speak so plainly before company, much less before a mere undertaker.

Frederick grinned wickedly and took another swallow. A few drops landed on his shirt, unnoticed. Perhaps this wasn't his first glass today. "Of course, Mother. Mrs. Harper, you should know that I am very marriage-minded, just not in the manner expected of me. Perhaps if I'm to be forced into a marriage I don't want, I'll choose to remain a bachelor."

"I hope you don't follow in your uncle's footsteps regarding marriage, my son," the baroness said.

Frederick laughed in derision. The rawness of his outburst was like a pistol shot in the room. "You think I'll end up like the mad duke, Mother? Not likely. I can hardly think he allowed himself to imagine he would marry an *opera singer*, of all things."

The baroness reddened at her son's exposure of a family failing but explained, "My brother fell in love with Miss Adelaide Kemble, back in the early '40s. She was the sister of Fanny Kemble, the actress, and therefore wholly unsuitable even if she weren't a stage singer, but she was. I'm sure John thought she would view him as her savior from a life of drudgery in the theater. Instead, she rejected him and ended up marrying some Liberal member of Parliament. My brother was permanently heartbroken."

Was there no end to the unlayering of the Duke of Portland? Violet had had no idea of the depth of the man's emotions.

Frederick had his own opinion on the situation. "He wasn't much of a man to have allowed it to turn him batty, which is probably why Miss Kemble spurned him in the first place. All the women who would have sold their souls to the devil to marry a duke, and he pined away for Miss Kemble. There were many other delicacies to have been sampled at the buffet table, but he decided to sit in the corner with a glass of water."

"Frederick!" Now the baroness was openly horrified.

He shrugged carelessly in the face of his mother's reprimand. "It's true. And he's been wasting his time and money ever since on those ridiculous tunnels. When I think of the racehorses I would have bought with just half the money my uncle has wasted, well, I would be the star of the Derby."

"You know your uncle is famous for his horsemanship."

The baron downed what remained in his glass and shook it back and forth to summon the footman for a refill. "Maybe, but he doesn't race them, which is the exciting part. He just foals them and breaks them, which is the drudgery side of things. Any stable hand can do that. Probably just as well, as if he were to race, he'd have trouble holding on to both his horse and his preposterous hat at the same time."

Violet knew little about horses except for their utility in pulling hearses, but she imagined that raising good stock was as important as putting them into actual races. That, however, was an opinion she would keep to herself.

Which was just as well, for Frederick had many more of his own opinions about his uncle that he didn't mind sharing with a mere undertaker. "Not only that, he never invites me—us—to Welbeck for parties—"

"Son, you know he doesn't host par—" The baroness attempted to interject.

"—where I could meet all of the heiresses of the Dukeries and their pretty little friends. It's damned unfair of him not to think of his family. After all, he's not producing an heir for the Bentinck line. The least he could do is give our side some assistance." He waved his empty goblet once more.

Violet noticed for the first time that Frederick had other wine spills on his shirt, and they were in various stages of fading. *His valet must be in permanent despair of him,* Violet thought.

Suddenly, she felt sorry for the Lady Howard de Walden, who was probably struggling to maintain her place in society and secure the family name on the back of a wild and unbreakable stallion.

Fortunately, the veal was just then served, and she was able to absorb herself in her plate and avoid further conversation with the baron. It was just as well, for he drank at least four more glasses of wine—complaining bitterly when the footman had to leave to ask the butler for another bottle—and continued to pontificate on horse races, pretty women, the execrable state in which his father had left the barony, and the injustice being served by his uncle. This spoilt boy, who was probably older than Violet, was giving her a headache worthy of at least two Beecham's Pills and a pot of chamomile tea.

Later, as Violet prepared herself for bed, the sounds of violent retching penetrated the walls around her, followed by spattering and coughing. She didn't envy the poor maid who would be required to clean that up, although she suspected that the servant was probably used to it. The vomiting was soon followed by angry bellowing and the breaking of glass, as well as a soothing voice.

Violet didn't envy the Lady Howard de Walden, either.

19

Inspectors Hurst and Pratt showed up the following afternoon while Violet was in her room, having just strolled through the rear garden to see for herself if the duke had a point in his desire for extreme privacy. She had to admit, it was rather pleasurable to be solitary among the now-sleeping shrubberies and trees—solitary except for probably the watchful eyes of the baroness, her son, and a myriad of servants.

A maid led her to a front parlor, but the baroness had made it there first and was already questioning the detectives. Fortunately, Hurst wore the expression of a stoic and refused to tell her anything. However, Violet's appearance made the Lady Howard de Walden dig her nails deeper into the arms of her chair, and the woman refused to leave the room. Perhaps it was time for Violet to confess the possible danger the baroness was in.

"My lady," she began, "there is something you should know. . . ." Violet proceeded to tell her about the attack the previous morning inside Cavendish Square.

"Impossible!" the baroness cried, all hardened expression of aristocracy wiped from her face and replaced with genuine alarm. "This is the most exclusive part of Marylebone. Such . . . such . . . a *common* thing wouldn't happen here."

"But it did, my lady, and my concern is whether it was a random attack . . . or if it was intended against a lady of quality and, seeing me, they thought I was . . . you."

"*Me?*" Lady Howard de Walden nearly screeched. "I am not acquainted with any street rogues. Unless . . . unless they are really after my Frederick. What has he done now?"

This piqued Hurst's interest. "Is there a problem with your son, madam?"

"What? Oh no. No, of course not." The baroness quickly regained her composure and folded her hands in the lap of her copper-colored dress, which caught the light from the chandeliers and made her glow handsomely even in the daylight.

Pratt was scribbling furiously in his notebook.

Despite the woman's astringent behavior toward her, Violet didn't want to see her swept up in an investigation. "Inspector," she said, addressing Hurst, "did you discover something regarding the men in the park?"

Hurst gazed thoughtfully at the baroness a few more moments before turning his attention to Violet. "Yes, and what we learned was interesting. It didn't take much to run down our informants and learn that a small-time thief by the name of Ian Hale had bragged of a 'job' in Cavendish Square. Does the name mean anything to you?"

Violet shook her head. She'd never heard it before.

"And what of you, my lady?" Hurst asked the baroness, who also shook her head.

"What is interesting about him, Inspector?" Violet said.

"He is a petty thief, but he also has a regular position at an orphanage."

"An orphanage!" Violet and the baroness exclaimed together.

"Yes. Not an important position, so to speak. He essentially serves as a clerk to the administrator there, checking children in and ensuring they are given tasks at local mills to keep them busy: lace making, wool spinning, that sort of thing."

"I don't understand," Violet said. "Why would an orphanage worker wish to attack me—or Lady Howard de Walden—in the middle of Marylebone?"

The baroness smiled tightly again, as she had during dinner the previous evening. "This is most disturbing, Inspector, as my husband left a considerable bequest to Coram's Foundling Hospital in his will, a bequest that was quite . . . onerous . . . on the family."

Pratt's fingers were racing across the page as he picked up on this tidbit of information. He stopped and flipped back through the pages. "It wasn't Coram's, my lady; it was Babbage's Home for Foundlings."

The baroness seemed relieved, but Violet was still confused. "It doesn't make sense that an orphanage clerk would spend his spare hours attacking women in parks." Nor that he would attack someone he thought wealthy, who might be a prospective donor to the institution.

"I agree with Mrs. Harper," Lady Howard de Walden said, in a move that surprised Violet. "I should think that orphanage staff are upstanding citizens, what with their holy duty toward protecting these children."

"My lady," Hurst said patiently, "perhaps you are not aware that orphanages are responsible for more than half of the criminal population in London. Some of these institutions are run by good Christian men, but many others turn their charges into thieves or prostitutes, and there are gangs of these children hiding in the alleyways of London. These occupations are the fastest way for them to earn money, and they bring plenty of it back to those in charge at the orphanage. Most donors—such as your husband, I'm sure, my lady—have no idea their generous contributions are used in this way."

"You seem to know a great deal about orphanages, Inspector," the baroness said. Somehow, the light wasn't shimmering off her dress so readily now, almost as if she were wilting.

"Commissioner Henderson is interested in starting a reputable orphanage, as well as a widows' fund, and is soliciting police superintendents to join him in the effort."

Violet had met the commissioner, who was also responsible for initiating the fledgling Scotland Yard. Somehow she doubted an orphanage started by this man would be permitted to descend into such shameful activities as those Hurst had described. "Is Babbage's one of these sorts of disreputable orphanages?" she asked.

"That's what makes it interesting. No, it is not. But there's more."

Hurst snapped his fingers at Pratt, who put aside his notebook, pulled a folded piece of paper from his coat pocket, and handed it to his superior.

Violet saw that the page had been addressed to a location in London, with no return name or address. Hurst handed the telegram to her, which contained just three lines. She read it aloud for the Lady Howard de Walden's benefit.

THE RAVEN IS AT HARCOURT HOUSE.

HER INQUIRIES ARE GETTING CLOSER TO MY TREASURE.

SEE THAT SHE DOESN'T LEAVE LONDON. EVER.

Violet looked up, returning the note to Inspector Hurst and trying to maintain a calm composure. "What does this mean?" she asked, although she had a fairly good idea what it meant. She was the "raven," a lady in black, and someone had instructed Ian Hale to kill her. But why? What "treasure" had she unknowingly stumbled upon? This note clarified that yesterday's attack had not been random. She shuddered to think what might have happened if a passing police van hadn't scared the men away.

Violet came out of her reverie as she realized Hurst was still speaking. "Hale got out of our grasp and fled after we checked his pockets, so we couldn't question him. No one has seen him since. The orphanage has been told to report to us if he shows up again. I expect he's gone to the Continent by now," he added with a grunt.

"He had a confederate. . . ." Violet said.

"We don't know who that may have been. Might have been one of the boys from the orphanage who has slipped back into his place."

Violet frowned. "He seemed like a full-grown man to me. And he referred to Hale as 'Ian,' a terribly familiar way to address his superior."

Hurst shrugged. "A mere detail. Suffice to say that we don't know where Hale has gotten off to, but it doesn't look like he'll be after you again, Mrs. Harper, and you were never a target, my lady," he said, turning and nodding to the baroness, whose color was already returning at Hurst's words.

Violet, though, was sure she was so pale as to be nearly invisible. Who wanted her dead, someone in London or at Welbeck?

Was it possible that Mr. LeCato heard of Violet's trip to London, and didn't want to be the focus of questioning and thus hired Ian Hale to silence her? But who would have told him about her trip? The only people who knew of it were Portland and Sam.

Wait. Wasn't she speaking of it to Sam a few days ago at Worksop Inn when Martin Chandler came in? But he went into the rear of the building, so he couldn't possibly have heard her. Then Violet remembered something else. Chandler had called her a raven to her face at Burton Spencer's funeral. He'd even said that the tails on her hat resembled a raven's wings. Who else had been present for that? Ellery Reed, Jack LeCato . . . and Colonel Mortimer.

The colonel had encouraged her to come to London. Had he done so in order to have someone set upon her outside the confines of Welbeck, where no suspicions would be thrown upon him?

Of course, she could say that Chandler or Ellery Reed could have arranged an attack on her, although for the life of her she couldn't discern a motive for either of them.

"Inspector," Violet said, "there is another man you might find of interest in this situation, besides Jack LeCato. His name is Colonel George Mortimer. He lived in London as recently as two years ago, and was once in the Grenadier Guards." There was no need to say that he was a close friend of Portland's in front of the duke's sister, lest she send a servant racing to the telegram office to inform her brother of Violet's seeming disloyalty.

As for Martin Chandler, Violet would have to investigate him back at Welbeck on her own.

20

The following morning, Lady Howard de Walden was once more seated alone in the breakfast room, nibbling idly at a dish of gingered apples topped with candied lemon peel, when Violet entered.

"Ah, Mrs. Harper, you may as well accompany me to Evensong service at St. Marylebone's this afternoon. Frederick is . . . not quite himself . . . today."

As Violet sat down and gratefully accepted a serving of the apples, she noticed that the baroness was as wan as she had been during the detectives' visit. Was their visit still upsetting her, or had Frederick Ellis conducted himself rudely again and embarrassed his mother?

"My lady, I would be happy to do so. Perhaps the baron will feel well enough by the time you leave to also attend."

The baroness nodded without enthusiasm. "Yes, perhaps."

After several moments of sterling silver forks clicking against Wedgwood plates, Violet said, "I have received a reply from my friend Mary Cooke and have plans to meet her tomorrow to visit the offices of Grover and Baker, to see their new sewing machines. Then I shall meet with Mr. Gladstone and be on my way back to Nottinghamshire."

"How nice for you. You will have dinner with us tomorrow before leaving, though, won't you?" The baroness didn't seem as happy about Violet's impending departure as she once had. It had been Violet's experience that many mourners relied on their undertaker for expressing their grief, but Lady Howard de Walden wasn't in mourning. Unless her son was causing her far more pain than even Violet could imagine.

Violet preferred to leave the moment she was done with Gladstone so she could get back to Sam, but acquiesced to the baroness's request. "Of course, my lady."

"You will speak well of your visit when you see His Grace?" the baroness asked, bringing her teacup to her lips and looking at Violet over the rim.

This surprised Violet, who had had no idea the lady was looking to secure a good report, or that her brother's opinion mattered to her.

Without waiting for Violet's reply, the baroness went on. "My brother has many quirks that the rest of us don't have, but he is still a good Christian man who takes care of his family and of those less fortunate than he. He is simply"—Lady Howard de Waldon looked up, as if searching for the right phrase to describe Portland—"simply less forgiving of fools and simpletons, and sometimes it makes him seem abrasive or peculiar. He doesn't appear to see you as a fool or simpleton, though, so I must assume you are neither since I have so little to go on."

Violet thought that Portland's actions and mannerisms went way beyond dislike of addle-brains, but there was much about the man she had yet to understand, so perhaps the baroness was right, although Violet wasn't sure whether she had just been insulted again or not.

"I remember a particular time not long ago," Lady Howard de Walden said, an actual smile making an appearance on her face as she put her cup down onto its plate with a delicate clink. "Our cousin William—who is the heir presumptive given that my brother is not likely to marry and beget heirs at his great age—went to visit John, to learn a little about the estate. I suppose William, sent there by his parents, of course, expressed little interest in the running of a ducal estate and more than likely demonstrated his utter boredom in eye rolls and sighs. Having had enough of the boy's impudence, my brother ordered him to stand in an empty room for hours on end until William was reduced to humbly apologizing."

At least, Violet thought, *the boy was sure to have had a chamber pot available to him, no matter in which empty room he stood.*

"He returned home chastened. Our uncle was outraged by his son's treatment, but he's still the heir and no damage was done, so that is that. Except there will be no more training, and William will be thoroughly unprepared to take the reins. I've no doubt he will end up like Fred—like so many others in his position."

Violet contemplated all that the baroness had told her. Portland was peculiar—of that, there was no doubt. But did his eccentricities cover up something deeper and more sinister? She began to question why he had been so eager to send her to London. Was it not Jack LeCato or Colonel Mortimer with a motive to attack her but the duke himself? Portland had been terribly vague about his reasons for sponsoring her trip to London. Perhaps she shouldn't have been so trusting of him just because he was a peer of the realm.

Moreover, should Lady Howard de Walden have shared such an intimate family detail with her, a stranger with no real connection to the Cavendish-Scott-Bentincks? Violet was beginning to realize something important. The dowager baroness was a first-order gossip, and not a discreet one at that. She now understood why Portland hadn't told his sister anything, for she suspected that anything that went into the woman's ear would be spilled out at her next card party.

Samuel Harper willingly met Portland at Worksop Priory for Sunday services—strange as it was to have to witness the proceedings through a wooden screen in the rear of the church—then accompanied him in the ducal carriage back to Welbeck. Sam was treated to the same experience Violet had told him of in her last letter, with the four-mile trek mostly inside an underground tunnel. They exited next to a European-style chalet, which Portland referred to as his Russian Lodge. With a sharply pitched roof that dominated the entire structure, it could have easily been a home in Sweden, where Sam had visited the dynamite inventor, Alfred Nobel.

The thought of Nobel reminded Sam of his ultimate purpose in meeting with Portland, and he girded himself for whatever conversation lay ahead. He had no idea what it could be since Portland had been utterly silent during their bizarre underground journey and, in fact, had stared out of the carriage the entire time, as though there was something fascinating in the miles of endless stonework they passed.

Portland wore the same old brown overcoat that he had worn at the dynamiting site. On his lap was the same tall hat under which the man could have hidden a giraffe. The duke didn't seem to be one for change in his life.

Sam refrained from grabbing at his own leg as he exited the carriage. Violet's rub of Mr. Johnston's Essence of Mustard had helped, but the autumn chill that seemed permanently set in the air meant that he was in for a painful few months. Colorado wasn't so damp, and it was easier on his leg there, but Violet was flourishing back here in her homeland, so he ignored the soreness, which would be over soon enough.

Nevertheless, he landed hard on the leg that had been wounded in the Civil War, and he couldn't help grimacing as he reached back into the carriage for his eagle-headed cane. Perhaps he shouldn't dread the trip to Egypt for the opening of the Suez Canal next month. Maybe the desert would be more agreeable for his bones, which weren't yet forty years old but sometimes made him feel older than Methuselah.

He shook off such morose thoughts. It was time for the thrill of a shoot, and the opportunity to talk to Portland about dynamite manufacture—that is, if the man would do more than stare off into space, avoiding him. Sam found the duke to be just as peculiar as Violet had described him.

They were greeted at the door of the lodge by a man who was as well groomed and sharply dressed as the duke was wild-haired and old-fashioned.

"Henry," Portland said warmly, offering the man a handshake, "this is Samuel Harper, the American I wrote to you of who is involved with dynamite. Harper, this is my brother, Henry Scott-Bentinck."

As Sam shook hands with the man, he noticed that, although Bentinck shared Portland's hooded eyes, he shared no other physical features. In fact, he appeared to be much younger than his age, which Sam presumed to be his midsixties, versus his brother's late sixties.

"Henry is a well-known hound man," Portland said with pride.

In response, Bentinck put his fingers to his lips and whistled. The sharp sound brought a pack of about eight dogs running from nowhere. It was hard to count them as they dashed excitedly around the men, sniffing the air, the men's trousers, their shoes, and whatever other item they could find. Some of the dogs trotted, as though they thought they were horses, while others wriggled their backsides enthusiastically as they moved.

Sam reached down to pat one on the head. It had a smooth coat of burnished brown, and its pink nose eagerly snuffled at Sam's hand as its unusually short tail shot out proud and erect behind it.

"They're vizslas," Bentinck said with pride. "The breed originated in Hungary, and holds a rare position among sporting dogs, as they are also good household companions and guard dogs."

"They have striking coats," Sam murmured, scratching the same dog behind its floppy ear. As his reward, the dog sat squarely on Sam's foot to better enjoy the attention.

Bentinck became more animated in his enthusiasm for the animals. "Yes, and they are not only excellent pointers but admirable retrievers, as well. They are absolutely fearless and make brilliant swimmers. Outstanding noses, too, and can be trained to perform nearly any trick. I once even trained one to pick out 'London Bridge' on a piano. Ha!"

With so many perfect qualities, Sam wondered if the dogs shouldn't be near to canonization.

With another whistle, this one not as piercing, the vizslas settled down on their rumps, expectantly staring at their master. "Stay here," Bentinck said and turned back to the lodge. Sam and Portland followed him inside, where servants waited to help them select weapons and ammunition, a luxury to which Sam was quite unused.

A half hour later, they had hiked to a remote part of the estate with an attendant who kept their rifles loaded and cleaned. Soon they were firing at a variety of game birds—pheasants, plump little gray partridges, and French partridges with their bright red eye rings. The pheasants made a loud *kok-kok-kok* noise as the dogs frightened them into bursting out of their cover of shrubbery. The birds' wings made a distinct whirring noise as they made a futile dash for cover.

The vizslas went wild with chasing the carcasses down and trotting back proudly with them gently cradled in their jaws, stubby tails wagging. The men rewarded the dogs with pats, then sent them on to the attendant so he could take the birds and string them together.

Sam enjoyed shooting the pheasants most. He was glad the duke kept them so well stocked on the estate, even if he was unlikely to be invited to partake in a meal that the estate's cook might prepare with them.

In between shots and moving to other locations for the vizslas to scare up more fowl, the men talked companionably. Portland spent considerable time talking about his skating rink project, while tactfully avoiding the subject of the late Edward Bayes. Bentinck, who apparently had no current occupation other than his dogs, talked about past accomplishments.

". . . then I was the member for North Nottinghamshire from 1847 to 1857. Our brother-in-law Evelyn Denison followed me into Parliament. Must keep things held close, eh? Ha!"

"Denison married our sister Charlotte," Portland said as explanation. "They live at Ossington Hall, about fifteen miles away, and have no children, either, so I suppose we are lucky the family has so many other members to carry on the name, eh, Henry?"

Bentinck reddened, and Sam noted that the man had made no mention of a wife or children, so he assumed Portland's brother was also a stopping point in the family tree. As disheartening as that was for commoners, how devastating was it for the aristocracy, what with their bloodlines and estates to manage and transfer? America certainly had her own aristocracy in industrialists like Commodore Cornelius Vanderbilt and Andrew Carnegie, but their wealth was self-made and not invested in the propping up of ancient edifices and pedigrees.

Is one any better than the other? Sam wondered. Perhaps one day the Vanderbilts and Carnegies would also worry about posterity and the continuation of family greatness.

Sam's contribution was to grouse about the state of banking in Great Britain. "With no offense meant, sirs, but it was nearly impossible to secure financing for my endeavor. Your new Debtors Act has fouled things up and made bankers frightened to loan money."

"Ha!" Bentinck said. "You can be sure the banks are continuing to shovel in gold coins like brass buttons, even if they never release a single ingot. Isn't that right, John?"

Portland nodded. "The same is true for other venerable institutions in this country."

Sam noticed a storm brewing in the man's expression after it had relaxed considerably while they had all been outside together. It cast a somber mood over the affair. Eventually, though, Portland guided their talk to the point of their excursion. "Tell me, how did you become an enthusiast for dynamite, Mr. Harper?"

"I'm a lawyer by trade," Sam explained. "I became interested in dynamite after meeting Mr. Nobel, though, seeing the value of it for safer mine tunneling. We worked diligently to get authorization to open factories in Wales or England, but most authorities refuse to consider the idea that a powerful explosive may actually be safer that what has traditionally been employed. My wife tells me that even in private the queen herself is vehemently opposed to it."

"Mrs. Harper knows the queen?" Bentinck asked, his mouth open.

The man's astonishment filled Sam with immense pride. "Indeed. She has performed many services for Her Majesty, from assisting with the Prince Consort's funeral to investigating suspicious deaths in the royal circle."

The brothers lowered their guns as they lost interest in the pheasants with Sam's revelation about his wife.

"I had no idea," Portland said. "And you say our government won't invest in dynamite? Hmm. I should definitely like to hear more about a substance Gladstone doesn't like. Explain it all to me in great detail, Mr. Harper."

This was Sam's moment, and he dove in with enthusiasm, explaining what dynamite was and how the combination of nitroglycerin, diatomaceous earth, and sodium carbonate, formed into short sticks and wrapped in paper, made for better shaft tunneling because the nitroglycerin was far more powerful than black powder.

"If you know the formula," Portland interrupted, "why don't you make your own and cut Nobel out?"

"Mr. Nobel obtained a patent for what he calls 'Nobel's Blasting Powder' in England in 1867, and is very serious about controlling his patents. Besides, I would never consider trampling upon my gentleman's agreement with him."

"I see." Portland nodded thoughtfully. "You know what your problem is, Mr. Harper? Besides the fact that you're a Yankee, of course."

Sam had heard that particular refrain hundreds of times and remained silent. What was he to do about his American birth?

"The problem is that you have no one of . . . substance . . . championing your cause. Naturally, it has been a lost one, and probably never had any hope of success."

Sam's optimism dwindled like a meteor crashing into the middle of the Atlantic Ocean. Was this a lesson he should have learned during his trials with the banks? Should he have hung up his fiddle after the first "no" he'd heard back in London? Giving up wasn't in his nature, though. If it were, he wouldn't have survived the Civil War, wouldn't be married to Violet now, and most certainly wouldn't be standing before the Duke of Portland, discussing his business aims.

"Sir," he replied resolutely, "I never give up hope. It defeats a man, and I am never defeated."

Portland didn't respond immediately but stared critically past

Sam, not quite making eye contact. Had Sam somehow sealed Portland's poor opinion of Americans?

When the duke finally spoke, though, his words were nothing Sam expected. "Yes, I suppose a man is defeated when he has lost *all* hope. It is deciding where hope is warranted and where it is best extinguished that is the conundrum. However, Mr. Harper, I believe that in your case, clinging to hope may have its reward. The sticking point here is what to do to make you acceptable in British eyes."

Bentinck nodded understanding of his brother's intent. "I'm a trustee for the British Museum," Bentinck said to Sam before turning to his brother. "Perhaps to elevate his status a bit, we should give Harper a position there. Perhaps . . ." He rubbed his chin and addressed Sam once more. "Perhaps you could be curator of our firearms collection. Ha! An American managing a collection of munitions for Great Britain. We shall have to ensure you don't decide to rebel against us again, won't we? Ha!"

Sam wasn't sure if the man was joking or serious about the position, so he remained silent.

"That may or may not be the right solution, but I believe it suggests that we can come up with one. Mr. Harper, I believe I should like to invest in your dynamite idea, and I can be of help in convincing the government to let you build. Would a thousand pounds be enough to start you on your way?"

Now it was Sam's turn for his mouth to drop open. "Pardon me? How much did you say?"

"A thousand. I expect a return on my investment, of course. Something far better than the infernal government bonds of which I cannot seem to divest myself. I shall also expect to be able to inspect your factory periodically. Have you considered building one in Nottinghamshire? Hmm, perhaps I can build a tunnel to it if it is close enough to Welbeck."

Sam couldn't believe what he was hearing. He was ready to exclaim that he would build his dynamite factory upon Welbeck grounds itself if the duke were willing to endow the project. Nobel would be beside himself when he read the news. Sam would have to send a telegram right away. But first he must attend to details.

"A dynamite factory in Nottinghamshire would be ideally situated, given the number of coal mines sitting atop the Nottingham coalfield," he said. "However, Your Grace, I don't know how close I can make it to Welbeck, given that I would put it far outside of town and I—"

Portland held up a hand. "I am not serious about the factory being close to Welbeck. Let us repair to the shooting hut to celebrate over a very old bottle of Taylor's I've been saving."

"What could you possibly be saving it for?" Bentinck asked. "A weekend card party? Ha!"

They returned to the Russian Lodge to drink port, with Bentinck joking about his brother's vast subterranean wine cellar, suggesting that they transplant themselves down there so that they didn't have to wait so long for another dusty bottle to arrive. Sam waited for a "Ha!" which for once did not arrive. Instead, Bentinck turned serious—perhaps it was the port weighing down his mind—and turned to the uncomfortable topic of the deaths that had occurred at Welbeck Abbey.

"They say that death comes in threes," he said, shuddering. "You've had two in the past week, John. You should expect a third soon."

"Come, brother, you're being superstitious, like my servants. My cook, Mrs. Garside, also frets over it. Ever since Aristotle died, she has—Ah, there you have it. There have already been three."

"A raven hardly qualifies as a noteworthy death. You mock me, John, but I warn you there is more to come. You would do well to heed me."

Portland shrugged in bland denial.

For someone who Violet said was concerned about his servants, Portland seemed rather indifferent today about the loss of two estate workers. Was he simply—like Sam himself—caught up in the moment of relaxation and camaraderie, or was he genuinely unconcerned about it? After all, he was a peer of the land with innumerable people under his charge. What were a couple of employees he had likely never met?

As the brothers changed topics once more to world events,

Bentinck's comments were soon lost in the smoky tendrils wafting upward from cigars Portland passed around.

Stretched back in a leather chair, his feet up on a worn ottoman shared with a softly snoring vizsla and a never-empty glass of savory port swirling in his hand as he and the brothers discussed the currently chilly state of trade negotiations between the United States and Britain, Sam decided that the aristocratic life might have its worries and threats, but it was certainly filled with physical pleasures not easily forgotten or forgone—unlike his coal mine, which, truth be told, he would happily be divested of.

Could he have enough success with a dynamite factory that one day he and Violet could have a country retreat? A place where he could shoot and she could . . . Wait, what did his wife enjoy other than working with dead bodies? Oh yes, Violet could lounge about in the sunshine, reading from her pile of books. In fact, she could have a room full of groaning bookshelves. All of these country estates had libraries, didn't they? The only difference being that Violet would make use of one.

Unfortunately, there would indeed be more death for Violet to contend with before the pleasant dream of a country estate could be realized.

21

Violet was happy to spend the day with her friend Mary Cooke. Despite their age difference of twenty years, they had much in common. Both had been widowed; both were in the funeral business, as Mary was a mourning dressmaker; and both loved to read.

Violet took a cab to her own shop in Queen's Road to check on the state of business with her co-owner, Harry Blundell, then went on to Mary's shop in Bayswater Road. Together the two women headed out, their first destination being Hatchards Bookshop in Piccadilly. After the seriousness of Welbeck Abbey and the attack upon her three days earlier, Violet was in the mood for something romantic in nature.

The clerk at Hatchards asked if she had read anything by Charlotte Yonge. When she said she hadn't, he immediately showed her to a shelf crammed with several titles by Yonge. "She writes the most heart-tugging novels. She's been popular for years. You're sure you haven't read her before, madam? No? Then I recommend that you start with *The Heir of Redclyffe,* her first and best-known work."

He pulled out a copy and handed it to Violet, who flipped through the pages, enjoying the feel of the thick, creamy paper that was always the immediate reward in purchasing a book.

Violet smiled at the clerk and handed the book to him. "Please wrap this for me."

The clerk bowed with the book in both hands. "Of course. Once you've read this, I recommend *The Daisy Chain*, then *The Chaplet of Pearls*, which was just published last year. I daresay that Miss Yonge's works are more popular than those of Mr. Dickens and Mr. Thackeray."

Violet tucked the book safely in her reticule, next to the knife that stayed with her at all times, despite its recent ineffectiveness. The two women were soon ensconced in a growler cab heading to Regent Street, where Mary wanted to visit Grover & Baker's.

"They are two American men from Boston who have developed a portable sewing machine, and have expanded their trade to London and Liverpool," Mary said. Violet leaned back inside the conveyance, one of the more comfortable carriages for hire since it had four wheels, not two.

"I read in one of my dressmaking journals that they offer tours so customers can see their machines being built. Misters Grover and Baker are making over a thousand machines per week! Can you imagine? How fantastic they must be." Mary's eyes shone with the excitement of a child being presented with a new flavor of ribbon candy.

"Is there anything wrong with your Singer foot-treadle model?" Violet asked.

"No, no, I just thought it would be fascinating to see a new type of sewing machine being constructed. The journal article stated that one day they will be even bigger than Singer."

However, Mary ultimately succumbed to the oily smell and rhythmic hum of the various machines on display and purchased one that Violet thought too pricey for Mary's circumstances, but hadn't Violet herself fallen victim to the bewitchery of a coffin salesman's samples before?

Later, after the man at Grover & Baker promised delivery of her specially made portable machine in two weeks, the women stopped at a coffee shop to celebrate Mary's purchase, which still had Violet breathless at the expense.

Mary, though, was undaunted. "Wasn't it marvelous?" she said, removing her hat and gloves and handing them to the hostess. "I can hardly wait to make my first dress with it. And I can even move it from my shop to my upstairs flat because it's *portable*, Violet dear. Have you ever seen such a thing?" She patted the puffy gray cloud of hair she wore.

Given the size of the wood box and its internal ironworks, Violet imagined that "portable," in this case, merely meant that the machine could be put on a lift and sent upstairs, but it couldn't exactly be carried about by a handle. It was as portable as one of her coffins. But she couldn't deny her friend's enthusiasm.

"You will have thousands of hours of sewing enjoyment, I'm sure," she said.

Once they had pots of coffee and raisin crumpets topped with butter and jam in front of them, the two women drifted into various points of conversation: Violet's daughter, Susanna; Mary's recent clientele; and Violet's upcoming trip to Egypt. Violet told Mary of the suspicious deaths at Welbeck Abbey and her subsequent trip to London for an investigation. As Violet recounted the attack in Cavendish Square, Mary spilled her cup of coffee, the brown liquid splashing into its saucer and onto the table.

"My dear, no! Not another dire situation! How do you manage it?"

Violet shook her head. "I don't know. Undertaking seems to have gotten more and more dangerous as time goes on."

"It's all of this investigating you do these days. Oh, honestly." Mary grimaced. "This coffee has obviously been *boiled*. Dreadful."

Violet agreed that it was atrocious. "I suspect they make it in quantity twice a week, to be heated up when ordered. This was probably made last Thursday."

Mary giggled, and Violet joined her. Seeing Mary express joy made Violet happy, as well. She was about to comment on her friend's seeming contentment when Mary asked a question that stopped Violet cold. "How is that handsome detective who has helped you in your investigative matters?"

Had Mary actually just batted her eyelashes? And did she think for one moment that she was convincing in her pretense of not remembering Hurst's name?

"Has he visited you or otherwise made contact with you?" Violet asked, too sharply. She wanted her friend to be happy, but why oh why did it have to be with Magnus Pompey Hurst? Inspector Hurst had developed a puppy-like devotion to Mary since meeting her several months ago, but Violet had been stern in warning him away from her friend, so recently in mourning for her husband, George. George had been an unfaithful fool, and Mary's grief was already perfunctory, but it was just . . . unseemly . . . for Hurst to express interest.

"Of course not, dear. I'm only in my fourth month of mourning. I just remember how kind and helpful he was with assisting me in hanging the draperies for your shop. Such a brave, chivalrous man. I don't wonder that it must be a delight for you to work with him."

Violet could see that Mary was refraining from asking the question she truly wanted to ask: Was Inspector Hurst attached?

The answer—that Hurst was a bachelor and obviously enamored of Mary—stuck in Violet's throat like an unchewed dumpling. Why was she so resistant to the idea of Hurst paying court to her friend? Did she believe that his gruff and overbearing manner would eventually assert itself and cause yet more heartbreak for Mary? Or was it that Violet was terrified for *herself* that a romance might bloom between the two? What sort of chaperone would she have to play? Would she and Sam be invited to dine with the other couple? After her last investigation—during which Sam nearly came to blows with Hurst—Violet wasn't sure a peaceable meal was possible. When had Mary taken notice of Hurst, anyway?

But Mary's hopeful expression was too much for Violet to bear. The woman deserved some happiness, and if it could be had with Inspector Hurst, well . . . Violet swallowed the lump and said, "The inspector is a bachelor, you know." Mary's eyes lit up, so Violet swallowed once more and continued. "I believe he finds you most attractive."

Mary's cheeks reddened, and she buried herself in the previously detested coffee as though it were suddenly apricot nectar.

Perhaps she would mention Mary's interest to Inspector Hurst. Much as she dreaded the thought of the bearish detective paying court to her friend when her mourning period was over, Violet didn't want to be responsible for preventing Mary's happiness.

Violet sighed and picked up her own coffee cup. She could

hardly believe she would willingly draw Hurst's cranky disposition into her own life.

After escorting Mary back to her dressmaking shop, Violet headed back to Marylebone, where she found Inspectors Hurst and Pratt sitting in the parlor with Lady Howard de Walden. Unlike her behavior during their first visit, this time the baroness politely excused herself from the room, leaving Violet alone with the detectives.

Hurst was more congenial today. He had been much more mercurial since meeting Mary, and Violet suspected he wanted to be cordial to her for Mary's sake, but it wasn't in his nature to do so, what with his perception that Violet was troublesome.

"You've returned quickly, Inspector," she said, taking the warm seat that the baroness had just vacated.

"Scotland Yard is always efficient, Mrs. Harper. Although I'm afraid our information isn't as salacious as you might have hoped it would be," Inspector Hurst said, waving at Pratt.

The junior detective flipped through his battered notebook. "Colonel George William David Mortimer, formerly of the Grenadier Guards, having served at the pleasure of His Majesty King George IV from 1818 to 1830, with fighting experienced during the Anglo-Burmese War from 1824 to 1825. Colonel Mortimer has a residence in Arlington Street overlooking Green Park."

"Green Park? How can that be?" Violet said, confused. How was it possible that Colonel Mortimer—who was relying on Portland's generosity for the very roof over his head—had a townhome in fashionable Green Park?

Hurst shrugged. "Many gents and ladies live there. Go on, Pratt."

Pratt ran his finger down the page until he picked up where he left off. "A year after leaving the army, the colonel married Esther Theodosia Bell, but she died shortly thereafter of unknown causes. The couple had no children. The colonel then became interested in railroads and invested a fair amount in them, making enough to enable him to move to Green Park. As far as anyone knows, the colonel has never again considered marriage. His neighbors say he is a quiet and considerate gentleman, even if he is a merchant up-start."

"No doubt," Violet said absently, trying to make sense of what Pratt had just told her. Was Colonel Mortimer's presence in Nottinghamshire as a poverty-stricken friend simply a ruse for him to keep an eye on his old army companion? Was it really the colonel looking out for Portland's well-being instead of the other way around?

Or was the colonel up to something that Violet couldn't fathom?

At this point, she was sure tongues in Green Park were wagging faster than a telegraph operator's finger making a war announcement. It wasn't often that Scotland Yard detectives came prowling around such a neighborhood.

"One last thing," Pratt added. "Most of his neighbors didn't recall him enough to have an opinion of him, but those who did said that Colonel Mortimer suffers from insomnia, for whatever that's worth."

It was worth much, for it explained the colonel's night wanderings around Welbeck Abbey. But was he somehow using that insomnia for some devious purpose? Violet had no idea what that purpose could be. Worse, was Portland fully aware of what the colonel was doing? Was the colonel doing it on Portland's behalf?

Violet was thoroughly confused, but Hurst was about to make her much more so.

"This Jack LeCato you asked about. He's a clerk who works for the chancellor of the exchequer and was installed at Welbeck Abbey for unknown purposes by the Speaker of the House, Evelyn Denison. Interestingly, Denison happens to be the Duke of Portland's brother-in-law. That was all we could get from our sources at the treasury. They were very secretive about whatever it is LeCato is doing."

Violet stared at the detective, speechless as her mind worked rapidly to make sense of what Hurst had just told her. She remembered Denison from an investigative matter she had worked for the queen, one that had her sitting through a parliamentary debate on the Contagious Diseases Act that Denison had overseen.

The duke was infuriated by the presence of Jack LeCato . . .

who had been installed at Welbeck by his own brother-in-law? Why would Denison have done something so egregious against his wife's brother?

Every time Violet sought an answer in this matter, a dozen more questions shot up as if she had riotous Guy Fawkes Day fireworks skyrocketing in her mind. Enough with the ongoing questions. She needed *answers*.

But Hurst had his own questions. "This Colonel Mortimer bloke seems harmless enough. What has you so agitated about him?" he asked.

Without the baroness present, Violet was more comfortable talking about him. "He resides at Welbeck . . . as His Grace's impoverished guest." She went on to explain the men's military experience together.

Hurst frowned. "Does His Grace know that the colonel is well-off?"

"I don't think he does. Curious, isn't it?"

"Maybe," Hurst said. "Do you suspect him of something other than taking advantage of his host?"

Violet sighed and echoed Hurst's own sentiments. "Maybe. I'm not sure."

"Well, there's nothing here for Scotland Yard to be worried about," Hurst said, rising. Pratt also stood, and Violet joined them.

"What about Ian Hale having attacked me here in Cavendish Square?" Violet said.

"First of all, he's left London without a trace. Second, you weren't actually murdered, Mrs. Harper, and so it isn't a case for Scotland Yard. It was a great favor to you that Inspector Pratt and I did the investigating that we did. We have to return to our real cases." He motioned to Pratt to leave.

As blunt as the detective had been, he was correct. There was no shocking murder to be investigated, so it was a matter for the police, not Scotland Yard. Violet knew she should be grateful for what he had done thus far. Well, there was one way to express her gratitude.

"I saw my friend Mary Cooke today," Violet said. Hurst turned back, standing up straighter, while Pratt arched his eyebrows in surprise. The junior detective knew of his superior's interest in Mary, and was also fully aware of Violet's disapproval.

"Oh yes, your dressmaker friend," Hurst said casually. Pratt rolled his eyes, out of Hurst's sight.

Violet took a deep breath. "She has been recovering well in her mourning. In fact, she's just purchased a new Grover and Baker sewing machine to assist her in her business. It's one of their new portable machines, which probably weighs a hundred pounds. It will be delivered in two weeks, and I'm not sure how she will move it around her shop."

Hurst perked up even further. "Does she need help setting up the machine? I'm sure I can stop by on my way home from the Yard one evening and—"

"Perhaps, Inspector. I shall mention it to her." Was that an actual bounce in Hurst's step as he left Harcourt House?

There. She had instigated . . . what? A romance between a centurion and a vestal virgin? Between the wolf and Red Riding Hood? Well, at least nothing would happen until Mary's mourning was complete.

In the meantime, she had an audience with Mr. Gladstone in the morning. Perhaps the answers she sought lay with him.

22

Violet waited for nearly an hour beyond her scheduled appointment until Gladstone's clerk called her into the prime minister's office. Fortunately, she had brought her copy of *The Heir of Redclyffe* with her, and was thoroughly absorbed in the misfortunes of poor Guy Morville when she was called back to sit before the prime minister.

William Ewart Gladstone was much as Violet had remembered him, with a scowl that was nearly buried under unruly white hair and elephantine ears. What she hadn't recalled was that he was missing most of the forefinger of his left hand.

Before acknowledging her greeting, he noticed what she had thought was her unobtrusive glance at his hand. "Lost it in a hunting accident back in '42," he said, opening a drawer in his desk and retrieving a black leather finger sheath from it, buckling it over his wrist.

Violet wasn't interested in Gladstone's prosthetics, however; she wanted information about Jack LeCato. She explained to the prime minister the situation at Welbeck Abbey and inquired about the government clerk's activities.

What Violet quickly realized was that Gladstone's scowl didn't mean he was angry or petulant, but merely that he was passionate about topics that concerned him. And he was concerned greatly about the Duke of Portland.

"Yes, Mr. LeCato is an agent of the chancellor of the exchequer.

You must understand, Mrs. Harper, that His Grace purchased nearly two million pounds in consol bonds a few years back from the government, and all of a sudden wishes to turn them in so that he can finance all of his ludicrous building projects. We need the money for those bonds to pay the ongoing debt from the expedition to Abyssinia."

Abyssinia? Violet reached into her memory, struggling to remember what she knew about that country.

Seeing her confusion, Gladstone explained, "Two years ago, we went on a rescue mission against Emperor Theodore, who kidnapped some Christian missionaries for propaganda reasons—appalling, given that the emperor was a Coptic Christian himself. We couldn't allow some minor despot to run roughshod over British interests, encouraging others to do the like. Locking away our citizens—can you imagine? We discovered later that they were chained and severely treated." Gladstone was working himself into a righteous high dudgeon.

"Of course you're right," Violet murmured, using the voice she employed for comforting the most aggrieved of mourners.

"Well," he continued, "it was one of the most expensive affairs of honor in our nation's history, as it required the transportation of a sizable military force across hundreds of miles of mountainous terrain that contained practically no road system. Savages, these Abyssinians." Gladstone stopped pacing long enough to pour himself a drink from a crystal decanter. He took a long swallow and a deep breath, then continued without offering Violet any refreshment. "Good Lord, we assembled a force of thirteen thousand British and Indian soldiers, built railways, purchased elephants for armament transport, and erected lighthouses and warehouses, all to rescue a half dozen men." He shook his head dolefully.

"You did rescue them?" Violet asked.

"Yes. For a mere cost of nine million pounds, we rescued the missionaries. Of course, this represented an enormous unplanned expenditure of one-eighth of our annual budget. We couldn't simply raise taxes to immediately collect the revenues, so we appealed to the patriotism of England's wealthiest to procure consols to permit the government to gradually ease in the eventual tax burden. Quite the news to deliver to the British subjects, eh, Mrs. Harper?" Gladstone started to pour more liquor, then put the bottle down, seeming to think the better of it.

"But it ended much worse than that," he continued. "On top of it all, the troops appropriated fifteen elephants and two hundred donkeys to load up with treasure they appropriated from churches and other buildings. Instead of sending it back to the Crown to pay for the war effort, the army simply divided it up as spoils of war and it all disappeared. When did we hire barbarians to serve Her Majesty?"

Violet could think of no words of comfort to offer the prime minister.

"I see you're reading one of Mrs. Yonge's novels," Gladstone said, completely changing the subject and pointing to the book that Violet had absentmindedly dropped into her lap.

"Oh, I forgot to put it away," she said, tucking it into her reticule.

"I am a great admirer of her works," Gladstone said. "Have you read *The Dove in the Eagle's Nest* or *The Prince and the Page*? No? I highly recommend them as excellent historical novels."

Violet was taken aback that the prime minister should be so interested in light novel reading and said so.

"Lord Tennyson, Lewis Carroll, and Anthony Trollope all read Mrs. Yonge's books," Gladstone said proudly, as if he were somehow responsible for these famous writers becoming Charlotte Yonge's admirers.

"Yes, but about Mr. LeCato . . ." Violet said.

"Right. No one knew how expensive the expedition would be, and there have been great debates in Parliament over new taxes and other ways to raise revenues. Meanwhile, while Britain is in this terrible quandary, I received word that Portland was demanding return of his entire investment in consols that were being used specifically to repay some of the debt from the Abyssinian venture. Hard to imagine Portland wants his money back just so he can build his godforsaken tunnels and skating rinks. I refuse to allow the empire to default on its good name so that a housemaid can scrabble around on wheels!"

Gladstone was once more working himself into a frenzy, and Violet still didn't have the answer she sought. "And Mr. LeCato went to Welbeck Abbey because . . ." She let the words dangle, in hopes that the prime minister would get back on course.

"Damned inconsiderate of Portland to do it, I say. Of what importance is an unnecessary building project compared to the financing of a military undertaking and loyalty to your country?"

Violet tried once more, attempting to tamp down her impatience, particularly since the man was making her dizzy with his rapid volleys around the room. Heavens, was this what she looked like when she paced? "Your frustration is understandable, sir. Perhaps you might tell me how Jack LeCato became part of your predicament?"

"Yes. Right. We needed to convince the duke to delay some of his building projects. If they were delayed, he might be less inclined to demand the return of his investment in the consols. So I told Denison to find someone he could put in there to do it. I didn't care what story he had to concoct. I needed to stop Portland from cashing in his bonds and work out a reasonable arrangement."

"You mean to say you asked the Speaker of the House to do this?"

"Of course. Who else would I mean?"

So Hurst's information had been correct. What did it mean that Portland's brother-in-law was involved in the whole mess? Perhaps nothing, perhaps . . . who knew?

"Why was Mr. LeCato chosen in particular?" she asked.

Gladstone shrugged. "It's none of my affair. You'll have to see Denison yourself for that answer. I suppose you'll want a letter of introduction?" He sat at his desk and pulled a thick sheet of paper from a stack, smoothed it with his finger-sheathed hand, picked up a pen, and began scribbling with his right hand. When he was done, he looked up. "That reminds me, Mrs. Harper. The queen says you're to be invited to the opening ceremony for the Suez Canal and invitations are to go out presently. Shall I inform her lord chamberlain that your current address is Nottinghamshire?"

"Yes, thank you." The way things were proceeding, Violet and Sam would have no time to return to London together before boarding a ship for Egypt. She only hoped that justice would be done for Burton Spencer and Edward Bayes before she stepped up the gangway and on to her passage to Africa.

Obtaining an audience with Evelyn Denison was much faster than getting one with Gladstone, and Violet was in front of the man inside of the hour.

Denison was tall and lanky like Portland, but much more self-assured. His office reminded Violet of a law office, with its book-case shelves bowed under the weight of heavy tomes, stacks of papers and documents on his desk, and long judicial wigs propped up on floor stands in a corner of the room. Violet remembered that the Speaker wore a special robe and hairpiece when he held parliamentary sessions.

Although the stacks on his desk were neat, they were still towering. Despite this, Denison overlooked it all, even from his seated position behind the massive piece of carved oak.

He glanced up distractedly at Violet. "A moment, please," he said, and went back to writing what appeared to be a very long letter. Denison was either angry or passionate about the topic, for he vigorously underscored words several times.

Eventually, he signed the letter and pushed it off to one side. "Mrs. Harper, I believe? You have come at Gladstone's request?"

"Yes, sir, thank you for seeing me." Violet had no idea what the proper etiquette was for addressing the Speaker of the House of Commons. "Sir" always seemed adequate when all else failed. "I've come about an agent of yours, Jack LeCato."

Denison's eyes narrowed. "What of him? How do you know him?"

Once more, Violet explained her situation at Welbeck, and also informed the Speaker of her conversation with Gladstone.

Denison sighed. "I tried to tell the prime minister that I have no control over what my brother-in-law does, but he insisted that I put a man in there to influence Portland's efforts. Does Portland know that I appointed LeCato?" There was genuine worry in his expression.

"No, sir, not to my knowledge. Actually, I think he believes Gladstone put him there."

Denison blew out a breath of relief. "Thank God. I knew LeCato was trustworthy, but one never knows how these things will go."

Violet foresaw eventual trouble between Portland and Denison. After all, for how long could this actually remain a secret, despite LeCato's supposed trustworthiness?

"You were placed in a most difficult position," Violet said, hoping to elicit more information.

"Gladstone was only trying to protect the party," Denison replied. "He felt that my brother-in-law calling in his bonds had the potential to stifle the British economy and he had to be brought to heel. There was simply no way to cover those bonds all at once. If the government is unable to cover its obligations, the economy will likely stall, meaning the end of Liberal Party rule. That couldn't happen, and Gladstone decided our best chance to stay in control of Parliament was to . . . influence . . . my brother-in-law."

"I would say that is an ambitious goal. His Grace is very . . ." Violet was at a loss for description.

Denison nodded. "I agree. Now, Mrs Harper, ordinarily I would not permit a mere undertaker to question me, but Gladstone's letter was most insistent. However, if there is nothing else, I must get back to my—"

But Violet wasn't nearly done. "In fact, sir, I have an important question. Who is Mr. LeCato? Why was he the man you appointed?"

Denison put down the pen he had just picked up. "Jack LeCato is an assistant to Robert Lowe, the chancellor of the exchequer. LeCato had a reputation of being very serious and very eager to do his duty, a trait probably carried over from his time in the navy. I also knew from various sources that he was very eager to leave Lowe's employ."

"Why is that?" Violet asked.

"Robert Lowe is wretchedly deficient. Spending has risen, and he constantly underestimates revenue. There are other issues brewing at the chancellor's office that might sweep LeCato out the door with Lowe, and LeCato wanted to rid himself of Lowe's stench, and the Welbeck situation provided a good solution for us both."

"I see." The explanation was quite . . . tidy, but was it perhaps *too* tidy? Or was Violet frustrated because there was nothing in what the Speaker—or the prime minister, for that matter—had said to implicate LeCato in anything that had to do with Spencer or Bayes?

She had one further question. "Do you know if Mr. LeCato has any association with Babbage's Home for Foundlings?"

Denison frowned. "An orphanage? I don't think so. Why?"

She decided against telling the Speaker about the attack. "Just a silly thought I had. Not worth mentioning. It appears that you have been working on some theological discourses," she said as a distraction. Several of the papers on his desk had biblical references on them.

Denison was easily led away from their previous discussion. "Yes, for quite some time I have seen the need for a plain but complete Bible commentary, something easily accessible by the public. After many meetings with some of the bishops, it was decided that the archbishop of York would undertake the production of the commentary. The canon of Exeter, Frederick Cook, has just been chosen to edit it. As the commentary has my endorsement and support, I am naturally most interested in all aspects of it, and I not only helped to put together the advisory panel for the project, but have been providing Mr. Cook with helpful suggestions." Denison tapped the letter he had just signed. "Today I am advising him to divide the Bible into eight sections, and for each section choose a different scholar to provide commentary."

Violet could only imagine how . . . appreciative . . . the canon would be of Denison's regular missives advising him on how to do his work. The Speaker and Reverend Appleton had much in common and would probably enjoy a good theological debate together.

She left Denison's office shortly thereafter. Later, as she reflected upon her meeting with him, it seemed to Violet that a man who was interested in assembling a biblical commentary couldn't possibly be involved with anyone or anything particularly depraved.

However, Denison had said something that was rubbing at the back of her mind, like the tide against a rock, wearing away layers as it tries to reach a central core. What was it?

Ah, now Violet remembered. He had said that LeCato had served in the navy. It reminded her of Edward Bayes, who, according to his wife, had also served in the navy. Had the two men known each other? Did LeCato have a similar tattoo?

Despite his association with the seemingly righteous Evelyn Denison, did LeCato's presence at Welbeck have a more sinister purpose?

23

*

Back in Worksop, Violet stopped first at the telegram office, as it had occurred to her that if the telegram to Ian Hale instructing him to assault her had been sent from someone at Welbeck, it would have been done here.

She handed the clerk her most recent *carte de visite*, which featured a photograph of her seated next to an upright coffin, with urns of lilies on the floor surrounding them and a spread of mourning cards arrayed in Violet's lap. Unfortunately, the clerk there had no helpful information in response to her questions and handed the card back to her, holding it between a thumb and forefinger as though it was a picture of a dead mouse. She turned to leave, but a strapping young man burst into the telegram office, nearly knocking her over.

"Telegram to London from Welbeck Abbey!" he shouted to the clerk, who smiled at the boisterous announcement.

"Right you are, Gilbert," the clerk said. The rest was lost to Violet as she stepped outside. She waited, though, for the Welbeck employee to leave the telegram office, where she fell into step with him as he made his way back to a horse and cart parked nearby.

"Pardon me," she said. "I heard you say you had a telegram from Welbeck Abbey."

The young man named Gilbert stopped in front of a chemist's shop. "Yes," he said, frowning as if trying to place who Violet might be.

"My name is Violet Harper. I was the undertaker for Burton Spencer's funeral. Did you know him?"

Gilbert's expression immediately turned downcast. "Of course, m'um, I'm Gilbert Lewis. I was at his funeral. We was all there."

This piqued Violet's interest. "We? Whom do you mean?"

"All of us home children."

"Home children? I don't understand." Violet had never heard this term before.

"There's this lady, Mrs. MacPherson. She pays for us to emigrate to distribution homes in Canada, and people hire us, for farms and factories. She says we will have a better life there than we can ever have in London."

"Where do you go in Canada?"

"Some of us go to Ontario, some to Quebec. I'm to go to Belleville, Ontario."

"I see." In reality, Violet had no understanding of what Lewis was talking about. Perhaps it was best to stick to her point. "I was wondering if I might ask a question about the tele—"

At that moment, a barouche drawn by two pairs of horses came trundling by, the wheels on Violet's side crashing through a deep rut and splattering mud against Violet's dress. Flecks of it splattered against her cheek.

Gilbert glowered at the passing carriage. "They was from Worksop Manor. It borders His Grace's land. The Dukes of Norfolk aren't always mannerly-like. May I fetch you a cloth of some sort, m'um?"

"No, I'm quite all right." Violet wiped under her eyes with a gloved hand, confident that she had only succeeded in smearing the dirt and turning herself into a good likeness of one of the raccoons she'd seen back in Colorado. However, her pathetic state earned her sympathy from the young man, who said, "You have a question for me?"

"Yes, about the telegram message you just delivered."

Gilbert resumed walking. "Yes, m'um, it was a rush order for machine parts from London. It's nothing special." He readily pulled the handwritten missive from his pocket and handed it over for Violet to examine. "Is there something wrong with it?"

As far as Violet could tell, it was indeed just an order for gears and springs to be delivered from the Charles Porter Engine Company. "Do you deliver these messages frequently?"

"Of course. There's always machinery breaking down and supplies to be ordered for His Grace's projects. Mr. Reed says I'm his best runner for telegrams because I am so quick about it. He says he will be short two men when I leave for Canada." This was obviously a point of pride for Lewis.

"Are the telegrams ever for anything other than the ordering of construction materials?"

Lewis was confused. "What else would His Grace need for his building projects?"

"No, you're quite right, of course." It appeared as though the telegram to Ian Hale had not originated at Welbeck Abbey—or if it had, Gilbert Lewis, the regular runner to Worksop, had not taken it to the telegram office. Yet another unresolved question to add to her rapidly growing list of them.

"So . . . how old are you?" she asked. She was still curious about Lewis's description of these so-called "home children."

"Sixteen, m'um."

"And how old was Burton Spencer?"

"He was older. Seventeen, m'um."

Poor murdered Burton Spencer was but a seventeen-year-old boy? He had been large and maturely formed, though, like Lewis. Were home children selected based on who appeared to be better suited for hard work?

But Violet was still confused. "If you're bound for Canada, why are you at Welbeck Abbey?"

"His Grace has agreed to take on some home children to learn a trade before we're sent over, so that we can have every advantage. We're paid just like regular workers"—the boy puffed his chest with pride—"and Mr. Reed saves it all for us orphan boys so we have plenty in our pockets when we get to Canada. I think I might even have my own farm one day."

This was yet another facet of the enigmatic Duke of Portland that Violet hadn't known. The man gave every impression of disliking the presence of others, yet he was very caring and involved when it came to his workers. And yet these home children could hardly be called his workers since they were essentially just stopping over at Welbeck on their way to a transatlantic voyage to Canada.

Actually, she could think of no benefit Portland derived by extending temporary positions to these unskilled boys. He must do it purely to do good. How would she ever comprehend the man?

She parted from Gilbert and returned to the chemist's for some cloths to take care of her face. Her bespattered gown would have to remain in that condition a while longer, as her curiosity about home children was growing with each passing second. Instead of going to Worksop Inn to change her dress, she immediately headed to Welbeck Abbey to visit Ellery Reed. Why had he concealed from her that Burton Spencer was a home child?

She wondered if Spencer's death had anything to do with his home child status. But why would someone want to kill a young man—a boy, really—for being an orphan?

Violet's breath caught. Ian Hale had worked for an orphanage. Was he somehow involved in the home children program? But even if he was, why had he tried to kill Violet? For heaven's sake, she hadn't even known about home children until a few moments ago.

She remembered what the note to Hale said. *Her inquiries are getting closer to my treasure.* But if the home children were the treasure in question, how was it that Violet was getting "closer" to them, other than that she had prepared Spencer's body for burial?

In no way could she even begin to fathom what Edward Bayes had to do with it all.

Nothing made any sense.

Ellery Reed was just coming out of his cottage when Violet arrived. He wore a brown vest already filthy from the new day's work, and held some odd hand tool with iron teeth. "Ah, Mrs. Harper, you are still with us," he said, putting the tool down to one side. "It looks as though you have had the worse end of a fight with a pig." He chuckled amiably, his words inoffensive.

"I'm afraid I lost against a passing carriage," Violet replied.

"Ah yes, there is no use going up against the wheeled beasts. How may I help you?"

"I met Gilbert Lewis in Worksop a short while ago. He mentioned something very interesting to me, that he was one of several home children on the estate." Violet watched closely for Reed's reaction, but it was bland.

"Yes, we have nine of them—no, eight. I can't seem to accept that Burton is gone now." Reed passed a hand across his eyes.

"You never mentioned this to me, sir. I didn't know that Burton Spencer was a mere boy of seventeen—as large as he was—and that he was part of the home children arrangement. Why didn't you tell me?"

Reed looked at her quizzically. "Mrs. Harper, was his orphan status relevant to his death? I try not to point out the orphans' status to others, lest the other workers look down upon them. The boys are only here for a short time, and there's no point in other workers viewing them as lesser beings because they are both orphans and not here permanently. His Grace wants them treated equally. They are paid just as fairly for the work they do as the other men, and they share the same meals."

"According to Gilbert, they aren't exactly paid. He says you are saving their money for them, and have promised to give it all to them upon their departure."

"That is true." Reed sighed heavily. "Would you care to see my accounting ledger for the boys?"

"Yes, sir, I would."

She followed him into his cottage, which was modeled much like Colonel Mortimer's, except that it was sparsely furnished and neatly kept. Disappearing momentarily into another room, he came back with a key attached to a long chain. He pushed aside a chair positioned against a wall and inserted the key into a lock recessed in the wall. Part of the wall sprang open on a hinge.

"His Grace likes certain things to be kept hidden from prying eyes. I must assume you are here on his business, and aren't just a nosy hen."

Violet swallowed a retort as Reed got onto his knees and dug around in the opening. "Here we are." He rose carrying a large ledger, similar to the one she used in her own undertaking business. He plopped the book down on a table, the thud reverberating through the largely barren room. Reed flipped through the pages and stopped in a certain place, pointing down for Violet to see.

"This is the current group of boys, who arrived back in March. You can see here that at the end of each week I credit each boy with his wages. I will total it all up in this column just before they leave."

Violet followed along, noting that there was a long line drawn through Burton Spencer's name. "What happened to Burton Spencer's savings?"

"I divided his money up among the other boys. You can see here where I added a portion to each boy's account. It didn't seem right for His Grace to just keep the money, and he agreed that it should be distributed among the others. A sad turn of affairs it was with Spencer, but I suppose there is solace in that the other orphan boys will have some benefit from his death."

"Yes," Violet agreed, although it seemed a high price for Burton Spencer to have paid for the dividing of his seven months' worth of spoils across eight other boys. Surely one of the other boys hadn't killed him for this reason. How could any of them have assumed even for a moment that Spencer's savings would be divided up this way? There would have been no benefit to such an act, anyway. They were all headed to new homes and guaranteed employment. There was no need to commit murder for just a few coins.

Violet still needed to know what connection the boys at Welbeck had to any London orphanages.

"Do the boys leave Welbeck at various times, or do they travel together?" she asked.

"Usually they all leave together, then Mrs. MacPherson arranges for another round of boys through various orphanages."

"Including Babbage's Home for Foundlings?"

Reed shook his head. "I don't know. Perhaps. Quite honestly, Mrs. Harper, I don't keep track of where they have come from because it doesn't matter, and I only make note of where they are going because it is important to the young men to look forward to the next place they will call home. I remind them regularly of their futures."

"Do any of them ever stay on here at Welbeck instead of going to Canada?"

"No, never. There is always a farmer or factory owner who has paid good money to have a strapping young worker sent to him. They always go, except of course . . ." Reed's words trailed off.

Except in the case of Burton Spencer. "Did His Grace reimburse Spencer's Canadian patron after the boy's death?" Violet asked.

"I believe there was some arrangement made to compensate the man, although I wasn't privy to the details."

Violet was empty of questions. It was certainly a striking coincidence that she was attacked by a man who worked for an orphanage and it turned out that a group of home children were in residence at Welbeck Abbey. However, she couldn't figure any way in which the coincidence had anything to do with Burton Spencer's death, much less that of Edward Bayes. She needed more information, and that meant another visit to Martin Chandler. She hadn't forgotten that it was he who had called her a raven during Spencer's funeral, and that Hale's telegram referred to her that same way.

She thanked Reed and said her farewells.

"I hope you are able to discover whatever it is you are seeking, Mrs. Harper," Reed said as he escorted her out and picked up his tool again.

"So do I," Violet said, wondering what exactly it was she was even searching for anymore.

Chandler was feeding the ravens and a couple of hawks from a pile of dead mice when Violet arrived. Some of the carcasses had been split open, exposing the rodents' flesh—and the odor of decay—to the birds, who were all grasping perches as they waited their turns for a tasty morsel, uttering various caws and mild screeches in their impatience to eat. Chandler had obviously trained them well, for none of them jumped at the falconer or attempted to steal food out of turn.

Violet was tired from traipsing across the estate from Reed's cottage to the rookery, and quickly became irritated that Chandler ignored her presence as he pulled a mouse from the pile and fed it to one of the birds, sometimes speaking lovingly and sometimes demanding a trick first, such as a whistle or a head bob.

After several moments of this, Violet interrupted, and soon found herself embroiled in a quarrel with the falconer.

"Mr. Chandler, may I have a moment of your time, please? I am here on important business."

"Still looking for what Aristotle may have choked on?" he asked, offering her his usual, lazy smile.

Violet had completely forgotten about that in the course of events. "No, I plant myself at your doorstep concerning something more important. Have you sent any telegrams to London recently, Mr. Chandler?" she asked directly, hoping to throw him off guard. Unfortunately, the only sign of discomfort in evidence was that Chandler paused momentarily with a particularly bloody mouse in his hand, causing the peregrine to protest loudly. "*Aah! Aah! Er-er-er-er-er!*" the bird sputtered in frustration.

With just a glance at Violet, Chandler tossed the entrails toward the falcon, which reached its head up and caught the mouse firmly in its beak, then placed the carcass between its talons and the perch, reaching down and ripping off small shreds with its sharp beak and swallowing them whole.

"Telegrams? To whom?" the falconer said, avoiding a direct response.

"Only you can answer that, sir."

He picked up another mouse from his pile on the table and once more tossed it up to the peregrine, which accepted it greedily.

"What reason would I have to send a telegram, Mrs. Harper? In any case, you haven't told me why someone else's telegram would have you in such a dither."

"I am not in a dither, sir. I am attempting to discover who—" Violet took a breath. "Never mind. Do you remember that you called me a raven during Burton Spencer's funeral?"

He shrugged with smug nonchalance. "Yes. Were you offended?"

"Of course not." Violet was growing more irritated by the second by his demeanor. "I am wondering if you have ever referred to me that way to anyone else."

"You are terribly consumed with yourself, madam. I am sorry to have to inform you that I do not spend my time talking about you. Perhaps you are disappointed to hear that."

Violet couldn't believe what she was hearing. "Of all the cheek! What arrogance to accuse me of such a thing."

"*Me* to accuse *you?* Madam, first you come here asking about some ridiculous telegram. It is obvious that you know specifically what telegram you are asking about, but you aren't sharing that with me, in hopes of trapping me into a statement of guilt. Guilt about what, I cannot imagine."

Chandler threw another mouse haphazardly in the air so that the peregrine was barely able to catch it. However, it went straight to work at mauling its catch. The falconer picked up another couple of carcasses and tossed one to each of two ravens also waiting their turns. "Then you wish to know if I have called you a raven to others, as though it is my secret pet name for you as I worship you from afar. Why should I have any interest in you? You're but an undertaker, barely above my own station. I have high aspirations, many of which will be realized soon, and wasting time yearning for a married rav—undertaker is not in my plans."

"I would blame your arrogance on your youth," Violet said quietly, trying to control the heat of embarrassment and rage inflaming her cheeks, "except that you are nearly my own age, are you not? You simply never learned any manners. In fact, that falcon is more polite than you."

"If you are quite done—" Chandler said, pointing the way out.

"Be assured, sir, that I am not done, and will never be done until I get to the bottom of this matter."

"*What* matter, Mrs. Harper? You talk in riddles and puzzles and criticisms, but all I know is that you were upset because one of the duke's ravens managed to choke to death on a piece of debris . . . just as probably thousands of ravens have managed to do over the years. You remind me of a harpy—a hungry, filthy winged creature with the face of an ugly old woman—because you torment people and bring stormy clouds with you wherever you go. Please be gone."

With that, Chandler scooped the remaining mice into the ever-present leather satchel at his waist and stalked off, leaving Violet and the birds completely outraged and unsatisfied. How had she managed to anger the duke's falconer, of all people, to the point of being dismissed from his presence? She reviewed what had happened in her mind. Was she guilty of provoking Chandler, or had he trumped up his own outrage in order to dissemble and obscure whatever it was he might be guilty of? She was so angry it was difficult to think clearly.

However, in the heat of her fury, a memory flickered to life. When Chandler had called her a raven at Spencer's funeral, hadn't Colonel Mortimer made some odd excuse and left, presumably heading back to Welbeck Abbey? She hadn't given it a second thought at the time, but was there something in Chandler's comment that had struck a nerve with the colonel, or, worse, given him an idea so wicked that he had to walk away from them?

24

Violet was already exhausted from the day's events and it was barely noon, yet she decided it was necessary to visit the colonel again, to see what he had to say about his fancy home in London. Back across the estate she went to Colonel Mortimer's cottage, just a short distance away from Reed's.

As she passed through a row of boxwoods on the approach to his cottage, she noticed the colonel exit his front door, a shovel in hand. Instinctively, she stayed inside the line of boxwoods and peered over them to observe his actions. Laying the shovel on the ground, he returned inside and came back out moments later with another digging implement.

Violet felt an unpleasant chill creeping up her spine. It turned into prickles of fear as she contemplated what to do next. *Calm yourself,* she thought. *His actions might be completely innocent. Perhaps he is planting a shrub or something.*

In the middle of October? the suspicious side of her replied. *He is up to no good, and you know it.*

He dropped the second tool and returned inside once more. When he came back out, he was muttering to himself as he picked the implements up and walked rapidly to the rear of his cottage.

What part of the estate was back there? The Greendale Oak was in that direction. So were some of the temporary construction buildings, which were scattered across the estate. Were there any tunnels in that direction? Violet wasn't sure.

She patted her reticule to assure herself that her knife was still there. This time, she wouldn't permit herself to be grabbed before she could reach into it.

If it came to that.

Violet emerged from the hedgerow and followed the colonel, who had already disappeared behind the cottage and out of her view. Violet picked up her skirts and walked quickly to catch up to him, all thoughts of her fatigue completely erased within the pounding of her heart. She slowed as she approached the rear corner of his cottage and finally stopped, peeping out cautiously to see if the man was still in view.

The colonel stood about a hundred yards behind his cottage, in an open space that might have been inhabited by another cottage were it not for a dilapidated little building that still stood there instead, tenaciously clinging to life despite the vines that threatened to consume it. The colonel was examining the area surrounding the structure, a tool in each hand. Violet hated to imagine what he might be planning to do.

From nowhere, courage welled up inside of her and she stepped out from the side of the cottage, taking large strides toward him. The colonel immediately noticed the movement and looked up. "Ah, Mrs. Harper, good afternoon," he said. "I was just, er, just having a bit of a walk, you see." The colonel made his way to her, except now he was weaving, as though in his cups again. Both digging implements fell to the ground as he approached.

"Any news on LeCato?" he asked, now standing before her unsteadily. "His Grace said he sent you to London."

"Yes, I just returned. Mr. LeCato appears to be a trusted—"

"Oh yes, I'm sure you found more than one bootlicker willing to vouch for him. Were you able to dig deeper than just getting a few government sycophants to tell you tall tales?"

Was the colonel trying to distract Violet from what he had been doing earlier? "I hardly think Mr. LeCato is of a position to have others fawning before him, sir. Both Mr. Gladstone and Mr. Denison themselves consider his conduct to be unimpeachable."

"Evelyn Denison? Is he wrapped up in this? Denison is His Grace's brother-in-law, you know."

Violet bit her lip. She shouldn't have told Colonel Mortimer that. Besides, it was the colonel who had explaining to do, not her. "What are the shovels for, sir?" she said, nodding back to where they lay haphazardly on the ground.

"Those? Oh." He made a vague attempt at a self-deprecating laugh. "Thought I might take down that old shed. An eyesore, you know."

"Did His Grace approve its destruction?" Considering how long it had been left there without falling prey to any of the estate's building projects, perhaps it had an actual purpose.

"His Grace?" The colonel was swaying again. "His Grace is my friend and permits me great liberties on the estate."

There was no smell of liquor emanating from the colonel, nor was he even wearing his bloodshot glass eye, although that wasn't conclusive evidence. "Yes, Colonel, but I wonder if those liberties extend to taking advantage of your friend. For instance, perhaps you are not in great need of assistance, yet you pretend to be a destitute army pensioner. Perhaps, instead, you own—"

"Well, if you'll excuse me, I must be off to bed. A little nap, you see." The colonel staggered off to the front of his house, leaving Violet in midsentence.

The man had clearly pretended to be intoxicated when she caught him bringing out his digging tools, which had certainly helped him to cut her off when she started to accuse him of manipulating Portland.

Taking the risk that he was watching her from a window and might come storming out at any minute, Violet walked over to the shed and inspected it for herself. As she had seen from a distance, it was old and decrepit, and was covered in a thorny rose vine relentlessly intent on destroying it. Patches of white paint suggested that it had once been a well-cared-for building, perhaps an artist's studio.

She walked completely around the building, but could find no evidence that there had been any recent digging going on here, so whatever the colonel had planned was new. She even picked up the tools. One was merely an average shovel; the other had a much narrower spade-like head. Both had dried dirt on them, which was not incriminating in and of itself, as shovels were meant to be placed into the earth. Neither had bloodstains that she could see, which she counted as a small blessing, and a point in the colonel's favor.

However . . . wouldn't this smaller shovel's head make approximately the same size hole as those that she'd found where she discovered Edward Bayes's body? Violet turned in the direction of the rookery and the copse of trees that would be between here and there. The trees were located in a direct line between the colonel's cottage and the rookery.

What was she to do now? Rapping on the colonel's door to demand answers might be safe, what with a shovel in her hand and a knife in her reticule, but he would undoubtedly respond with loud snores. He also wasn't likely to confess to any grand plot, either. No, Violet had to see Portland.

As she walked back, intent on reporting her encounter with Colonel Mortimer as well as her trip to London, Violet noticed a curtain move inside the cottage.

Once more, Violet sat on the other side of the screen in Portland's suite. With a great knot of guilt resting in her rib cage, she omitted telling the duke that Denison had hired LeCato, fearful of his reaction. However, she did relay the real purpose in LeCato's presence at Welbeck.

She saw the outline of Portland's head nodding from behind the carved-out wood. "Yes, I'm not surprised that they would do such a thing. It explains why LeCato was so worked up when Mr. Bayes's body appeared during the dynamiting. Anything to slow down progress. I thought I would never get him out of my presence. Well, Mr. Gladstone is in for quite the surprise when he finds that Mr. LeCato no longer has any influence here. In fact, I shall have the man thrown out."

Knowing that such a reaction would only serve to notify Gladstone and Denison that she had run back to Welbeck and tattled on them, Violet spoke at length, urging caution and circumspection. "After all, Your Grace, we don't know yet whether Mr. LeCato had anything to do with Spencer's or Bayes's death. Sending him away would spoil any opportunity for determining that."

Portland grunted, but slowly nodded once more. "I suppose you're right, Mrs. Harper. So no one other than Gladstone has been party to putting this irritating vermin on my estate to chew me to distraction? You have no other information about him other than that he works for the chancellor of the exchequer?"

Fortunately for Violet, Portland continued on without waiting for an answer. "If Gladstone believes he can save his party upon my flea-bitten back, he is sorely mistaken. I need more, though, Mrs. Harper. So you still believe he is connected to Spencer's and Bayes's deaths?"

"I'm not sure, Your Grace. However"—Violet stepped through the opening provided for her—"I am currently concerned with another person on the estate. Someone who is rather close to you."

"Close to me? Who could that possibly be?"

"Sir, I mean Colonel Mortimer."

Portland made no verbal response, but Violet felt the reproach and disapproval that permeated the resulting silence. It hung in the air like a cold December morning's mist. She plowed on, telling Portland of the colonel's nice home in London, and of catching him with digging tools near the shed on the grounds behind his cottage and his subsequent pretense of inebriation.

"What shed?" Portland demanded.

Violet described it, and Portland harrumphed. "I know the structure," he snapped. "George wouldn't do anything to destroy it."

"Please understand, Your Grace, I wasn't suggesting that he was planning to demolish it, but he had shovels and it seemed to me that he was about to—"

"Let me be clear, Mrs. Harper. George Mortimer is no more a criminal than I am a hippopotamus. He was undoubtedly doing some necessary digging. He knows of my concern for the servants, and I've often talked of creating a small ring toss field for them. George might have taken it on as a project, as some small repayment of my providing him with a home. I'm sure that we will soon see the charitable result of his seemingly suspicious behavior, and we will have a good laugh about it."

Violet couldn't imagine Portland smiling, much less laughing, about anything. "Yes, Your Grace, except that he doesn't seem to need a home."

"If George says he needs my assistance, then he does. I'll hear no more on it. If there is anything devious going on at Welbeck, I'm certain it can be laid at the feet of Jack LeCato."

Violet left Portland's presence thoroughly frustrated by how obtuse the man was on the subject of his friend. Why did he refuse to listen to any facts whatsoever about the colonel? Why was he obsessed with LeCato? Not that Violet didn't have her share of suspicions over the man, but there were others acting just as dubiously at Welbeck Abbey, too.

The swirl of speculation made Violet's head hurt. The pain reminded her of the attack in London. Was it related to the deaths, or to the projects at Welbeck Abbey, or to the buyback of the consols?

It all brought her around to Portland again, and a new thought occurred to her. Was it possible that Portland was trying—in his own clumsy way—to lead her silently to some conclusion he'd already made? Worse, was she being led away from the colonel because it also led her away from the duke himself? Maybe, but she couldn't see a reason for it. For that matter, she still couldn't understand why *anyone* at Welbeck would want any of the estate's workers dead.

If only she could figure out a small piece of this puzzle, she was certain the other pieces—no matter how irregularly shaped— would fall quickly into place.

That evening, Violet enjoyed supper—her usual fish pie—with Sam at Worksop Inn. Mr. Saunders was particularly jovial this evening, and the fire burned merrily in the fireplace. With her husband across from her and a glass of sherry in her hand, Violet relaxed for the first time in days. Even with having to repeat everything that had happened in London and then back at Welbeck earlier in the day, she felt none of the anxiety that had been plaguing her. Perhaps it was the comfort she felt from witnessing Sam's outrage over the attack on her person, an outrage that far outweighed his elation over his new business prospects with Portland.

"By God, if I ever lay my hand upon whoever did that to you, I will beat him within an inch of his life. He will lie on the ground, begging me to kill him. This will be my battle-ax"—whereupon he picked up his cane from where it leaned against their table— "and my fists will do what it cannot. If anyone ever again tries to . . ."

Sam's tirade went on for several minutes, and included some choice words for the incompetence of Inspector Hurst, with whom he had bickered in the past, as well as a round of cursing for every London street criminal, those currently operating and those to be born in the future.

Violet allowed herself to be cocooned in her husband's fierce defense of her, letting it wrap her like a warm blanket and giving her a sense of safety from the world. She could only wish that every woman had a husband like Sam. Poor Mrs. Bayes had a less than sufficient husband, although the woman herself . . . Violet shuddered and drained her glass. Mr. Saunders's daughter, Polly, was immediately on hand to refill it.

Violet had to be careful. She was still struggling with her weight after an overindulgence in fine food during a recent stay at St. James's Palace. Too much fish pie and sherry while in Nottinghamshire might mean another trip to the dressmaker's before they left for Egypt.

Of course, she had done so much energetic walking across the Welbeck Abbey estate today, so perhaps a little bit of dessert wouldn't hurt. . . .

"How about some plum pudding or Neapolitan cake, Mrs. Harper?" Polly asked, as if reading Violet's mind.

Violet glanced at Sam, who, still beside himself with indignation, could barely sputter, "None for me." She bit her lip. It was so much easier to indulge when Sam went along with her. "Well . . . perhaps just a tiny slice of the Neapolitan," she said, promising to herself that she would take a brisk walk through town in the morning. Polly returned with the confection in mere moments.

Violet sliced into the colorfully layered dessert as Polly moved away to help another customer. It was sugary and iced to perfection.

She paused with the fork near her mouth as she caught what Polly was saying at the next table: ". . . work for my father anymore when I come into some money soon . . . live in a fine house . . . better dresses than this old stained thing . . ."

Violet was so engrossed in Polly's statements that she actually put down the cake-laden fork. Hadn't Martin Chandler said something similar about coming into a fortune? She decided she would talk to Polly later in the evening after the dining room had cleared itself of patrons.

Unfortunately, by the time Violet decided the time was right and came back downstairs from reading and talking over Polly's comments with Sam up in her room, Mr. Saunders was turning out the gas lamps, and informed her that Polly had gone off to a friend's house for the night.

As she walked back up the creaking oak steps to her room, Violet made a decision that she shared with Sam, who had just completed his nighttime ablutions. "I believe I need to go back to Welbeck Abbey tomorrow," she said, unbuttoning the bodice of her dress to prepare for bed herself.

Sam slid into bed, sitting back against the pillows and crossing his fingers on his bare chest. "For what reason?" he asked sleepily.

"I want to go see Colonel Mortimer again, to confront him once more when he isn't ostensibly in his cups," Violet said, removing her skirt and corset, then sliding into her Welsh flannel nightgown. "Also, since Polly is gone for the evening, I believe it might be beneficial to visit Martin Chandler again to inquire further about the fortune he believes he will inherit. I have no idea if his grandiose idea is pertinent to anything, but I don't want to ignore it, either. Mr. Chandler may have dismissed me from the rookery today, but I won't allow him to do so tomorrow."

"Hmm," Sam said absently, his eyes closed. "Well, there is one thing for certain."

"What is that?" she asked, sitting on her side of the bed and loosening her hair from its pins.

"You won't be going without me." He opened one eye and looked at her sternly.

"Sam," she began, "I think I am reasonably safe on the estate grounds. Besides, I carry my knife—"

"Safe on the estate grounds?! Need I remind you that the whole reason for your inquisition is two deaths on those same grounds? A fat lot of good that knife did you in London, either. I'll not hear any excuses or pleas, nor make any bargains with you, woman. I will stand next to you while you interview these dolts, and that is the end of the conversation. Now, all of my anger has made me very overwrought. Come, Wife, and calm me down."

Violet laughed as she shook out her hair and tumbled into her irresistible husband's arms.

25

The next morning was windy and overcast, but Violet thought maybe the clouds would drift away without drenching her in a deluge. With Sam steadfastly at her side as he had sworn he would be, she removed a glove and rapped upon Colonel Mortimer's door. To her surprise, the door fell open at her touch.

Exchanging a puzzled look with Sam, she replaced her glove and stepped into the cottage, calling out for the colonel. She received no response, and thinking he might have truly become intoxicated after she left and was therefore still sleeping it off, she called out louder.

Still no answer.

Violet started to move farther into the cottage, but Sam took her elbow and shook his head no, stepping ahead of her into the small house. "Wait here," he commanded, and went to search the rest of the cottage.

While she stood inside the front door, she craned her neck to see if anything was amiss. Nothing seemed out of place, but who could really tell inside this overstuffed habitat?

Sam returned. "There's no one here."

"Curious that he left his door open," she replied. "Perhaps the wind blew it open. I wonder where he is."

"This is your opportunity," Sam said. "Have a good snoop around."

Violet hesitated. "Do you think we should? Aren't I . . . we . . . trespassing?"

Sam looked at her incredulously. "The man is almost certainly a sot and a liar, and may or may not be a murderer, and you're worried about poking about in his cottage for a few moments?"

Well, when he puts it like that . . . Violet thought.

Together, they systematically went through the house, looking through drawers and cabinets. Violet's immediate conclusion was that the colonel lived like a genuine bachelor. The man really needed a wife to bring some semblance of order to his life. Not that Violet could claim to have engendered great neatness in Sam's life, but she was an undertaker, after all, and that meant . . .

Well, she supposed it didn't mean much at all when it came to caring for the home. Perhaps it was best to disregard that line of thought—an easy task, for as she went through the colonel's liquor bottles, lifting them up individually and noting with surprise how far down most of them had been consumed, she came across a folded sheet of thick paper.

As soon as she had unfolded it, she knew she had struck upon something significant. "Sam!" she called out urgently.

He rushed out from what was presumably the colonel's bedchamber as quickly as his limp would allow. "What did you find?"

"This," she said, showing him the paper. He took it and placed it on the colonel's dining table, the only clear surface available.

Sam frowned as he smoothed it out. "This looks like a map of the estate. This represents the house, and this looks like the skating rink site," he said, pointing at two hand-drawn symbols.

Violet bent down over the map to study it more closely. "There are some very strange marks on the map. They look like three arrows—no, triangles—over in this area. I wonder what they could possibly mean? Do they indicate—oh!" Violet jerked straight up.

"What is it?" Sam asked. "What are they?"

"I'm not sure, but I have a good idea the area being marked."

"Which is . . . where?"

"They signify places inside the copse of trees between here and the rookery. It's where I discovered the glass eye shard . . . and Mr. Bayes's body."

Sam put a hand to her back, as if to steady her. "What do you think this means about Colonel Mortimer?"

Violet felt her worst fears being confirmed. "This seems to prove that the colonel had known where Mr. Bayes's body was, and my discovery of the shard proves that he was there with the body."

"Are there marks where Burton Spencer's body was found?"

Violet traced a line with her finger from the shape representing the house to approximately where she'd found Spencer. "Oddly enough, no. Maybe the mark indicates a grave. Bayes was loosely covered in leaf debris whereas Spencer was not buried at all, but does that mean there are other shallow graves I missed?"

Sam nodded grimly. "I wonder if the colonel has fled the estate."

"None of his belongings seem to be missing."

"How can you tell in this mess? Besides, I imagine that a murderer running for his life doesn't bother with much other than the clothes on his back."

Violet couldn't argue with that. The lingering question in her mind was, what reason could the colonel possibly have had to kill Edward Bayes?

Violet and Sam proceeded on to the rookery to visit Martin Chandler, with Colonel Mortimer's map in Violet's hand. They kicked against the curled brown leaves that swirled around their feet, and Sam tapped his cane along the crunchy gravel.

As they neared the area of the copse, Violet tugged on Sam's arm. "Let me show you where I found Mr. Bayes and the glass eye." She led him off the gravel path, across a patch of lawn, and into the cluster of trees. "The eye was here"—Violet pointed down—"and farther back, near this bramble, was Edward Bay—" She gasped at what she now saw. This simply wasn't possible.

"What's the matter?" Sam asked. "You said—good Lord!" He knelt down and Violet dropped next to him, as if a closer view might convince them that they weren't staring at the body of Colonel George Mortimer. His eyes were half closed, and his balding pate was bloody and covered in bits of dirt and leaves.

26

Violet could hardly comprehend what she was seeing. "But . . ." Her voice trailed off on the now implausible thought that the colonel had been her primary suspect. Within moments, though, her undertaking senses took over and she began examining him.

First, she removed her gloves and picked up the colonel's hand, manipulating the fingers. His hand was cold but still flexible. He hadn't been here long, although the mere fact that she'd just seen the man the previous afternoon was proof enough of that. "Colonel, who has done this to you? I fear I must apologize to you for my suspicions of you, although I don't suppose we can completely absolve you of everything."

Violet sensed Sam moving restlessly next to her, then returning to his feet, dropping his cane, and walking a short distance away.

"Sir, forgive me while I lift your head, like this. . . ." Violet gently cradled the colonel's neck in one hand, as she inspected the rear of his head. It was a sticky morass of pulp that made her queasy, but she swallowed the acid rising in her throat. "You've been battered, sir, far worse than Mr. Spencer was. What did you do to anger someone enough for this? What evil is running unchecked on this estate? And what part might you have played in it?"

She removed her hand from the back of his head and gently lowered him back down, apologizing quietly to the colonel for her tactless behavior as she wiped her hands across her skirts to remove some of his blood. "Here's the weapon." Sam was standing alongside her again. He offered a hand, and she stood up, too, to see what he held in his other hand. It was a shovel, and if Violet wasn't mistaken, it was the same wide shovel she had seen the colonel with yesterday.

"It belongs to him," she said.

Sam shook his head. "Is there a greater insult than to be done in by your own weapon?"

Violet, remembering that the colonel had had two digging implements with him the day before, asked, "Did you find another, smaller shovel?"

"No, there's just this."

Violet's mind was racing. All three of these deaths—Spencer's, Bayes's, and now Colonel Mortimer's—had no link as far as she could see, except that they had all occurred on Welbeck Abbey property, over the space of about two weeks. It was madness. It was also maddening that she couldn't seem to unearth a motive or the correct suspect. Names and the memories of isolated incidents boiled and churned in her brain, but instead of giving her answers, she was merely left with a faint feeling of nausea.

How was it that the curse of the raven the cook had warned her of had come true?

She turned her head in the direction of the rookery, which was only about a couple of hundred yards away. What of Chandler's claim—and Polly's—that there was to be an inheritance soon? Did Chandler know that the colonel was actually well-off?

Once more, she swallowed the bile in her throat.

"Sweetheart," Sam said softly, interrupting her agitated state, "I believe it's time we notified His Grace."

"Yes, of course." Violet shook her head to clear it of its squawking accusations. Her first priority must be the colonel, who had to be removed from his insulting circumstances. Portland, though, would be devastated at the loss of his friend. She dreaded this confrontation, but it was one she had to make without Sam's presence. If Sam delivered the bad news, how might it unintentionally impact Portland's view of her husband, and thus Portland's interest in investing in dynamite? Violet didn't mind being the bearer of bad news. . . . She frequently was.

"Sam, I will go back to the house for His Grace. Will you wait here so that the colonel won't be alone, nor spirited away like Mr. Bayes?"

Sam nodded, and Violet took off to report to Portland, ready to accept whatever consequences there might be.

Portland's reaction was not only the total disbelief that Violet anticipated; he practically went into a stupor over the news. Violet employed everything she had to comfort him, or to at least bring him around to communicating with her.

Finally, he seemed to come to a silent decision and summoned his valet, Pearson, to have him dressed in his usual heavy brown coat and tall hat. He then argued for several moments with Violet over summoning Molly Spriggs to bring his lantern to guide them both, but Violet was adamant—there was no time.

Portland settled for just his umbrella, and Violet then led him to the copse. Or, rather, Violet scurried to follow on the heels of his long-legged stride.

When they arrived, it was no longer just Sam standing watch over the body. Martin Chandler had joined him, and Sam looked as though he might snatch the man by the neck if he attempted to go anywhere. As if they had gathered to protect their master, ravens filled the trees above the two men, perching silently as ebony witnesses to whatever drama was about to unfold.

The birds would not be disappointed.

"I presume this is your falconer, Your Grace," Sam said, jostling Chandler so that the two of them blocked the colonel's body from view.

"Yes, what is the meaning of this? Where is George?" Portland addressed Chandler in rough tones, but it was Sam who answered, though he kept to his own topic.

"Mr. Chandler came traipsing through here," he said, "which I found most interesting, given what my wife just discovered here a few moments ago. Thought I'd corral him to see if he also knew what lay here."

"Y-y-your Grace," Chandler stumbled. Faced with his master, he lost his easy smile and self-assuredness. "I was just d-d-doing some training and s-s-stumbled upon this man, who threatened me with force if I were to leave."

Chandler seemed almost . . . panicked. Violet knew that a panicked man will commit irrational acts and it was best to confront him now before he did anything more foolish than he already had. She hadn't anticipated facing him in front of Portland, but there was nothing she could do about the timing of it.

"You just happened to be out with your birds, and chose this particular copse of trees to wander through?" Violet asked, more sharply than was necessary.

Chandler pointed up, his finger trembling. "They like it here."

"It would seem that Colonel Mortimer, too, once liked it here, but found quickly that it was not a particularly safe location for him," Violet said, noting that Portland winced as she mentioned his friend's name. "I know of a few men who might wish to track his whereabouts . . . or who might have an interest in his death."

"Are you mad, woman? I have no interest in the colonel's death. How could I possibly want him dead?"

Violet dug into her reticule, retrieving both the map and the telegram Hurst had taken from Ian Hale, and handing them to Chandler. She regretted doing this in the midst of Portland's grief, but it was vital that a murderer be caught. Chandler paled visibly at both the map and telegram, refusing to take either one. She offered them to Portland instead, who shook open the map with one trembling hand and cocked his head to one side as if to decipher what it was. Propping the umbrella against his leg, he then shook open the folded telegram with his other hand and scanned it quickly.

"'The raven is at Harcourt House.' How very dramatic. I presume you are the raven, Mrs. Harper?"

"Yes, Your Grace. Mr. Chandler referred to me as such at Mr. Spencer's funeral, and it certainly makes sense that he would use such language." She pointed upward, as Chandler had moments ago. One of the ravens on a nearby branch ruffled its feathers in response.

Portland handed the telegram back to Violet. "Yes, but this is certainly not *proof* of any kind. What is this other document, though? It appears to be some kind of map."

Violet showed him the landmarks of his estate and various other markings on the map, including the strange triangles in the copse—one of which, she supposed, might mark where the colonel's body now lay. "You may find it interesting to know that Mr. Chandler has claimed that he is coming into an inheritance soon. It is my suspicion that that inheritance was something promised from the colonel, and Chandler got impatient waiting for it."

"You don't know what you're talking about," Chandler protested. "I have no inheritance coming."

"And as I've stated before," Portland said in stubborn insistence, "the colonel had no fortune. He was dependent upon my beneficence." His voice cracked on that last word, but he maintained his aristocratic stoicism.

Violet shook her head. "I'm afraid I will have to disagree with you, Your Grace. Scotland Yard told me personally of the home the colonel had in Green Park."

"So you've said. I refuse to believe that. It is simply not possible that George lied to me." Portland handed the documents back to Violet, who wasn't sure what to do next. Fortunately, Sam was more than willing to lead, and shifted the subject to what was uppermost in his mind.

"Did you have anything to do with my wife's attack in London?" he growled at Chandler. Violet was thankful Sam's cane wasn't in his hand at present.

"What attack is this?" Portland asked, pushing his hat back on his head to get a better look at Chandler.

"My apologies, Your Grace," Violet said. "I wasn't seriously hurt—"

"Only by great providential mercy," Sam thundered, far more aggravated now that he had the man potentially responsible in his hands.

"—and so I thought it best not to worry you by mentioning it."

Portland's expression was one of shock, but his response was not what she expected. "I can hardly believe my sister didn't thrash the telegram office clerk in her haste to send me the gossip. I received no news of it at all from London."

Actually, come to think of it, Violet was rather surprised by that herself.

"Perhaps the baroness didn't wish to dishearten you regarding your decision to send me there," she offered.

"You did meet my sister, did you not, Mrs. Harper?" Portland said, in the closest thing to humor Violet had seen yet in the man's demeanor. She was actually glad to see it in the midst of his misery. "Now, what was this attack to which Mr. Harper refers?"

Violet explained what had happened in Cavendish Square, while Portland frowned and grunted several times. "And were you responsible for this, Chandler?"

The falconer's forehead beaded with sweat, despite the chill air surrounding them. "Your Grace, no! I—I—I hardly know Mrs. Harper or the colonel. Why should I wish harm on either of them?"

Violet jumped on the stammering falconer's words. "I think you are involved in some monetary scheme involving the colonel, and when he did something you didn't like—perhaps he refused a demand, or informed you that his will was to include someone else, or maybe he discovered your involvement in other mischief on the estate—you decided to murder him before he could cut you out or tell on you."

"You don't—I—This is all wrong," Chandler mumbled in desperation, red-faced.

"Were you here to move the colonel's body, just as Edward Bayes's body was moved a week ago? Who else but you—what with your accompanying the ravens here on what I presume is a regular basis—would not draw suspicion, and would know this to be a good hiding place for a corpse?"

"I don't know anything about hiding corpses. Your Grace, please let me explain. You see, the colonel occasionally came to see how the birds were doing in their training. He particularly liked the ravens. So I let him help sometimes—"

"Yet you said you hardly knew the colonel," Sam interrupted. "You've just started your tale and already it's a lie."

Violet was worried that the falconer wouldn't survive his own story if her husband had anything to do with it. "Sam, please," she said, pleading.

Sam glared at Chandler but motioned for him to go on. The falconer took his case back to Portland.

"And so, Your Grace, I came to know the colonel a bit, but 'tweren't as though we were friends, if you understand. Now I do remember the colonel saying to me—oh, probably a month or so ago—that he knew a great secret. A secret that could bring down the estate." Chandler glanced furtively at Sam.

"What secret is this?" Portland asked gently, as though to blunt Sam's anger.

"I don't know, he never said. That's the truth, Your Grace. I don't know what he meant."

Violet was absolutely certain there was very little truth in what Chandler said, but she had no way to prove it. She also couldn't prove that Chandler had anything to do with the colonel's death— just a strong suspicion combined with the man's unexpected appearance at the crime scene.

Violet saw the reluctance on Portland's face to do anything about disciplining his falconer.

"Mr. Chandler," Portland finally said, gravely, "you have had serious allegations lodged against you in relation to my dear friend. Yet I believe it is in my best interest—and that of everyone who lives here—if we continue to investigate the matter further and not assume you to be guilty."

Chandler's relief was palpable, as was Sam's disappointment.

"However," Portland continued, "I think it might be best if you confined yourself to your quarters in the rookery for a time, eh? Until this is all sorted out, so that no one worries that you might flee."

"But, Your Grace, the birds . . . Odysseus has been training on rabbits, and Sophocles has almost completely finished a maze I've built for him. I must be able to—"

"Very well. You may go from your quarters to the rookery."

That was it? It didn't seem like much of a confinement to Violet, given that that was how the falconer spent most of his days, anyway. Portland was terribly quick to grant leniency in this situation, but grief didn't lend itself to good decision-making. Perhaps it was time the police were brought in. There was certainly no question whatsoever this time that a man had been murdered.

Apparently resigned to Portland's pronouncement, Sam retrieved his cane, which now resembled a menacing weapon in his hand, and took Chandler by the arm to escort him back to the rookery, leaving Violet alone with Portland . . . and Colonel Mortimer's body.

"Your Grace," she said quietly, "would you like a moment alone with your old friend?"

Portland took a deep breath. "Poor George. Always such a tragic fellow." He took a few steps forward in the direction that Violet was indicating, but then held back, refusing to approach too closely, and removed a black-trimmed handkerchief from his pocket, which he held to his nose.

That is odd, Violet thought. *Does His Grace keep a supply of mourning handkerchiefs at his elbow, to be prepared in case of an unexpected death?*

The duke stood quietly, gazing off in the direction of the colonel's body, which was partially obscured by leaves and plant matter. Violet stepped away as quietly as possible to give him privacy. After several minutes, Portland called for her and she hurried back to his side.

"Return tomorrow morning at eleven o'clock to discuss George's funeral with me, Mrs. Harper. I'm afraid such decisions are best left to a new day. I presume you will take care of his . . . more immediate needs?"

Violet knew that that was the duke's way of telling her he needed time to grieve, and she would never argue with a mourner's need for it. She turned to leave, but Portland was not quite finished. "Mrs. Harper, you must understand that I have never fired an employee here at Welbeck. Anyone who secures employment here has it for life. Everyone knows it, and I shouldn't wish to have any other reputation."

Violet nodded, although she didn't agree with the duke's philosophy. He turned back to the house, and she went to retrieve Sam to prevent him doing Chandler any great harm, before going on to arrange for the colonel's body to be moved to his cottage.

27

Instead of escorting her to Portland's private rooms the next morning, Kirby showed Violet into the cavernous dining room, and there she found Portland waiting for her. They sat down face-to-face in the location where Burton Spencer's body had been laid out not two weeks ago. Violet suspected it was a measure of Portland's respect for Colonel Mortimer that he was willing to spend such a lengthy amount of time outside of the protection of his privacy screen in order to discuss the man's funeral.

Or perhaps he was finally getting used to Violet.

"George is . . . comfortable?" Portland asked. His expression was certainly more haggard than it had been yesterday, but he seemed to be bearing up stoically, especially given that this was the third death on his estate in just over two weeks, and this one involved his oldest friend. Actually, Violet wondered if Portland now considered anyone else to be a close confidant.

"Yes, Your Grace. He is laid out nicely on the dining room table in his cottage. Would you like to visit? I can accompany you—"

Portland held up a hand to stop her. "No, no, that will not be necessary. I cannot bear to see him in any manner other than the jovial fellow he was. He was my friend and comrade in arms, as you know, and he understood me like no one else ever has. George was the only man alive who knew of my affections for Miss Adelaide Kemble all those years ago, and never thought the worse of me when she married elsewhere."

Apparently His Grace was not aware that just about everyone knew about his great passion for the opera singer.

"As you wish." Violet moved on with the preliminaries of the funeral, mainly what class of service the duke wished to purchase, given that the colonel had no other family to do so for him. Portland held up a hand again. "I'll spare no expense on it. Provide the best of everything for him."

Violet withheld a sigh. It was commendable that Portland wanted to do well by his friend, but the colonel wasn't entitled to, say, a society funeral. However, there were ways to work around this. For example, the colonel could have a fancy coffin, but not the extras such as multiple ostrich-plumed horses and dozens of professional mourners, which were visible hallmarks of an upper-class funeral. This had to be broached delicately, so as not to offend Portland regarding the status of his friend.

"Your Grace, may I recommend that we honor your friend with an elegant coffin? I can obtain one in perhaps an elm burl—very popular with the society set—or perhaps in a finely finished mahogany."

"Hmm. Those are nice choices, yes, but I've heard of glass coffins rrimmed in brass. Very elegant and rare. Have you access to any of those?"

"Yes," Violet said hesitantly, dreading the very thought of such a coffin. They weighed around three hundred pounds empty and were exceedingly fragile. The weight made them difficult for six pallbearers to manage, and their fragility meant that the slightest slip could result in shattered glass everywhere. They were the bane of an undertaker's existence. She had to steer him away from the idea.

"Such a coffin will require eight pallbearers, not the usual six, because of the weight. Who do you think would be appropriate men to do this? They must all be of good size." She couldn't imagine that the colonel had eight men who would be considered friends on the estate and that this conundrum would veer Portland off of the idea.

Not so. "I'll have Kirby select some strapping young men for it, not to worry, Mrs. Harper," he said, clearly warming to his own idea. "Decorate the top with the flag. I'll find some army mementos to lay on it, as well."

Violet tried once more. "Your Grace, a glass coffin will require special casing around it inside the grave, a large effort for the grave diggers."

Portland waved her off, in the manner of the wealthy who never understand the work required of their whims. "Not to worry, Mrs. Harper. I have plenty of diggers who can assist with a simple grave."

Violet repressed a sigh once more and made notes. *Adult brass-and-glass coffin. Additional lifting straps. Union Jack.*

"Will you have all of the staff come out for the colonel's funeral?" she asked.

"No," he replied quickly. "This will be a very private affair."

"Then . . . just you and perhaps a few of your chief employees, plus the pallbearers?"

"No, no, the employees have been under enough anxiety and worry. We won't trouble them with this. We will just bury George as quickly as possible so that we can, hopefully, dispel the aura of gloom that has hovered over Welbeck these past days." Portland nodded, as if declaring it would make it so. Violet had her doubts that a quick funeral would make fifteen hundred estate workers forget about the death surrounding them all. In fact, remembering Mrs. Garside's hysterical reaction to just Aristotle's demise, Violet was quite certain that it wouldn't.

"Very well, Your Grace. Shall I hire any professional mourners?"

"No, no, that's just more fuss, especially in town."

"I see," Violet said, wondering whether there was to actually even *be* a funeral. "So, other than the pallbearers, you will be the only mourner, sir?"

"Hmm," Portland said, resting his chin in his hand, his elbow on the polished surface of the intricately inlaid mahogany table. "No, I believe I shan't go outside that day. Besides, I've already attended one funeral in recent days. You may start the procession at the front door, and I will view it from an upstairs window."

Violet was flabbergasted. The duke planned to pay for an elaborate funeral, to be attended by . . . no one. Well, it was her responsibility to put the deceased into the ground in a dignified manner, and she could certainly accomplish that. It just seemed a shame that he wouldn't have anyone attending his interment except the pallbearers, Reverend Appleton, and Violet.

A discreet clearing of the throat alerted them that they had company. Kirby, the butler, had entered the room with the noiseless stealth of a cat. "Yes, Kirby?" Portland said.

"Your Grace, pardon my interruption of your discussion. Mrs. Neale and I were just consoling each other over your terrible loss." He said this with the blandness of someone mentioning that tea was served. "It reminded us of the celebrations for All Hallows' Eve that the staff have been preparing for. Do you wish that we should stop? We do not wish to intrude on your grief, and Mrs. Neale and I thought perhaps it would be an unseemly amount of frivolity."

"Ah, you always have my best interests at heart, Kirby," Portland replied warmly. "However, I do not wish to steal away the joy the servants have each year with the festivities. You may proceed as planned. Hold the events down in the ballroom."

Kirby bowed and departed, and Violet thought she saw a hint of a smile upon the butler's lips.

After talking through a few more details with Portland, Violet stood. She still had to make final preparations to Colonel Mortimer's body, then head over to Worksop to telegram Harry and visit with Reverend Appleton. Portland, however, waved her back down.

"One more thing, Mrs. Harper. I plan to release Mr. Chandler for the funeral. In fact, he shall be a pallbearer."

More disappointment for Violet. "Are you certain, Your Grace? After all, we haven't cleared his name in connection with the recent deaths."

"Is Mr. Chandler your suspect in all three deaths?" Portland asked.

"At the moment, sir, he is my best guess," Violet replied truthfully. "Except that I cannot be sure of his motives."

"He is not the culprit."

"Your Grace? How do you know?"

Portland put a finger to the side of his nose. "I know it isn't possible for my falconer to have committed such acts. Anyone who cares for feathered creatures the way he does could not possibly wish to commit violence against a living being."

Violet considered that a weak conclusion. Many a brutal murderer had a pet kitten at home on whom he doted. "Your Grace, perhaps it is time we called the police—"

"It won't be necessary, Mrs. Harper. I am confident you will quietly find the culprit. I prefer not to have the commotion that involving the police would bring. When the police come, the press are typically right upon their heels, and soon there would be engravings and photographs of everyone from the lowest laundry maid to my own self splashed through every paper in England. This was always my concern, but now that I know the government is looking for ways to avoid repaying my bonds in a timely fashion, I am doubly concerned about the estate's reputation. I don't want them to figure out a way to use distress here as a mechanism for refusal to pay—or, worse, as a reason for sending in more busybodies."

Violet realized that Portland's care for his workers was considerable, but would not extend beyond his own . . . what was the word? Oh yes, his *dignitas*, she thought, remembering the ancient Roman word used to describe a nobleman's sum of his clout, personal reputation, moral standing, and entitlement to respect.

With that understanding, she knew that she would have to continue bearing the responsibility of justice for three men on her own. Very well, then, that was what she would do.

Taking her leave of the duke, Violet rushed back to Worksop and met with Reverend Appleton, working patiently to overcome his consternation that a funeral would be held so quickly with no time for visitation of the deceased. It was a delicate dance she performed, explaining the urgency of the funeral without revealing that the man had been murdered, nor that there were simply to be no mourners. Reluctantly, he agreed, but would not permit her to leave before he pressed a bound collection of his sermons into her hand.

She then rushed off to telegram Harry for a glass coffin, hoping he could ship it on a train this evening. At the last second, she also added in a request for him to send along the finest elm burl coffin in the shop. Just in case the glass one failed to contain its occupant.

* * *

Violet had never held her breath so much during a funeral before, a great irony given that it was just her, a coachman, and eight pallbearers making the trip from Welbeck to Worksop Priory. It was just short of a miracle that the glass coffin had survived the handling and train trip from London, and she supposed that as long as it survived the distant viewing by the duke, she could let out a small sigh of relief.

She had worked diligently upon returning from town the previous afternoon to put the colonel into a condition ready for display within a glass coffin. Along with copious amounts of cosmetic massage, his red-jacketed Grenadier Guards uniform, with its enormously tall, furred hat, hid the damage that had been done to poor Colonel Mortimer.

Portland offered a wave from an upper-story window as the pathetic little procession departed. Violet didn't know any of the men that Kirby had selected as pallbearers except for Martin Chandler, who avoided even glancing in her direction. Normally, Violet would have walked at the back of a procession, but this time she climbed onto the box with the driver, and once they had exited the long estate driveway, the pallbearers loaded the coffin onto the carriage, and all found places to hang from on the side of the conveyance, to speed their trip to town.

Violet attempted to muse about her investigative matter as the horses clopped along, but they found every rut in the road to drag the hearse's wheels through, rattling her bones and driving her to distraction with worry that the coffin would shatter into pieces. Dear God, how she hoped she wouldn't have to return to the storage locker at the train station to retrieve the elm coffin.

However, they made it to the churchyard without any damage, and the good reverend did his part well. Violet probably stopped breathing for a full minute as the pallbearers slipped the lifting straps around the coffin to pick it up and lower it into the hastily constructed enclosure in the ground. Each sway of the flag-draped coffin caused her to restrain a gasp. With a sickening clank it finally made it to its destination.

Violet hoped to never deal with a glass coffin again.

As the party made its way back to the hearse, Chandler finally acknowledged Violet's presence. "Mrs. Harper, if I might have a word. . . ." he said, a spark of his old self-assuredness back. "May I ask that you visit me at the rookery upon our return? I would offer to visit you directly, but of course my present circumstances make that impossible."

Would he remain confined until Violet solved this case? If so, she needed either to conclude definitely that Chandler was the killer or to quickly find another culprit. "Yes, but what is it you wish to see me about?" she asked.

His lazy smile had returned. "Believe it or not, I wish to tell you a story that you will find most interesting."

Violet sat across from Chandler inside his cottage, which was just a single room. They sat at a worn oak table, with an oil lamp between them providing an incongruously merry light for their discussion.

"I suppose I owe you an apology, Mrs. Harper," Chandler began. "I haven't been entirely honest with either you or His Grace."

Violet was silent. This much she knew.

"You see," he continued, "I thought that if I pretended not to know the colonel all that well, I could continue my own . . . investigations, shall we say . . . in the background while you continued with yours. I figured my confinement would only last a few hours until His Grace realized how unfair it was and I would be free to act as before. But now I'm not so sure that will happen. And I have information you need in order to do some intelligent questioning about the colonel's death, because I can tell you, Mrs. Harper, that you are as far off the path as an eagle hunting for a fox in a bog."

Violet ignored the jibe, waiting to see if Chandler had anything valuable to say.

"I confess I feel right bad about His Grace, thinking the colonel was such a dear friend of his. The colonel had his plans the minute he moved onto Welbeck estate."

"What plans were those?" Violet asked.

Chandler interlocked his fingers on the table. "I guess I should start from the beginning. Do you know about the Cavendish sisters?"

Where had she heard about them before? "Oh, you mean the seventeenth-century Royalists, Jane, Elizabeth, and Frances? Yes,

His Grace told me that they protected Welbeck from Cromwell's men during the war."

Chandler nodded. "Was that all he told you? There's far more to the story than that. The Cavendish sisters were very clever. When word came that the Roundheads were on their way, their father fled like a coward, but the girls set to work protecting the house. One of the first things they did was to gather the servants together to help them bury all of the silver. Well, all of it except for enough forks, knives, and serving bowls to convince the Roundheads that they had done no such thing."

Violet was intrigued. "Where did they bury it?"

"No one knows. It might have been in one place, or it may have been scattered around. Legend has it that the girls made a pact to leave it buried until their father came home. Of course, he never did, and as the sisters began making good marriages with wealthy men, they simply forgot about the enormous treasure they had buried."

Events and conversations began clicking together rapidly in Violet's mind. "So you and the colonel were working together to try to find this supposed treasure."

Chandler nodded. "The colonel heard of the legend, and used his old friendship with His Grace to his advantage, pretending to be down on his luck. Knowing His Grace's good nature in certain circumstances, he was right to assume His Grace would invite him to stay on the estate."

Now it was Violet's turn to nod. This confirmed her suspicions about the colonel. "I found some strange holes on the property, particularly in the area where his body was found. They must have been his attempts at testing the earth for locations containing storage trunks."

"Yes. Sometimes he used his cane, which made less-noticeable holes, and sometimes he used a special, narrow shovel he had purchased."

Colonel Mortimer must have been affecting to be much more of a drunkard and an insomniac than he really was, in order to stumble about the estate without anyone being suspicious, Violet thought.

"The last time I saw the colonel alive, he was standing outside his cottage with a couple of shovels, and when he saw me, he feigned being in his cups. I presume now that that was to throw me off track. He was hunting around a dilapidated shed behind his cottage."

"Yes, I know the one," Chandler said. "It's smothered in a rose vine. I hear that Miss Kemble, the lady His Grace fancied many years ago, visited here a couple of times and commented on how much she adored the roses on the building. They are some unusual shade of yellow, I think. He has never allowed the building to be removed, nor does he maintain it, and that's why it just rots on its own. Like his heart, I expect."

"Was there something about the cottage that made the colonel think there was treasure there?"

Chandler shrugged. "He never told me how he decided on locations. I always figured he chose them randomly. It was only when you showed me the map that I realized he was doing something more methodical."

That reminded Violet of a large question to be answered. "How did you become involved with the colonel? I'm surprised he would share the treasure with anyone."

"I think he realized it wasn't possible to search the entire estate alone. I told the truth when I said he liked to spend time with the birds. We talked, as men do, and I told him that I wanted to be married one day but didn't want to take on a wife on a falconer's paltry wage. It gave him the idea that he could help me realize my plans while getting himself a helper who wouldn't be likely to blab. He offered to split the haul evenly with me when we found it, so there would be no arguing over percentages.

"I suggested to the colonel that I could train the ravens to do some overhead scouting for us, and he agreed. Told me it was a brilliant idea." Chandler said this with pride in his own ingenuity. "So I did. Aristotle was the best seeker of them, but that really only meant he was the best at finding unusual objects. It was difficult to figure out how to train them to look for odd rises or depressions in the land. When your husband grabbed me so roughly—and unjustly, might I add—I had followed the ravens to that copse of trees because they were behaving excitedly and I thought perhaps they'd found something. What they had seen was Colonel Mortimer. I was just as surprised as you were to find him there, all done in."

Chandler seemed to have no grief over the loss of his friend, but perhaps friendships developed in the bonds of thievery didn't tend to be firm and enduring. Remembering back to her first encounter with the falconer, then subsequent events at Worksop Inn, Violet asked, "Have you a lady in mind to take as your wife?"

"Yes, I promised Polly Saunders that once the treasure was found and sold, my half would make me well-off enough to support her and she wouldn't have to work in her father's inn anymore."

"Your interest is in Polly, not Olive, the housemaid?"

"Olive? That little mouse? Why would I be interested in her?"

Why indeed. Poor Olive would be most disappointed to learn that the object of her adoration had no eyes for her, although Violet suspected Chandler would no longer have his position here at Welbeck, and Olive could find someone else less . . . unsavory . . . to pursue.

"How did you know the treasure would be extensive enough to make you wealthy?"

Chandler waved a hand in the direction of the house. "A place like this? Full of people that have always been rich and powerful? I knew." He offered another sardonic smile.

"But why would Colonel Mortimer, a man who had an army pension, secure investments, and a comfortable home in London, need to dig up his friend's estate to find a few pieces of silver? Unless . . ."

Chandler nodded. "The colonel wished to remarry, too. His wife died a long time ago, Mrs. Harper. He thought that a larger fortune would make him more appealing. What with that eye of his and his age, I expect society debutantes weren't falling all over themselves for him."

Violet thought that his fondness for liquor might have more to do with women's reticence toward the colonel, but kept that to herself. Chandler must have taken her silence as belief in his confession, for he finished with, "So you see, I was in partnership with the colonel, but I had nothing to do with his death. I was just as surprised to find him there as you were. There's an actual murderer still on the loose while I'm shut away like a petty thief."

Violet shook her head at his audacity. It was time to deflate his rubber balloon. "Well, for one thing, you *are* a petty thief, or a potential one, at a minimum. And you've proved nothing to me, as it makes perfect sense that you would wish to kill the colonel so that you wouldn't have to split the treasure with him when it was found."

Chandler gasped. "That's not true. Mrs. Harper, I've told you everything."

"Once you knew of the legend, what use was the old man to you?" Violet continued. "He was just an inconvenience. Perhaps you had returned to the copse to move his body, and were surprised by my husband. Isn't it ironic that Mr. Bayes was found in the same location, as well? Almost as if it is your own personal graveyard."

"What do you mean? Mr. Bayes was found at the skating rink site, killed by your husband's dynamite."

Ah, a fine jab and twist of the knife Chandler had executed there. "Don't attempt to befuddle me, Mr. Chandler. It won't work."

The falconer shrugged and Violet stormed off, irritated that she had once again permitted Chandler to annoy her. As she got farther away from the rookery and Chandler's derision, her mind wandered over what he had told her. In reality, his story of having partnered with the colonel for some sort of ephemeral buried treasure might sound like a child's story on the surface, but it explained much. And would Chandler have risked being caught and hanged merely to double the enormous fortune he already thought he would find? Chandler was cocky, but didn't strike Violet as an idiot.

If she accepted Chandler's entire story as true, though, then who killed the colonel, and why? Was it coincidental that he was murdered in the same location where Bayes had been found? Had the colonel and Bayes been privy to something illicit, something that had resulted in their deaths to ensure they never revealed what they had seen?

Had she not dug far enough into Edward Bayes's past? Perhaps it was time to pay his widow another visit.

28

In front of Mrs. Bayes's home, several burly men were shoving crates into a van emblazoned with "Whipman-Wood Transport" on the side of it, while her children chased one another through the piles of belongings waiting to be loaded. Since the door stood wide open, Violet rapped several times on the door frame and let herself in. "Mrs. Bayes?" she called out.

"Edward's clothes is outside in the green trunk, Mrs. Meadows," called out a voice from somewhere inside the home.

"Mrs. Bayes, it's me, Violet Harper."

"What?" In moments, the widow appeared in the front room, dressed in a garish lime-green-and-red dress, the sleeves of which were too long. "Oh, I thought you was Mrs. Meadows from the Prisoners' Aid Society. I'm giving all of Edward's clothes to 'em. I'm moving into my new cottage today and my income starts next week." She frowned. "Where's Charlie?"

"I believe he's outside with his brothers."

Her expression completely distracted, Mrs. Bayes swept past Violet and went outside, giving Charlie an earful about not breaking anything or getting himself hurt. The widow returned, breathless from her lecture. "'Ow may I 'elp you, Mrs. 'Arper?" she said.

"My apologies that my timing is so inconvenient. I didn't realize you were moving today. In any case, this couldn't have waited until you were settled onto the estate. I was wondering if you could tell me what your husband's job duties as purser were at

Welbeck?" On her way into town, Violet had decided that perhaps she might establish how the man's duties might have caused him to interact with others on the estate. If she could establish links between Bayes, Colonel Mortimer, and Spencer, perhaps she could then figure out who the murderer or perhaps *murderers* were.

"'Is duties?" Mrs. Bayes said, her expression bewildered. "'Ow would I know? 'E just scribbled in 'is book all the time when 'e was 'ome. I don't know what 'e did when 'e was at Welbeck."

"His book? Was he writing a novel? A memoir of his time in the navy?"

Mrs. Bayes shrugged. "Can't say as I much paid 'im attention."

Of course not. The widow Bayes would not be one for being interested in her husband's work, although Violet suspected that Edward Bayes wasn't the type of man that women could be that interested in generally.

"Do you have this book? I would like to see it."

Mrs. Bayes sighed and offered Violet an exasperated look. "Now 'ow am I supposed to know where it's packed away?"

No, she wasn't likely to remember where she had tossed her late, but not lamented, husband's personal belongings. "Perhaps you might allow me to search for it? It might be important to my investigation of your husband's death."

The widow's gaze narrowed. "What investigation? Is this about all them questions you were asking about before? I'm still to get my cottage, aren't I?"

"Mrs. Bayes, this has nothing to do with your cottage. I just want to ensure your husband gets the justice he deserves."

Margaret Bayes paused, as if weighing the truth—and, more importantly, the value—of Violet's claim, then shrugged. "If you can find it, you can gawp over it."

It didn't take long for Violet to find a shabby trunk with Edward Bayes's personal items hastily thrown inside it. Among the items tossed on top of a nicely tooled leather volume were smoking pipes, tobacco, a ship's compass with a cracked dome, and an old leather collar, making her wonder if he had been in charge of the care of a ship's cat when he was off in New Zealand.

Kneeling next to the trunk, Violet pulled out the book that she assumed had to be Bayes's mysterious work, and was surprised at how fine the gold-embossed burgundy leather was. Such a volume must have cost someone like Bayes a great deal, an indicator of how valuable the contents were to him.

With the book propped up against the lip of the trunk, Violet opened it to the middle and flipped backward through the creamy pages filled with sepia-brown ink. This definitely wasn't a novel. Nor was it a memoir.

She then flipped through the pages from the middle to the end. The book was only about two-thirds full of scribbling. As Violet continued studying it, understanding finally dawned. Her vision blurred, and she felt sick to her stomach at the realization of what had really happened to Edward Bayes, and how Colonel Mortimer and Burton Spencer played into it all. What made her even queasier was the realization that she had been right about one thing: there was more than one murderer involved.

What was she to do now, with Bayes's widow in the next room, waiting for Violet to leave so she could resume her journey to her new cottage at Welbeck? Violet couldn't leave this in Mrs. Bayes's possession, as there was no telling what the woman would do with it if she realized what Violet now understood. With her heart hammering, she returned to the outer room.

"Mrs. Bayes, I was wondering if I might borrow this for a short time, to study it further."

As Violet had feared, the widow became suspicious. "For what? Did 'e write something stupid? Are you planning to show it to 'Is Grace? I won't be denied my—"

"No, Mrs. Bayes," Violet said patiently. "This won't impact your move to Welbeck today. In fact, I can return the book to your new cottage once I am finished with it."

"Oh. Well, that's all right then, I suppose." The widow still eyed Violet suspiciously, as though Violet somehow had the power of denial over Portland's generosity toward his worker's wife.

Violet carried the book back to Worksop Inn to share it with Sam, holding it as though it were precious cargo, like a newborn infant. In fact, the book *did* carry the power of life and death for someone at Welbeck Abbey.

* * *

Sam agreed that she now held the answer in her hands, even if there were a few missing pieces. However, he urged caution. "Don't run back to Welbeck with your gun half out of its holster," Sam cautioned. "You have to show this to His Grace first."

"But what if he doesn't grant me the ability to accuse the right parties of their crimes? You know how peculiar the man is about any whisper of scandal." Had Violet raised her voice at her husband? She was becoming jittery over her newfound knowledge.

Sam smiled at her. "My love, the one charge we can confidently level at the Duke of Portland is that he cares about what happens to his workers. He entrusted you with finding the answer to these deaths, and you have found it. He will comply with your desire to call out the enemies of his estate."

Violet nodded. Sam was right; she was bordering on hysteria for no reason.

"However, what *I* will not comply with is the idea that you will make any accusations outside of my presence." Sam tapped the ground with his cane for emphasis. "Is that understood?" He cupped a hand around the back of her neck and kissed her forehead.

"Well then, you should plan on a very busy day tomorrow," she replied, hoping she herself would be able to achieve at least ten minutes of sleep during the night.

29

Not only was Portland amenable to Violet's plan for confrontation, he expanded the idea, suggesting that she do so in the ballroom, where most of the household staff were gathered making final preparations for the All Hallows' Eve festivities.

"It eliminates any rumors being spread about the estate if most of them hear it with their own ears. And this way they can go straight from the unpleasantness into the joy of their apple bobbing and such," Portland said confidently as he pulled another black-edged handkerchief from a cache of them at his elbow. Apparently, he really did keep mourning handkerchiefs on hand.

Violet thought Portland's idea made about as much sense as going from a funeral directly to a fancy ball, but she was glad that the duke would participate in her plan.

Even if it was from behind a wood screen especially set up in the ballroom for the purpose.

Violet had discussed with the butler the specific people who needed to be present, and he rounded them up—as well as other estate staff—using some form of excuse known only to him.

Sam, too, was given a particular role to play, although he was none too happy at the thought that it required him to be out of Violet's presence for even a short while.

At noon, Violet traveled through a tunnel into the ballroom, where dozens of servants were moving their planned games and activities from the center of the open space to locations lining the wall. Upon seeing the undertaker, most of them frowned in confusion. Kirby must have told them just enough that they knew Violet was responsible for disrupting their plans.

By one o'clock, everyone had drifted in. Mrs. Garside was bent over a vent, sniffing, while Judith stood patiently nearby. In a corner, Mrs. Neale was lecturing Olive, who gazed over the woman's shoulder at Chandler. The footman, Miles Hudock, stood rigidly at one of the entrances to the ballroom.

A group of young men whom Violet suspected were the resident home children, since Gilbert Lewis was among them, were on the floor to one side. They were huddled over a staking board, playing Pope Joan, almost as if they had known in advance there would be a wait. She noticed a house servant kick one of them for being in the way. The home child looked up, oblivious, then returned to his hand of cards.

Ellery Reed watched the home children's play from a distance, and started when the servant placed his well-aimed kick, but the anger left his face quickly. Violet knew Mr. Reed was probably working out for himself that a confrontation with the house servant in this tense and uncertain situation wasn't worthwhile.

Jack LeCato stood apart from everyone else, gazing at Violet speculatively. She didn't care for his scrutiny. Margaret Bayes, however, stood eyeing LeCato with overt interest. Violet was amused to imagine the government agent fending the woman off.

For once, Molly Spriggs didn't hold a lantern, but a deck of cards, which she constantly rearranged in her hands while nervously licking her lips.

Even Parris, the head gardener, was down here, looking completely ill at ease in his palatial surroundings, but not as apprehensive as Martin Chandler, who might as well have been under arrest already, what with the shadow of guilt darkening his face.

William Pearson, the duke's valet, stood guard in front of the wood screen, behind which sat his master like an eerie specter. Henry Bentinck had even been summoned from his own home, and stood chatting amiably through the screen, as though his brother's detachment in public gatherings was perfectly normal.

Once she saw that everyone had been assembled, Violet nodded to Hudock, who rapped sharply on the door to get everyone's attention. She took a deep breath before beginning her story. It was awkward that she was leading this discussion, but Portland had refused to take center stage, and no one else was privy to the answers to what had happened at Welbeck over the past two weeks. She just hoped that guilt and fear wouldn't cause someone to commit an unfortunate, stupid act.

Violet raised her voice, and it reverberated off the walls and ceiling of the subterranean room. "You all know me as the undertaker who first came to Welbeck Abbey to bury poor little Aristotle, His Grace's favorite raven."

"Poor little bird," Mrs. Garside echoed, pulling a handkerchief from her sleeve and dabbing at her eyes.

Violet ignored her. "Remarkably, the story of Aristotle's death reaches far back into the previous century, when the famous Cavendish sisters defended Welbeck Abbey from the Roundheads."

"That old legend?" Henry Bentinck scoffed. "How could that possibly have anything to do with the evil going on here today?"

Violet calmly accepted the rebuke. "I understand your skepticism, sir, as I, too, was quite astonished when I learned the truth of it."

She explained the falconer's conspiracy with Colonel Mortimer to locate the buried silver, then turned to where Chandler stood, nodding miserably at her revelation of his perfidy.

"It was an unfortunate way for Mr. Chandler and Colonel Mortimer to repay His Grace's generosity to both of them. Regardless, shortly after Aristotle's death, the body of Burton Spencer was found, and it appeared that he had fallen and struck his head on a nearby rock. When I arrived at the scene, Mr. Kirby and Mr. LeCato stood over the body. When I later inspected Mr. Spencer, I realized that he hadn't been killed by an accidental fall, but that he had been violently struck in the chest, then again in the head by the rock, as evidenced by the terrible bruising on his chest that accompanied his mauled head."

Several female servants gasped. Perhaps Violet shouldn't have been so graphic.

"The next morning, Colonel Mortimer came to His Grace, reporting that he had witnessed a murder—a strangulation. But he admitted that it had been dark when he saw it, and he knew neither who the attacker was nor who the victim was. I made the mistake of assuming that Spencer was the victim. He was not. The victim the colonel had witnessed being killed while he was out searching for dig holes in the dark was actually Edward Bayes, and Bayes was killed almost immediately after Spencer."

"What? That's not possible," Ellery Reed interjected. "I was summoned from town to bear witness to Spencer's body, and that was days before you found Bayes."

Violet nodded. "Yes, Spencer was found days before Bayes, but in fact he died only a short time before Bayes."

"How could you possibly know this?" Reed asked.

"I initially suspected that the colonel had something to do with Spencer's death, although I couldn't fathom what it was. When I discovered a piece of a glass eye at Bayes's murder scene, I realized that Colonel Mortimer had been mistaken in the murder he had witnessed. However, it was the fact that he *had* witnessed Bayes's murder that made him a victim, as well. Perhaps he confronted the murderer on his own in an attempt to bring him to justice. I don't know." In Violet's opinion, it was most likely that the colonel had actually demanded a bribe to keep quiet, but she might never know the answer to that question, and she had no desire to disparage the colonel's memory in front of Portland.

"So the murderer would eventually kill the colonel to prevent him from revealing who had killed Bayes. What confused me, though, was whether I was dealing with one killer or two."

"Two?" Margaret Bayes's eyes were wide with fear. "You mean one person killed Colonel Mortimer and Mr. Spencer, and someone else killed my beloved Edward?"

Now he was her "beloved Edward." Was that bit of affection for Jack LeCato's or Portland's benefit?

"No, Mrs. Bayes. I don't mean that at all. I mean that one person killed Colonel Mortimer and your husband, but it was your husband who murdered Burton Spencer."

A chilled silence descended on the room like a graveyard fog.

Margaret Bayes's voice was barely a squeak now. "Why would 'e do that?"

"Why indeed. I was very confused by the entire scenario myself until I ran into Gilbert Lewis at the telegram office a few days ago. There, I learned that there is a home children program that has been established in Great Britain that offers orphans a chance for new lives through relocation to farms and factories in Canada."

"Mrs. Harper," Reed interjected, "please . . ." He cast a glance at Lewis and the other boys, as if pleading with her not to embarrass them by calling out their status. It was unfortunate, but she had to expose the ugly details of what had happened.

"His Grace knew about these boys, and was pleased to offer them a chance to learn construction skills before they left for their new homes, but he didn't know that the housing of these young men at Welbeck was a sad state of affairs. His Grace insisted that they be paid fairly, like every other worker, and Mr. Reed developed a plan to have their wages saved until such time that they were to depart, in order to provide them with a good start in Canada.

"Mr. Bayes, though, revealed his dirty deeds to me in death, inside a ledger he kept, which detailed the manner in which he was altering Mr. Reed's savings records, to remove a little for himself out of each boy's pay. When it came time for their departure, he would see to it that they received less money, and how were they—or anyone else, for that matter—really to know the difference? Mr. Bayes wisely kept this ledger at home, out of the sight of anyone at Welbeck, lest he be immediately dismissed. After all, even a man as generous as His Grace would be unable to tolerate that."

"Dear God," Reed said. "The effrontery of the man!"

The boys stared at one another, open-mouthed. Violet hated that she had to shock them all further. "Burton Spencer figured it out somehow. Perhaps Mr. Bayes had taunted him over it one day while in his cups and more likely to wag his tongue. Spencer was a sizable young man, and probably assumed he could bully Mr. Bayes into more money for him to keep him quiet about Bayes's scheme. But poor Spencer underestimated Bayes's strength, and it resulted in his death."

The cook spoke up once more. "But, Mrs. 'Arper, if Mr. Bayes was the one responsible for Spencer's death, why should anyone want to kill 'im afterward? And 'ow would the next murderer know to do it right after Mr. Bayes killed Spencer?" Mrs. Garside put a hand over her mouth, as if the thought of two murderers at Welbeck Abbey was simply too much to continue discussing.

Violet nodded. "A troubling question, indeed. I had many other questions to ask myself, as well, Mrs. Garside. Who else might know of Bayes's scheme? Who might think I had discovered it and arrange to have me attacked while in London? For that matter, who knew I was heading to London?"

Parris spoke up for the first time. "You were attacked?"

"Yes," Violet said curtly. "I was set upon by a thug who worked in a local orphanage, which I realized later was no coincidence, given Bayes's chicanery with the home children. But back to your question, Mrs. Garside, the only person who would wish to kill Mr. Bayes was whomever he was in collusion with. It occurred to me that only one person could possibly have known about Bayes's scheme, have had connections in London to attack me, and had reason to kill Colonel Mortimer. Yes, there was only one person who could have been responsible for it all, and ultimately, it was the one person who was the most obvious from the start." Violet turned slowly until she faced the murderer.

"It was you, Mr. Reed. You were really the intellect behind the scheme to cheat the boys."

"What?" Reed gasped. "What are you talking about? I have treated Burton and the others as if they were my own children."

"That's true, Mrs. Harper," Gilbert Lewis piped up. "Mr. Reed is very kind to us. Much better than it was at the orphanage."

"Yes, the worst of men can present themselves as the most innocent of lambs before they reveal themselves as wolves to devour you," Violet said dryly. "Nevertheless, Mr. Reed is guilty."

She whirled back on Reed, who continued to protest her accusations. She cut him off. "You maintained your own false ledger—very cleverly hidden in a safe, to convince any curious eyes that you were serious about keeping the boys' savings sacred. I admit, I was most convinced when you eagerly showed it to me."

"You're wrong; that was the actual ledger of the boys' savings."

"You mean, sirrah, that it was the ledger that accurately reflected what would have been saved for each boy . . . if you had actually intended to give it to him."

Reed didn't respond, and Violet pressed on, now pacing to burn nervous energy.

"I speculate that your agreement with Ian Hale of Babbage's Home for Foundlings was that he would ensure that the strongest of boys be sent to Welbeck. You would then recommend to His Grace that they be paid an older man's wages, for their ability to lift, push, and carry. How much were you paying Hale for the right sort of boy, Mr. Reed? Furthermore, what did you pay Hale to kill me? You must have been quite put out when he was unsuccessful and then fled town."

"Surely you are joking, Mrs. Harper? Why would I pay a man to kill you?" Reed implored, spreading his hands to demonstrate his innocence.

Violet gave him a grim look. "I was your raven, the one who was too close to your secrets about the home children. What I couldn't understand was why you had to murder Edward Bayes. You couldn't possibly have known that he was maintaining a separate ledger," Violet said, trying to draw as much out of him as she could.

"Of course I knew he had one. What sort of fool do you think I am?" Reed snapped before catching himself. "I mean, I'm not surprised that he had one. I never trusted Bayes."

"No, and I doubt he trusted you, either." Violet realized that Reed was not owning up to anything, and decided that a quick deception was in order.

"Of course, Edward Bayes's ledger was a fake, and you kept the real one inside your hidden safe."

"Don't be ridiculous. He kept the real one and I held the fake—" Reed stopped as he realized his own admission of guilt. Several people in the room gasped, and Mrs. Garside burst into tears.

Violet felt a tumultuous blend of satisfaction and deep sadness at knowing herself to be right.

Reed dropped his voice, and Violet feared that it meant he was becoming dangerous, like a cornered tiger. "Of course Bayes's ledger was the real one, which reflected his cut of the proceeds. How could you think for a moment that I didn't have control over my system? Yes, Mrs. Harper, I had to kill Edward Bayes, but not because of the ledger. No, I had to dispose of him because he killed Spencer."

Now it was Violet's turn to gasp as she tried to work through what this heartless monster was telling her. "Do you mean to say that you were *avenging* Spencer's death?" she asked, incredulous.

Reed sighed. "No, my dear. I was not *avenging* Spencer's murder. Why would I care about such a thing? I had plenty of other boys to profit from." He nodded back to the remaining home children.

"Bayes was as frightened as a silly little maid who has burned her master's toast. He was overwrought with guilt after accidentally killing Spencer, blathering about wanting to confess his crime and that it was a divine sign that we should halt our plan. He was too unstable, and I couldn't have him committing some stupid act that would have ruined it all. Once he showed me where Spencer was, so that I could arrange the boy's body as I wished, I then convinced Bayes to walk awhile with me so we could talk everything out. Then I took care of him."

Reed's calm as he confessed to his heinous deeds was chilling. However, his revelation caused Violet to realize something else. "You moved Bayes's body for two reasons, then. One was to make me think I was completely confused, and the other was to make his death look to be the result of the dynamite."

"Actually, I had intended to bury Bayes where you found him, but when I returned to do so, you were already poking around. So I waited until you were gone and moved him. By then, the dynamiting was planned and I realized how to use it to my advantage." Reed's expression didn't offer any hint of remorse.

Swallowing her disgust, Violet said, "It was a callous manner of treating your partner, someone you had known from your time in Her Majesty's navy." This was a wild shot in the dark, but based on Reed's startled reaction, she knew she had found the target.

"If you were to undo your shirt, sir . . ." Violet said.

He frowned and glanced at one entrance to the ballroom, which Hudock still guarded. "For what reason, Mrs. Harper?" Reed glanced back at the rear entrance of the ballroom. No one stood there, but Violet didn't dare call attention to it, lest Reed attempt to bolt through it. She wasn't sure he didn't plan to do so, anyway.

"I am interested in whether you have followed in what so many jack-tars do."

Reed narrowed his eyes, but as several other men stepped toward him menacingly, he waved them off, unbuttoned his vest, and shoved his open collar to the right. "Is that what you wish to see?" he asked.

There it was. A tattoo of a volcano with a flourishing tree atop it, just like that adorning Edward Bayes's shoulder. Now Violet fully understood how Bayes came to be employed at Welbeck. LeCato must have realized it, too, for an expression of utter contempt came over his face, and Violet knew he was contemplating the shame Reed had brought upon the navy.

What a terrible tragedy had descended on Welbeck, a fine estate that might be owned by a very peculiar man, but also one where employees were cared for and the local economy flourished. Violet sighed heavily, so very saddened at the destruction Reed had wrought. It was yet another terrible addition to the long line of tragic events in the Welbeck legacy. Perhaps this episode could be stricken from the Abbey's history.

"Thank you, Mr. Reed. I'm sure the other men in your prison cell will be most impressed by it."

Reed frowned, as if he didn't understand what Violet was telling him. Then, as realization finally dawned, he gazed at her, the color draining from his face as he began babbling.

"There will be no prison for me. I'm Ellery Reed, a competent estate manager who has effectively run all of His Grace's projects here as well as maintained Harcourt House. Do you think that another local dukery won't hire me for my skills? Just because His Grace might be offended doesn't mean I can't get work else-where."

The man was completely delusional. As though his offenses only amounted to some minor infraction.

He interrupted his own nonsensical stream of thought to dash toward the rear door that led into the tunnel off which were the guest bedrooms. Parris made a dash for him, but Reed anticipated him, turning and connecting his fist with Parris's jaw and sending the gardener sprawling to the ground.

One of the home children also sprang up and attempted to tackle Reed, nearly causing the estate manager's knees to buckle, but he was able to throw off the boy, who yelped as he crashed to the floor.

Mrs. Garside's sobbing grew noisier as Reed bolted out of the ballroom and into the passageway, with several more estate work-ers close behind him, but within moments came the sounds of a scuffle through the open doorway, blocking out the cook's wailing. Several sickening thuds against the stone left Violet trembling without an explanation of who, exactly, was meeting his destiny with the ground. In moments, though, Sam appeared in the door-way, triumphant, as he dragged Reed behind him. Sam's cane was nowhere to be found, as if his injured leg was completely forgotten in the pleasure he took in bringing down the man responsible for trying to kill his wife. The workers who had rushed out behind Reed now followed behind Sam, glowering at the man Sam had unceremoniously hauled back into the ballroom and occasionally glancing up at Sam with burgeoning respect.

Sam dropped Reed, his face bloodied and his voice reduced to a mere gurgle, in the center of the elegant ballroom, then went to stand at Violet's side. His knuckles were scraped and bruises were already forming, but his expression suggested a complete eupho-ria. It was enough to silence Mrs. Garside.

"Ahem," Sam said, clearing his throat. "If someone would be so kind as to summon the police?"

Hudock dashed out the opposite door as everyone else gathered to observe Reed's quivering form, inspecting him as though he were some new form of insect. One of the home children spat at him, the glob landing squarely on the murderer's forehead and dribbling into his eye. Others standing around cheered the boy, and an anonymous foot connected with Reed's hip, causing the man to grunt roughly in pain.

Now it was Portland's turn to clear his throat from behind his wood screen, where presumably he had successfully witnessed all that had transpired in the room. Violet thought his timing fortuitous, as she feared Reed was going to be served a violent justice before the police arrived.

Pearson stepped behind the screen and returned with a sheet of paper in his hand. The valet handed it to Kirby, who opened it and walked over to where they all stood around the enfeebled estate manager. He read aloud to the prone figure. "'Mr. Reed, you will be presently transferred into police custody. Let me assure you, sir, that you are a disgrace and no longer in my employ.'"

Reed was now whimpering in pain, so Violet wasn't sure whether he'd heard Portland's unnecessary pronouncement.

Portland sent out another note through Pearson. Kirby read this one out for Mrs. Bayes. "'You are not responsible for your husband's actions. You may remain at Welbeck Abbey for the rest of your natural life.'"

The duke's correspondence was certainly terse and precise.

Mrs. Bayes sniffled, now looking bedraggled and droopy, and not at all the brazen wench she presented herself as. Violet supposed that Portland was performing the kindest of deeds for her, as many an aristocrat would have thrown a criminal's widow and her children to the street, or recommended them for the workhouse. Even though she likely had no idea what her husband's ledger was about, the widow would have had good cause to destroy it after his death, as it might have ruined her chances for her much-anticipated pension and cottage. Without it, Violet would have never figured everything out.

Mrs. Bayes dashed to the wooden screen, prostrating herself on the ground before it. "Your Grace, I'm forever indebted to you. You are such a kind and wonderful gentleman, and I don't know 'ow I could ever repay your charity. But what with Edward's passing, my children and me . . . we 'ave so little except for your goodness, and if we don't 'ave—"

The woman's desperate prattling was cut off midsentence, as the duke began rapping his cane loudly on the wooden screen, whereupon Pearson quickly grabbed Mrs. Bayes and pulled the sobbing woman away.

A third note was issued. This time, Kirby didn't open it but brought it to Violet, cupping it in both hands as he presented it to her. It was sealed in red wax with the duke's coat of arms. She read it to herself, with Sam reading over her shoulder:

Mrs. Harper, my gratitude for your help with our small trouble at Welbeck. To think that you solved our predicament, and now I shall earn money from your husband's dynamite production. A happy turn of events, although I am disappointed not to be rid of LeCato. I had so hoped he was the culprit.

Violet figured that was probably the highest praise Portland had ever given anyone, outside of the colonel and perhaps a few siblings. She thought that LeCato might soon leave of his own accord to avoid what Violet suspected would soon be Mrs. Bayes's smothering attentions.

She also presumed that Chandler would be publicly dismissed from service, but she was shocked when Portland passed a final note through Pearson for the falconer. This one Kirby also read aloud: "'Mr. Chandler, you should be dismissed from service at Welbeck. However, if the Cavendish sisters buried silver on the property, I should like to find it. You will find it for me, and will still be responsible for the falconry. You are no longer confined.'"

Chandler looked as though he might faint dead away from his good luck as he thanked the duke profusely for his generosity. Personally, Violet would have sent him packing and whispered so to Sam.

Her husband chuckled, his expression still one of great cheer among everyone else's countenance of shock, anxiety, and sadness. "So says the woman who is terrified of her own servants," he whispered back.

"I am not," she replied indignantly.

"Hmm, remember the time you refused to send a burnt apple tart back to Mrs. Wren, for fear of her reaction?"

Violet frowned, remembering the incident. "Well, that was a different circumstance altogether."

"I see," Sam said solemnly, but there was still mirth spread across his face.

"It was. I'm not a peer in charge of thousands of acres and people who must retain a reputation so as to keep things in order." She knew Sam was teasing, so why was she defending herself? Besides, wasn't it true that servants intimidated her? It was why she was thankful she and Sam lived in quarters small enough to just require day help. Violet hoped to never again have a home large enough to require live-in staff.

She turned her attention back to the room as Portland cleared his throat from behind the screen and spoke a single, baritone sentence. "Now, good people, we will dispense with our troubles and let the All Hallows' Eve festivities commence."

30

To Violet's surprise, Portland had been correct about the staff diving into All Hallows' Eve once Reed had been hauled away. Within a short time, it was as if the lurid details of the estate manager's deception and murderous deeds had been completely forgotten, relegated to the dusty pages of some ancient history book.

Which was fine with Violet. She and Sam joined in on the apple bobbing and other games the servants had set up, laughing uproariously with the others when Kirby took his turn as "it," stumbling around the room in an undignified manner, grasping for someone to tag.

"I tell you, my prayers worked," Mrs. Garside said, coming alongside Violet and startling her as she stepped outside the ring of play to catch her breath. "I went to the priory on several afternoons and near wore my knees out, asking for the curse to be lifted from Welbeck, and now it 'as been. Perhaps I was wrong about Aristotle, Mrs. 'Arper. Perhaps 'e was an 'arbinger of good luck, not bad."

"Perhaps you're right," Violet murmured, reflecting that it was only because of Aristotle that she'd managed to find the glass eye shard—and therefore Bayes's body—before he showed up in Sam's dynamiting of the skating rink. How ironic to think that Aristotle had been instrumental in preventing Sam's reputation from being thoroughly ruined.

As everyone lost interest in blind man's bluff, someone suggested that they all play pin the tail on the donkey. Violet noted with amusement that when it came to Olive's turn to wear the blindfold, Hudock volunteered to cover her eyes, and did so with the utmost gentleness and a whisper in her ear, causing her to blush prettily. Thank goodness it looked as though she would recover quickly from her devotion to Martin Chandler.

Violet avoided Molly Spriggs, who now sat at a table with tarot cards spread in front of her, a staple of All Hallows' Eve celebrations. She invited Violet over for a reading, but Violet was still shy of the cards, which had been the precursor to several deaths during an investigative matter for the queen several months ago. Undaunted, Molly called to Mrs. Garside, who happily plopped herself before the table.

James Appleton, the vicar, had been making rounds, greeting and offering blessings to everyone in the room, and finally arrived in front of Violet and Sam, red-faced in his exertion. "Such a wonderful celebration, isn't it?" he asked. "I have always encouraged His Grace to sponsor All Hallows' Eve amusements. I find them to be a theologically sound way of remembering our saints, martyrs, and all of the faithful departed believers, especially when the games use humor and ridicule to confront the power of death. Ah, see here, we have someone dressed up as a court jester to scare away Death. Amusing, isn't it?"

Violet was speechless because it was Jack LeCato in the costume, prancing about in an undignified way to the delight of several women—Margaret Bayes in particular—who taunted him in playful voices and squealed when he came after them, the bells on his pointed hat jingling wildly. Perhaps it was more than just the actual Welbeck staff who were relieved that the murders had been solved.

Next came Kirby's announcement that the scavenger hunt was to begin. Everyone paired up to seek out items hidden throughout the tunnels and rooms surrounding the ballroom. Sam grabbed Violet's hand and led her through the rear door of the ballroom and into the tunnel, dodging past other couples who were searching the unused guest rooms for hidden treasures. Violet avoided looking down, worried that she might find traces of Reed's blood spilled during Sam's rage.

Sam peered into various rooms and finally stopped before the Gothic arches of the chapel's doors. He stared at them a moment, then said, "Perfect."

He held open one of the doors for Violet to pass through, then shut them behind her with a resounding thud. "Why are we—" she started, but he put a finger to his lips and backed her up against the door.

"I'm very proud of you," he whispered. "You doggedly stuck to your investigation and ensured justice for those who deserved it. The police couldn't have done so fine a job."

Violet warmed at her husband's words. "You helped me. You advised—"

"Shh," he whispered, placing his hands on either side of her face and putting his lips to hers.

"That's for being such an intelligent undertaker," he murmured.

Violet's stomach twirled with pleasure.

"This," he said, coming in for a much longer kiss, "is for being the kind of wife that makes a husband proud to share his name with her."

"The others," she demurred weakly. "They will want to search the chap—"

"And this," he continued, wrapping his arms around her waist, "is just for me." He captured her in a kiss that made her forget not only about any of the other revelers barging in on them but also about why she had even come to Nottinghamshire in the first place.

Author's Note

Located south of Worksop—the largest town in Nottinghamshire's northernmost district—the **Dukeries** is a district so named because it once contained four ducal estates totaling some eighty-eight thousand acres: Worksop Manor, seat of the Dukes of Norfolk; Clumber Park, seat of the Dukes of Newcastle; Thoresby Hall, seat of the Dukes of Kingston and later the Earls Manvers; and Welbeck Abbey, seat of the Dukes of Portland. The parklands of these four magnificent estates are largely contiguous, making this area notable for the number of English ducal families who once lived in such close proximity.

The Duke of Norfolk sold Worksop Manor to the Duke of Newcastle in 1839, preferring to spend more time at Arundel Castle. Newcastle demolished the main part of the house. Later, in the 1930s, Newcastle demolished Clumber House because of the expensive upkeep, although the park now belongs to the National Trust. Thoresby Hall is today a country house hotel.

Welbeck Abbey was built as a religious house in 1153 to 1154. It flourished, but by February 1539 it was largely destroyed under the order of Henry VIII, who waged a war against the Vatican to assert his own supremacy over the church in England. In 1584, it came into the possession of Gilbert Talbot, who later became the 7th Earl of Shrewsbury. He was a stepson of the infamous Bess of Hardwick, who arranged his marriage with her daughter. Through Bess's machinations, Welbeck Abbey came into the hands of her third son, Sir Charles Cavendish. Sir Charles's son, William Cavendish, was the father of Jane, Elizabeth, and Frances Cavendish, who grew up at Welbeck Abbey and who would courageously defend it during the English Civil War when their feckless father abandoned them there. The story of the girls burying silver on the estate is my own invention.

Lady Margaret Cavendish-Holles-Harley inherited Welbeck in 1741, and brought the home into the Bentinck family by marrying William Bentinck, the 2nd Duke of Portland. The Bentincks were a noble Dutch family descended from Hans Wilhelm Bentinck, groom of the bedchamber (a highly coveted position) to William of Orange, who made him Earl of Portland.

The 3rd Duke of Portland, William Henry Bentinck, became prime minister twice during the reign of George III. He inherited Welbeck from his mother, and married Lady Dorothy Cavendish, daughter of the 4th Duke of Devonshire and herself also a descendant of Bess of Hardwick. It was at this point that the family adopted the name Cavendish-Bentinck.

The home went through various stages of repair and expansion through the nearly three centuries between the 7th Earl of Shrewsbury and **William John Cavendish-Scott-Bentinck, the 5th Duke of Portland** (1800–1879). It was this duke who launched one of the most remarkable building projects in England, mostly underground. Over the years, he added a ballroom, a warren of guest rooms, a chapel, and a library—all underground. He also built miles of tunnels to take him to various places, including the train station in Worksop, and these tunnels were always built in pairs—one side large enough for workers to walk four abreast, and the other side large enough to accommodate the ducal carriage. It is estimated that the duke spent £2 to £3 million on all of his projects.

Portland served in the Grenadier Guards prior to his elevation as Marquess of Titchfield upon the death of his elder brother, William Henry Cavendish-Bentinck, in 1824. The Grenadier Guards is the most senior regiment of infantry in the British Army and traces back to the mid-seventeenth century. During the Victorian era, the regiment took part in the Crimean War. It was involved later in the Anglo-Egyptian War, the Second Boer War, World War I, and World War II, and has been involved in various peacekeeping missions since then. Portland reached the rank of captain in this prestigious regiment. For the sake of the story, I portray the guards as having participated in the First Anglo-Burmese War (1824–1826), which resulted in British control over Burma.

Portland was one of nine children, of which three died prior to

1869. I have chosen to include three of his remaining siblings in the story.

One of Portland's younger brothers, **Lord Henry William Scott-Bentinck** (1804–1870), was an enthusiastic hunting man and as much an authority on hounds as his brother was on horses. Lord Henry sat as a Conservative Party member of Parliament for North Nottinghamshire from 1847 to 1857, and was also a trustee of the British Museum.

One of Portland's younger sisters, Lady Charlotte Bentinck, married **John Evelyn Denison** (1800–1873), Speaker of the House of Commons from 1857 to 1872. Denison is particularly known for having championed *The Bible Commentary*, later known as *The Speaker's Commentary* in his honor, a plain but complete and accurate commentary on the Bible that was assigned to Frederick Charles Cook for producing. Denison also picked up the seat as the member of Parliament for North Nottinghamshire after his brother-in-law, Lord Henry, vacated it in 1857. Denison was made the 1st Viscount Ossington in 1872, a title he only enjoyed for less than a year until his death. As the couple was childless, the title went extinct.

Another of Portland's sisters, Lady Lucy Joan Cavendish-Scott-Bentinck (1807–1899), married Charles Ellis, 6th Baron Howard de Walden. The baron was a British diplomat and politician, and together they had five sons, the eldest of whom was **Frederick George Ellis** (1830–1899), who became the 7th Baron in 1868. As a young man, Frederick assisted his father in overseeing the family's holdings of Jamaica sugar plantations and later became a major in the 4th Light Dragoons. Unfortunately, the elder Ellis died with his estate in debt, and Frederick inherited this debt.

Lady Lucy managed to discharge her husband's debts, but Frederick's life was not to prove a smooth one. In 1876, he married Blanche Holden, and they had a son, Thomas Evelyn. By 1893, though, the couple had become engaged in a bitter divorce suit. Frederick accused Blanche of "undue intimacy" with Count Jean de Madre of Paris and with a Captain Winter. In return, Blanche accused Frederick of physical abuse and cruelty, alleging that he had threatened to shoot her. Press reports of the trial described testimony of Frederick frequently returning home drunk and vomiting in bed, developing "filthy and hoggish habits" that prevented Blanche from sharing a bed with him. Although these events happened two decades after my story, I chose to use the accusations made against Frederick as the basis for describing him as a younger man. I do not know if Lady Lucy and her son lived at Harcourt House—which was indeed brought into the family through a card game—but I don't think it is unreasonable to think that her brother might have given her the use of his London home since her husband left her essentially destitute. Today, Harcourt House is a mix of commercial offices and medical spaces, as well as several residential units.

William Ewart Gladstone (1809–1898), a British Liberal politician, had an exceedingly long political career of more than sixty years, of which more than ten years were spent as prime minister in four separate periods. He also served four times as chancellor of the exchequer. Gladstone's administration was most noted for reforming the haphazard poor relief system, and working with charities to instill the Victorian values of self-reliance and self-discipline. An interesting tidbit about Gladstone is that he lost the forefinger of his left hand in a hunting accident while reloading a gun in 1842. After that, he always wore gloves or a finger sheath. Gladstone was also a great admirer of Charlotte Yonge's romantic novels, I suspect primarily because they had religious and moral undertones to them.

Robert Lowe, the 1st Viscount Sherbrooke (1811–1892), was chancellor of the exchequer from 1868 to 1873, and then home secretary from 1873 to 1874. Gladstone appointed Lowe as chancellor, expecting him to rein in public spending. Instead, public spending rose, and Lowe repeatedly underestimated revenue the Crown would receive, thus enabling him to resist demands to implement tax cuts and reduce the national debt. Gladstone pronounced Lowe "wretchedly deficient."

Portland purchased a vast amount in consols from the British government. Consols are high-grade bonds, or "gilts," with low risk and low yields, and virtually no maturity date. The consols

Portland purchased were issued in order to help the government finance an expedition to Abyssinia to rescue several missionaries and two government representatives from the emperor of the Ethiopian empire, to be followed by a punitive invasion. Portland's investment in these bonds was critical to the success of the British mission. However, his building projects were requiring vast sums for completion, as well, and Portland began calling in the bonds in 1868 during the tenures of both Gladstone and Lowe. This probably caused no end of irritation to the government, which was counting on Portland's money to finance the venture. I used this as a basis for the fictional Jack LeCato's involvement with Welbeck Abbey and his attempt to slow down Portland's building projects to, in turn, prevent the duke from needing so much money at one time.

At first blush, Portland appears to have been an eccentric among eccentrics, what with his bizarre building projects, extreme reclusiveness, and odd personal habits. However, a closer examination of the duke reveals a man who was kind and considerate, and cared deeply for his workers. Although he is remembered as the "mad duke" and the "prince of silence" who was completely out of touch with the world, it should be noted that he sent out a whole shipload of food and beer for the British troops in the Crimea—an extraordinarily expensive venture—and also gave £4,000 to help Turkish hospitals in the Russo-Turkish War of 1877. He was well known for generosity with his money, and did indeed provide all of his estate workers with an umbrella and a donkey to enable them to get to work safely and without fatigue. He also established a widows' and orphans' fund to care for the families of workers who had died, even providing widows with cottages for life after the deaths of their husbands.

Unfortunately, it is mostly his quirks that history notes: the chickens roasting at all hours, the salmon-painted walls of empty rooms, the old-fashioned clothing, and the secret tunnels and bizarre warren of unused, underground rooms.

Portland's involvement with his workers seems excessive to us today, but would have been welcomed and celebrated in his time. He did indeed install a roller-skating rink for his staff, and encouraged them to use it for their good health. He also liked them to row on the lake, and would even coach them in oarsmanship.

He was a keen hunter and a renowned expert in horses, even building a riding school that was second in size only to the Spanish Riding School in Vienna, Austria. He regularly inspected his stables, and enjoyed watching young horses being broken. His naming of rooms after extinct horse breeds, however, is my own invention.

I have described many of his tunnels and structures—the ballroom, the chapel, the skating rink, and so forth—but not everything existed in 1869, as tunneling operations had just commenced in 1864. For example, the ballroom was not completed until 1872. However, I wanted to show the reader the breadth of the duke's building ambitions. The unusual contents of the subterranean ballroom—the drop earrings and chalice from Charles I, the letters from the Stuarts—have been documented.

Sadly, for all of Portland's kindheartedness, he was thwarted in love. Early in his life, he fell for and proposed to Adelaide Kemble, an opera singer and sister of Fanny Kemble, the famous actress. She refused him, and it does not appear that he ever courted another woman after that deep wounding.

An interesting note for history buffs who enjoy the most minute pieces of trivia, as I do: Adelaide Kemble married Edward John Sartoris, a landowner and member of Parliament (being an opera singer didn't close *all* doors to you). In 1874, their son, Algernon, married Nellie Grant, daughter of President Ulysses S. Grant, in the East Room of the White House.

Portland died in 1879 at his London home, Harcourt House, at the age of seventy-nine, and was buried in Kensal Green Cemetery in London. True to his unprepossessing nature, he instructed that his tomb be surrounded with shrubs, which soon completely obscured it from view, thus rendering the duke completely anonymous in death. Welbeck Abbey passed to his cousin William, who actually used the home and its structures for parties and guest visits. The house was used by the military during both world wars, and from 1953 until 2005, part of it housed an armed forces college.

In his 1907 history of the Cavendish-Scott-Bentinck family, Charles Archard describes Portland as an ogre and a cynic who was nonetheless kind and considerate. I have attempted to portray Portland as the genuinely multidimensional—and unusual—man that he was. I like to think that he would approve.

The **Reverend James Appleton** was the vicar of **Worksop Priory** in 1869, but little is known about him, so I was able to have some fun in his characterization.

The **Nottingham coalfield** was a relatively new coalfield in 1869, having had its first serious mine sunk in 1841. As a result, Nottingham tended to be at the forefront of technological advancements in coal mining, leading the way in mechanization of coal mining and eliminating pit ponies in favor of underground transports for both men and coal.

"Home children" is the term used to refer to the child migration program implemented by Annie MacPherson in 1869, devised to rescue poor and orphaned children in the United Kingdom and send them to Australia, Canada, New Zealand, and South Africa for a chance at a better life and to alleviate the shortage of labor in those countries.

Such practices began as far back as 1618, with the transportation of a hundred vagrant English children to the Virginia Colony to work. This, of course, led to the kidnapping of other children to work in the Americas, and large numbers of children were forced to migrate until the scheme was exposed in 1757.

Annie MacPherson was a Scottish evangelical Christian who pioneered a new form of child migration in the late 1860s. MacPherson was appalled by the virtual slavery that children in the matchbox industry lived in, and resolved to do something about it. She bought a workshop and turned it into a "Home of Industry" where poor children could be fed and educated. Later, MacPherson decided that the real solution for these children was migration to a country of opportunity, so she started an emigration fund. Children were trained in London homes and then shipped to Canada, thus beginning an extensive campaign to find homes and careers for fourteen thousand of Britain's needy children.

As one might imagine, there was plenty of criticism for MacPherson's project. Not only were there rumors of ill treatment of the children by their new employers and of profiteering by those involved in the training and transport of children (although Mac-Pherson herself was always held in the highest regard), but also it was held that grouping together "good" children from the workhouses with "street" children, who were mostly considered thieves, caused nothing but trouble.

Child emigration was suspended for economic reasons during the Great Depression of the 1930s, but not completely stopped until the 1970s. During a 1998 parliamentary inquiry in Britain, the full extent of the home children scheme was exposed. In 2010, Prime Minister Gordon Brown issued an official apology for the resettlement program.

I have written before on workhouses in Victorian London. Orphanages were different but similarly bleak. They were intended specifically for foundling children, whereas workhouses contained adults, children, and sometimes entire families who did not want to be separated. However, orphanage children were frequently farmed out to mills and other workplaces during the day, embracing the workhouse idea that all residents must be productive. Both workhouses and orphanages could be dreary, forbidding institutions. Coram's Foundling Hospital was founded in 1741 and generally ceased operations in the 1950s, as British law trended toward more family-oriented solutions to the problem of orphans. Edmund Henderson, the commissioner of police, was indeed instrumental in starting the Metropolitan Police Orphanage, which opened in October 1870 and closed in 1937. By all accounts, it was a humanely run institution, and Henderson was known for his kindness and charity, as well as his foresight in developing Scotland Yard. Babbage's Home for Foundlings is my own invention.

You might think that I completely invented Colonel Mortimer's playful manner with his glass eyes. I actually took this idea from Prince Christian of Schleswig-Holstein, husband of Princess Helena, one of Queen Victoria's daughters. The prince lost his left eye in December 1891 while on a holiday shooting party at Osborne. Friends later recalled that he kept a large collection of replacements, which he brought out to show—and shock—favored guests. He was particularly attached to a bloodshot version, which he wore when he felt poorly. Unfortunately, this event happened more than twenty years too late for me to actually write the prince into the story, so I attributed his antics to a fictional character.

You might also assume that tattoos are a twentieth-century affectation, particularly in the West, but that is not so. In 1862, the twenty-year-old Prince of Wales received his first tattoo while on a trip to Jerusalem, just a few months after the British nation had plunged into mourning for his father, Prince Albert. His tattoo of five crosses forming a Crusader's Jerusalem cross started a fad for tattoos among the aristocracy. Although tattooing was largely the practice of seamen, with most British ports having a tattoo artist in residence, there were certainly others who had designs inked into their skin. Many leading figures of society criticized the fashion, associating it with the rough life of sailors, port towns, and prostitutes, not the well-mannered life of the ordinary citizen.

Ravens have a special place in English history. Legend holds that the White Tower, the old keep within the Tower of London, will crumble and a great disaster befall England if the six resident ravens ever leave the fortress. It was Charles II, the legend continues, who first insisted on having ravens protect his kingdom, as England was so hard-fought and -won for him. It is a lovely story, but more than likely a Victorian-era invention. However, the requisite six ravens (plus a spare) are continuously kept on the grounds of the Tower of London today, and are accorded great respect, as evidenced by the special ravens' graveyard kept at the Tower. I thought it only appropriate that Violet Harper have an opportunity to work with one of these magnificent birds, even if she isn't quite happy with the honor.

SELECTED BIBLIOGRAPHY

Archard, Charles J. *The Portland Peerage Romance*. London: Greening & Co., Ltd., 1907.

Beeton, Isabella. *Beeton's Book of Household Management* (Facsimile Edition). London: Jonathan Cape Limited, 1968.

Bentley, Nicolas. *The Victorian Scene: 1837–1901*. London: George Weidenfield and Nicolson Limited, 1968.

INTERNET REFERENCE

Victorian Web:
www.victorianweb.org
A deep compendium of quotes and facts from the Victorian age.

Turn the page for a special excerpt of Christine Trent's

THE MOURNING BELLS

One of Victorian London's most respected undertakers, Violet Harper has the duty of accompanying coffins on the London Necropolis Railway for respectful funerals and burials in Surrey. But on one fateful trip, the mournful silence of the train is shattered by the shrill ringing of a coffin bell—a device that prevents a person from being buried alive.

Inside the noisome coffin Violet finds a man panicked and wide-eyed with fear chattering incoherently. When a second coffin bell is rung on another trip Violet grows suspicious. She voices her qualms to Inspector Hurst of Scotland Yard, only to receive a puzzling reply that, after all, it is not a crime to rise from the dead.

But Violet's instincts are whispering that all is not well on the London Necropolis Railway's tracks. Is this all merely the result of clumsy undertaking, or is there something more sinister afoot? Determined to get to the heart of the matter, Violet uncovers a treacherous plot and villains who will stop at nothing to keep a lid on her search for the truth . . .

A Kensington trade paperback on sale now!

1

Until today, undertaker Violet Harper would have sworn that it was impossible for corpses to rise out of their coffins.

Now, she wasn't so sure.

The sun was just breaking over the dome of St. Paul's Cathedral when Violet entered Waterloo station to stand on a dedicated funeral train platform with her undertaking partner, Harry Blundell. They were both watching as six coffins, including one under their own care, were loaded into the long compartments on the railroad hearse van, which contained twelve total slots. Each compartment in the van had a door in the side of it, past which a coffin was pushed so that it lay perpendicular to the train's length. The coffins, stacked in individual compartments, were three high and four wide in the wood carriage. These special carriages were made especially for the London Necropolis Railway and painted chocolate brown, edged in an orange-red vermilion, to match the carriages of the London and South Western Railway, upon whose tracks the LNR ran.

Coffins were placed on large biers with hand cranks by the coffin porters, who wore simple dark-blue uniforms and matching hats with large brims and flat crowns. With one man on the ground cranking the bier up, the second coffin porter rode on the bier and pushed the coffin into its compartment, and was then cranked to the ground for the next coffin.

As the last coffin was pushed into its compartment on the ground level—a little too carelessly, in Violet's opinion—she noticed that it bore a maker's plate from Boyce and Sons Cabinetmakers. It reminded her that she wanted to set up dealings with Putnam Boyce again, now that she was permanently back in her London undertaking business.

But the coffin was hung up on something, and as one of the coffin porters pulled it back out to reposition it, she noticed something disturbing. She held up a hand to stop them.

"What's the matter, Mrs. Harper?" Harry asked in irritation. Harry's wife was expecting, and although she wasn't due for at least a month, he was always impatient to return to the immediate area surrounding their shop.

She waved him off as she moved closer to inspect the coffin. It was one of those confounded "safety" coffins, intended to give loved ones comfort with the idea that if the deceased were not truly dead, he could send an alarm aboveground and be rescued even after burial.

Violet heartily despised these so-called safety contraptions, which took the form of bells, trumpets, and even ladders in vertical coffins, by which someone who awoke to find himself mistakenly buried could literally climb up a ladder and out of his grave.

No matter how often Violet railed against these foolish mechanisms, firmly telling people that only the return of the Lord Christ would cause people to waken in their graves, people still wanted them as a measure of comfort. And as always, unscrupulous undertakers were happy to sell them.

This one had a bell apparatus, with a bell attached to a string following along a folding brass pole that would be unfolded after the coffin went into the ground so that the bell sat above the freshly shoveled dirt.

Violet's insides churned. If she opened the coffin, she would undoubtedly find a string tied to the deceased's fingers and toes, so that with the merest of tugs, he could set the bell jangling.

More frustrating was that this coffin had been made by Putnam Boyce, a respected cabinetmaker whom Violet had used in the past. Most cabinetmakers made coffins during their slow times, for there was always demand for them in a mortal population. Mr. Boyce's coffins were well crafted, with tightly fitted lids and smooth surfaces. Why, then, was he peddling safety coffins?

Perhaps she would have to rethink her plan to purchase coffins from him.

"Thank you," she said simply to the two coffin porters, who were still looking at her in bewilderment as to why she was halting their work. They pushed the coffin off the bier and into the compartment. With the last coffin now placed inside the hearse van, the train was ready for its journey from Waterloo station to Brookwood station in Woking, Surrey.

Violet climbed into the passenger carriage with Harry. They would accompany Mr. Harland's body to the cemetery, making final arrangements at the chapel until his family arrived later in the day for the funeral.

The LNR had been in operation since 1854, but Violet had only recently become involved with it. Although she had sold Morgan Undertaking to Harry Blundell and his partner, Will Swift, four years ago, Will had recently asked her to buy him back out so that he could join his wife's floral business. During his time with Morgan Undertaking, though, Will had built up a considerable business with wealthy patrons who wanted to start family crypts far outside the stench and overcrowding of London.

Not content with some of London's garden cemeteries, such as Highgate and Kensal Green, they were flocking to Brookwood, which its owners bragged had enough spaces that London need never build another cemetery again. Clearly the gentlemen had no experience with what happened in a cholera or typhoid outbreak, where deaths in the thousands could occur in the space of a few weeks.

However, coffins at the 2,200-acre Brookwood didn't have to be buried in the crowded manner that they did at these other cemeteries, and certainly didn't need to be stacked up to six high as they did inside the ancient and overflowing church graveyards. The owners' idea of creating a cemetery that could accommodate millions of bodies when fully developed—thus alleviating the need to ever build another London cemetery again—was commendable.

The funeral train pulled out of Waterloo with a steamy snort and a jarring lurch as Violet settled into her third-class compartment with Harry. This special train was only comprised of an engine, the hearse vans, and six passenger carriages. The passenger carriages were divided into two sections, conformist and nonconformist, with first-, second-, and third-class carriages within each religious section.

Conformist carriages were for those passengers who belonged to the Church of England, also called the Anglican church. The nonconformist carriages typically conveyed Presbyterians, Methodists, Baptists, Congregationalists, Unitarians, and Quakers, but might be those of other sects, as well. Special care was taken to ensure that people from different social backgrounds and religious leanings didn't have to be distressed by having to mix with others of a different class.

The train ran a single, hour-long route from Waterloo to Woking, southwest of London, so it certainly had no beds or Pullman dining carriages, but it did have comfortable enough seats for the hour's ride, even in third class. The first-class seats included plush cushions, chandeliers, filigreed ornamentation, glass windows instead of bare openings, and doting attendants, but such fripperies were never Violet's concern when there were bodies to be looked after.

The only real inconvenience was having to travel at dawn with the bodies and wait at the cemetery for the train to return to London to pick up mourners at the more civilized hour of eleven thirty in the morning. If the number of mourners for the day justified it, later trains followed.

There were always details to attend to at Brookwood, but it was still earlier in the morning than Violet cared to rise.

The train conductor stepped into their carriage, nodded at Violet, Harry, and the other two undertakers in the car, and passed on through to the next carriage via the open platform between them. The undertakers were always recognized by their severe black dress and tall hats with black crape wrapped around the base of the crown and trailing down their backs. However, the conductor had to dutifully check for any stowaways who might attempt to board the train for a free ride.

Now that they were in relative privacy, seated across from each other, Harry asked, "Do you feel well, Mrs. Harper?"

Violet had had violent experiences with trains in the past, having been involved in a wreck and also having witnessed a train hitting a murderer who had fallen from a platform. She had largely overcome her resulting fear of the hulking, steam-breathing beasts, but always felt an unwelcome twinge as the whistle shrilly blew and the engine started its laborious forward motion.

"Yes, I'm fine," she assured him, even as she swallowed the unpleasant taste in her mouth.

Harry nodded knowingly and then proceeded to change the subject. "What did you notice on the platform?"

"A bit of false hope by loved ones preyed upon by an unscrupulous undertaker. A bell safety coffin."

"Really? How fascinating. I was reading in the latest issue of *Funeral Service Journal* that an American named Vester has developed a new safety coffin that adds a tube connected to a viewing glass inside the coffin." He seemed eager to share both his knowledge and the evidence of his willingness to research the latest in undertaking. "That way, the face of the corpse can be viewed from above. An interesting solution to the inadvertent bell-ringing problem."

Harry referred to the fact that the swelling or position shifting that naturally occurred when the body began to decay would frequently cause the body to ring the bell and send people into a frenzy of grave digging. A viewing tube would enable a mourner or cemetery worker to look down and determine whether the coffin's occupant was still alive.

Not that it mattered, for coffins held very little air, perhaps two hours' worth at most, and so unearthing a coffin in time to rescue someone buried alive was nearly impossible.

Violet was displeased with her own grumpiness but unable to condone even a discussion of the infernal contraptions. She turned dismissively to the window to avoid any further discussion of safety coffins and the deceptive reassurance they gave grieving families. Instead, she contemplated the packed and soot-covered hovels of south London. That dreary cityscape soon opened up to impressive country estates, the rich red-brown coats of Sussex cattle, and the spires of crumbling country churches.

Brookwood station's main platform was deserted except for a few LNR workers, as to be expected so early on this August morning. There were two separate substations serving the cemetery: The North station was located in the center of the nonconformist section, whereas the South station was situated on the east edge of the Anglican cemetery.

The train chugged gently past the main platform and on to the North station, where Violet and Harry remained seated as the nonconformist coffins were unloaded from their hearse van. They then continued on to the South station, where Mr. Harland and the other remaining bodies were unloaded.

Undertakers sometimes neglected to accompany bodies to Brookwood, a failure Violet found shameful and a dereliction of their moral duties. The deceased certainly deserved the respect of an attendant, but many undertakers did not want to rise before the cock's crow to take a third-class ride an hour outside of London.

The nonconformist third-class carriage always carried whatever undertakers were accompanying the train to Surrey so that they were immediately on hand for the coffin unloading. Also, since they rode for free, the LNR wasn't about to provide them with luxury accommodation.

Violet suppressed a yawn. Perhaps the lazy undertakers did have a point about these arduous trips.

Soon, she and Harry stood on the South station platform amid a scattering of coffins, waiting for the LNR's horse-drawn biers to arrive from the company's stables. It was unusual for these conveyances to not be at the ready.

Harry looked particularly irritated. Violet touched his arm to comfort him. "All will be well, you'll see. We cannot return until after the funeral anyway, remember?"

He dropped his scowl. "You're right, Mrs. Harper. I'm just anxious over what the next month will bring. . . ."

"I understand." Violet moved to sit on a backless bench, and Harry followed. The coffin porters were just cranking down the last box from the third level of the hearse van.

Violet watched their work in fascination, almost missing a man in a tall beaver-skin hat poking about one of the coffins as if looking for something. Violet would have thought he was another undertaker except he hadn't been on the train, and his jacket was a light camel color. Perhaps he was a local fellow.

She paid him no more mind, for her attentions were diverted by a distinct sound that at first she unconsciously attributed to a servant's bell. As it penetrated further into her senses, though, the hair stood up on the back of her neck.

Ting. Ting. Ting-a-ling.

Impossible!

Wide-eyed and with only a horrified glance at Harry, who looked as dumbstruck as she was, Violet jumped up from the bench and rushed to the sound.

It was coming from Mr. Boyce's coffin. The bell, dangling down from the tip of the folded brass tubing, danced insistently now. Dropping her reticule to the ground, she knelt down and tugged ineffectively on the coffin lid. It was nailed down in several spots.

Harry was now at her side, and with the burly strength that enabled the man to single-handedly lift empty coffins and move them with effortless ease about the shop, he ripped the lid off as though he were merely opening a tin of biscuits. The two undertakers gasped in unison at the sight of the body inside. Instead of a lifeless corpse there was a man of about thirty years in a rumpled but high-quality frock coat. His coppery beard, mustache, and hair were flecked with early gray and closely cropped, but his bloodshot, pale-blue eyes were wild with panic as he struggled to sit up.

"Havfindabang," the man slurred, weaving where he sat as he squinted in what was now bright morning light, like a mole popping out from its burrow.

Violet stared at him, speechless. She had been undertaking for more than fifteen years and had never, ever come across a body resurrecting itself. Dead bodies sometimes moved on their own, or made noises through the expulsion of gases, but this—this—was inconceivable. This was actually a body sitting up after having been dead for presumably at least a day. She shivered involuntarily, overcome by the implication of what it meant. Surely it was not possible that she herself had ever buried someone who was not truly, irrevocably dead. . . .

She looked over at Harry, who obviously shared her shock in his unblinking eyes and gaping mouth.

"Sir, can you hear me?" Violet said, her voice quavering as she knelt next to the coffin, still in complete disbelief that she was actually witnessing a body arising from a coffin.

He recoiled from the sound of her voice. Harry, shaking his head in complete incredulity, reached in and lifted the man out effortlessly.

"May I be of help?" came an awestruck voice from behind Violet. It was the man in the light coat. She now saw that he was in his forties, and had thick, curly muttonchop whiskers. He, too, must have realized what had happened, for his face was drained of all color. "I am Byron Ambrose. I'm a doctor with offices nearby. I witnessed the, er, disturbing thing that just happened and can hardly believe my eyes. I cannot comprehend how this gentleman could have possibly—" Like Harry, the physician looked incredulous. "If I might have a moment with him to—"

"Misser 'Brose, havfindabang," the man from the coffin repeated senselessly, still tottering and struggling to fully open his eyes.

The physician peered into the man's eyes and pulled open the man's mouth without asking for permission. "Fascinating," he muttered as he looked inside. "Sir, can you understand me?" he asked.

"Yuh," the man said dully, his eyes now darting about wildly. Violet couldn't blame him. How must it feel to wake up in a dark coffin, with no room to move and with no understanding of why you were sequestered into such a tight space?

She shook her head in bewilderment. It was absolutely inconceivable that a dead man could have risen from his coffin. Wasn't it?

The doctor was clearly as baffled as she was. "Sir, if you'll come with me, I'd like to examine you." He turned back to Violet. "I'll help this man recuperate back at my office. His . . . recovery . . . is quite unusual, don't you think? I'll also help him back to his family."

At that moment, the stationmaster arrived to see what the commotion had been. After Violet explained what had happened, the doctor interjected, "I'll help the poor man home, Uriah."

The stationmaster nodded. "That's all right then, Mr. Ambrose."

As the physician offered a supportive arm to the seemingly reincarnated man and the two walked unsteadily away, Violet turned to the stationmaster, who didn't seem particularly surprised by the supernatural event they had just witnessed. "I am Violet Harper, and this is my associate, Harry Blundell."

"Uriah Gedding, at your service, madam." He politely touched the brim of his hat at her and shook Harry's hand. He wore a dark blue uniform with red stripes up the sides of his trousers. His jacket, with brightly polished silver buttons running up both sides and a large red lapel, marked him as the important railway man he was.

"Sir, I presume you have never seen such a—a—such an *extraordinary* occurrence at your station before," Violet said.

Gedding shrugged casually, although whether this was intended to convey that bodies sprang routinely from coffins at Brookwood or that he had no real answer for her, she couldn't be sure.

"May I ask you a few questions, Mr. Gedding?" she asked. Surely the stationmaster would have answers about what had happened.

"Of course, madam." Gedding led Violet and Harry into the one-story station, which was built around a square courtyard filled with pebbled pathways and flowering urns for viewing from anywhere inside.

One side of the square contained the first-class reception room for mourners dropped off by the late-morning train, while the other side housed the ordinary reception room for second- and third-class mourners. Gedding took them through the ordinary room to the offices that lay along the back side of the station. She knew that beyond the offices lay lodgings for certain railroad staff, Gedding included.

Gedding's office was plain, with badly whitewashed walls covered with timetables, maps, and a single drawing obviously made by a child's hand. There was an out-of-place floral tablecloth thrown over the table that served as his desk. A gift from his wife, no doubt.

As Violet and Harry settled into seats across the distracting fabric's profusion of roses, lilies, and hyacinths, Gedding offered them tea. Violet waved a dismissing hand and instead pressed directly to the point. "Mr. Gedding, have you ever experienced what we just saw, a man seemingly rising from the dead out of his coffin?"

Gedding pondered the question only momentarily. "I can't say that I have. I'm just glad there was no one else about for it except you two. Imagine a funeral party witnessing what happened. *The Times* would have flown reporters in on brooms for that news item, and the LNR would have been accused of intentionally shipping live bodies for profit or some such thing." Gedding shuddered, presumably imagining reporters in warlock garb blocking out the sun as they swarmed into his station, laughing menacingly in low-pitched voices.

As if on cue, a sleek tan cat, with chocolate-colored paws, ears, and face, appeared from nowhere and jumped gracefully onto the tablecloth with a plaintive meow. Gedding absentmindedly reached out a hand to pet the animal, which turned to face Violet and Harry. The cat sat down, lazily blinking its sea-green eyes at them.

"Do you keep records about the bodies shipped on your trains?" Violet asked.

"Records?" the stationmaster asked, his face reflecting the confusion in his voice. "What kind of records?"

"The name of the deceased in each coffin, for one. Who the undertaker is, in which part of the cemetery the body will be buried, and so forth."

Gedding scooped up the cat and embraced it to his chest. The cat climbed up and draped itself like a fur stole casually thrown over the shoulder by a wealthy woman. All Violet now saw was a pair of dangling legs and a swishing tail, although the animal's purr resembled an incoming train.

"Mrs. Harper," Gedding began, drawing himself up importantly in his chair. He put up an arm for the cat to prop its back legs on. "We are in the business of moving bodies, not doing an undertaker's job. As you can imagine, anyone who can afford to pay to have a body shipped here is probably not going to abandon that body. We have never had an instance where a coffin went unclaimed."

"But surely you—"

Gedding shifted the animal to his other shoulder, but the cat became irritated by the movement and leaped from its owner's shoulder to the floor, disappearing out of the room in a feline huff. The stationmaster leaned forward and, with his elbows on the tablecloth, brought his hands together in a triangle. "Please understand. The LNR has not had a single complaint yet of a body being mishandled or disappearing. Families and undertakers hire us to put coffins on board, and they always—always—show up to collect them. It is vital that we maintain our sterling reputation, for we are not yet profitable, given our presently limited number of runs each day. Any bad publicity would . . ." Gedding spread out his hands expressively to indicate the disaster that would befall the company.

"I don't think the London Necropolis Railway can be held accountable for what happened," Harry assured the stationmaster.

Gedding immediately seized on this. "Yes, Mr. Blundell, you are absolutely correct. Besides, there has been no crime committed, has there? A man believed dead now lives. Mr. Ambrose is a respectable physician who will see to the man's reunion with his loved ones. His family will rejoice, as will we. I consider the matter resolved, and so should you."

Violet and Harry left Gedding's office. She knew the stationmaster was correct in his assessment, but it bothered her that not only had some undertaker somewhere been careless with a body, but that it was actually possible that those dratted safety coffins might work.

The horse-drawn biers arrived, with the drivers offering apologies for their tardiness, having been delayed with coffins at the

North station. With Mr. Harland now securely resting on the bier, Violet and Harry walked on either side of it to the Anglican chapel, a sweet and peaceful structure surrounded with columns. The driver and his assistant unloaded the coffin into the chapel, with a promise to return later for the ride to the grave.

Violet asked Harry to stay behind to compare final notes with the cemetery director, while she went to inspect the grave site. Ordinarily, she enjoyed such interactions and Harry, who was still young and lacking experience, preferred to take care of the manual aspects of funerals. Today, though, Violet wanted to enjoy the walk under the tree canopies and through the winding pathways on her own, to settle her mind over what had happened back at the station.

The August day was warm but not uncomfortably so. The oak, hawthorn, and elm trees in the cemetery were mostly along the borders of the cemetery, working together in their varying heights to serve as sentinels over the graves, blocking views from outside the cemetery and providing mourners with a sense of peace and steadfastness. Thus far, only around five hundred acres had been excavated and put in order for graves, with only a fraction of those graves occupied. Beyond that, nearly fifteen hundred more acres awaited eventual preparation.

Violet tripped over a tree root but caught herself by grabbing on to the edge of a crypt, this one in the unusual Gothic-inspired shape of a large bed frame. At the head of the "bed" were pointed arches topped with crosses and gargoyles. It was a fantastical crypt, unlike any of the usual oblong boxes with weeping angels resting atop them, or the tall obelisks and crosses marking the occupants beneath them.

She continued along the path to the section containing Mr. Harland's grave site, with only chirping birds for company as she paused to examine the names and dates on some of the graves. Nothing was more than fifteen years old, except for a few ancient graves that had been transferred out of London to alleviate the overcrowding of churchyards there. Most of the sites also lacked the soot and lichen stains that plagued older cemeteries. It was almost as if this cemetery breathed life, not death. For now, anyway.

Violet found Mr. Harland's site, which had been freshly dug. His family already had a crypt, built to resemble a Greek temple, a common style for those who had the money to spend on it. Mr. Harland's grave was dug between two of the columns. She pulled out her measuring tape from her reticule and unrolled it down into the grave. It stopped at the twelve-foot mark. Very good. This was a fresh dig in the Harland family site, so Mr. Harland would rest at the bottom, leaving room for two more family members to be buried on top of him in the future.

She rolled up the tape, satisfied. Several urns of lilies surrounded the temple, and a few chairs were positioned around the grave for the widow and elderly family members, as she had requested. Violet was pleased with Brookwood's efficiency. No wonder Will had started engaging in funerals with them, despite the trip involved.

She strode quickly back to the chapel. She was happy enough with how things were turning out for this funeral, and was ready to forget about the unfortunate, yet fortunate, man who had staggered out of his coffin. Harry was waiting for her outside, and he, too, indicated satisfaction with the proceedings.

They walked back to the station to wait for the family. The reception room was not furnished with gas, but instead relied upon oil lamps for light and a cavernous fireplace on one wall for heat in the winter. Here they would wait another two hours for the mourners to arrive, then accompany them back to the chapel.

Violet paced restlessly inside the reception room, discussing the various details of the funeral with Harry. It wasn't long, though, before their conversation turned back to what had happened on the station platform.

"What do you think?" Harry asked, animated and no longer irritated with his temporary exile from London as he leaned casually against the fireplace mantel and watched her pace. "That seems proof that safety coffins do have some merit. I look forward to posting a newspaper advertisement about it." He became invigorated by his own words. "Imagine the favorable publicity the undertaking profession will receive once people realize that someone has been rescued by a safety coffin. Why, it could erase a hundred years of notoriety. We should order a great sampling of these coffins before the other under—"

"No," Violet interrupted, her voice firm. "Absolutely not." She stopped pacing and whirled on him. "Whatever happened back there was . . . was . . . incomprehensible. Harry, we both know it's not possible for a dead body to come back to life, except for the Resurrection."

Harry straightened to his full height. "Ordinarily I would say yes, you're right. But we saw it occur with our very own eyes. You cannot deny that the man arose, quite terrified and babbling, but also quite alive."

Violet frowned. Yes, it had occurred just as Harry described. But even if—if!—the man had not been truly dead and was saved by a bell coffin, it was a rare circumstance. So despite the excitement it would generate among mourners who imagined they could hold out hope that their loved one might come out of the grave a week or two after death, it would ultimately prove to be a leaden disappointment to all of them. And eventually it would bring shame to the undertaking profession, which was already tarnished by the few charlatans who practiced it.

She softened her tone. "Harry, we must think this through. Whatever medical condition that man experienced was not typical. We have both seen enough bodies in our lives to know when they are dead. The ashy skin, the vacant eyes, the odors. Don't you think it more likely that the undertaker who put him in a coffin was incompetent?"

Harry considered this. "Yes, perhaps, but—"

"If we want to maintain our reputation, we have a responsibility to keep quiet about this until we know for sure who put that man in a coffin before he was ready."

"How would we do that? We have no authority, and no undertaker is under obligation to talk to us."

Violet had encountered more difficult situations than this before, and even uncovered killers in the process. This was no murder, just a simple case of bad undertaking. How challenging could it possibly be to ferret out the inept funeral man in their midst?

"I'll take care of it, Harry. Meanwhile, we have a funeral to perform, to make sure Mr. Harland is sent off well. We must stop such talk, at least until we know for certain what happened."

Harry shrugged. "As you say, Mrs. Harper. I'll keep quiet. But after what we just witnessed, I have to say I'm convinced."

Mr. Harland's funeral went off well enough except for a problem with a relative who availed himself of a little too much gin inside the reception room and almost stumbled into the grave before Mr. Harland himself was laid in it.

It was with tired relief that Violet and Harry made the hour-long train ride back to London in silence. Violet's peaceful walk through Brookwood was now but a distant memory as she was consumed with the bell coffin experience.

The stationmaster had stated that no crime had been committed. Perhaps in the eyes of the law, no. But in Violet's mind, a careless undertaker had perpetrated an inexcusable act on an innocent person.

Whatever undertaker had put that man in his coffin no more deserved to wear his hat and tails than a Newgate Prison inmate did.

GREAT BOOKS, GREAT SAVINGS!

When You Visit Our Website:
www.kensingtonbooks.com
You Can Save Money Off The Retail Price
Of Any Book You Purchase!

- **All Your Favorite Kensington Authors**
- **New Releases & Timeless Classics**
- **Overnight Shipping Available**
- **eBooks Available For Many Titles**
- **All Major Credit Cards Accepted**

Visit Us Today To Start Saving!
www.kensingtonbooks.com

All Orders Are Subject To Availability.
Shipping and Handling Charges Apply.
Offers and Prices Subject To Change Without Notice.

31901056675715